Skeletons in the Closet

(Phantom Rising #2)

by Davyne DeSye

© 2014 Davyne DeSye

All rights reserved. No part of this publication may be reproduced or transmitted in any form or by any means electronic or mechanical, including photocopy, recording, or any information storage and retrieval system, without permission in writing from both the copyright owner and the publisher.

Requests for permission to make copies of any part of this work should be mailed to Permissions Department, Illuminus Publishing, PO Box 75459, Colorado Springs, CO 80970-5459.

Ebook ISBN: 978-0-9988747-3-9

Cover art by Biserka Design.

BOOKS BY DAVYNE DESYE

HISTORICAL ROMANCE

The Phantom Rising Series:
For Love of the Phantom
Skeletons in the Closet
Phantom Rising (forthcoming)

SCIENCE FICTION

The Aggressor Queen Series:
Carapace
Warmonger (forthcoming)
Aggressor Queen (forthcoming)

Short Story Anthology:
Soap Bubble Dreams and Other Distortions

PRAISE FOR
FOR LOVE OF THE PHANTOM

"*I recommend this book to all fans of Phantom of the Opera and to those who believe in unbridled true love.*"
Readers Favorite – 5-Star Review

***

"This is a love story unlike many that have been written ... The entire book is rich in atmospheric detail, with enough twists and turns to keep me eagerly turning pages."
K.C. Willivee, author of *The Wrong Man*

***

"This sequel to Phantom of the Opera is fantastic!! ... The same magic that the opera had is continued in Davyne DeSye's story. This story gushes with the same extreme romance as the opera did."
Tassa Desalada, author of *Sex and Sushi*

***

"Bravo! Highly recommended for lovers of historical romance or those simply infatuated with the Opera Ghost and his beloved Miss Daaè."
Jessica Jesinghaus, author of *Mirror, Mirror*

For Bit
Thank you for putting the idea in my head.

CONTENTS

CHAPTER 1 – LONELINESS	1
CHAPTER 2 – YOUTH	12
CHAPTER 3 – A DECISION IS MADE	22
CHAPTER 4 – SET BACKS	32
CHAPTER 5 – A HINT OF TROUBLE	43
CHAPTER 6 – OPPORTUNITIES	54
CHAPTER 7 – TREACHERY	64
CHAPTER 8 – PETTER AND CONSTANCE	78
CHAPTER 9 – ERIK COMES HOME	91
CHAPTER 10 – LOVE AND FRIENDSHIP	104
CHAPTER 11 – ERIK WAKES	115
CHAPTER 12 – CHRISTINE'S TRAVELS	127
CHAPTER 13 – ERIK AND PETTER	133
CHAPTER 14 – PETTER LEARNS PART OF THE TRUTH	148
CHAPTER 15 – MEETING WITH THE PERSIAN	159
CHAPTER 16 – CHRISTINE MEETS THE SULTANA	173
CHAPTER 17 – PLANS ARE MADE	183
CHAPTER 18 – CHRISTINE TAKES CONTROL	194
CHAPTER 19 – THE OPERA HOUSE	203
CHAPTER 20 – CHRISTINE AGAIN	216
CHAPTER 21 – THE SULTANA FINDS ERIK	228
CHAPTER 22 – THE VOYAGE	241
CHAPTER 23 – CHRISTINE AND THE SULTANA	256
CHAPTER 24 – IN MAZENDERAN	271
CHAPTER 25 – CHRISTINE PLANS FOR ESCAPE	282
CHAPTER 26 – ERIK ENTERS THE PALACE	293
CHAPTER 27 – CHRISTINE ESCAPES	305
CHAPTER 28 – ERIK AND CHRISTINE	316
CHAPTER 29 – MOTHER AND CHILD	323
CHAPTER 30 – ERIK FINDS THE SHAH	336
CHAPTER 31 – THE SULTANA	350
CHAPTER 32 – PETTER RETURNS TO LONDON	361
CHAPTER 33 – PETTER AND HIS LOVE	370
CHAPTER 34 – CHRISTINE AND ERIK	380

Davyne DeSye

CHAPTER 1
LONELINESS

The wildflowers Erik clutched in his long white fingers were an absurd gesture.

He dipped his nearly nostril-less nose toward the small bouquet and inhaled of its almond scent. His shoes still bore traces of his trek through the nearby woods to gather the small flowers for his beloved, his Christine, and he tapped them against each other where he stood in the short green grass. Before him in the far distance rose their manor house, strong and stately against a backdrop of the blue-white Swedish sky. The house stood at the edge of a cliff top that dropped toward the gulf waters, but at this distance, Erik could not hear the soothing sound of the waves beating at the cliff base.

He moved his eyes to where Christine knelt in the freshly turned earth, and then lowered them again to the flowers in his fist. A smile turned up the corners of his thin lips. As absurd as his small gift was, it might help ease Christine's mood, her loneliness. They would serve as a gentle reminder that even with Petter gone, she was not alone, not unloved. He missed his son as well, but Christine's prolonged melancholy was worrisome.

SKELETONS IN THE CLOSET

He walked toward Christine along the white pebble path, careful not to step as silently as was his wont – he did not wish to startle her. She turned toward him as he approached. Suddenly shy of her – Erik had never lost his amazement of her affection even after their score years of marriage – he dashed the small bouquet behind his back. He was rewarded with a tentative smile.

"What have you, my husband?" she asked as she rose to her feet. Even in his concern for her, Erik could not help but admire the figure he knew so well – it had not much changed in the years between when he first saw her – as a young girl of seventeen – and now, as she was approaching forty. She was still a beautiful woman.

"Come and see," he answered. His tone conveyed a lustful quality he had not intended, but Christine cocked her head, and raised one eyebrow. Her tentative smile grew to the teasing smile of a young girl pretending to coyness.

As she approached, Erik's knowing eyes searched her face. Her smile did not reach her blue eyes. She was pretending to good humor for his sake.

When Christine reached him, she raised her hands to his chest, and rising to her toes, kissed him, a warm feather-brush against his thin lips. Her eyes moved over his deformed face with the same unfaltering acceptance of their years together. Her hand stole to his head and smoothed his still thick but silvered hair.

"What have you?" she whispered toward his ear. He had won that much at least: the listlessness that had so often dulled her voice of late was gone.

Presenting the aspect of a young boy come a-courting, he stepped back from Christine and presented her with the bouquet, his arm jutting between them, his chin ducked in mock embarrassment. His reward was immediate. Christine threw her head back and shaking her golden lustrous hair from her shoulders, laughed fully, melodically. When she lowered her head her eyes sparkled as they had not in weeks.

"Erik, you sweet, sweet, silly man!" She laughed again – a smaller tinkling sound – as she took the flowers from his hand. "You felt I needed more flowers?"

Erik's eyes danced over the garden in which they stood – tall colorful ranunculus in myriads of colors bobbing in the gentle breeze, smaller daffodils, straight and yellow in the morning sun, the small anemone, luminous and white against their dark foliage.

"You didn't have any of these," he said.

"Oh, Erik. I love you so," she answered. She lifted the delicate dangling pink blossoms to her nose, and slipped her arm into his. "Come, let us see if we can find a vase for your silly, wonderful gift." As he led her toward the large stone manor house, she raised the flowers to her nose again, giggled, and tilted her head against his shoulder.

Yes, the flowers had been absurd, but their absurdity had broken through to her. He hoped the transformation would last, although he feared it would not. But, it was a start, and he would be satisfied with that. He had left her alone with her grief for too long

SKELETONS IN THE CLOSET

– he hoped now to draw away the shroud in which she was smothering.

***

Erik lay sprawled across the blanket under a large poplar, enjoying the rare grace of a warm Swedish summer afternoon. Christine sat at his head; her feet curled to her other side, hidden under the folds of her blue skirt. The open book from which he had been reading lay forgotten on the blanket beside him.

Christine fed him morsels from their picnic, teasing him with the food bits. They had not picnicked in some time. Christine seemed carefree, younger than her nearly forty years, released of the aging that had crept upon her in the past months.

Erik closed his eyes and tilted his head back as Christine moved a grape toward his mouth. When the grape did not enter his mouth, he smiled and opened his eyes expecting to see that Christine was teasing him again. She was not.

The grape still dangled from her fingers, but her eyes were not on his. She was gazing, unseeing, past Erik. He knew from the cloud that had descended over her features that she was thinking of their son, Petter, again. His certainty was answered with her quiet statement.

"I wish Petter could be here with us. He always enjoyed our picnics." She sighed, and turned her sad eyes to Erik, a small apologetic smile twisting her lips before she turned away from him. The grape, now forgotten, fell to the blanket.

Erik had to restrain himself from sighing in answer. He rose from his elbow and propped himself in a sitting position with one hand. With his other hand, he caught Christine's chin, and turned her face toward his. Her eyes were dark with her sadness. He kept his voice gentle as he spoke.

"Petter is not dead, Christine, he is merely in London. They have trees in London, and blankets, and picnic baskets…"

"But he is just a child!" Christine answered. "He needs us!"

Or you need him, he did not say.

"He is a man of one and twenty, Christine, off to seek his fortune, to seek adventure," Erik answered, hoping for her understanding, her acceptance.

She pulled her chin from his hand, and looking toward her hands in her lap, she whispered, "He needs us." She raised her eyes to Erik, and the pleading in her eyes was painful to him. "We have sheltered him so. He has no knowledge of the world."

In one sense she was correct. They had sheltered and protected Petter – Christine because of a mother's love, and Erik because… because Erik of all people knew the dangers and evil in the world. He would have given his life – would even now give his life – to protect the woman he loved, and the son he never thought he would have. But Petter also needed to live and grow. Protecting him further would weaken the boy of whom they were both so proud.

"You were married before you were his age, Christine," Erik said. "Married and traveling the world." He raised his eyes to hers to see how she would react to this gentle reminder of her imprudent marriage to her first husband. He was pleased to see a smile playing at her lips.

"Exactly," she said. "I was a foolish child. If not for your… persistence, I would not be the happy woman I am today." She leaned toward him and kissed the cloth of his coat at his shoulder.

Are you happy?

"We must give Petter the chance at his own happiness," he said. Christine pulled away from him, and a small pout replaced her smile.

"It's different," she said. She tried to marshal a reason for her statement, but he knew from her pout and her posture that she had none. She always pouted like a child when she knew she had lost an argument – a habit that, even after all these years, charmed him. He kept his silence.

She shrugged and lifted her hands from her lap to throw them to either side of her skirt. Then with a sigh, she lifted her hands again and smoothed at the blue fabric.

"I know," she said. "It's not different. Petter could not stay with us forever." She sighed in defeat. "But I miss him so. He was such a bright, funny child. He will make mistakes and we will not be there to help him."

"We are all entitled to our own mistakes," Erik answered. He tried to catch her eye, but she refused to raise her head and meet his eyes. She busied herself replacing their luncheon in the large basket. He kept watching her – her face, her eyes. When she finished packing the basket, she brought her eyes to his.

"I know," she said. She gave him a hesitant smile, and said again, "I know. I shall try not to worry."

As they walked toward the house, she said, "I love you, Erik."

"I love you, my strong wife," he answered. He emphasized the word, *strong*, hoping to remind her of her true character.

"Will you sing with me?" Erik asked, as she delivered the remains of their luncheon into the hands of the young maid, Aina. Aina's youthful eyes moved to Christine, excitement evident in their depths.

"Nothing would please me more," Christine answered, with a smile and a glint of the same excitement in her blue, blue eyes. Erik smiled as Aina dashed from the room, and he knew from experience that the young girl would inform all the servants who could be spared of the upcoming performance.

"Which would please you? Something by Strauss, or perhaps Puccini?" Erik took Christine's hand as he led her to the music room.

Christine wrinkled her nose as she answered. "Not Strauss – he is too heavy for such a lovely afternoon. Puccini better suits the lightness of the day."

Erik preferred the dissonance of Strauss, but was not surprised with Christine's answer. He knew she was struggling against the discord within herself. He smiled and bowed over her hand.

"I shall be Rodolfo," he announced, his lips brushing her hand as he spoke the words.

She waited until he was looking into her eyes again before answering, with an obvious expectation of the ecstasy that still overwhelmed them with their song. "Mimi shall make love to you with song."

With no further preliminaries, he seated himself at the piano and they flew into song, swept away by the rapture so akin to that which they found in lovemaking. Even through the rapture, Erik watched Christine, pleased to see that despite her longing and worry for their son, she could still touch her fountainhead of happiness through song.

***

It was two weeks later that Erik found Christine weeping over a stack of Petter's letters – two weeks during which he had lavished his dear wife with affection and attention, singing and activities, and listened to the laugh returning to her voice. And now this distressing relapse. He lowered himself to the cushioned bench on which she sat and put his arms about her. She leaned into his embrace. Under the ministrations of his soothing words and soft strokes to her hair and back, her tears soon subsided.

"Forgive me, Erik," she said.

"Why the tears, wife?" he asked, moving the letters aside to make more room upon the bench for them both.

"I can't read this one!" she said, thrusting the letter she clutched in her fist toward Erik. "Why must he write in Persian?" she continued as he took the letter from her. "I can read the letters he writes in Swedish, and French and English… why must he also write in Persian?"

Erik chose to respond in Persian, to remind Christine of their long habit of speaking the different languages. While she understood and spoke Persian, she had never mastered the script. "To maintain his fluency in the language of love and poets, my desert rose."

The stricken look left her eyes, leaving only sadness. Responding in Persian, she said, "You are the poet of my heart." Her thankful eyes roved over his malformed face. She straightened her posture and smoothed the crumpled letter on her skirts. She pointed to the beautiful script and said, "I can recognize the salutation." She pointed to the few other words and phrases she recognized, as intent as a schoolgirl at lessons, and then held the letter out to Erik. "Will you read it for me?"

Erik read. The letter contained information similar to that in the other letters they had received – the letters Christine could read: News of his efforts to find commissions befitting the master stonemason he was, news of his landlady and of other acquaintances, tales of his adventures in London. Christine sighed as Erik finished with Petter's closing remarks, rendered all the more affectionate by the florid language in which he wrote.

SKELETONS IN THE CLOSET

"He doesn't sound as though he is having success with gaining commissions," she said at last.

"He is a fine stonemason, and can certainly find work, even without his own commissions," Erik answered.

"I know," Christine answered, disconsolate.

"Even I worked for others when I began," Erik continued.

"I know, I know," Christine answered, slumping against his side.

"He has not written that he needs money, which is a sign that he is…"

"Prideful!" Christine finished with surprising vehemence. Her posture collapsed as she whispered, "Like his father." Erik could hear the small smile behind her words.

Erik put his arm about her shoulder, and whispering into her ear quoted the Persian poet, "'Ah, my beloved, fill the cup that clears today of past regrets and future fears.'"

Christine pressed herself farther into his embrace, and again answering in Persian, said, "My husband, though the great poet Khayyam speaks to my solace, it is but you, my pillar, my lion, that stills my heart's fears and fills my cup." She turned her face to his and kissed him. He pulled her closer and she pressed her face to his shoulder.

"Fill my cup," Christine whispered, then rose and pulled him from the bench. He was pleased and excited by her lascivious suggestion, for in her recent sadness she had been less inclined toward lovemaking.

Even in his mounting ardor, he found room within himself to maintain his concern for her. He took her to bed in an earnest attempt to both satisfy his hunger and lift the sorrow from her heart.

After, as she lay sleeping in his arms, he thought of the veneer of melancholy that seemed, even in sleep, to shroud his bright and beautiful Christine, and knew… knew something needed to change.

CHAPTER 2
YOUTH

Petter paused before stepping from the covered building entrance into the gray London morning. He glanced down at the two portfolios he clutched in his hands, one heavy with drawings and small photos of his completed stone carvings, and the other filled with the architectural plans he had labored over in the past weeks.

At least he had not been laughed out of this meeting. It was a sad measure of his flagging optimism that he considered this a consolation.

He took a deep breath of the dank air, and pulling his head high, stepped into the fog and stood for a moment, his feet reluctant to step away from yet another failed attempt to gain a commission.

"Beg your pardon, sir." This from a round-shouldered older man who almost collided with Petter due to the large black umbrella tilted before the man as he hurried into the fine mist. The man stopped and bowed to Petter before tromping away on his squat legs. Petter watched him until he melted with startling suddenness into the surrounding gray.

Sir.

After the undisguised condescension of his latest meeting, Petter was surprised at the off-hand politeness of the stranger. With an internal shudder, he threw off the demoralizing reaction.

I do deserve "Sir." I do.

He had fought against "young man," or worse – "boy" – through his months of determination to win a commission of his own. A commission his work deserved if only the moneyed gentlemen he solicited could overlook his apparent youth. He knew he cut a fine figure, tall, and with a manner and bearing far more courtly than many of the men to whom he spoke. But his youth was exaggerated in the length and thinness of his limbs, which bespoke a young boy just coming into his height; in the smooth youthful skin of his face which despite his twenty-one years had never needed the scrape of a razor. Like his father, Petter could not grow facial hair.

Or at least not yet. The thought burst upon him with wishful boyish fervency – had he had a free hand, one finger would have rubbed at his upper lip.

Petter put one portfolio down long enough to pull his coat collar up against the dampness and then retrieved the leather case from the wet ground. *I know my craft. I will succeed.* Without a backward glance toward the façade he had approached with such hope not one hour ago, he turned toward the offices of his current employer. As though weeping for this latest failure, the mist turned to rain before he could take a dozen steps.

SKELETONS IN THE CLOSET

***

"Petter, m' boy!" The high-pitched voice of Edward Evans greeted Petter as he stepped, dripping, through the door into the shop. Petter winced at the man's choice of words – "boy," again – as much as he winced at the stilettos in the eyes of the journeyman over whom the master stonemason stood.

"Mr. Evans, sir," Petter answered his employer with deference. He removed his handkerchief from his pocket and began wiping the rain from his face and hair.

"Any luck, m' boy?" Evans asked, moving his enormous, muscular bulk toward Petter with the ease of one long accustomed to moving great blocks of stone, and finding himself – empty-handed – free to float across the floor. The glistening baldness of his great head and the flapping of the long, free-floating mustache as it bobbed toward Petter enhanced the impression that the man floated. Petter had often wondered if the lush mustache was nurtured to counterbalance the lack of hair upon the skull.

Before Petter had quite finished drying his face, the man's massive arm was around his shoulders, and then removed in almost the same moment. "Good gracious, but your coat is soaked."

"Yes, sir," Petter said. "Forgot my umbrella." He shrugged out of his topcoat, making sure not to look toward the abandoned journeyman, certain he would find the man's eyes still smoldering his resentment.

"Good day to you, Petter," said a sweet lilting voice at his other side. Petter turned toward the young lady while wrestling his waterlogged coat over one arm.

"Good day to you, Miss Evans." He bowed his head to the rather plain daughter of the master mason, returning her radiant smile with a more subdued smile of his own.

"Phoebe, Petter. I have asked you to call me Phoebe," she answered, her clear eyes meeting his. Her eyes were her best feature – large and luminous even in their darkness, and surrounded by luxurious dark lashes.

"Phoebe, take Petter's coat, dear," her father said as he clapped Petter's shoulder with one massive hand. It struck Petter that the pitch of the man's voice was very close to the high register tones of his daughter's, although the man was three times the size of the girl. "Come, Petter, m' boy, tell me how you fared. Have I lost my best journeyman?" He pulled Petter toward the office to the side of the work area.

Petter coughed into his hand to avoid answering, both because he loathed to confess his most recent failure to the journeymen working in the room, and because he knew Evans' careless praise only increased the jealous contempt with which the journeymen regarded him. While he appreciated the effusive compliments of the good-natured man, he also regretted the tension the praise caused among the men who would be Petter's fellows.

SKELETONS IN THE CLOSET

"Sit, m' boy, sit. Which did you show them? Have you got your commission?" Evans motioned to the chair on Petter's side of the great desk, and began folding architectural drawings and illustrations of carved stone cornices and frontispieces to one side.

"No, sir, no commission," Petter said, "although one of the gentlemen seemed quite impressed with my latest plan."

"Ah, the only aesthete in the group then," Evans answered, and patting the desk, said, "Come on then, show me. I don't believe I've seen the final version."

Petter placed the drawings of the hotel he had designed on the table, and turned them to face Evans. Starting with a rendering of the façade of the building and moving through the architectural plans beneath, Evans bowed his glowing pate and leafed through the plans.

"Magnificent," he said at last.

"Magnificent," echoed Phoebe, startling Petter, for he had not heard her enter the room.

"Thank you, sir, miss," Petter said.

"I am especially impressed with the design of the main floor – the flow you achieved with the open arches between the foyer and adjoining rooms. The placement of the main reception area… And the planned carvings!" Evans' voice squeaked at the final word, and he cleared his throat before finishing, "Magnificent!"

"Thank you, sir." Petter glanced at Phoebe, and gesturing to one section with a sweeping hand, said, "This particular section was planned at Miss Evans' suggestion."

"Oh, Petter! I simply...," Phoebe began, a pretty blush coloring her otherwise plain features.

"Ah, yes, Phoebe!" Evans interrupted, and he raised a marble-block of a hand to Phoebe's face and rubbed a finger along her cheek. "If her womanly attributes did not leave her without the bulk or strength needed, she would be a fine mason, but I daresay she shows promise in architecture. I am sorry for your sake, dear, that you were not born a son."

The blush on Phoebe's cheeks warmed anew, and she uncharacteristically cast her eyes down, and back at Petter with an expression he could not name, before saying, "I'm not sorry, Father."

"No, no, neither am I, my dear." The man patted at his daughter's arm as his eyes returned to Petter's plans. Petter gazed at Phoebe – trying to decipher the meaning of her odd expression, and failing – before returning his attention to Evans and the part of the plans the man was examining. Phoebe's suggestion for the main foyer was insightful – both an artistic and functional improvement to his original design – but he wondered if her father was doing the girl a disservice to allow her to spend her days in his offices learning a man's craft. The girl's mother was deceased for some years and she would benefit more from the company of women – an aunt, perhaps, or cousins – where she might better learn the feminine arts. Lord knew, if Petter was being frustrated by his youth, the girl could only be educating herself into a life of dissatisfaction and disappointment. Petter glanced toward Phoebe again.

And perhaps in the company of women, she could learn to be less plain.

Petter was wrenched from his reverie by another exclamation from Evans: "Magnificent!" The man brought his palm down on the desktop with a bang, and then moved around the desk to place an arm around Petter's shoulders again. With the other hand pounding Petter's chest, he said, "There will come a day when you overcome your youth, m' boy, and then I will need to worry over my own livelihood. I hope when the time comes, you'll remember that I proclaimed your genius first, and take pity on me." He loosed a high-pitched twittering laugh setting the flaps of his mustache flying, before releasing Petter to gather his drawings. "Now where was I?" he said, as he strode out of the office and back toward the abandoned journeyman.

Petter watched Evans' broad back as the man first filled and then moved through the doorway, feeling much lifted by the tonic of the man's gracious tribute. When he turned to the desk, Phoebe was gathering up Petter's plans.

"Your father is right, you know. Your suggestion was truly inspired." He opened the portfolio to allow Phoebe to place the plans within.

"You are kind, Petter." From any other girl he would have expected the words to come with a coquettish bat of eyelashes, but when he looked up, her large brown eyes met his.

"No, I am..." He faltered under her gaze, and began again. "Miss Evans, I am not..." She did not let him finish.

"Phoebe," she said. "If you mean what you say, we are co-workers, and perhaps even friends, and you could do me the favor of calling me by my given name, as I have asked." Rather than revealing any petulance with her words, she smiled as she spoke.

Petter smiled in return, as though they shared a joke.

"Phoebe, then." He glanced over his shoulder toward the workroom, and the journeymen about their various tasks, realizing that other than his employer, Phoebe was the only person on the premises who treated him in a friendly manner.

"Friends, then," she said, and held her hand out as if to shake his hand in the fashion of a man.

Petter hesitated, and then with a laugh took her hand and shook it once. "As my friend and co-worker, perhaps you should look at more of my plans – to help me improve them where I fall short," he said.

"It was a lucky inspiration; that is all. The plans are yours and are truly splendid... beautiful." She paused, shifting her weight between her feet, seeming embarrassed. She cleared her throat and said, "And perhaps, if it would not be an imposition on your time, you could look at my own fledgling plans."

SKELETONS IN THE CLOSET

"You've drawn your own plans?" Petter asked, and then saw the folly of his surprise. Until now, he had thought her suggestion regarding his own plans to be blind luck supported only by her familiarity – through her father – with various architectural drawings and devices. Now it occurred to him that her father's statement that she showed promise in architecture insinuated much more than that. Before she could answer his question, he said, "I would be pleased… Phoebe."

She smiled at his use of her name, but said nothing more.

"Now I must earn my keep as your father's journeyman, or soon seek other employment. Please excuse me."

Petter worked the remainder of the day, sleeves rolled up. With mallet and chisels, rifflers and sanders, he masticated the immense marble block on which he had been working for some days until the elaborate carved column capital stood gleaming and ready for delivery. He stood back, pleased to be finished with the piece, glowing with his exertion and the pleasure he took in his craft. His failure of the morning was forgotten for the moment. His self-satisfied smile faded as he turned toward a neighboring journeyman – wanting to share his triumph – and met a sneer. He glanced away and around the room, seeking refuge in a friendly face, before remembering – or realizing anew – that as Evans' obvious favorite, he would find none. Even the two people who had extended friendship to him did not share his momentary pleasure: Evans had left his establishment for a meeting, and

Phoebe sat at a drafting table in the far corner engrossed in a project of her own.

Drawing architectural plans? It amazed him that he had not considered the possibility before today, as she was often ensconced behind the same table.

Just as his eyes were releasing her to turn to his next project, her head lifted and her eyes fixed on his. His smile was born anew, and was answered with the warmth of her own.

A friend. It is good to have a friend in this place. In silence he turned, and began with ropes and rollers and wedges to move the next piece of roughed-in stone into place. The page attached to the stone described it as part of a frieze to be mounted above a bank entrance. He began the process of preparing the surface for the carving of the large letters.

Through the rest of the day – whether stopping his work for water or for a brief rest – he sought Phoebe's steady gaze and warm smile. For reasons he could not name, a certainty rose in him that today was a turning point to his time in London, and that success soon would be his.

CHAPTER 3
A DECISION IS MADE

Christine ran her fingers through the loose, ruddy mane of her mare as she waited for Erik to dismount. Her breathing was returning to normal after their gallop back to the stables, although her mare still puffed and blew and stamped as the handler patted its muzzle. The exhilaration of the final gallop and the pleasure of their morning ride together still glowed within her.

Erik came around to her side of the horse, smiling up at her, his eyes searching her face. She knew why he examined her so intently, and a spasm of guilt knifed through her. She hoped it did not show on her face.

What is wrong with me? The thought was followed by another, more vehement inner voice. *There is nothing wrong with missing your child, with worrying about him… with wanting to protect him!*

Erik reached his long-fingered hands up as she pulled her foot from the single stirrup and lifted her top knee over the saddle horns. She slid from the saddle into his waiting arms, and he lowered her to the ground. His careful tenderness and his closeness pulled her away from thoughts of Petter, and, grateful, she pressed her cheek to his chest. She could feel his own ragged breathing as he embraced her and held her close.

I do love this man so. I am happy with him. She lifted her face to his, and looked into his large, round eyes. The small wrinkles at the corners of his eyes deepened as his smile grew. She concentrated on losing herself in the love reflected there, and to focus for the moment on Erik, only Erik. She barely noticed as the handler led the horses away, the animals nickering their affection at the capable man.

"Gazelle was in rare form today," Erik said, turning and taking her arm to lead her from the stable entrance.

"She is a beautiful mare," she answered. "We should ride more often. That last gallop was glorious!" She put all the enthusiasm into her voice that she felt, and forced herself not to think of the third horse in the stable – the horse that had not joined their ride today.

"Then we shall!" Erik responded. She thought his exuberance a bit forced, but could not blame him. Even she found her despondency over Petter's absence confusing and annoying at times and she knew Erik was trying to help her overcome her surprising feeling of loss. Unfortunately, there were times, like now, that his forced cheerfulness brought back the loss, rather than alleviated it.

"What shall we do now, wife?" he asked, turning to face her, and walking backwards before her as they made their way down the path toward the gardens and the manor. "You could read to me – the new book by that Doyle fellow is rather interesting." When she did not answer, he continued, "Or if reading strikes you as too mellow, perhaps we could make another trip to Stockholm – the excitement of the city…"

Erik would continue in this vein if she did not answer, so she put him off as gently as she could. "Erik, my love, what I want most is a pleasant walk with my husband, and a moment to catch my breath before we begin another enjoyment." She smiled as she spoke, and hoped that Erik could read the love and gratitude in her eyes, rather than the mild exasperation – directed at herself or at Erik, she could not tell – which was growing as he planned the next distraction.

Erik smiled and kissed her cheek, and then strode beside her, hands gripped at his back, eyes roving over the sky and the surrounding scenery, down to the white pebbles of the path on which they trod. His wholehearted effort to do as she had suggested settled as a weight against her, and she wondered if any of his apparent pleasure of late was genuine.

If not, it is purely my own fault. She could acknowledge this much, although she felt helpless to change.

The past months had been full of time together; singing and reading and trips to both Korsnäsborg and Stockholm, dinners with the few close friends who accepted Erik's deformed features as of no more consequence than the clothing he chose to wear. Erik was unstoppable in his efforts to fill her every waking moment with activities and distractions, all meant to keep her from brooding on Petter's absence and worrying about their son's fate in London. As she thought through the last months, she realized that Erik had not even taken the daytrips he usually took to see his old friend, Mattis, the sailor, and to work on the man's boat as a common fisherman – an escape Erik enjoyed. She spoke without thinking.

"You have not been to see Mattis lately."

"No," Erik answered, and a brief cloud crossed his features. Then he turned to her, smiling again, interpreting her statement as a suggestion for an activity. "Would you like to sail? Mattis would be more than happy to see you again, or take you out on the water, if you wish." The childlike eagerness reflected in his face at the thought of seeing his friend while also providing another activity in which to engage her drew a laugh from Christine.

"No, dear," she answered, and laughed again. "I just thought you must be missing his easy friendship. If so, you should go." The tone of her last statement was sharper than she intended, sounding in her own ears as if she were asking him to leave her in peace for a time. She put her hand on his arm, and continued, softening her suggestion. "I love you, Erik, truly, but I need not monopolize your time – especially when doing so steals your time for relaxation and denies your companionship to a man who loves you, as Mattis does." She rose to her toes to kiss his chin.

Neither of them spoke, and she saw in Erik's eyes both his desire to visit with his friend and his concern for her. When he spoke, his concern carried the greater weight.

SKELETONS IN THE CLOSET

"I would rather be with you, my love." The quiet sadness that crept into Erik's voice confirmed Christine's suspicions about the forced nature of his constant cheerfulness of late, although his face still bore the stale leavings of a smile. Lifting her hand, he bent and brushed his lips against her riding glove.

This must stop. In her sudden frustration, she almost pulled her hand from Erik's gentle grip. Then it came to her that Erik was entertaining the identical thought – *this must stop* – and her heart filled with compassion for her husband's effort; an effort made necessary by her own melancholy behavior, and made possible by his love for her.

This must stop. But how?

Erik released her hand, and she brought her palm to his face, where he covered it with his own.

"Then I shall be happy to oblige you, husband. I am still winded from our ride, so… something quiet. Would you be interested in besting me in a game of chess?"

Erik laughed, and Christine felt thankful that this expression of delight, at least, was caused *by* her instead of *for* her, and bore no traces of being forced.

"I do not win every time," he answered, taking her arm to resume their walk.

"No, you don't," she answered. "You only win when you are not allowing me to win."

"I never deliberately lose," he said, with a tone of outrage at her scandalous suggestion. He lifted his chin as though injured by an unfair accusation. She smiled and tilted her head against his shoulder, hoping like a vain child that in this he told the truth, and yet doubting the statement nonetheless.

They walked the rest of the path to the manor in silence, Erik apparently lost in his own thoughts, and Christine hoping that a game of chess would give her time to think on their situation, and to find a way to break the unhappy rhythm in which they were locked.

I wonder if Erik's mind is engaged in solving the same dilemma.

***

Christine was no closer to a resolution when, during dinner, Erik took up the effort toward distraction he had avoided since their ride that morning, and their game of chess. He had won, of course.

"What would you think about having a party?" he asked. Before Christine could answer, he continued, excitement and enthusiasm bubbling through his words. "We could have all of our friends over – Mattis could bring his wife, she would be delighted – and perhaps hire entertainment… fireworks… that sort of thing? Hmm?"

Frustration bloomed in her again, and the words were out of her mouth before she knew what she was saying. "I want to move back to London." Even as she said the words, she could not believe she was uttering them. She had hated London while she lived there – hated the weather, the crowds, the city… even hated her relationship with her first husband, Raoul. The only pleasant memories that she had of the city were those that centered around Erik prior to Raoul's demise (and even those memories were colored with moments of fear and uncertainty), and then their final year spent together there, married under the guise of Lord and Lady Bastion. Thankfully, the manor in which they then lived was outside the horrid city.

The silence between them grew as her words echoed in her ears.

"You hated London," Erik answered, echoing her thoughts. His surprise was evidenced in the sudden furrows that creased his forehead. His mouth drew down into a thin bow of confusion and disappointment.

"Yes," she answered, and then said the only words that would explain her statement, the reasoning which they both understood as the motive behind her statement. "I miss Petter. I worry about him. Perhaps if we were there…"

"Petter is a man now, Christine," he interrupted. "He does not need, nor will he likely appreciate, being coddled." The sharpness with which Erik spoke startled Christine – she had become so accustomed of late to his gentle tones and obsequiousness. Rather than irritating her, she decided that she preferred his current tone – at least it was honest.

Finally, some of the rubbish between us is being cleared!

Sudden tears pricked her eyes at the recognition of the barrier between them, and the knowledge that her behavior was the reason for the building of that barrier.

"I know, Erik. He is a man in the eyes of the world. But in my eyes, he is a child who cannot know how to move through the world as a man, let alone the dangers it holds." Her tears spilled over, tears that were for Erik, for her, but she knew he would see them only as more weeping for the loss of Petter. She wiped at her cheeks, her eyes, as Erik stared at her, frustration and disappointment tainting his features.

She lifted the linen napkin from her lap and dabbed at her eyes, determined to gain a better control over herself before she continued. "I… I know you are worried about me. I know how hard you've worked to help me. I wish I could control or even understand my melancholy. I was trying to think of a way of… of alleviating it, of helping. Perhaps if we were nearer Petter…" Her voice began to tremble and more tears escaped to trip down her cheeks. "I love you, Erik, I love you! I don't wish to push you away. I couldn't bear to lose you, too!" She almost shouted this last into her napkin as she covered her face.

Erik dropped on his knees at her side, his arms around her, the velvet returned to his voice as he soothed her and told her again and again that he loved her. He lifted her from her chair at the dining table and carried her to the next room, to a couch, where he held her like a child until her sobbing came under control. He crooned a melody, and rocked her until she quieted. He pressed a handkerchief into her hand and waited while she dabbed at her face. He put a hand under her chin and she let him draw her face up toward his.

SKELETONS IN THE CLOSET

"You will never lose me, wife," he said, answering her last heartbroken cry as though she had uttered it only moments ago. "Never."

Another tear escaped Christine's eye, but she dabbed at her eyes and blinked in an effort to clear them.

"I have had a thought – something that may… heal wounds and perhaps even bring joy." The small smile that moved his lips seemed a sad one. Christine could not bring herself to smile in return as she recognized his admission of the wounds she had inflicted in him, the barriers that had risen between them. She clenched her lips in determination that she would hear him out without weeping again.

"Why do we not visit Petter in London?" he asked. His subtle emphasis of the word "visit" stabbed at her, but even so, she nodded again, her excitement rising at the thought of seeing her son again, and being able to see with her own eyes how he fared. "And then, we can continue our travels." Erik paused, gauging her reaction to this last statement. When she looked her confusion at him, he continued. "When first we… were together," he smiled at the reference to the affair they carried on prior to her first husband's death, and Christine flushed with the memories of that passionate time, "we talked often of traveling. You made me promise to take you to the places I have seen in my wanderings. Why do we not make London our first stop, and then see the world?" Instead of seeing the false gaiety that had so often painted his features of late, she saw only pleading – a bare hope that this might help Christine where his other efforts had failed, that she would accept his suggestion.

    Christine bent her lips into a sad smile, and placed her hand against his cheek. She nodded and tried to raise the liveliness of her smile for his sake. She thought of all the hopes Erik must have with this suggestion: that she would be distracted from her melancholy by the new and exciting sights and sounds; that they would have time together, alone, to tear down whatever barriers were growing between them… it was a good plan. Her excitement grew as she considered the adventures to come, the exotic people and places she would see. But the part of the plan that excited her most, that caused her to sit forward and throw her arms around her husband, was the fact that she would be seeing their son again. And soon.

    "I love you, Erik," she murmured. "Thank you."

    "I love you, Christine," he answered, and clutched her closer.

    She heard the miracle of his forgiveness in the words.

CHAPTER 4
SET BACKS

Despite his exhaustion, Petter walked through the evening toward Evans' offices. He had spent the evening at leisure, enjoying a meal with an acquaintance, planning to retire early. But on leaving the pub, his feet had turned him toward the offices again. He was drawn to complete his latest carving – his own work, his own design, and one he could not labor over during his working hours. He hoped – knew! – this latest carving would provide yet another proof of his excellence and his qualifications to call himself a master stonemason. He hoped to be able to photograph the completed carving before returning to his rented rooms for the night. The Brownie camera he always carried thumped against his chest as he walked, keeping time to his slow steps.

Petter thought through the small triumph of the day as he walked. He had spent the day in the Elite Gardens section of the Bush Exhibition building site with Evans, at first appreciating the cloudless day, and later, as the sun wilted him and drained his energy, wishing for the usual London weather to smother the sky. Evans had flattered his "good eye," and at the end of the day, had introduced him to a banker with connections to the kind of investors who had interest in and money for building. The banker had promised introductions, and Petter hoped to receive the commission that would allow him to stop working as a journeyman in another stonemason's shop. Hope fluttered in his stomach as he recalled the conversation with the banker, and the man's surprised but respectful comments.

Petter stumbled in weariness as he approached the shop, and muttering chastisements at himself, decided to turn around and go home. He was too fatigued to get much good work done tonight in any case. He stood for a moment, enduring the battle between the energy of his mind and the exhaustion of his body, then turned to begin the walk back to his flat.

Tomorrow will be soon enough. The piece is nearly finished.

He threw a glance over his shoulder for a last look at the shop as he started away, and stopped again.

In the light of the streetlamp, a figure approached the door to the shop, and then a lamp was lighted within. His curiosity changed the balance of the battle within himself, and he strode with new purpose to investigate.

He entered the shop expecting to find Evans, perhaps laboring to complete office work, but the light did not come from Evans' office. Instead, the light came from the near drafting table – *Phoebe's table* – and Phoebe stood over the table, eyes already roving over half finished plans as she worked to remove her overcoat. Petter strode toward her.

"Phoebe?" he asked, his voice loud in the darkened shop.

SKELETONS IN THE CLOSET

The girl emitted a loud shriek and startled in a most unladylike fashion, almost upsetting the stool near which she stood.

"Who is it!" Her usually quiet voice was harsh and laced with anger. Her fists clenched at her sides as she leaned forward and tried to peer into the darkness.

"It is I, Petter," he answered, still striding toward her. "What can you possibly…?"

"Petter! You just gave me the fright of my life!" There was still the anger, but some of the harshness had left her voice. Her hands came to her chest and pressed there as if to control her fluttering heart. Sharp breaths burst from her lips, and Petter could see the lifting and falling of her ample breast beneath her hands.

"I'm terribly sorry, Phoebe. I didn't mean to startle you." His steps brought him into the light and he stopped at the side of the table, hand reaching toward her before dropping to his side again.

Phoebe gazed at him for a moment longer, before puffing a small embarrassed laugh in his direction and dropping her hands to her sides.

"Petter," she breathed. "Good Heavens." A smile grew on her lips, and he returned it, careful not to allow it to develop into the laugh he could feel building. He did not wish to give insult by laughing at her after startling her.

"What are you doing here at this hour?" she asked, her eyes holding his as she spoke. Her eyes were even more magnificent in the low lantern light, and again he concluded that they were the best feature of the plain girl.

"I came to see about the light, about who might be working here at this time of night," he answered.

"You were just passing by?" she asked, sounding incredulous, with a lift of one eyebrow and a look that suggested she had caught him in a fabrication.

"No, actually. I originally planned to come in and work, and then decided – when practically on the doorstep – to leave well enough alone and get some much needed sleep. Then, I saw the light."

"Ah," she said, satisfied with his answer. As if only now remembering his question, she said, "I had a sudden inspiration for an improvement to my plans, and could not let it wait until morning." She gestured toward the plans spread on the drafting table. His eyes followed her gesture, but before he could take in what he was seeing, she gripped the near corner and doubled the drawing over on itself. "I'd rather you didn't see it until it is finished," she said.

Petter flushed with the feeling that he had been caught spying or eavesdropping, and took a step backward with a small bow of his head.

Phoebe took a quick step toward him, and said, "What work were you planning? Something for Father? You are faster and more skillful than any of his other men. You can't possibly feel you must work at this hour."

SKELETONS IN THE CLOSET

"No." A smile returned to his face. "Something of my own. It's in the back."

"Shall we?" she asked, eyes again on his. She lifted the lantern with one hand, and offered her other arm to him. "Unless, of course, you'd rather I didn't see it until it is finished…" A smile lifted the corners of her mouth as she offered him the excuse she had used regarding her own work.

"It's nearly finished now. I wouldn't mind," he answered, and began leading her toward the back of the shop.

"There," he said, and pointed, falling back a step, allowing her to approach his piece alone, proud of his work, and hoping for – waiting for – her exclamation of praise.

"Oh, Petter!" she said with an appreciative gasp, as the light from her lantern fell on the large and intricately carved stone bracket. She lifted the lantern higher in her hand, the better to see the top of the man-tall stone. Petter looked with renewed pride at his work in the unsteady light, the carven leaves appearing to dance with the movement of the lantern. The modillion he had carved was ornate in the extreme, and did not even have the linear rectangular bottom of the usual corona bracket – the long sides of the rectangle flared outward with flat-bottomed fern leaves curling away from either side like feathers. The fragile protuberances would make the modillion more difficult to maneuver and hang, but he thought them beautiful in the extreme.

He brought his hands together in delight as she turned to him. Appreciative wonder glowed from her features before she turned back to walk further around the stone. He took a step toward her.

Then, "Oh, no, Petter!" – and this time her exclamation was laced with horror.

Petter rushed to her side, unable to imagine what could have elicited her second anguished exclamation.

He gasped. The modillion was broken in two along the center grain. The break had not been visible from where he had been standing. The plugs used to feather and tare the great stone still remained in the top of the piece, difficult to see at first due to the intricacy of the acanthus leaves and palmettes carved there. Petter could not form a coherent thought or movement as he stared at the deliberate vandalism of his work, unable to move his mind past the incomprehension of the act. He stood staring, for an immeasurable length of time before he was startled from his stupor by something touching his arm. He jerked his head toward the touch in desperate need to look away from ruined piece. Phoebe was next to him, gazing at him, her dark eyes laced with pity.

"Petter, oh Petter," she said. "Who would have…?" Her eyes followed his own as they were drawn back to the wreckage.

Petter knew who would have done the incomprehensible – any one of a number of the jealous journeymen who glared their hatred of him as he worked among them. The skill of his work, and the speed with which he could accomplish it only added to the enmity in which his fellow workers steeped each time Evans praised him.

SKELETONS IN THE CLOSET

Anger choked his throat like a swallowed fist, and battled against his desire to cry out in pain. He took several panted breaths in an effort to clear the obstruction in his throat, as Phoebe stepped away from him and again approached the broken piece. Her fingers ran over the curled leaves he had so labored to make complex and fragile in their beauty. He blinked back tears as her fingers ran over the still beautiful portion of the spoilage. He watched her fingers, transfixed; horrified by her ability to touch what to him seemed a corpse. When she turned to him again, there were tears in her eyes.

"Petter, it was beautiful." Her voice broke as she spoke and her tears overflowed to her cheek. In a moment of grotesque clarity, he watched as Phoebe's tongue moved to the corner of her mouth and caught at a tear. The image remained clear in his mind even after she brought her handkerchief to her face to gather the remaining wetness. For a brief instant, Petter tasted her tear on his own tongue, tart and reflecting the bitterness of the moment. Still unable to speak, and in a sudden need not to see what lay before him – the destruction of weeks of work – he closed his eyes and turned his back to Phoebe and the broken stone silhouetting her.

Phoebe's shoes tapped on the concrete as she walked toward him, and he inhaled her warm, pleasant scent – like that of a fresh meadow – as she moved past him. The lantern she held turned the blackness behind his closed eyelids to red as she moved to stand in front of him. She said nothing. He was thankful for the time she granted for his grief, but was also ashamed that he needed it.

Exhaling through pursed lips, Petter forced himself to let go of his disappointment and accept.

They will not beat me. Nothing will stop me. And forcing his thoughts forward and away from this hideous moment, *What can I recover from the wreckage?*

He breathed again. Calmer, feeling more himself, he opened his eyes to the disconcerting gaze of Phoebe's pain-laced eyes on his.

"I am quite myself again. I apologize."

"Apologize?" she asked, incredulity twisting her features.

"If I worried you," he explained.

"You didn't worry me," she answered. "This senseless… this terrible…" she stammered, unable to find the right words. "*This* worries me!" she finished, one hand flung to the ruin behind him. "I don't understand why…" Again words seemed to fail her and she stopped speaking, looking away from his work and into his eyes again, something like pleading in her eyes. She took a step closer and raised the lantern, brow now crinkled with curiosity. "Your eyes…," she said. Petter knew what she saw: the strange reflectiveness that also shone in his father's eyes in low lamplight. He looked away.

"I will find another place to work on my own projects," he answered. *They will not beat me.*

SKELETONS IN THE CLOSET

"Father will help you. He will be so angry! He will…" In her indignation, she seemed ready to spit or stamp, the matter of his eyes forgotten.

"Your father can do nothing, nor should he. That would not help me," Petter interrupted.

Phoebe looked her exasperation at him, and then her face cleared with sudden inspiration. "Father has store rooms you could work in. I am certain…"

"I will ask him in the morning." Petter's calm statement broke through Phoebe's anger and outrage.

"Oh," she said. "Good." She seemed to shrink in size back to the small, plain girl she was.

"And tonight, I can at least take several close photographs of the carvings," he continued. "The parts that are not *ruined*." Almost growling the last word, anger tinted his words away from the calmness he had achieved in his determination. He took another deep breath to quiet himself again. "Would you be willing to assist me?"

"Of course!" Phoebe answered. "What can I do?"

"Hold the lantern, if you would. The photographs will likely be better in daylight – I can take additional photographs tomorrow – but perhaps the shadows and glow of lantern light will lend themselves to a more interesting photograph."

"Of course," she said, with a shy smile.

After taking several photographs, Petter approached his drafting table, half expecting to see his unfinished architectural plans ruined as well. Nothing was disturbed. In all likelihood, the vandals had not known whether the plans were Petter's own or a task assigned by Evans, and they would not have risked damaging Evans' work. Petter folded his plans, and locked them into a drawer beneath the drafting table, vowing as he did so to do the same every day before leaving the shop. Phoebe remained at his side as he returned the key to his pocket. She did not question his reasons.

Turning to Phoebe, Petter said, "Thank you. For everything."

She nodded in acknowledgement, and turned to her desk to retrieve her abandoned overcoat.

"May I see you home?" he asked, moving toward her to assist with her coat. He wondered what he had not questioned in his surprise at finding her here: that she had come to the office unescorted. Now, given the lateness of the hour and her kindness of the past hour, felt compelled to see her home.

"Yes, thank you, Petter," she said. "Unless it would be an inconvenience. I am perfectly capable of…"

"It would be my pleasure," he answered, and presented his arm. They walked in silence the few blocks to the brownstone residence she shared with her father.

"Please get some sleep, Petter," she said when they reached her door.

"Hah!" he answered. "Tired as I am, I could not sleep just now." Phoebe turned back and looked at him with such concern in her eyes that he felt compelled to explain further. "I think I will take in a silent picture. There is a theater not far from here. A dose of banal humor should do the trick."

Phoebe hesitated, before saying in a rush, "Petter, if you would like company…" She stopped, and in the lamplight, she flushed. Petter could not imagine why she would.

"No need to worry about me, Phoebe. Thank you. I have imposed upon you enough this evening." He bowed in an attempt to show his thanks and appreciation for her friendship.

Phoebe hesitated again, and Petter thought she would say something more. Instead, she said, "Good night then, Petter."

"Good night, Phoebe." He waited until the heavy door of her residence closed behind her before turning away.

He wondered as he walked if he should relay all that had happened this evening in his next letter to his parents. Before he reached the theater, he had decided he would not. His parents had probably never experienced these kinds of malicious behavior, and would worry. As he paid for a ticket to the silent picture, he thought again:

I am stronger than they think. They will not beat me. They stole my work from me this time, but not my skill. Nothing will stop me.

Minutes into the picture, he fell asleep.

CHAPTER 5
A HINT OF TROUBLE

"Oy, Lucky!" The voice boomed across the docks toward where Erik stood wearing a tattered, hooded rain cloak, the large hood covering his head and pulled forward to cover most of his face.

Smiling and shaking his head inside the over-sized hood, Erik turned toward the tall broad-shouldered man moving up the pier. He had not seen his friend in too long a time, and only now realized how much he had missed the cheerful sailor.

"Mattis," Erik said, as the two men closed to arm's reach. "It is good to see you, old friend." His words came out in grunts as the large man threw his arms around Erik and pounded his back.

"Why do you still wear this worn old thing?" Mattis asked, pulling at the hooded cloak. "No shame in being lucky, Lucky." The great man threw back his head and boomed a great laugh.

"Nostalgia," Erik answered. "Believe it, if you will – this is the same cloak I wore when I first met you." Erik recalled the day of their first meeting, more than two decades ago, when the sailor had first unhooded him and thought his deformed face the result of a shark bite – and Erik had never corrected the misconception.

SKELETONS IN THE CLOSET

Mattis had dubbed him "Lucky," and had used the epithet exclusively since. Mattis would forever hold a special place in Erik's heart for the complete acceptance of his deformity and the quick friendship that followed between the two — the first real friendship of Erik's life. The once golden hair of the man was now shot with silver, and his girth had grown, but Mattis still wore the same bright blue eyes, and the lines that bordered his eyes were all drawn by smiles over the years.

"Oh, ho! I'd believe it. Looks it." Mattis paused, and then said, "Smells it, too." The old sailor laughed again. He tugged at the cloak again, feeling his question unanswered.

"I know most everyone at the docks is aware of my... features. I just do not feel the need to discomfit them," Erik said.

"You're no uglier than I, and we both have managed to keep beautiful wives...," he grinned, then shrugged. "But suit yourself, eh?" Mattis threw an arm around Erik's shoulders, and together they began walking toward the small outdoor dock café where they always took lunch. "So, how's the boy? What brings you here today? Up for a bit of fishing?" Mattis asked.

"Petter's fine, if his letters are to be believed. Although his mother worries..." Erik began.

"'S mother's job to worry, and Christine always did dote on the boy. But he's a fine man — so help me — better man than my youngest, the lazy git! Them being grown doesn't stop Mama from worrying 'bout them all. But Petter'll make you proud, mark my words." Mattis stopped to take a sip from the mug of beer that had just been delivered to the table, and continued. "Fishing? Eh?" He licked at the rim of foam on his upper lip, his eyes bright with anticipation as he looked back at Erik.

Erik could not suppress another smile, and a flush of gratitude at the simple pleasure of sharing an afternoon with the happy man. A tension that he did not realize had been gripping him over the last days – or weeks – lifted, and he felt lighter under his cloak. He lifted his own beer in silent toast to Mattis, before answering the man.

"I'm afraid not. Not today, Mattis, my friend." Erik smiled again as an accepting resignation settled over Mattis' large features. "I would like to hire your services, however."

"Hire?" Mattis said, and a slight frown of confusion and disapproval clouded his sunny face.

"Christine and I would like you to take us south, if you would, where we can catch a larger ship – we are going to London for a visit." Even here, without Christine to hear his words, he needed to reinforce that the trip to London was merely a visit.

"Ah, to see the boy! Excellent, excellent!" Mattis pounded a hand on Erik's shoulder. "I can take you to Stockholm." Another sip of beer, and Mattis said, "And when do you return? I will meet you to bring your tired bodies home!"

"From London, we plan to travel for some months. I don't know when we'll be returning."

"Exciting, exciting. Mama doesn't care for travel, but to each their own, eh? When do you want to leave?"

SKELETONS IN THE CLOSET

"In a week," Erik answered.

After giving Mattis the details of their plans, Erik settled into a haphazard discussion with his friend, discussing the latter's newest fishing boat acquisition, his wife and sons, and the weather – which for a sailor was no trivial subject. They both enjoyed an excellent fish stew and shared a dark, heavy loaf of fragrant bread. Erik relaxed as the two talked and laughed away the better part of the afternoon.

"I must get home, Mattis," Erik said. "Christine has had the unpleasant task of shopping for clothes and sundries we will need in our travels, while I have had the day to while away in the pleasure of your company." Erik's eyes roved the docks as they had throughout the day.

"Finish your beer, Lucky, no sense in wasting it, although I reckon it will be on its way out again soon enough." Mattis laughed, and touched his own near empty mug to Erik's.

"Yes… of cour–" Erik stopped mid-word as his eye caught on the dark robes and turban of a Persian leaving a small passenger vessel at the far dock. The man's furtive movements would have been enough to interest Erik even without the exotic clothing, but the sight of a Persian here, in a small fishing village in Sweden, seemed surreal and unnerving.

Erik had not seen a Persian in garb since his escape first from Mazenderan and then from Constantinople more than four decades hence. In both cases he had escaped the death sentences that had been levied upon him – death sentences that undoubtedly were still in place. The sultans of both Mazenderan and Constantinople had used Erik's expertise to build or add to their magnificent palaces, but then sought to erase his knowledge of their interiors, secret passages, and protections by ordering his death. It was the reason he had left Persia forever. And now a Persian appeared in this small Swedish fishing village. Intuition caused his skin to prickle with chill even in the warmth of the afternoon.

Erik's unease heightened when the Persian, with a last cautious look about, moved from view behind a small shack at the far end of the dock. He returned his gaze to Mattis.

"There's a strange one," Mattis said. "Don't see the likes of Moors in these parts often."

"No," Erik answered.

"In the big ports, sometimes, but then usually with a crew." Mattis sipped at his beer and said, "Wonder why he's here. Think he got on the wrong boat?" He chuckled at his feeble joke.

"Perhaps we should stay a bit, and see," Erik answered. He pulled his hood farther over his head and yanked at its edge to better cover his face.

Mattis grunted in reply, and Erik realized that his own uneasiness was infecting the jovial sailor.

As the minutes passed, Erik's curiosity and frustration nearly propelled him from the table to question the Moor – perhaps a simple introduction to the Persian would alleviate his suspicions – but a sense of foreboding kept him seated. He waited for the man to reappear. Mattis stopped his attempts at continued conversation when Erik answered him with brief and distracted comments. The sailor finished his own beer, and then Erik's, as Erik waited and watched, unmoving.

Finally, another man approached the same shack behind which the Persian had disappeared. Erik sucked in his breath as he recognized the man as a servant from his own household, and also took in the man's stealthy posture and cautious looks from side to side.

Too much coincidence.

Erik was certain he was still a wanted man in the two kingdoms – and now his own servant was meeting with a Persian! He pulled at his hood again and sank lower into his seat.

"Friend, what–?" Mattis began, but Erik interrupted, leaning forward to place a hand atop the giant hand of the other.

"Mattis, how long are you staying? There is trouble in the making," Erik said. He kept his eyes on the far shack as he spoke.

"I'll stay a month if it will help you. What sort of trouble?"

Erik pulled his eyes from the shack to look into the earnest eyes of his friend. "Trouble in which I do not want you involved. But Christine and I may be leaving much sooner than I thought. Maybe tomorrow."

"Tonight, if need be," Mattis said. "I'll make ready right away."

"Thank you, friend, most sincerely," Erik answered. Mattis looked alarmed when Erik accepted the idea of immediate departure. "Don't speak of this or of me to anyone. I will come to you soon. Where will you be staying?"

"On my boat!" Mattis answered. "There'll be no delay on my account. I'll be ready to push off in just two hours. Where do we go?"

"I don't yet know." With a final look toward the shack, he stood, threw money to the table enough to cover their meal and more, and raised his hand to the other man's shoulder. "Thank you again." Then Erik was off, hurrying toward his home and Christine, leaving his friend standing confused and concerned at the small dockside table. When he looked back over his shoulder, the sailor was already moving toward his boat to make ready.

***

"Christine!" Erik startled the young maid Aina as he burst through the front door of the manor house. Looking to her, he said with uncharacteristic sharpness, "Where is your mistress?"

Alarmed at Erik's evident agitation, she pointed toward the stairs to the second level. Erik had no time to apologize or calm the poor girl, but instead ran up the stairs, two and three at a time, undoubtedly alarming the girl further.

"Christine!" Erik shouted again, as he reached the top of the stairs. "Christine!"

"Here," she answered from their bedroom. Her muted voice sounded to his ears like that of an angel, his relief at her unconcerned reply causing him to gasp. He walked to the open door and huffed through a small smile at the tranquil scene of

SKELETONS IN THE CLOSET

domesticity he found there, as Christine folded and stacked and organized items atop their large bed. She looked so calm and happy.

"Did you have a nice visit, dear?" she asked, and raised her smiling face to his. Discerning his anxiety from his posture or some telling expression on his face, or perhaps from some other clue of which he was unaware – they had been together long enough to make such intimate knowledge seem natural – the smile fell from her face. She dropped a coat she had been folding, and coming around the bed toward him, concern now blanching her cheeks, she said, "What is wrong? Is it something with Mattis?"

His arms came around her as she rushed to embrace him, and he kissed her on the forehead, holding his lips there longer than necessary, cherishing her anew, thankful that she was in his arms, only now realizing how much he had feared for her safety.

She released him, and taking his hand and pulling him to the large window seat, she said, "Come, you must tell me." Aina appeared in the doorway as they crossed the floor, and Christine said, "Aina, tea please." And to Erik, "Are you hungry?" and before he could answer, again to Aina, "And biscuits." She pushed Erik onto the cushioned seat, and sat beside him, taking his hands in hers. Worry creased her brow.

Erik took a deep breath, closed his eyes, and shook his head from side to side, as if to deny what he prepared to tell her.

"I am found," he said.

"Were you lost?" The statement sounded as if she meant it to be humorous, as if she meant it to be followed by a small laugh, but her tension denied her any levity.

"It seems we may be moving from Sweden after all, Christine," he said, dropping his eyes from her needy gaze and squeezing her hands in his own.

"Erik, please speak sense," she said. "You're frightening me!"

He sighed and kissed her. She responded with a perfunctory meeting of their lips, and drew back again. He could not blame her. He could see the fear and worry in her eyes, and he had not, in fact, explained himself yet.

"There was a Persian at the port," he said. He waited, letting the implication settle in her mind, and then continued, "And Jacob met with him. Secretly."

"Jacob? But why would he meet–?" As understanding dawned, she shook off the irrelevant question. Outrage at the servant's betrayal flashed across her face. "They cannot still seek your death after all these years," she said, but there was no conviction in her voice.

"I am under a death sentence twice over, my dear. You know that."

Christine turned to look out the window, toward the flower garden she had nurtured, but her gaze did not seem to take in the view. She stood, pulling her hands from his.

SKELETONS IN THE CLOSET

"Then we are moving. I have a start on the packing." She paced to the bed, and took up the coat she had been folding when he entered the room. "When do we go? Where?" she asked. "And before you say it, I know we will not be moving to London. You would not endanger Petter so."

Erik's throat closed and his eyes blurred as he filled with pride at Christine's immediate acceptance and action, at the strength of his bride, at her abandonment – for a time at least – of her melancholy obsession. For a moment he could do nothing but watch her purposeful movement.

"What on Earth could have you smiling?" she asked. A smile grew on her own face in response. He rose and came to her, taking her in his arms.

"I am smiling at you, wife." He kissed her, and this time she returned his kiss with fervor. When they broke, he tried to keep his hold on her, but she pulled from him and turned back to stacking clothing.

"What can we take? When are we leaving? How do we travel?" she asked.

"Mattis." He answered. No further explanation was necessary. "He will be ready to leave before we are, and will take us wherever we choose. It may be best if we board under cover of darkness. Can you be ready by this evening?"

Christine nodded her response as she crossed to the dresser, and began pulling open drawers.

"I have certain financial matters I must attend to. Will you be all right here without me?" he asked.

Moving from the dresser to the wardrobe, she again nodded.

"I'll tell the servants to come immediately to your assistance. And I'll have them lock up after me." He continued to watch as Christine discarded a party dress, took up another, more practical dress, and began to fold it.

"I am sorry, Christine," he said.

She stopped her packing long enough to meet his eyes across the room. "I love you, husband." Smiling, she held his gaze a moment longer, and then turned again to the wardrobe. "Now go. Come back as quickly as you can."

Erik turned and left the room, not bothering to explain to Aina, who was coming down the hall with tea and biscuits – Christine would explain soon enough. He did give orders to Pontus, the aged butler. He paused outside the main door to listen for the lock before running for the stables.

CHAPTER 6
OPPORTUNITIES

Petter turned where he stood, eyeing the magnificent white buildings of the Bush Exhibition site at which he and Evans had been laboring through the day. As he waited for Evans to finish a conversation with a foreman, he rolled his shirtsleeves down, and wandered toward one elaborate building whose Oriental style intrigued his imagination. While he still had not achieved his own commission, he had to admit to himself that the work at the fair site intrigued and fulfilled him – it represented building on such a grand scale. Petter was certain that it must be the largest exhibition site ever constructed, covering as it did one hundred and forty acres, and including an artificial lake and numerous gardens. With the construction underway in the neighboring district for the upcoming Summer Olympics, he felt himself involved in a monumental undertaking.

Petter put his coat on, and pulled a small sketchpad from the pocket. He sketched a portion of an arch above a portico and the carvings and details that illuminated the supporting columns – he would not copy them in his own work, but they intrigued his imagination toward something he knew he would find in his own work later. Replacing the sketchpad, he rejoined Evans, who had finished with the foreman.

"Astounding, isn't it, Petter, m' boy?" the giant man said as Petter approached. Petter smiled and turned a circle again, allowing his face and eyes to reflect his appreciation for the grandness of the project.

"Indeed, Mr. Evans. I must thank you for the opportunity of…"

"Nonsense," Evans squeaked. Raising his beefy hand as he walked and bowing his smooth, shiny head, he greeted a well-dressed, silver haired man. "Good afternoon, Lord Pendleton." He looked to keep walking, but the man turned and held a hand out toward the large mason.

"Ah, yes. Good afternoon. Evans, isn't it?" he said.

Evans bowed again before answering, mustache bobbing and ruddy face flushing with pleasure at the Lord's recognition. "Yes, m' Lord. Mr. Evans at your service." After a pause, Evans continued, "May I introduce my colleague, Mr. Petter Nilsson."

Petter flushed with pride and gratitude that Evans had not introduced him as his journeyman – which he would have been well within his rights to do – but as his colleague. "Lord Pendleton," Petter said, and bowed.

"I find myself quite pleased," Pendleton said, and as Petter had done, the man turned in a circle to take in the multitude of ornate buildings, surreal in their whiteness against the half-finished gardens.

SKELETONS IN THE CLOSET

"Thank you, sir," answered Evans, although he could not claim more than a small part of the credit for the extravagant display.

"Quite worth my investment, I should say," Pendleton continued.

"Oh, Father. Are you discussing investments again?" This latest statement was delivered in a dulcet voice that carried a hint of both chastisement and affection. Petter looked toward the voice, and almost gasped at the sight of the beautiful girl that approached the graying lord. His mouth opened – in awe or disbelief of the vision before him – then closed again, as he forced himself to swallow and breathe. His eyes took in every detail of her loveliness. Her dress was a bright golden yellow – not one of the somber colors preferred by most of the ladies in London – and she carried a matching parasol, which she tilted to one side as she kissed her father's cheek. Petter nearly bent his head to look around and under the parasol as it blocked his vision of her face. Then, as if answering his most fervent wish, the girl turned to face him, parasol cocked over one shoulder, and smiled at him.

This was no girl. This was a goddess!

Golden hair limned her perfect face, and fell in shining ringlets to her shoulders. Ocean blue eyes mirrored the smile she directed at him with her rosebud lips. Petter's face warmed as he smiled in return. He could not take his eyes from her and continue living, while at the same time, he had to pull his eyes from hers or never breathe again.

"May I present my daughter, Constance," came the disembodied voice of her father from what seemed quite a distance, but still Petter could not take his eyes from the girl, or stop smiling.

Constance. Petter clutched at the information with all his mind. *The name of perfection is Constance.*

"Constance, this is Mr. Evans," the voice continued, and the vision before him looked away from him, to the spot at his side where he now remembered his employer was standing. Petter shuddered as her eyes left his, but still he could not look away from her, his entire being willing her to turn back to him.

"Delighted," Mr. Evans said, as he took her delicate, gloved hand in his own, and bent over it. Petter moistened his lips with his tongue as he noticed the fragility of the slim wrist at the base of the glove, imagined the glove removed, imagined his lips pressing to the back of her tiny bare hand.

"Mr. Evans is one of the master masons who are responsible for the splendor you see about you," Lord Pendleton continued. Petter listened to the words, not interested in the meaning of them – only listening in the hopes of gleaning anything more about the beautiful girl before him.

"How wonderful," the girl answered, and Petter could not help but agree with her statement.

She is wonderful!

She turned her blue eyes to Petter again – he felt a shock as though she had touched him, or whispered into his ear – and then she dropped them to flutter her golden eyelashes. Drawn to her as though hypnotized, he took a half step toward her.

"And this is Mr....," Pendleton said, apparently not remembering Petter's name. Tongue trapped behind smiling lips, Petter could not speak to answer him.

The high-toned voice of Mr. Evans came to his rescue. "My colleague, Mr. Nilsson."

"Ah yes, Mr. Nilsson," Pendleton said.

Petter accepted the outstretched hand of the golden angel before him, and bowed over it. "Constance," he murmured as he raised his eyes to her face again.

She blushed and giggled as she pulled her hand from his, and her father and Evans cleared their throats. Like a slap to his face, Petter jolted back to himself, to reality, appalled at his familiarity.

"I beg your pardon! *Miss Pendleton.*" Petter's darting eyes took in the stern face of her father, and the amused expression on Evans' face. "Miss Pendleton," he repeated, turning to the girl, and bowing again. "I am pleased to make your acquaintance."

The rosebud mouth turned up again in a smile, and she said, with a slight tilt to her shoulders and another flash of golden lashes, "Are you a master mason as well?"

"Yes, Miss," Petter answered. He hoped his misery – misery as terrible as his ecstasy had been sweet only moments ago – did not sound in his answer.

"Oh, Father. Don't glare at Mr. Nilsson so. He meant no harm," she said, flashing her eyes to her father and back to Petter. She giggled again behind one gloved hand.

Lord Pendleton sighed, and then, a slight smile turning up one side of his mouth, and his voice laced with humor, said, "I am glaring at you, my dear. You take too much pleasure in Mr. Nilsson's attentions."

"Father!" The briefest of frowns creased her porcelain forehead, and her lips came together in the most delectable moue. Petter imagined kissing the pout from her pursed lips. Instead he managed to look away from the girl, to her father. Thankfully, the man was directing a raised eyebrow of affectionate rebuke toward his daughter.

"We are working on a rather classical building in the Elite Gardens," Petter said, hoping to recover some semblance of propriety, "but I find myself quite intrigued by the often Oriental styles of many of the buildings and pagodas." He clasped his hands behind his back to keep from the temptation of taking Constance's hand in his own.

"Indeed," answered Pendleton. "The overall effect is quite pleasing. Quite."

"Thank you, sir," Evans said. After another moment of silence, Evans said, "A pleasure, Lord Pendleton – Miss Pendleton," and bowed again to man and girl before moving away from the two.

Petter murmured his own words of leave-taking, but could not remember what he had said. He hoped he hadn't made an even greater fool of himself.

As he walked, he was startled from his catalogue of Constance's perfection – he could not bring himself to call her Miss Pendleton in his mind – by the high-pitched giggle of the large man at his side, and a jog to his elbow.

"Love at first sight, eh, Petter, m' boy?" Evans asked with another giggle.

Petter staggered as Evans put a name to the turmoil within him. "Love…," he answered, and then as an afterthought, "Is that what it is?" He felt sure of the answer even as he asked the question.

Evans laughed again.

After another immeasurable length of time lost in his thoughts, Evans clapped him on the back and said, "See you in the morning, m' boy."

Somehow, Petter found his way home for the evening.

***

It was late, and – as was now usual – Petter and Phoebe were the only two left in the shop. Phoebe sat at her drawing table and Petter at his, although of the two, only Phoebe was getting any work accomplished. Petter gazed over the top of the lamp, not seeing the shop at all, not thinking of the plans spread before him. He tapped his pencil on the leg of the table.

"Do you know Constance Pendleton, Phoebe?" Petter asked into the silence. The name – Constance Pendleton – sounded like a prayer in his ears, and he spoke it with reverence. It had been mere weeks since that fateful meeting at the Bush Exhibition.

"I know of her, Petter," she answered. She did not look up from where she ran her pen along a straightedge.

"What do you know of her?" he asked. "Tell me everything."

"What everyone knows, I suppose, Petter. What you know," she answered. "I know who her father is, and in what area of town she lives, and…"

"No, no. I mean, yes, I know all of that, but I want to know about Constance." Petter's gaze shortened when Phoebe did not answer. She sat at her drawing table looking at him across the space between them.

"This morning, her father gave permission for me to court his daughter, and I wish to woo her completely." He grimaced as he thought through the uncomfortable meeting with Lord Pendleton that had – to Petter's surprise – ended with the father's permission to see the girl. The man had said, "Constance must have her suitors," as Petter had risen to go. Even now he did not know whether the statement was meant to indicate that Petter was one of many, or that Constance had insisted on being allowed to see Petter. He preferred to believe the latter.

SKELETONS IN THE CLOSET

Petter lowered his gaze again to see that Phoebe had resumed her drawing. "Do you know if she likes flowers, or chocolates? Does she like the opera? Do you know?"

Phoebe sighed before answering. "Most young ladies like flowers and chocolates, Petter," she answered. "I know that she often attends the opera, but I do not know whether her attendance translates to an appreciation of the art."

Petter sat, still attentive to Phoebe's words, waiting for her to continue. After a moment, she spoke again.

"She likes pretty frocks," she said.

"Phoebe! I cannot buy frocks for Constance." His tone was indignant, but Phoebe laughed, and then sighed again.

"I know that, Petter. I'm telling you what I know about Miss Pendleton, as you asked."

"Yes, of course," Petter answered.

"She seems to like the outdoors – she likes to take a turn about the park with her gentleman friends," Phoebe continued.

Petter's mood darkened at the mention of gentleman friends, but the glorious image of walking in the park with Constance's arm in his own brightened him again.

"Perhaps roses, Petter. Roses are flowers for courting. Roses, and a walk in the park." Petter glanced at Phoebe again, thinking her voice sounded diminished somehow – laced with sadness or resignation, or some other emotion he could not name. But when she lifted her dark, luminous eyes to look at him, she smiled the warm smile of friendship.

"Thank you, Phoebe. I think the idea is grand." And then more to himself than to Phoebe, he murmured, "Roses." He pictured a delicate bouquet of pink tea roses, clutched in Constance's small hand; the delicate sniff she would take, and her blue eyes turning down, before rising to meet his.

"You are a true friend, Phoebe, to help me with a woman's perspective," he said. She held his eyes for a long moment before dropping her gaze to her work again.

"Yes, Petter, I am a friend," she said, and this time, he was sure he heard sadness in her tone. If she still seemed unhappy tomorrow, he would find a way to ask her the reason. Perhaps he could return the favor, and as a friend, help ease whatever might be troubling her. Yes, tomorrow. But tonight, he would get no good work accomplished. He stood, determined to dine quickly, and retire – in all likelihood to moon over Constance, which was his favorite occupation of the moment.

"Can I escort you home, Phoebe? I'm of no use this evening." He pulled on his overcoat.

"No, thank you, Petter. Father knows I am here, and I will be quite all right." She did not look up from her drawing.

He hesitated, feeling deflated by Phoebe's unswerving attention to whatever lay before her. "Good evening, then," he said.

"Good evening, Petter," she answered.

CHAPTER 7
TREACHERY

Christine stepped back from the travel trunk as Aina and Annika placed the last pieces of clothing within and pulled down the heavy lid. The latches clicked into place under their fingers. She would miss the two ubiquitous, ever-pleasant girls. Today, despite her curt – and sometimes confusing – instructions to them, they worked with diligent effort to follow her directions.

"Now the other," she said to the girls, as she gestured toward Pontus, the faithful old butler, who in turn, gestured into the hall behind him. The girls moved to the next trunk, and began loading the nearby articles, making the most of the space in the trunk through judicious stacking and arranging.

When Christine looked up, Pontus was bent over one end of the loaded trunk, while Erik's assistant valet took the other end.

"Pontus," she said, rushing toward the older man, "you needn't do that. Wait for one of the others to come back." She wondered why none of the others had returned.

The man straightened, and with raised chin, said, "I am quite capable, Madam, and loyal to your welfare. I can and will do what must be done." He did not bend again, unwilling to resume his self-appointed task until having at least her tacit permission.

Christine clutched the man's arm, and gave him an affectionate squeeze. "Yes, Pontus, I know. Your loyalty has never been and will never be in question." She smiled as she continued. "I will not interfere. I am quite certain of your capabilities." She was not altogether sure that the man would not injure himself moving the heavy trunk, but under the circumstances, she could not wound his pride by expressing her doubt.

After hearing of Jacob's treachery, each of their servants had approached her professing their loyalty, and damning Jacob for his defection. Several had confessed to disliking or distrusting the man, and Pontus had even confessed – much to her surprise – that he had discussed the matter with Erik. Christine had thought Jacob to be rather pleasant – although she was now furious over his betrayal – and his hand in the kitchen was nothing short of miraculous. She sighed, thinking that she would have done with a lesser chef, if only to avoid the current danger.

If Erik was correct that there was a danger.

The two men maneuvered the trunk through the doorway. She was pleased to note that Pontus appeared to be handling the heavy load. She turned back to her supervision of the two girls, again wondering with annoyance why the other menservants had not returned. She shook off her irritation, reminding herself that she did not need them until this next trunk was full.

SKELETONS IN THE CLOSET

The sound of breaking glass from the floor below caused all three women's heads to rise in unison. Christine dashed for the door, assuming that the latest trunk had been dropped, and hoping that no one had been injured. She heard a deep-throated shout, and she uncharacteristically swore under her breath.

Not an injury. Not now.

She froze at the head of the wide curving staircase as she heard another shout, and an answering stream of Persian. She covered her mouth with both hands to stifle a scream of her own, and moved with all possible haste back toward the bedroom and the two girls there. She closed the door, turning the handle and easing the door shut before locking it.

Erik had been right to worry after all!

"Annika, Aina, you are in danger." The girls' faces were stricken, and they clutched at each other and looked to the locked door as another muffled shout sounded from below. As Christine rushed to the two girls, she prayed that none of the servants had been killed, while knowing from the shouts that her prayer had little likelihood of being answered.

"Quiet," she said, as she gathered the girls in her outstretched arms and pushed them to the far corner of the room. She left them there, still clutching each other, eyes widened in wooden terror as she ran to the window. She searched from side to side, looking to see if any of the villains appeared in the gardens below. She saw nothing, no one, although with the maze of manicured shrubbery beyond her flower garden, anyone could be hiding. She looked a moment more, but the only movement she could detect was the glitter and shine of water dancing in a fountain. They must take the chance. She rushed back to the girls.

"Go," she whispered, gesturing behind them to the servant's entrance to the room. The girls shook their heads, now clutching at her as well as each other. She ignored their unspoken protests. "You must! Take the stairs to the back of the house and hide in the garden. Cut your way into a hedge, if you can find nowhere else, but hide. I would not have you harmed."

Or worse.

"But, Mistress…," Aina whispered, and then stopped as a great crashing in the upstairs hallway caused them all to jump. The villains must be breaking down the first door near the top of the stairs. They would soon be outside this room. She reached behind the girls, and pulled open the servant's door.

"Go!" she whispered. "Go now!" She pushed them toward the opening.

"Mistress, come!" Annika grabbed at Christine's sleeve with such terror and urgency that the seam at Christine's shoulder tore.

"I will be fine. Please! Trust me and GO!" She pushed again at the girls, and as another loud crash sounded in the hall, the girls turned and fled. Christine closed the servant's door, and placed a chair in front of it, knowing as she did that it was a useless gesture – it would provide no physical protection to the girls, nor any helpful delay.

SKELETONS IN THE CLOSET

Christine spun away from the chair, nearly upsetting it, and hurried to the large bed. She crawled onto the bed, upsetting the coverlet, and falling to her face as her knees caught in her skirts. She freed herself, and crawled further, toward the wall at the head of the bed. At a touch, the enormous carved wooden headboard slid down, revealing a door in the wall, only large enough to allow a person to crawl through. She pressed on the door, and it swung inward revealing darkness.

As voices sounded in the hallway outside the bedroom door, Christine flung herself into the darkness, the pressure of her weight on the tunnel floor beneath her causing both the small door and headboard to return to their original positions. Within moments she heard a nearby crashing sound which must be her bedroom door smashing into the room.

She squatted in utter blackness, not daring to breathe, unable in her fright to move. She listened to the muffled voices of men moving through the bedroom on the other side of the wall, unable to make out words, but knowing by the lilting music of the cadence that they were speaking Persian. She heard a shout of triumph as the men discovered the servant's door, and heard several go pounding down the stairs in search of… Whom? The servants? Herself? Erik? Were they all to be killed?

She waited further, until the voices of the men became inaudible as they moved again to the hall. After a time, it seemed the only sounds in the house came from the lower floor, with occasional shouts from the gardens and yards about the house.

She stood and made her way into the black passage and down a slender staircase, guided by her hands against the tunnel walls and her memory of the interior labyrinth Erik had insisted she learn by rote. She moved through the tunnels of the lower floor, stopping at room after room, using only those passive methods of watching that did not require the opening of any traps or peepholes. She did not light any of the candles or lanterns that were stored in abundance, for fear a glint of light from a crack or from behind a mirror would give her away. She blessed Erik for his insistence on her ability to move through the passages blindfolded – she now understood the need for what she had considered a silly exercise.

Most of the men were gathered in the kitchen, helping themselves to what foodstuffs they found there, although several lounged in the drawing room – some even sleeping – while one restless man still wandered from room to room. All were dressed in the Persian garb. She could find no evidence of any of the servants, and she prayed again that this was because they had escaped, and not because their corpses had been moved out of doors. She did not worry about Erik coming back to the house and being captured unawares. The beasts had broken out several windows in entering the house, and the main doors now stood open. She hoped that he would not be foolish enough to worry after her welfare and attempt a rescue. He knew as well as she that these tunnels provided numerous points of ingress and egress should she find an opportunity to escape, and were also well stocked with food and water should she need to stay hidden for long. She could leave from any of several hidden exits once she knew the gardens were free of the searching men.

She settled herself in front of – or rather behind – a large piece of glass that, from the room on the other side of the glass, appeared to be a massive gilt-framed mirror. She studied the men she could see from her position.

Despite her predicament and her fear of the situation, Christine's eyes soon grew heavy. She wondered if it was in response to the blackness that surrounded her and a normal instinct toward sleep when it grew dark, or if it was a reaction to the quiet exhaustion that came after fear and exertion.

She was awakened by a nearby commotion of yelling and crashing noises. For a breathless moment, she could not recall where she was, or why, and she nearly cried out. The Persians limned in the glass before her brought her back to her monstrous reality. One tall, dark Persian she had not seen before seemed to be shouting curses or instructions, while gesturing at the walls of the room, and kicking those few men who were unfortunate enough to have been caught dozing on the various couches and lounges. Christine pressed as close to the mirror as she dared, hoping to be able to make out the words, and cursing her inability to open the vent that would allow her to hear.

The tall Persian stood, legs firm and slightly spread beneath him, fisted hands resting on his hips, immobile except for the swivel of his head from side to side. Most of the men hurried from the room, and soon Christine could hear knocking and pounding coming from various rooms of the house, and echoing through several of the tunnels around her. It was not until the large Persian lifted a chair and began approaching the mirror that she understood what they were doing.

Horrified, worried for her safety for the first time since entering the tunnels, she scrambled to her feet – tearing some portion of her petticoat as she did so – and ran toward one of the hidden exits. She must take her chance now for escaping the house. As she turned the corner from one tunnel to the next, she heard the crashing, tinkling sound of the great mirror shattering behind her, and heard the unmistakable shout of triumph followed by the words, yelled in Persian: "I have found the passages! I told you the monster would have passages!" Christine did not pause in her flight to hear more.

She heard sounds of men ahead of her, and realized that the Persians were in the tunnels between her and the exit she sought. She turned and retraced her steps to another tunnel, toward another exit, only to hear again men yelling in the tunnel ahead of her. Trapped like a frightened mouse in a maze, she turned toward her final hope for escape.

She stumbled into the hidden room she sought, unable to see anything, but knowing what she must do – and with little time left to her. She felt along the wall to her right, until her hands met a solid wood obstruction. She felt along the top until she found what she knew would be there – match sticks and a lantern. She closed her eyes before striking the match, not wanting to blind herself in the sudden flare, and then opened them and lit the lantern. The room burst into muted color around her.

She had always thought the room sweet, but given her fear and the horror of voices yelling through the tunnels, she now thought it ridiculous. It was a woman's bedroom, complete with pink lace coverlet and canopy, overstuffed chairs, lace curtains over non-existent windows, and a vanity. The vanity was covered with cut glass perfume bottles in various iridescent colors, a hairbrush and comb, and face powder. It was backed by an oval mirror, unattached to the wall. The stool that sat before it was slanted out into the room instead of tucked beneath the vanity, as if a woman had just left her seat before the mirror.

Yes, a foolish room, but with an indispensable purpose. Christine ran toward the vanity, and moved the stool aside. She wanted to throw the stool in her hurry and fright, but even in her panic, she knew she could not allow the noise to lead the beasts to her. She removed the top to one of the perfume bottles, and tipped it to wet her finger with a clear, odorless liquid. Then, trying to think through all that she knew and all that she must tell Erik, she began writing invisible letters on the mirror.

She had just finished her message when a voice began shouting that he could see a light ahead. The trampling of converging feet told her the men were not far – but far enough, considering that the tunnels were unknown to them. She still had a chance to escape. She replaced the top on the perfume bottle to insure that no attention was paid to the contents and the special odorless solution it contained. She bent, and with shaking fingers, loosed the buttons of one shoe. The footsteps pounded closer, and Christine dove from her position before the mirror to climb under the bed. If should could reach the trap door concealed under the bed, she could still make her escape from the house. She hoped all the men were involved in searching the tunnels, and that once outside of the house, she would have some chance to hide or escape.

She pulled herself further under the bed, until her hand found the small lever that would open the trapdoor beneath her. As soon as she pushed the lever, the portion of the floor beneath her face and arms fell away, and the wet rock-scented air of the tunnel came into her face, smelling of freshness and freedom and the sea. This tunnel, she knew – even though she had only traversed it once – led to the cliff face well below the house and her last possibility of escape. She slid inward with as much speed as she could, preparing to lower herself the short distance into the safety of another blackness.

Her breasts were over the gaping hole. With one more pull, she would be far enough to bend from her waist into the tunnel and pull her legs after her. Her hands tightened against the edge of the trap door and again, she pulled. Instead of sliding forward, her dress snagged on some protrusion poking from the underside of the bed. Nearly screaming her frustration, she felt backward with one hand, trying to loosen the snag. She could feel where the dress was caught at the full top of her skirts, but could not untangle it. She pulled again on the edge of the trap door with the greater strength of her terror, and heard her dress ripping.

One more time! God, help me – one more time and I shall be free!

She grunted with the effort to pull herself free, and the dress tore loose. She braced her arms for the headfirst plunge into safety, and then screamed as a hand gripped her ankle and held her from goal. Her scream echoed down the dark tunnel, escaping without her, leaving her behind as it fell toward the sea. She kicked at the hand with what little leverage she had, to no discernible effect. The iron hand locked around her ankle did not loosen, and the floor slid against her as she was pulled from under the bed.

She rolled to her back, needing to face her captors as they pulled her into the light, hoping for the strength or the luck to perhaps strike a blow. Her progress was arrested as the front of her blouse caught on the same snag that had caught her skirt earlier. For a brief moment, foolish hope filled her.

They cannot pull me out!

Her other ankle was entrapped, and with another great tug and the sound of tearing fabric, she was yanked from under the bed, and pulled halfway across the floor of the small room. She was mortified to notice as she struggled to push herself up to a sitting position, that the front of her dress between her breasts was torn open, and only her chemise remained to protect her modesty. She lay back and brought both hands to the front of her dress. Panting full breaths, she looked up at the men surrounding her. Their strange dark faces seemed twisted with evil sneers, and she began to swoon with a dangerous light-headedness.

I will not faint. I will not! Somehow, her body obeyed her command.

After what seemed an infinite moment, one of the men bent toward her, and laughing, grabbed her wrist and pulled her to her feet, wrenching her arm. He pulled her close, keeping a tight hold on her. Mere inches away, he laughed in her face, and she saw in a flash before she closed her eyes and turned her head that his teeth were crooked and stained. She kept her free hand pressed to her torn dress front, and squeezed her eyes together, waiting for a blow or a stab from one of the many knives she had seen in the hands of the men. Believing her end near, she eased her loosened shoe from her foot.

Her eyes flew open again as another rough hand pulled her hand from her bodice, and another tore at it, opening it to the waist. Raucous laughter filled her ears as she screamed again. She struggled anew, prepared to bite, or at least to spit upon her attacker.

"STOP!" The volume of the order, and the unquestionable command in the voice caused even Christine to stop her struggles. It took a moment for her to register that the word had been spoken in Persian, and could not be any kind of rescue. Several of the men before her moved aside and the tall, dark Persian who had broken the mirror stepped into her view. He looked at her for a long moment, expressionless as his eyes took in her disheveled hair, torn dress – every detail of her, down to the tip of her remaining shoe. He lifted the edge of his tunic and reached beneath it toward the waistband of his baggy pants.

Just as Christine began to struggle anew, fearing the worst, he pulled out a section of cloth that had been tucked into the side of his waistband, and held it to her. The men to either side of her released her wrists and the tall man before her mimed wrapping the cloth around her shoulders. She unfolded the cloth, discovering that it was quite long and wide enough to act as an adequate shawl. She draped it over her shoulders and pulled it around to cover her torn bodice. She could not bring herself to thank the man, in his or any other language.

The tall man ordered the others to examine the room. Two men entered the hidden tunnel under the bed. Christine held her breath as one man moved to the mirror, but he only passed his hand behind it to show the leader that it could not be hiding another passage.

Satisfied that the room held no surprises, the tall Persian turned back to her. In broken Swedish, and pausing between each word as if to insure she understood, he said, "We. No. Harm. You." He raised his eyebrows and nodded, seemingly asking if she had understood his statement. Shaking with fear and hope that his statement was true, she nodded in return. Without another word, he began to lead her from the room. At the door, she turned, and forgetting that the men would not understand Swedish, she said, "My shoe," and pointed. One of the men brought her shoe, and she clutched it to her chest. She was led from the room, through the tunnels, and out of the house.

CHAPTER 8
PETTER AND CONSTANCE

Petter's head swam with the giddiness of a balloon lost in flight. Constance was his… or at least more nearly his than he could have hoped for so soon. She must love him as much as he loved her.

His day had begun with a morning call upon Constance. He had reasoned with himself that if he wished to luncheon with her, he could not call too late, but the truth was that he had awoken before dawn, and by mid-morning, had exhausted his ability to wait any longer to see her. Given the early hour, he was rather chagrined to discover that he was not the first caller of the day. However, Constance put him quite at ease before his insecurity could rise to crush him.

He was led into a small sitting room, quite pleased to be afforded such an intimate setting. He held a small bouquet of yellow roses (he had decided on yellow upon remembering the color of her dress), and the smile he wore stretched his face to the point that he felt it might reach his ears. His smile faltered – but did not fail him – when he entered the room to find another man in the room with Constance. Not merely in the room, but sitting quite close to her on the couch, leaning toward her in an intimate and thus disturbing manner.

"Mr. Petter Nilsson, Miss," the butler announced, his eyes fixed upon a spot on the far wall. The man turned and left the room without any answer from Constance.

"Petter. How wonderful!" she said. The glowing smile she directed at him as she held her hands out to him took his breath away, and almost made him forget that another man sat at her side. He stood transfixed before uttering her name, careful this time to address her by her proper name.

"Miss Pendleton," he said, and bowed.

"Tosh, I was Constance to you when first we met and I simply must be Constance now and forever." She giggled and turned to the man beside her. "Petter was quite charming."

Petter's face reddened at her words, and then reddened further as the man reached for her hand and grasped it in both of his. When he spoke he pulled her hand to his heart and held it there. "Constance, *please!*"

Petter's instinct was to charge the man, but before he could take so much as a step, Constance acted.

"Do not be so familiar," she said, pulling her hand from his. She flashed Petter another glowing smile, as she said, "I asked Petter to call on me." Petter could not remember ever seeing so beautiful a sight in his life. She glanced at the man, who seemed about to fall on his knees before her, and said in a lowered voice, "Michael, don't be such a bore."

SKELETONS IN THE CLOSET

The man dropped his chin to his chest, then rose to stand at her side, the pleading expression on his face turning to something meaner. He spun and strode toward the open door of the room, murmuring as he passed Petter, "Just you wait until she decides you aren't *rich* enough or exciting enough."

Petter could think of nothing to do but nod toward the man, for his words made no sense. He turned back to Constance. She had moved toward the broad window seat, and now stood facing him, her lavender skirts still dancing with the movement that had brought her to the spot, her golden hair glowing like a halo in the sun through the windows. He stood, again hypnotized by the vision of her beauty, until she held her hand out to him. He crossed the carpet toward her with what he hoped was not too much haste.

He presented the small bouquet, and the movement with which she dipped her face to inhale the scent and raised her eyes to him matched his earlier fantasy of her perfection.

"Constance," he murmured, unsure of what he would say, but certain that gazing at her in silence would not suffice.

"*Are* you rich, Petter?" she asked. She smiled and tilted her head as she watched for his reaction. She lowered herself to the window bench and indicated with a nod that he could join her.

"Rich?" he asked, somewhat startled by the question, and wondering what had prompted it before he recalled the murmured statement of the rebuffed suitor.

"Yes. Are you rich? This is something a young lady may wish to know about a gentleman caller," she said. Her smile was so dazzling Petter almost wished she would stop so that he could focus on her words. He coughed into his hand before answering.

"No, not yet. But I shall be… Constance." He could tell her that he was rich, since his parents were quite wealthy by all the standards he knew, but he had determined to make his own wealth on coming to England, and he determined it anew now. He would win Constance on his own merits.

"How shall you be, Petter?" Her interest in his future plans seemed quite innocent.

"I am a master stonemason and an architect – the best I know," he said immodestly. "This is quite an accomplishment at my young age, and it is only my youth that holds me back from success." He hoped he didn't sound the braggart – under normal circumstances, he would not speak in so boorish a manner – but he also felt that Constance was a woman who needed reassurances, and Michael's warning rang inside his head again. He waited for her response, his breath held within him, hoping he had not gone too far.

"Lovely," she said. "Father does so adore his buildings – 'investments' he calls them. Somehow, spending a ridiculous amount of money on buildings makes him a ridiculous amount of money – not that I care to understand it all." Keeping her eyes on Petter's, she bent her head to the roses again, and then dazzled Petter with another winning smile. Petter imagined kissing the pink lips that smiled at him.

"Father could help you. Father's friends could help you," she said. Petter wondered what she could mean, before catching the thread of the conversation, and realizing she was referring to assistance in his profession, in getting the illusive commission he so desired.

"I… I would be grateful – indebted," he stammered, "but I…."

"I could speak to him, but it is you who must prove to be as talented as you say," she continued. Her smile puckered into a delectable pout, and she raised a curved golden eyebrow and tilted her head at him, as if challenging the veracity of his earlier self-praise.

"I will prove my skill," he answered, and then feeling that the statement was too immodest, he said, "I believe I can prove it. Of course, your father must be the judge."

Constance threw her head back and laughed, and then clapped her hands around the stems of the bouquet. Petter could do nothing but smile at her, happy with whatever he had said to so win her approval. He was ready on the instant to declare his love for her, and thought to take her hand, but again, the image of the rebuffed suitor flew into his mind, the moment when Constance had pulled her hand from his grasp. He kept his hands in his lap, afraid of being too familiar with her, not wanting to earn her disdain after earning her golden laughter.

"I called here today for the pleasure of your company," he said, "and would do so again, if you permit me." Again he had to force himself not to take her hand as she smiled at his words. "Naturally, I would be grateful for any assistance with your father, although I cannot conceive of why you would intercede for me so, knowing so little about me…"

"I wish my… friends… to be successful," she answered, looking away from him and shaking her head in such a way as to make her curls bounce about her shoulders. She returned her gaze to his, and asked, "You do wish to be my friend, don't you, Petter?"

"Yes. Oh, yes!" he answered, and this time, he could not restrain himself, and he took her near hand in both of his. As his fingers closed over hers, Petter remembered himself, and almost pulled his hands away again, but the pretty blush that colored her features reassured him that he had not taken an unwanted liberty. He was lost in the dizzying sensation of her skin against his own, and lost in her blue eyes as she turned toward him. He might have sat there for days, without need of food or drink.

"Shall we walk in the park, Petter?" she asked, as she pulled her hand from between his. He stood, and offered his arm.

"I would be delighted," he answered, still feeling under a spell, wondering if sunshine and mild exercise would deliver him of it. He hoped not.

That was how his day had begun. He had walked with Constance, accepted her invitation to luncheon, and later basked in her attention over tea, thinking as the afternoon passed that perhaps he had imposed on her for too long, but unable to bring himself to leave her. When he began to excuse himself, not wanting to wear out his welcome, she would hear nothing of it.

"Nonsense," she said. "Father will be home soon, and I would have you speak with him." She smiled and leaned toward Petter. In an intimate voice, she said, "I would have you stay. I don't know when next I'll have such a handsome man in my parlor."

Petter blushed at her compliment. He wanted to jump for joy, and shout that she could have him tomorrow and every day thereafter if she said the word, but instead he answered, "I would be most pleased to speak with your father of my work."

"And I would be pleased to see to your immediate success," she answered. Petter could only smile at her again, stunned and pleased at her unselfish interest in his own happiness and success.

True to her promise, her father arrived a short time thereafter, and Petter set an appointment with the man – two days hence – to which he would bring photographs of his carvings, and several of his most ambitious architectural drawings. He took his leave of father and daughter, his head spinning with the euphoria of his successes of the day. Although it was now evening, he raced with all haste to Evans' shop to begin preparations for the meeting.

***

"Petter!" Phoebe enthusiastically greeted him as he entered the shop. She rose to approach him. "Father told me you would not be in today. I didn't think to see you this evening either." She seemed quite happy to see him.

"Good evening, Phoebe," he answered, distracted, moving toward his own drawing table, but then remembered himself. He did not wish to be rude to his friend – especially after so wonderful a day.

He turned back to her, and her faltering smile came to life again under his attention. "How are you this evening?"

"I finished with my plans today," she answered. She gestured toward her table with obvious excitement. As she turned back to him, her dark eyes held his. When he made no response, she said, "Would you…?"

"Yes! Yes, of course," he answered, and began moving toward her drawing table.

"I didn't mean this moment, Petter," she said, laughing. "Take off your coat. I did not mean to interfere with whatever task you had planned. I simply meant that I would appreciate your insights, or suggestions." She laughed again at the quizzical expression that grew on his face as he stopped and looked down at his half-removed coat.

He shook himself, befuddled, as if Constance's spell still held him in thrall – which, he supposed, it did.

"Of course," he said again. He turned back toward his own drawing table and finished removing his coat. He threw the coat over his stool, lit the lamp at its head, and stood, torn between whether to look over Phoebe's plans now, or whether to do as his mind insisted – to begin putting together the portfolios he intended to take to Lord Pendleton. After a moment of thought, he realized that his portfolios were already in excellent order, and he could complete whatever additional preparations he needed rather quickly. Completed portfolios would not bring the date and time of the meeting any nearer than two days hence.

When he raised his eyes, Phoebe had returned to her drawing table, leaving him to his thoughts or his work, rather than pressuring him to her request by hovering. She was truly a good person and good friend.

"At your service, Phoebe," he said, as he approached her across the dim room. Her dark eyes were luminous in the lamp light, her appreciative smile turning up the corners of her eyes as she looked up at him.

"Thank you, Petter," she said, and moved off her stool to allow Petter to sit.

He knew enough from examining earlier of her plans to know that her structure would be properly supported, and set out with an eye to proper flow and placement of rooms, hallways, stairways. He almost never needed to give suggestions with regard to those essentials of construction, and Phoebe always seemed to remember his suggestions and to incorporate them into her future designs. He no longer questioned her abilities, although her ambitions were futile in such a masculine field.

His eyes and fingers traveled over the drawing of the building he found before him. He moved the top page aside, and then the next and the next, as he took in the layout of the plans. His astonishment and appreciation grew with the details he took in.

"This…" he said, and could say no more, as he flipped the pages back and forth again. "This is like nothing I've ever seen," he said. He looked again at the plans, confused by the combination of uses she had introduced into the building.

"The top looks to be apartments or hotel rooms… no, apartments," he said, "and then a central layer of offices, and then a ground floor which is restaurant or men's club, and offices combined. You've… you've…." He raised his head to look at Phoebe where she stood above him, quite near. Her eyes looked a question at him, and she seemed apprehensive and yet eager. "What made you think of combining the uses?"

"Something you said, Petter," she answered.

"I…?"

"You spoke of your favorite restaurant, and lamented that it was so far from your flat, and from this shop. I thought at the time that it would be wonderful to have everything one desired close at hand. Home, work, restaurant." She took a deep breath, and added, "Is it…? Is it terrible?"

"It is fantastic!" He looked down at the drawing again, bringing the top sheet to the front again. "Now, I don't know whether it is saleable, but it is fantastic." He looked up at her now smiling face. "It is certainly an improvement to the apartment over the shop, or any number of the single-use buildings we have: Flats or offices, take your pick."

"Oh, thank you, Petter!" She bent toward him and put her arms about him for a quick embrace. Petter stiffened, startled at the sudden intimacy. Just as quickly as she had embraced him, she straightened again, and he could see the immediate flush of her cheeks.

"Oh, excuse me, Petter, I forgot myself," she said, both hands moving to her mouth.

"Quite all right, Phoebe, I assure you," he answered, wanting to put her at ease. "I was merely startled, not discomfited." He smiled, and wondered at himself, at the tone in his voice that suggested he was pleased with her familiarity – which he was.

Well? After all, we are friends.

He turned his attention back to Phoebe's plans in an effort to relieve the sudden awkward silence. He made some few suggestions – the widening of an entrance here, a rearrangement to the apartment spaces that would provide for a more efficient use of space – but his suggestions were more artistic than necessary, and when she questioned him over one, he admitted that her original design was better than his suggestion. Finally, there seemed nothing more to say.

"I've kept you from your own work," Phoebe said as he stood and stretched his back.

"Not at all," he answered, but his eyes moved to his desk. "I was going to assure myself that my portfolios are in the best possible order. I can do that tomorrow."

"You have another presentation?" she asked. Her straightforward gaze was full of excitement for him.

"I do," he said. His mind filled with Constance, and all that the day had meant to him – to his heart, to his hopes for a commission and professional success. He told Phoebe everything about the day, about his walk, his luncheon, his meeting with Lord Pendleton – even to including the ousting of the other suitor upon his arrival.

Phoebe murmured something at this latest detail, which he could not hear or understand. It sounded as though she had said something to the effect that Constance was not very constant, but he could not believe Phoebe – or anyone – could say such a thing about his dear Constance.

"What was that?" he asked.

"Hmm? Oh, I said that Constance must have been quite taken with you." For once Phoebe did not meet his gaze with her own. Then she raised her eyes to his again, and said, "Which is quite understandable."

Petter flushed, and said, "Oh, well. Thank you." This time it was Petter who could not meet Phoebe's gaze. "I can't for the life of me imagine why Constance would be so helpful with her father, but I am quite eager for the meeting. This could be the meeting I have been hoping for since my arrival in London."

"From what you've told me, she gave you the reason, Petter," Phoebe said. Her voice was quiet and her tone gentle. "She wants you successful," she finished, and turned away to return to her drawing table. She began to roll her plans.

Suddenly, Petter heard Constance's voice in his head. *Are you rich? This is something a young lady may wish to know about a gentleman caller.* This was followed by the other man's warning. *Just you wait until she decides you aren't rich enough…*

A frown settled onto Petter's features, at the same time that he denied Phoebe's insinuations – her accusations. He did not like them, but perhaps she had misinterpreted what he had told her about the day. To his mind, Constance was the soul of consideration. He put his coat on, refusing to doubt his Constance, his love. He shook himself, also refusing to be angry with Phoebe.

"I must be going, Phoebe," he said, as he walked to where she still worked at her desk, returning tools to their proper places. "May I escort you home?"

"Thank you, no, Petter. I have some things to finish up. Notes I wish to make."

"All right then," he answered. "Good evening, Phoebe."

"Good evening, Petter," she answered, and as he turned from her, "Be careful."

"I shall," he answered. It did not occur to him until he had reached the street, that perhaps she had not been warning him to be careful on his walk to his flat, but warning him about something else altogether. He refused to think of what that might be.

CHAPTER 9
ERIK COMES HOME

Erik reached the border of his own land as darkness was falling. He was frustrated with the length of time needed to accomplish his business in town, and frustrated with the fact that he could not push his horse any faster without harming the poor creature. He hoped that Christine had been able to complete the preparations for their journey – it would be safest if they could be away this night. Christine was capable of the feat, but he worried that she had not had sufficient assistance from the servants. He had not been of any help.

He approached the manor house through the orchard, waiting for a glimpse of the light from the windows, hoping that Christine had been vigilant in keeping the doors locked against any possible intrusion. He doubted there was any real danger yet, but better to be safe than suffer the consequences of being lackadaisical at a time like this. He could have misinterpreted what he had seen at the docks with Mattis, but he could not make himself believe it.

Erik was disoriented as to his location as the trees thinned. He must have lost his way in the orchard – he had not yet caught sight of the lighted windows of the manor. The horse must have turned in its path through the trees.

His heart stabbed with fear and his breathing stopped as he saw his error. The manor stood dark before him. He had not seen the lighted windows because none of the many windows was illuminated. Christine and the servants were either huddling in the dark, or…

Erik slipped from the horse and patted its rump, sending it home to the stables. Staying to the edge of the orchard, he moved toward the side of the manor house, searching each window, each shadow within and without for any sign of movement. Nothing. As he approached the front of the house, he saw the muted velvet blackness of windows open to the night instead of the slight gleam of glass he should have seen. Lowering his eyes to the ground below the windows, he saw the glitter of broken glass shards. The heavy front doors stood ajar, removing any hopes that all was well. He fought the instinct to scream Christine's name to the night sky, as an animal might bay its loss.

He swallowed, and held tightly to hope. Christine could have escaped, or she could be hiding. He refused to entertain the thought of his Christine lying as cold and lifeless as the manor house now appeared to be.

Erik entered the house through one of the secret entrances into his tunnels, hoping to find that Christine was safe – safe and hiding there, as he had planned. He was not far into the tunnel labyrinth before this hope was extinguished. The tunnels had been breached, through mirrors, through walls. His lantern showed shadowed debris flung across the floors of the tunnels and the house itself. Sensing more than hearing the emptiness of the house, he stopped his attempts at silence, and began his search of the house.

He lit lamps as he went – those that had not been smashed or broken – lighting the ruined house as he went. He found the bodies of two of his servants behind several packed trunks in the foyer. He discovered another body in the kitchen, crumpled in the far corner. Upstairs, he found a trunk – not yet packed – in their bedchamber. The candle of hope burned in his chest with every room he entered that did not contain the body of the one person he could not bear to see.

Certain that Christine was not in the main house, he returned to the tunnel labyrinth. He searched it as carefully as the rest of the house before making his way to the final room – the room with the tunnel to the cliff face. His heart rose into his throat choking him with despair. This room, like the others, had been disturbed.

She may still have escaped! This destruction could have been done after she escaped!

His eyes moved from the tipped up bed and the open tunnel mouth to the mirror over the vanity.

Please! Please have left me a message, Christine!

Erik lifted the bench from where it lay across the small room and pulled it before the vanity. He turned the silver hairbrush over in his hand and removed the back cover, revealing a secret compartment full of red powder. He lit a candle and ran the flame over the surface of the mirror, and then used the large brush from the face powder to brush the red powder over the surface of the mirror.

There!

He could make out words on the mirror, and brushed more of the red powder against the surface, heating the mirror face as needed with the candle when the words would not come clear. He closed his eyes and took a deep calming breath before reading the message Christine had left him there.

Mazenderani, she had written at the top. He might have guessed as much, but at least now he was certain.

I love you, were her next words, and his eyes burned with love and pain, and the frustration that she would have wasted any time on the words.

"I love you," he whispered into the dim silence of the room.

My shoe, were the next senseless words, but Erik knew an explanation would follow – a code, a sign of some sort.

I will escape with two – meet me at the old tree. Erik understood. She would not escape with only one shoe, and if she should escape, she would meet him at the tree that stood on her old farmstead in Korsnäsborg, her childhood home.

I will be taken with two – Mazenderan. Erik translated again, understanding that if she was captured – kidnapped – they would not take her with only one shoe.

If I am to die – you will find my shoe – I love you.

Erik's eyes blurred as he read the last words, loving his wife and damning her for the second foolish waste of time and words.

A shoe! He spun as he rose from the chair and lifted the lantern, swinging it to and fro, searching the floor of the small room. His pulse slowed when he did not find a shoe, but he determined to be certain. He emptied the room of its entire contents, filling the tunnel leading to the room, and then descended into the escape tunnel and searched it to its far end. No shoe.

Erik admired Christine's choice of code signals in what must have been a moment of terror and despair. No one would consider the loss of a shoe – or the retrieval of one – to be anything more or less than it appeared. The code was not perfect, he realized, nor could it be. Christine could have escaped through the tunnel, and then been killed before she could reach safety. She could have been killed before she was able…

Stop!

He refused to allow his mind to move in those death-shrouded circles.

First, to Korsnäsborg, willing Christine to be there, at the old tree, waiting for him – picturing their tearful reunion, feeling the warmth of her skin on his lips as he kissed her beautiful face.

SKELETONS IN THE CLOSET

Climbing over the detritus in the tunnels, he re-entered the house, moving to gather the few supplies – and weapons – he intended to take to Korsnäsborg. He threw the few implements into a satchel, and gathering up two half-eaten loaves of bread, he turned from the bright kitchen to the blackness of the open door to the yard, ready to run to the stable to determine whether Christine had been able to take a horse.

"You hurry like a man running on coals." The husky feminine voice washed over Erik like ice, speaking Persian. He spun in the open doorway to the yard toward the speaker, hand on the knife at his belt.

There, between the two large preparation tables stood a woman, the lower half of her face veiled in the Mazenderani fashion, her body wrapped in colorful silks. Behind her stood two enormous, muscular Persian men, neither as tall as Erik, but both outweighing him. When Erik did not move or speak, the woman threw her head back and delivered a rich, thrumming laugh.

"Have you forgotten our language?" she asked in Persian. Changing to French, she said, "Would you prefer I spoke in another?"

"Sultana," he said, for it could be no other. When last he had seen her, she had been a precocious – and dangerous – child of ten, not the voluptuous woman who now stood before him, but the shape of her eyes, and the velvet venom in her tone betrayed her to him.

"Erik, my beloved," she answered, again speaking Persian. She detached one side of her veil and pushed it aside. "When we knew each other so well, you called me by name." She took two provocative steps toward him, moving her hips as she walked in an insinuating dance.

"We no longer know each other well," he answered, stifling the anger that threatened to color his words. He must tread carefully if he had any hopes of discovering Christine's fate, or of extricating Christine from the Sultana's clutches if she yet lived. He entertained no doubt that this woman was responsible for the wreckage surrounding him and the disappearance of Christine.

"Say it," she said sliding closer to him, one hand brushing from hip to hip across her stomach. "Call me by name, beloved."

Erik clenched his teeth against the curses and oaths he meant to utter. After a moment's struggle during which she moved closer and closer to him, he said, "Naheed." It came out as a croaking whisper, and knowing she would not be satisfied, he cleared his throat and said her name again. "Naheed."

"Thank you," she said, lowering her eyes in apparent gratitude, as if he had granted her a great favor. Closing the last of the distance between them, she stopped, a mere handbreadth from him, and raised her face to his. It seemed to Erik that she expected an embrace or a kiss, as if they were old lovers reunited after more than forty years – a ridiculous and revolting notion, considering her extreme youth when last they parted.

"Where is my wife?" he asked, his voice quiet and toneless.

SKELETONS IN THE CLOSET

The Sultana exhaled in apparent disappointment, and turned from him, although she did not step away. "Ah, yes." After another sigh, she turned to him again. "Am I not beautiful, Erik?"

"Yes," he answered. A smile of cunning satisfaction grew on her face. "You look much like my wife – although older." The statement was both cutting and true. The Sultana's features were similar and the shape of her face was the same. Her skin tone was darker than Christine's. They both had lustrous hair although of opposite tones – Christine's golden and full of curls while the Sultana's was black and straight – and the same large eyes. The glare those eyes directed at him now took away from their beauty, but they were still remarkable: clear amber, with a darker green ring at the outer edge, and brown flecks throughout. Just as they had when she was a mere child of ten, they sat in striking contrast to her otherwise dark features.

Erik wanted nothing more than to see the clear, deep blue of his wife's eyes.

"Where is my wife?" he asked again.

The Sultana spun and began walking away, hips moving from side to side in an exaggerated motion, leaving Erik with the impression of a snake moving through grass. She stopped as she reached her bodyguards, and looking over her shoulder at Erik, said, "Come. I have a proposition for you." The guards moved aside as she began walking again, then followed her as she left the kitchen.

Erik followed as she picked her way around overturned furniture and scattered debris to settle in a lounge chair in the large drawing room. An ominous gaping hole into his tunnels darkened the room once made bright by a massive gilt mirror. Erik shook with anger as he imagined Christine's fear when the tunnels were breached.

The Sultana reclined and stretched before she spoke. "She lives," she said, smiling at Erik as though she had told a joke. Erik tried to suppress the shudder of relief that ran through his body. "But others also live, whom I would have die. A life for a life, then." And again the sly smile.

"Explain yourself," Erik said, lowering himself to a chair.

The Sultana sighed as though she were bored. "My exquisite father – you remember him, beloved – he wanted you dead after your service to him, for the simple crime of your own genius." She paused to raise a hand, palm down, fingers splayed, and examined the rings on her fingers. "My father has taken a new wife," she said, and for a moment, Erik thought ludicrously that she was referring to Christine. "And now, that twice-damned spawn of a three-legged dog has borne my father a son." The statement was delivered in a singsong tone that belied the venom behind the words. She continued to examine her hands, rings, fingernails. "A SON!" Her hand became a claw that scratched at the cushions as she shrieked the final words. Her face transformed into a face he remembered from long ago – a vicious rictus of anger and hatred painted on the face of a young girl.

SKELETONS IN THE CLOSET

"And?" Erik asked, allowing a small amused grin to curl his lips, knowing well enough that the Sultana would have preferred a response of nervousness or weakness at her outburst. The evil woman recovered herself and her mouth smoothed into a coy, sweet smile.

"You must know I have no intention of allowing a son to threaten my position," she answered.

"So kill him," he answered, knowing the statement would not shock the Sultana, and knowing also that the deed would not be outside her ability – or her pleasure.

"I cannot," she said, with a sudden pout. "Oh yes, I have helped others of my father's son's to Allah, but my father begins to suspect treachery. He guards the insipid woman and her squalling son day and night." She smiled again and said, "So you see, I cannot."

Erik feared that he did see. "And?" he asked again.

"You have become obtuse in your old age," she spat, sitting up, and pointing an exquisitely manicured finger at him. She smiled and sank back onto her side across the lounge. "As you will," she said. "I have your wife. She has not been harmed – and you must remember how extraordinary that is for a woman of my… habits." She winked at Erik, and he clenched his fists and the muscles of his body to keep from lunging at the monstrous woman. "You will kill my father's newest wife, and her wretched son, and your wife will be released."

Erik closed his eyes in a prolonged blink as he heard the explanation he feared.

"Or, my beloved," the Sultana continued, her tone now one of intimacy and invitation. She rose from the lounge and crossed the room to where he sat, then lowered herself to her knees before him. "We can be reunited. You can have your old position with me. Perhaps over the years you have learned new methods of torture with which to entertain me." She placed her hands on his knees and began moving them up his thighs.

Erik stood so abruptly that he overturned his chair, and the Sultana fell back on to her bottom. She looked at him in hurt surprise for a moment before she recovered herself, and licking her lips, smiled again from where she sat at his feet.

"And if I refuse?" he asked.

"Why should you refuse? I know the sort of entertainments you like, the sort you devised for me. We could have that again..."

You make me ill. He did not say the words. His memory of the angry young man he had been, how he had helped the little Sultana, sickened him with regret and shame. He took several breaths to calm himself, aware that he was dealing with a deranged woman – a woman who held his beloved's life-threads in her hands.

"I am no longer engaged in the business of torture, nor do I wish to be," he said through clenched teeth.

The Sultana raised one hand into the air and one of her bodyguard moved forward to help her rise to her feet.

"Then do as I ask. Kill the woman and the boy." She turned away from him as she spoke, again affecting boredom.

"Again, if I refuse?" he asked.

She turned back to him and studied him, as if he were an interesting insect trapped under glass. She flipped a hand at him as if dismissing the question. "You will not refuse." She turned away from him. "I will not permit it."

"My wife. Where is she?" he asked. The Sultana behaved as if he had not spoken, beckoning to her guards and gesturing toward the open front doors of the house.

"Naheed," he growled, elongating her name through clenched teeth.

She turned at the sound of her name from his lips.

"Beloved," she said, and raised her cupped hand as if to caress his face across the distance between them. "Thank you for making it so clear to me how much you care for her," she said sweetly, and with sudden iron in her voice, "and remember that I hold her in my palm." She clenched her outstretched hand into a fist, turned again, and continued walking away from him. She threw her final words at him over her shoulder: "I will keep her until you have done as I have asked. Take years if you wish, but do not expect me to restrain myself from… enjoying her… for too long."

Erik stood, impotent in his rage and frustration as she left the house, her undulating hips wagging at him in mockery.

"Christine!" he howled, head thrown back, voice tearing at his throat like glass shards. He knew even as he screamed that he was fueling the Sultana's resolution, but knowing also that his own resolution to find Christine would fail him only upon his death. He would rescue her. And he would not become a murderer of women and children to win her life and freedom. He would not be the man Christine loved, nor would he deserve her love, if he did as the Sultana demanded.

"Christine!" He screamed her name again and again. With his own voice raging in his ears, he did not hear the men approaching him in the open foyer until he was surrounded. He managed with fists and feet alone to dispense with two of the Persians before pain exploded in the back of his head. He fell to his knees and then onto his face, struggling all the while to maintain his consciousness. His last vision was that of booted feet moving toward him.

CHAPTER 10
LOVE AND FRIENDSHIP

Petter closed the door to his flat and slumped back against it. With his work for Evans at the Bush Exhibition site during the day, his work on his own carvings and plans in the evenings, and Constance in every other spare moment he could find, it was a wonder that he didn't sleepwalk. Not that he wasn't enjoying himself. He felt proud of the work he was involved in at the Bush Exhibition, and he had promised Constance to take her on the Flip Flap ride once the exhibition opened. He was exhilarated by the new plans he was designing at the request of Constance's father, Lord Pendleton, although he had not received a guarantee that a commission would be forthcoming. And Constance. Ah, Constance.

Constance was a labor of love, in the truest sense of the word. He was so infatuated with the young, exciting beauty that he thought of little else through his waking hours, and often dreamed of her as well. But the girl required work. Her taste for expensive meals and entertainments, her desire for the new and exciting, tested both his energy level and his purse. But she was worth it – worth every moment of his effort.

He removed a long slender box from his inside coat pocket, and opened the lid to look at his latest gift for Constance. He hoped she would recognize it for the love-gift it was. He closed the lid and sighed, thinking of the thing she would appreciate even more — the knowledge that he had received a commission, that he had started on the road to success and riches. He could not blame her for her ambitions. She was a Lord's daughter, and accustomed to the finer things in life. What choice had she but to ensure her future through a provident match? He was determined that he would prove himself the man to win her.

He sighed again, knowing that despite his current exhaustion, he should go to the shop and attempt progress on Lord Pendleton's requested design. He would not obtain the hoped-for commission with the plans still unfinished. He placed the lidded gift box on the side table, and turned to leave his flat again. On a whim, he retrieved the box and returned it to his coat pocket. He would like to show Phoebe his gift to Constance, and perhaps preen himself in her praise. Phoebe always seemed able to return energy to him with the comfort and constancy of her friendship.

He stopped on the way to the shop to buy bread and cheese, knowing the simple food would revive him. He bought more than enough for himself so that he could offer some of the plain fare to Phoebe, knowing that she — with simpler tastes than Constance — would not be offended by the poorness of the meal.

"Petter!" Phoebe's happy greeting hailed him as soon as entered the shop. "I was hoping you would come tonight. I haven't seen much of you with your work at the exhibition." She bent to retrieve a bundle at her feet, and rose, coming toward him. "My goodness, you look wretched. Do you ever sleep?" Petter smiled at her banter.

"I brought some..." she started, lifting her bundle toward him, at the same time that he said, "I thought you might..."

He stopped and said, "My apologies. Go on. You brought..."

She smiled and unwrapped her bundle, revealing a loaf of brown bread and a hunk of cheese. "I had an early supper and found myself hungry again. Would you like nourishment? You look to need it."

Petter pulled a sack from under his arm, and reaching into it, brought out a still warm loaf of white bread and a block of cheese. Phoebe's dark eyes glittered with good humor, and then both of them were laughing. Phoebe, still giggling, broke her loaf in half, and then broke his in half. She exchanged the two pieces and returned to her drafting table.

"There. Now we are sharing our meal," she called over her shoulder. Petter put the two loaf halves into his own sack and moved to his table. They spoke as they worked, of the plans upon which they were laboring, or of his work at the exhibition. Petter ate as he worked.

"I like your bread better," he said at last, realizing that he had nearly finished her half loaf.

"As do I," she said. She flashed him a smile – in the dimness of the room between them he could not tell if she was teasing him, or apologizing for her slight of his purchase. He put his own bread and the remaining cheese away, thinking to save it for morning.

As soon as he stopped eating, his eyes grew dim again. However, he was determined to finish the explanatory notations on the current page before he retired for the evening.

"Petter?" Phoebe's voice and a hand on his shoulder woke him some time later. He raised his head and examined his page to assure himself that he had not ruined it. He had not.

"You should get more rest," she said.

"Indeed," he answered, leaning back on his stool and stretching in an undignified manner. As he put on his coat, the weight in one pocket reminded him of his gift to Constance, the gift he had wanted to show Phoebe.

"I made something. I want to show you." He avoided mentioning Constance – she was the one topic that he now felt uncomfortable discussing with Phoebe. Not that Phoebe was at all cold toward the topic, but even so, he felt an inexplicable unease when discussing the one woman with the other. He pulled the long box from his pocket and placed into Phoebe's open hands. She opened the lid.

"Oh…" The utterance was more a sigh or an exhalation than a word. She placed the box onto the surface of the table, eyes riveted to the white marble rose that lie within, a barely opened bud on a long, leaved stem. Her eyes moved from stem to leaves to flower. Her hands hovered above it.

"May I?" she asked, her eyes still looking at the delicate carving.

"Of course," he said. He flushed with pride as he imagined presenting the gift to Constance and her similarly admiring response.

Phoebe lifted the flower from the cushioned box, and held it, turning it as she did. "Petter. My Heavens, it's... perfect. I can see the veins in the leaves, the texture in the petals..." Her eyes lifted to meet his. He was surprised to see tears glistening in her eyes, making them even more luminous than usual. His smile faded.

"Ah, well. I'm glad you like it, Phoebe," he said. His discomfort grew as she looked back at the rose, smiling through her tears. "Ah... Um...," he stammered, unsure how to explain – without causing Phoebe hurt or himself humiliation – that the gift was not for Phoebe but for Constance. "I, ah, made it for Constance," he blurted. He put his hands in his pockets and ducked his head. When Phoebe did not respond for a time, he raised his head again. The rose lay in the cushioned box again, and Phoebe's shining face floated before him, still smiling, eyes still tear-filled. He huffed a quick breath of relief and embarrassment.

"Petter, I wasn't thinking of who will own it," she said with reverence. "I was marveling over its existence." She looked back at the rose a last time, and then reached out and closed the lid. She lifted the box to him, and said, "Thank you for showing it to me. Constance will be very pleased."

"Thank you," he responded, taking the box, unsure why he was thanking Phoebe. For her awe, for her understanding, for her friendship – for all of those. He returned the box to his coat pocket.

"Do you intend to keep working?" he asked. He yawned behind his hand, and said, "As you know, I need to sleep. May I escort you home?"

"Yes, thank you, Petter," she said, her smile as she met his eyes so genuine that it erased all vestiges of his discomfiture.

***

Petter waited in Constance's now familiar sitting room, pacing, feeling every minute pass as an hour. As he paced, he moved from statuary to vase to painting, looking again at the beauty with which Constance surrounded herself, vowing anew – as he did each time he visited – that he would win her, and be able to keep her surrounded with objects just as beautiful as she.

"Petter, how nice," she said, as she swept into the room. "I hope I haven't kept you waiting." He pulled his eyes from her smiling face, and bent over her hand.

"All time is waiting between those moments when I can see you again," he said, raising his head to her face again. Constance blushed prettily, and turned away from him, walking toward the window seat.

SKELETONS IN THE CLOSET

"No flowers today?" she asked turning back to face him, and then she laughed. "You always bring flowers. Does your affection wane?"

"No!" Petter said, mortified at her suggestion, taking a step toward her, a pleading hand held out to her. "Certainly not." He regained his composure, and pulling himself straighter, he said, "As a matter of fact, I brought you a very special flower. A flower that will never die – like my affection for you." With a flourish, he produced the lidded box, and held it out to her.

"Never die? Oh my," she said, and she granted him a curious smile as she took the box from him. She lifted the lid, and said, "Oh, isn't that pretty!" Her hand rose to the flower as if to snatch it from the box.

"Carefully," he said, his own hand rising with hers. "It's very fragile."

"Oh," she said again, then raised the flower from its cushioned bed.

"I carved it for you," he said as she brought it to her nose.

Her eyes flashed up to him and back down to the rose at her nose. She giggled. "It doesn't have any aroma," she said.

"No," he answered, laughing.

"But I suppose it will last forever," she said, and with a nod toward a vase of flowers near the window, "unlike the flowers I receive from other suitors."

Petter's face darkened as his eyes moved to the vase and the large bouquet rising above it.

"Your gift makes any others unworthy," she said, and she twirled the carven rose between two fingers. "Those will wither and die, and yours won't. Oh, Petter, thank you. I will treasure it." She smiled at him and shaded her eyes with pale golden eyelashes, before returning her eyes to his. He bowed to her, too dazzled to say anything in response.

She returned the rose to the box and closed the lid. She pressed the box to her chest and smiled again before placing it on the side table beneath the large bouquet.

"I shall find a special place for my special flower," she said, turning away to take a seat in the window box. Gazing at the closed gift box sitting under the large spray of fragrant flowers, inexplicable disappointment dimmed his pulse, but he shook himself and joined her at her gesture.

"So tell me, Petter. Have you finished your plans for Father? He tells me he was very impressed with your presentation," she said, taking his hand in hers. Petter warmed at her touch, and looked down to commit to memory the sight of her hand grasping his.

"Nearly," he said.

"And is the building a grand one? Will the commission fetch a very grand price?" she asked.

"Your father has made no promise of a commission," he said. Smiling at her girlish and hopeful questions, he said, "and yes, it is a very grand building."

"Oh, but he shall!" she answered. "And one grand commission will follow another, until you are the most famous architect in London!" Her face glowed. With her genuine and selfless eagerness for his own achievement and advancement, he felt she had made a declaration of love.

Without thinking, with eyes focused on the full softness of her mouth, he leaned toward her, closer, closer, until his lips met hers in a chaste first kiss. The surprise he felt at his own action so overcame him that he could not cherish the kiss as he had always thought he might – in truth it was over in the same instant it was begun. The surprise in Constance's widened eyes froze him in mortification, but before he could pull away from her, or voice any apology, a small smile spread over her lips. Her eyes lowered, and then rose to his again. He thought he must be dreaming as she leaned toward him again, but he would not rebuff her by rejecting the opportunity she was presenting to him.

He placed his hands on her arms, and pulled her nearer, watching her eyes close as she presented her rosebud lips to him again. This time, a spreading warmth suffused his body as their lips met, and then a shock that traveled from his mouth to his loins as her lips parted, and her warm, moist tongue entered his mouth. She moved her mouth against his, and he attempted to move to match her. His nose bumped hers and, awkwardly, he turned his head again. His eyes were still closed, his lips still reaching for the missing warmth of hers, when she laughed. He opened his eyes, and her hand rose to her delectable laughing lips to stifle the end of her laughter.

"That was rather clumsy," she said from behind her hand, and covered another small laugh. Petter fell from the heights of his euphoria into a seething black swamp of humiliation. Apparently seeing the devastated look that he could not keep from crossing his face, she said, "You were very sweet, though." She lowered her hand into his, and leaning toward him again, said in a whispered intimacy, "I shall have to let you kiss me again tomorrow." She rested her head against his shoulder, before straightening again. As quickly as he had fallen, he was lifted again to ecstatic happiness, ready to pull her to him and kiss her again, but controlling himself.

Tomorrow, he repeated the word to himself. *I would not be a gentleman if I pressed my advantage upon this beautiful, darling girl.* Even admonishing himself to courtliness, he did not know how he would live through the interminable eternity until the next day. *Perhaps before tomorrow, I will solve the dilemma of how to avoid bumping noses.* He smiled at Constance, and squeezed her hand, having no ability to speak in his untethered state of happiness and hunger.

Constance rose and walked to the side table where his gift lay. She raised it to her chest, clutched in both hands, and said, "Thank you again for your gift, Petter."

He stood, and with a small bow of his head, said, "I am happy it pleased you, for I hope only to please you, now and always."

SKELETONS IN THE CLOSET

In his inner vision he saw Phoebe's tear-filled eyes as she gazed at the carven flower. He raised his bowed head, his eyes searching Constance's own, hoping to see appreciative tears there as well. But the box remained closed, and she turned to replace it on the side table.

Constance smiled into the awkward silence that descended between them, and stepped toward him, extending her hand to him.

"Thank you for coming, Petter," she said.

Startled by the realization that his visit was at an end, Petter hesitated before bending over her hand. "Until tomorrow, then," he said, hearing the promise in his voice, seeing the promise in her sudden, shy smile.

He thought of nothing as he walked the streets, nothing as he ate a dinner he did not taste, except Constance and the kiss. The perfect kiss.

No, not perfect, he reminded himself. A small frown creased his brow as he made his way to his flat thinking of his parents, kissing. *With Father's nearly non-existent nose, he and Mother never have the problem of bumping noses when they kiss.* Petter mused if being nose-less wouldn't be more convenient.

Thinking again of kissing Constance, of tomorrow and the promise of more, he laughed, the sound ringing through the street. He wrapped his arms about himself in an embrace and turned full circle. He ignored the few looks the passersby threw his way, and laughed again.

CHAPTER 11
ERIK WAKES

Erik awoke with a crowning ache in his skull as his body jolted from the moving surface upon which he lay. Through the pounding of his pulse in his head, like a painful, palpable siren, Erik tried to assess his location and condition, despite the fact that he could not see. Location came – in a general sense – as he recognized the motion of a moving cart or carriage, and heard the squeak of leather harnesses and the pounding of hooves over packed dirt. The rhythmic jolting of the surface on which he lay did not seem to translate to great speed, which meant the journey was not a short one. He had no notion of how long he had lain trussed as he was within the cart, nor how much time had passed between when he had lost consciousness and the moment they had begun this journey. The hunger that gnawed at his innards did not help his assessment, as he had not eaten since his meal with Mattis, and had been hungry when he met the Sultana.

The Sultana.

He had little doubt the Sultana was responsible for his capture – trying to speed him to Mazenderan for his task – but he determined to wait for confirmation through the unfolding of events.

He moved where he lay, bundled on his side like a game carcass, trying to determine the extent of his injuries beyond the obvious blow to his head. With slow and careful movements and stretches, he discovered a wrenched shoulder, and various minor bruises, and a burning area on one shin that might be a gash. Besides the thrumming pain behind his eyes and at the back of his head, he was not in altogether terrible condition. His eyes were blindfolded, and his mouth tied with a bulky gag. His hands were tied behind him with a rough length of rope, and although he could not be certain, he thought his knees and ankles were similarly tied only with rope. He hoped this was the case, because it would be far more difficult to rid himself of chains. He raised his ankles and dropped them again, the movement timed to coincide with another jolting of the cart, and listened through pounding head for the sound of metal against the surface on which he lay – a sound he did not hear. He became even more certain that it was rope that bound him.

For some minutes, he lay still as stone and tried to listen for the sound of breathing in the space surrounding him – to determine if any one shared this space with him. He could hear nothing of breathing over the pounding of hooves, and the jolting of the cart and the squeaking, clanking sound of the harness, but with the clarity of those sounds, he determined that he likely rested in the bottom of an open cart, and not an enclosed carriage. There would be at least one driver in plain view, and quite likely another man charged with watching Erik.

Still needing to determine if any guards shared the cart with him, Erik stretched his legs and lengthened his body until his shod feet came into contact with the edge of the cart. Again, moving slowly so as not to alert any watcher to his wakefulness, he moved his legs and feet to front and back along the walls of the cart, trying to determine if any other person or object shared the space with him. Satisfied that no one occupied the portion of the cart below his waist, he could think of no easy or unobtrusive way of determining whether or not anyone sat near his head or to either side of his upper body. The knowledge that he was not guarded head and foot – but only possibly at his head – gave him some small measure of comfort.

Erik gleaned another helpful bit of information through the movement of his legs: he was covered by a cloth or horse blanket of some kind. The coarse cloth had moved across his face and pulled against his clothing as he moved. This helped his chances of escape, as his movements until the instant when he revealed himself would be hidden from view.

Moving as little as possible, he began working at the knots that held his wrists. They were well tied, and high on his wrists, making it impossible for his fingers to do more than touch or scratch at the rope, especially given that his hands were tied palms together, leaving his fingers the least amount of flexible motion. He flexed and twisted his wrists in an attempt to loosen his bonds, ignoring the pain as the rope cut into his skin. Even after many minutes of his silent struggle, the ropes were no looser, and Erik was no closer to freedom.

He sighed as he realized that he would have to raise his arms over his head. If he was being watched, this movement would alert the guard both to his wakefulness, and to his attempted escape. Also, the wrench in his shoulder would not make the difficult task any easier, and depending on the level of damage to his muscles and tendons there, may make it impossible. Unwilling to accept the alternative of remaining captive, Erik slowed his breathing and began the self-hypnotic meditation that would allow him greater muscle control and flexibility. The pounding in his head lessened as his heartbeat slowed, and the deep breathing seemed to alleviate some of the more immediate pain in his skull and limbs.

Reaching the appropriate level of relaxed control, he rolled his upper body onto his face, removing the pressure from the shoulder on which he rested. Rolling his shoulders and raising his arms behind him, he rotated his arms until first one, and then the other, lifted over his head. The ropes tore into his wrists, and his injured shoulder felt as if it would dislocate, but he would accept even that to escape. He could not rescue and free Christine if he was a captive himself!

He rolled onto his side again as he brought his still bound hands down in front of him. Only with great effort did he manage to maintain his relaxation and deep breathing, while remaining alert to a shout or a blow that would indicate he had been discovered.

After another several minutes in which he rolled his wrenched shoulder to relieve the stabbing pain there, he raised his hands to his mouth and pulled off his gag. With the rough rope tearing at his lips and gums, he began with his teeth to loosen the knot that bound his wrists.

His hands free, he pulled his blindfold over the top of his head. The blackness around him did not lessen with the gift of eyesight, and this confused him until he lifted the blanket covering him, to find that this did not relieve the darkness either.

It is still night! Relief flooded him with the realization that even if he was being watched, his movements would also be veiled in darkness.

Erik lowered the blanket to his head again, determined to loose his remaining bonds before making any attempt to further explore his surroundings. Still moving slowly to preserve whatever safety the night provided, he pulled his knees toward him and curled forward. With a patience borne of his determination, he labored for what seemed an hour against the impossible knots at his knees and ankles, until the ropes fell away. He gathered the three lengths of rope to his chest, and with long practice, twisted each into a Punjab lasso.

Ready to investigate the situation outside of his protecting blanket, Erik took several calming breaths, and relaxed again to listen. As yet, he had heard no one speak, but he felt sure from the sound of the hooves that several mounted men rode to either side of the cart – he estimated no fewer than two to each side of him. He could not determine if additional riders rode ahead or behind the cart.

Gathering the ends of the short lassos in one hand, Erik pulled the blanket down over his face. One mounted, turbaned Persian rode to the side of the cart. The man's dark face was barely visible in the glow of a lantern hanging just behind and to the side of the driver of the cart. Erik tilted his head back and lifted his eyes toward the driver. Two men; one driving, one sharing the bench, head slumped forward as though asleep.

Erik sprang up, and slinging the blanket around his body like a great winged cape, he flung it over the head of the sleeping man, and threw him from the side of the cart. The startled man's waking shout stopped abruptly as he hit the ground. At the same moment, a cry of alarm sounded from one of the riders. Losing no time, Erik shouldered the driver off the other side of the seat to the ground, jerking the reins from the man's clutching fingers as he fell. Standing in the cart behind the riding bench like a mad charioteer, Erik yelled at the two horses, and flicked the reins, urging them to speed.

Hearing a rider approach to his side, a stream of obscenities flowing from the man's lips, Erik separated a lasso from the rest, and with a glance to his side, caught the man about the neck and yanked him from his horse. Before Erik could catch both hands to the reins again, a hand clamped on his shoulder from his other side.

Erik grabbed the man's wrist, and using the momentum provided by the man's momentary lack of balance, Erik stepped back and to the side and pulled the man from his saddle and across the driver's seat before pushing him forward and off the cart. Erik was nearly thrown from the cart when it careened and bumped as one wheel rode over the fallen man. He dropped the lassos and nearly dropped the reins as he fell to his knees and crashed against the side of the cart, a hoarse yell escaping him with the sudden explosion of pain in his injured shoulder. Panting through clenched teeth, he righted himself and drew unsteadily to his feet again, blinking away the red-blackness that threatened to close over his vision.

Another yell alerted him to an additional rider approaching from his right side, and Erik spared a quick glance in that direction, hoping to determine how many riders still pursued. He could only see the one. He turned to the front and snapped the horses on, knowing as he did that the rider had the greater speed, and would be on him in a moment. He bent, groping the space around his feet, hoping to retrieve the lassos that had fallen from his grip. He gasped in relief as his fingers closed around one end of rope, and he rose to his feet again, turning his head to gauge the proximity of the closing rider.

Erik yelled in surprise as he was felled by the weight of another rider, apparently leaping from an unseen horse at his left. Bright starbursts exploded in his sight as he grappled with the man, fingers now lost to both reins and lasso, both hands and all his remaining strength struggling to keep the man's hands from his throat. Erik managed to push to his knees and then his feet as he struggled against his attacker, both he and the enraged Persian stumbling from one side of the cart to the other in the uncertain footing of the runaway cart. Even in the midst of the struggle, Erik noticed with despair that there remained two riders. The closer of the two would be near enough to join the fray in less than a minute. He would not be able to resist both men – the man he now wrestled and the near rider – and certainly not the three. Erik's despair rose as the cart slowed, giving the riders the more definite advantage. He must rid himself of the one he now fought.

In the hopes of throwing the man overboard, Erik twisted in his grip, and using an extended leg, kicked the man's feet from under him. As the Persian fell, Erik threw him toward the edge of the cart. With his own waning strength and his upset balance, the Persian did not go over the edge. Instead, the man's head smashed into the wall of the cart, leaving the man dazed. Thankful for even a brief respite in the wrestling fight, Erik turned his attention to the two remaining riders.

The near rider was preparing to leap from his horse to the cart. In no fewer than half a dozen paces of the racing horse, he would be near enough to do so. The farther rider was not so near, but seemed suddenly the greater danger, as he raised a pistol and took aim. Erik threw himself to the floor. The other man in the cart rose, a long curved knife in hand, and supporting himself on the sides of the far end, prepared to lunge once more at Erik.

A shot rang through the air. The man before him gasped, an expression of disbelief contorting his features before he fell. Erik bellowed as the Persian's knife sank into his thigh. The heavy body of the dead man pinioned Erik's legs to the cart bottom.

They've missed their shot! Even through the pain of the knife wound, Erik felt a burst of ecstatic gratitude for the far Persian's poor marksmanship.

With a shout, Erik pulled the knife from his thigh and struggled to loose himself from the weight of the fallen Persian. The gash on his shin tore open as he pulled his legs free. He remained crouched, still unwilling to expose himself to the faltering aim of the galloping Persian. Grabbing one of the lassos at the side of the dead man, he secured it about his upper thigh to stop the main flow of blood. Finding the third lasso, he raised his head until his eyes cleared the edge of the cart, looking for the near rider.

To his surprise, the near rider was no longer alongside. Instead, the near Persian had turned toward the far rider and was raising his own pistol.

Are they fighting each other?

Before Erik could begin to make sense of the two charging riders, shots rang from both pistols, and both men fell from their horses – the near man falling cleanly to the ground, while the farther was dragged a short distance, his foot tangled in his stirrup.

Seeing no more riders, Erik leaped toward the head of the cart, but the reins were out of reach. He yelled for the horses to stop, to no avail. Taking the dead Persian's curved knife and pistol, and bracing himself against the pain to come, he leapt from the cart, rolling several times before coming to a stop. Still confused by the two dueling Persians, he limped toward the fallen men and their now quiescent horses.

He came first to the Persian who had abandoned his leap into the cart. The man was dead, shot through the heart. Erik patted the rump of the nearby horse as it whinnied and stamped. Erik crept toward the second fallen man. As he neared the man, he heard a groan. Erik stopped and raised the pistol. The man before him groaned again and raised his head. The grayed head was bare of the usual turban, and Erik assumed that the rider had been unhatted as he fell. It was not until he approached that Erik took in the man's clothing – not Persian garb, but the clothing of a well-dressed man of Sweden – and finally, the man's familiar face.

"Pontus!" Erik leapt to his butler's side as the old man moaned, and again attempted to raise his head. "Good gracious, man!"

Erik searched his servant's body, finding the bleeding wound just under the man's heart. He pressed one hand to the bloody hole as he pulled the butler into his lap, cradling his head.

"Master Erik," Pontus said weakly, and coughed, spewing flecks of liquid into Erik's face. A thick fluid trickled from the side of his mouth, appearing black in the light of the moon. "You are safe," Pontus gasped.

"Safe, yes," Erik answered, raising his head to look about the dark terrain, confirming that no other persons were approaching, "but you…"

"I followed…," Pontus continued, and his whispered words faded to nothing before he coughed again, the sound trailing into a moan. Erik's mind raced for what he might do to help the loyal servant, although from the warm blood still flowing under his hand, no manner of help could prolong the man's life much longer.

"Nothing I could say can express…" Erik began, but on feeling Pontus' shuddering body in his arms and listening to his labored breath, he knew that the old man would not live through the gracious words Erik wished to lavish upon him.

"Thank you, Pontus," Erik said at last. "You have saved me."

Erik's eyes burned and blurred as a slow smile stretched Pontus' blood blackened lips. The smile turned to a rictus of pain, as the old man's eyes squeezed shut and his body shuddered through another cough.

"I promise you this," Erik said. "Your wife, your children, your grandchildren, will want for nothing for as long as I live." Erik took the old man's hand and squeezed it as he uttered his oath. It was the least he could promise the servant who, in his loyalty, had traded his own life for Erik's. Erik hoped, and not out of simple self-interest, that he would live a life long enough to make the promise worthy of Pontus' sacrifice – not that anything would.

SKELETONS IN THE CLOSET

"I can tell you…" Erik stopped, sentence uncompleted, as Pontus opened his eyes, and convulsed with a last shuttering breath. Erik lowered his head.

He held the old man for a short while, and then lowered him to the ground.

The faithful, brave butler deserved a proper burial, but Erik had no tools to perform the task, and no time in which to perform it. Limping, he pulled Pontus to the side of the dirt road, and laid him in the low ground cover under a tree. He straightened the old man's clothing as best he could, crossed his hands over his chest, and closed his eyelids to the dark foliage above him.

"Rest in peace, friend," Erik murmured.

His own pains from bruises and gashes began clamoring for his attention again as he moved back toward the horses. His own horse – the horse Pontus had ridden to his rescue – nuzzled him as he approached. He turned and rode back in the direction from which they had come, not wanting to ride forward to meet the waiting enemy, and reckless enough in his anger and pain to hope to meet trailing Persians behind him.

And now to find Christine.

CHAPTER 12
CHRISTINE'S TRAVELS

Christine was unsure if she still dreamed, or if the vertiginous feeling that gripped her body was real. She did not open her eyes. Her body swayed to and fro in rhythm to a regular sound that she could not identify. Her stomach twisted within her, but she could not be sure whether the twisting was an indication of hunger or a desire to be ill. Somehow it was both. She tried to lift her hands to her stomach to press there in brief investigation, but she could not lift her hands. In fact, she could not feel any part of her body other than the pit that was her stomach and the feeling that she swayed, floating.

A dream then. I have had this dream before, this dream of helplessness. I wish I could wake from it.

After some time wherein she did nothing more than count the beats of her heart, or count the pulsations of the other swaying rhythm which seemed syncopated with her heart, she became aware enough of her body that she knew she was reclining on some lumpy, uncomfortable surface. She could feel the lumps under her back, another pressing against her legs, something supporting her arms. She tried again to lift her hands to her roiling stomach. Her heavy hands moved and then rested on a soft surface which must be her abdomen, for she felt a weight resting above the pit within her.

I want to wake.

She heard a strange mumbling in her ears as she tried to make her thought take the form of words, tried to say the words aloud.

"She is waking." She heard the words near her, a man's voice, the words spoken in Persian, and reaching her ears as though through cotton.

She felt hands under her body, under her heavy limbs, lifting her into a sitting position. Her head was too heavy for her neck to hold, and it flopped forward until her chin rested on her chest. She tried again to open her eyes, but could not. For some time, she sat, feeling nothing more than hands securing her in her upright position. She returned to counting her heartbeats.

After another passage of dreamtime, she tried to speak again.

I want to wake.

She tried to force her tongue and lips to make the sounds that would echo her thought. "I wan do way…" she heard, in a voice that sounded like hers might if her mouth were stuffed with sausages. At the thought of sausages in her mouth, the pit that was her stomach deepened. She wanted to weep, and she heard a sad keening noise which frightened her because it sounded as if it was issuing from within her own body.

A hand lifted her chin from her chest, and something pried at her closed eyelid. She tried to focus her open eye and could not. She tried to keep her head raised as the hand released her chin, but she could not.

More time passed, and again she tried to open her eyes. This time she succeeded. She was looking at the front of a skirt she recognized as her own, although the bodice above her waist did not look familiar. She tried to raise her head again to take in her surroundings, and found this time that she could, although not without loosing another wave of dizziness that caused her to close her eyes again. She swallowed and fought the vertigo hoping that it would not cause her to be ill. The dizziness subsided and she opened her eyes again. Her vision was clearer this time, and the dizziness did not return.

She sat in a coach, three Persians looking at her, the men packed across the bench seat she faced.

Now, why would I dream of Persians?

She could feel the bodies of two others pressing against her on either side. She turned her head to look to her right, and then clamped her teeth together as another, milder wave of dizziness returned with the movement of her head. Her breath came heavy through her nostrils. She could not see the face of the man beside her. His head was turned to look out the curtained window of the carriage, through the small space made as he held the curtain aside in one hand. The sunlight through the window stabbed her eyes. She turned to face forward again.

SKELETONS IN THE CLOSET

This time she recognized the tall man facing her. She recalled him from… from somewhere. His inscrutable gaze held hers as she tried to remember.

Suddenly, she recalled where she had seen him before. The tunnels in the house… the foolish room…

I am not dreaming! Erik! Erik!

She wanted to shriek his name, but did not. She recognized the moan this time as her own.

The tall Persian leaned toward her, and holding her chin in his hand, looked into her eyes. Apparently satisfied with what he saw there, he reached behind him and pounded on the carriage wall. The rocking of the carriage slowed, and then stopped.

She knew what would happen now. This had happened before. Food. Her mouth filled with saliva and she swallowed to keep it from cascading on to her dress.

The door of the carriage opened. The Persian standing outside the door dipped a cold stew into a bowl and handed it in – lamb, Christine thought, as she caught sight of the first bowl. Her mouth began to water as the smell of strong spices infiltrated the carriage interior. Six bowls of stew were passed in, one for each of them. Christine lifted her hands as a bowl was passed to her. With deliberate motions – for she feared spilling the stew held in her uncertain hands – she ladled the pungent mix of meat and vegetables into her mouth.

As she ate, her strength returned, and the vagueness of her senses began to fade. She shook her head in an effort to dispel the last of her confusion.

I am awake. I have been captured by Mazenderani.

She leaned over the nearly empty bowl in her lap to see if she could catch sight of her shoes. The toes of both shoes peeked from the hem of her skirt, and she sighed as she leaned back in her seat again.

Erik! I hope you understood my message!

She sighed again and dropped her eyes to her lap.

Catching sight of the remainder of her stew, she thought, *I must keep up my strength*. Her stomach did not require her logical deduction of necessity to accept the last of the stew, and too soon her bowl was empty. Her eyes moved to each of the bowls in the hands of the men surrounding her as her greedy stomach hoped for more.

She handed the bowl out as the man outside the carriage came to collect them, uncertain whether to break her silence to request more. She accepted the flask that was passed in to her, and drank of the warm, delicious water. She turned her eyes to the tall man across from her, feeling somehow that even in this terrible circumstance he might be the most receptive to her request for more food. She opened her mouth to make the request, but before she could speak the words, the man removed another small flask from within his sleeve. He removed the lid and held it out to her. She did not know what the flask might contain, but she was quite ready to accept whatever additional food or drink might be offered. As she lifted the flask to drink from it, a delicious rose-scented aroma came to her, and she sucked in a deep breath of it.

Her entire body went slack, and the flask was removed from her failing fingers. Her vision blackened at the edges, and her body slumped sideways to rest against the man to her side. The last thing she heard before she was swallowed by a frightening blackness was the raucous laughter of the men within the carriage.

CHAPTER 13
ERIK AND PETTER

It was night again when Erik abandoned his horse near the docks. After a night and a day spent in flight and in scraps of stolen sleep, Erik felt as if the horse had ridden him. He crept toward the docks hoping to find Mattis still moored, but ready to forgive the man if he was not. The heavy pant of breath that escaped him when he caught sight of his friend's boat was cut short as a stabbing pain shot through his chest. He brought a hand up to press against what he was sure were broken ribs.

After a long moment during which Erik watched for movement on or near the darkened boat, he crept toward it. He boarded, ignoring his various pains, and hunkered down out of sight of anyone who might venture dockside at this late hour. Avoiding the planks above the sailor's sleeping quarters, he limped a circuitous route to Mattis' private cabin. He eased the door open, and smiled at the large man's stentorian snores. Slipping into the room, he closed the door behind him, and turned to wake his friend. He was not surprised that the man still slept – the rumble he was producing would camouflage any sound Erik had made in entering the small cabin.

SKELETONS IN THE CLOSET

Erik listened through another cycle of rumbling and whistling, loathing to wake his friend, feeling that he might slide down the wall to the floor and sleep himself. Without any sound or any indication of movement in the near perfect darkness, suddenly one large oak-like hand closed around Erik's throat and his head slammed against the wooden wall behind him.

"Oy, friend, you've got the wrong cabin." Mattis' voice rumbled as though in a ragged continuation of his snore.

"Mattis," Erik whispered over the constriction in his throat. "It's Lucky." He hoped his words would be understood, and soon.

The pressure on his throat eased on the instant. "Lucky! You crazy loon!" came the immediate response. Erik bent forward from the waist and coughed through his ruined throat. He brought his hand to the back of his head to determine if his wound had begun bleeding again. Erik examined his hand as a lantern light flared across the tiny room. He did not see fresh blood.

"You nearly ran out of luck, old friend," Mattis admonished as he brought the lantern toward Erik. Then, as he raised the lantern to look at Erik: "Gracious, friend! Looks as though you already have!" In the lamplight, the sailor's incredulous face became uncharacteristically somber and creased with worry. Erik laughed weakly, then clutched again at his ribs.

"Sit, sit, friend," Mattis said, and put a great arm around Erik to help him to the bunk. Mattis settled the lantern near the bunk and sat in the solitary chair.

"Christine?" asked Mattis, painful dread reflected in his features.

"They've taken her," Erik growled, the violent rage that had been cutting at him over the last hours slicing through him again like pain.

"Tell me what you need. Whose neck you need broken," Mattis answered. He clapped his massive hands together and squeezed until his knuckles grew white. Having just experienced those enormous hands about his own throat, Erik did not doubt that Mattis could do the job – although he had never known the man to be in the leastwise violent.

Erik choked back the angry oaths that threatened to join Mattis' own. When Erik did not answer, Mattis spoke again, his tone laced with worry, his eyes moving over Erik's ruined and bloody clothes.

"Do you need a doctor?" he asked.

"I need sleep. Do you have food? I am too tired and angry to think," Erik answered.

Mattis rose without another word and left the room. Erik longed to lie back and rest, but refused even in his exhaustion to take his friend's bunk from him.

Erik awoke from a half-sleep still sitting upright on the edge of the bunk when Mattis re-entered the room.

"Dried fish and hardtack," Mattis answered. "Thought it best not to make a ruckus."

SKELETONS IN THE CLOSET

Erik ate as if asleep, not tasting the meager rations. When he awoke, stretched out in Mattis' bunk, he could not remember finishing his meal. He stood with a groan, each of his aches awakening with his movement, but he felt well-rested and stronger.

Before Erik could straighten his tattered clothing, the door opened and Mattis backed into the room, and then turned bearing a washbasin and steaming pitcher of water.

"Ah, good. You're awake. Slept the sleep of the near-dead, I'd say." Mattis was again full of good cheer, and he laughed as he put the washbasin on the small table. "Need help?" he asked as he handed Erik a pile of clean white bandages and a wash linen.

"Thank you, no," Erik answered as he took the linen and began to pour hot water into the basin.

"What can I do?" Mattis asked, sitting on the edge of the abandoned bunk.

"I need to go to London," Erik answered. Mattis raised his eyebrows. "I am too old and injured to do this alone," he paused and grimaced as he passed the warm cloth over his battered face. "I am going for the one man I can trust to be of assistance."

"Petter," said Mattis.

"Mm," Erik answered, nodding. "I will find it hard to explain… Petter does not know all I have done and been in my life."

"No son knows his father – thank the Heavens," Mattis said, with another laugh. "But Petter is a good son. He will never believe that you are anything but a virtuous man."

"Virtuous," Erik repeated, with a snort and a wry smile. "Oh, Mattis. In my youth…" Erik's mind filled again with ancient bitter memories made clear again by the Sultana's reappearance.

"Follies of the youth are best left there. We each have our own. I know the man you are now, Lucky, and he is a good man, a good friend." Mattis coughed into his hand as if embarrassed at his own effusiveness. He said, "Friend, what can I do?"

"I will not involve you in these dangerous matters, Mattis." The man struggled between curiosity and acceptance. "But I do need supplies and a way to Stockholm."

"As good as done," Mattis said, and grinning, he shook Erik's hand.

After Mattis left with a list of supplies and two letters of instruction, Erik removed his clothing and bathed and bandaged the remainder of his wounds. He paid special attention to the knife wound in his thigh and the bone-deep gash in his shin. Mattis returned with two bowls of the fish stew they both favored, and some of his own over-sized but clean clothing for Erik to don as they waited for the arrival of Erik's requested supplies. By the following morning, the boat was sailing for Stockholm.

Despite Erik's unbearable need for speed in his journey, he relished the time spent with his friend. The pleasure was bittersweet, as Erik knew what he had failed to explain to his friend – that whether he lived or died in his attempt to rescue Christine – he could never return to Sweden again. He could not. And so he cherished each of Mattis' loud laughs, each painful clap on the back, each joke, with the appreciation of a man on his deathbed clutching at his last moments with loved ones. The pain in his heart surpassed the pain of his wounds and he spent every minute he could basking in the warmth of his dear, dear friend's companionship.

Erik was in a black mood as he prepared to debark in Stockholm. Mattis stood at his side at the railing, one heavy arm slung about Erik's shoulders, his eyes combing the docks and the part of the city visible from his vantage on deck.

"Mattis," Erik started, and had to stop to swallow past the lump in his throat. He began again. "Mattis, my friend, I…"

"I'll see you again, friend," he said, and he clapped Erik on the back, face still turned to the teeming docks. He bent and raised a duffle to Erik's hand and turned to Erik, eyes boring into Erik's own. Erik tried to smile at his friend, but could not. Mattis repeated, "I'll see you again." The statement had the sound of a command rather than a wishful statement.

Erik hesitated, and then nodded. The two men embraced without shame, the strength and length of Mattis' embrace belying his belief in his hopeful statement.

Erik limped down the gangplank, the sad knot again in his throat. He refused to turn back for a last sight of his friend.

***

Erik checked into a hotel in London with the surreal feeling of having traveled through time. Many of the buildings and roadways in London were as he remembered them from over twenty years ago, but the trams and motorized buses that moved through the streets among the horse drawn carriages were out of place in his memories. Despite the lowering weather, he felt invigorated by the bustle and business surrounding him, and smiled as he thought of how Christine would react were she beside him. The smiled was short-lived.

I will find you, my love. Nothing will keep me from you.

He did not consider how the Sultana might be entertaining herself with Christine, focusing on the hot hope that the Sultana would not go so far as to kill his beloved. She could not expect to obtain the service she had asked of Erik if she went so far.

Once ensconced in his suite, Erik indulged his mischievous sense of humor, and sent a messenger to Petter, giving a false name and asking the boy to come for an interview regarding a possible commission. He received an immediate answer indicating that Petter would be available within the hour. He removed his hooded cloak. As he donned a mask he had not worn since leaving London twenty years ago – a mask Petter had never seen, as Petter had never seen any of his masks – he looked forward to seeing his son once more, and to his son's presentation.

"A pleasure to meet you, my boy," he said to the empty room, as he gazed into a mirror, and straightened his coat. "A pleasure to meet you, my boy." He was satisfied that his English and its accent were correct. Gripping the cane he used to support his injured leg, he walked to the door when the knock sounded.

"Petter Nilsson, sir, at your request," Petter said, presenting his card, and bowing.

"A pleasure to meet you, my boy," Erik answered, stepping back and gesturing into the room. "Thank you for coming on such short notice." He took the card Petter presented, and introduced himself, using the name he had used when last in London. "I am Lord Bastion."

"At your service, my Lord," Petter answered.

"Please," Erik said, after shaking Petter's hand. He gestured to a low table, and seated himself on the facing couch.

"Right away, my Lord," Petter answered.

As Petter presented his architectural drawings and photographs of several magnificent carvings, Erik was torn between watching his son and looking through the presented materials. He was proud to see that Petter's presentation was smoothly delivered, and that his plans and carvings had only improved during the months since he had left Sweden. He did not feel the need to suppress his smile.

As the presentation concluded, Petter arranged several of his most admirable drawings on the table, and placed small photographs of his carvings strategically – artistically, Erik thought – among them, and stepped back.

"Very impressive, young man," Erik said.

"I am so pleased you like them," Petter answered. Cocking his head to one side and smiling, he said, speaking in Swedish, "So,

Father, when shall this charade end, as I am certain you are not here to hire me."

Erik paused, surprised, before he threw back his head and laughed. He rose, and closing the distance between them, embraced his son.

"How?" he asked, matching Petter's Swedish and smiling at his son.

"Your perfect teeth – unlike an Englishman's. Unmistakable, really." Petter leaned in to peer at Erik's eyes. "And your English is too proper," he finished, and laughed. He reached a finger up to pluck at the fleshy cheek of the mask. "Why are you covering your face?" he asked.

"Ah, a habit of old," Erik said, awash in memories, both pleasant and otherwise.

"The cane? Another part of your disguise?" Petter asked with a laugh.

"I am afraid not. I have injured my leg," Erik answered.

"Where is Mother?" Petter asked, glancing around the room.

"I… I hope we will be joining her soon," Erik answered.

"Joining her?" Petter asked.

"Would you be willing to make a quick jaunt to Paris with me, Petter?" Erik asked. He knew he must tell the boy of his mother's predicament, but he hoped to be on his way before divulging the full extent of the problem.

"Paris! When?" Petter asked.

"How soon can you leave?" Erik asked, smiling, allowing the taunt in his question to twist his smile.

"I… Father, I have work, and I have…," Petter answered, leaving the statement hanging.

"A woman friend?" Erik asked, reading the flush rising to Petter's cheeks.

"A magnificent woman friend!" Petter finished in an enthusiastic burst.

"I should love to meet her," Erik said, and winked. Then: "But can you not leave your work? Even to see your mother?"

"I…," Petter paused. "Yes, I am certain that I can. Mr. Evans – my employer – is gracious, and would grant me a leave of absence, I am sure." He glanced sidelong at his father, and said, "This is important?"

"Fairly," said Erik, aware that Petter was reading his own suppressed anxiousness.

"I will go now to speak with Mr. Evans," Petter said, and began gathering his presentation materials. "Did you like them?" he asked, nodding toward the pages.

"I could not be more proud," Erik answered. "And I would meet your Mr. Evans, if it would not be inconvenient."

"Certainly," answered Petter, now smiling again. "Shall I present you as," and here Petter lowered his voice and drew the syllables out, and with a strong English accent, said, "Lord Bastion."

Erik laughed. "No, I shall be proud to be your father."

"And your mask?" Petter asked, flicking a finger toward it as though he thought it a silly affectation.

"It is for the best, son," Erik answered. Petter shrugged.

***

Erik took an instant liking to the gregarious Mr. Evans, who reminded him of his friend Mattis in size and good humor, despite the incongruously high-toned pitch of the former's voice, the shining, hairless pate, the humorous mustache. Or perhaps he saw the similarity out of a wistful longing for the friend he had just left.

After confessing to being a master stonemason himself, he allowed himself to be shown around the shop, and to be introduced to several of the working journeymen. He declined a tour of the Bush Exhibition site, despite being quite interested in seeing the place – he rather hoped to be leaving with Petter too soon to have the time, although he did not say so aloud.

Finally, and at Petter's insistence, Erik was introduced to a rather unassuming and plainly dressed young woman standing near a drafting table.

"My daughter, Phoebe," Evans said.

"My dear friend," Petter said. "Phoebe, this is my father."

The girl curtseyed, and turned her smiling face toward Petter again. It was quite obvious to Erik that the girl was enamored with his son.

"She's quite a good architect," Petter said, gesturing to the drafting table beside which she stood. "She's helped me with several improvements to my own plans."

"May I?" Erik asked, as he stepped toward the table.

"Oh, Mr. Nilsson, my plans are nothing as good as Petter's," she said, but she stepped aside to let him look, blushing. Erik bent over the top drawing and examined it.

"Hmm," he said after a moment. "You have quite a good eye." He raised his head, and with a small groan, straightened his back, gazing at her. "And quite beautiful eyes, if you don't mind an old man saying so."

Again, Phoebe blushed, but her eyes remained on his as she curtseyed again, and said, "Thank you, sir. I don't mind in the least."

Erik followed her gaze as it moved to Petter. His son rolled his eyes.

"My father always speaks his mind," Petter said with a smile and patted Phoebe's hand where it rested on the table. In that instant, Erik knew that this charming and talented girl was not his son's love interest.

Petter left Erik to talk with the girl as he took Mr. Evans into the office and obtained the necessary leave of absence. When they left the shop, Erik was even more impressed with the girl, as she spoke quite knowledgeably about not only architecture, but also of masonry, world history, music, and any other subject Erik had cared to introduce.

"I am to dine with Constance this evening," Petter said, as they walked to Petter's flat, again reverting to Swedish. Erik heard the fervent infatuation and excitement in his son's voice. "I would be proud to have you make her acquaintance."

"I would be pleased to meet the inestimable Constance," he answered, quite eager to meet the woman who could surpass Phoebe in wit and charm.

"Yes, quite!" answered Petter.

At Erik's insistence, Petter agreed to bring Constance to Erik's hotel dining room for dinner, and Erik retired to his suite to "freshen up." In truth, he wanted an hour out of the retched mask he was so unaccustomed to wearing.

Constance proved a disappointment to Erik, but he made certain not to show it. She was a pretty girl – prettier than Phoebe – but her prettiness was just that. Not beauty, and not backed with the same kindness and intellect he had seen in Phoebe. Constance was charismatic in a charming and haughty way, and Erik laughed several times through the meal – although not always for the same reasons as Constance and Petter. She obviously had Petter's heart in her clutches.

The meal concluded, and the three stood. Constance took Petter's arm, and said, "My goodness, Petter! You never told me your father was so… charming." Her eyes took in the remnants of their rather lavish meal, and then Erik's tailored suit. Erik nearly flinched at the calculating avarice that shone in her eyes in that telling moment.

"Expense account," Erik said, with a tilt to his head that he hoped conveyed a mild embarrassment. "But I am pleased to have been able to use my employer's money in the company of such a lady as yourself."

Petter's omnipresent smile faltered as he looked to his father, confusion plain on his face, but he said nothing. Constance fluttered her eyes at Erik in disingenuous coyness before she turned to Petter.

"I shall see Constance home," Petter said, smiling again, eyes locked with Constance's.

"Of course," Erik answered. He stood at the table as couple left, hoping for his son's sake that Petter did not expect to find happiness through a liaison with this girl. He sighed as he left the dining hall, knowing from painful experience that matters of the heart were ungovernable.

Constance came to the dock to see them off when they left. Petter waved like a madman from the rail. Erik had to admit that the girl, standing under a parasol and waving a small lace handkerchief, made rather a pretty picture. But again, it seemed to Erik that that was all the girl was: a pretty picture, painted over a small soul.

"I so hate to leave her," Petter sighed, as they turned from the railing.

"Do not trouble yourself," Erik answered. "You will find your dearest one waiting when you return." He, of course, was not thinking of Constance as he spoke.

"Yes. Yes, of course," Petter answered. Love-struck as Petter was, Erik heard the uncertainty in his answer. He smiled as he led Petter from the rail.

CHAPTER 14
PETTER LEARNS PART OF THE TRUTH

They were entering the Strait of Dover, and the white cliffs of the southeast coast of England could be seen across the water when Petter left the deck, knocked at the door to his father's cabin, and announced himself. The lock disengaged, and the door swung open. As soon as he entered the room, the door was closed behind him and locked again. At no time had Erik stood where he could be seen.

"I am pleased you finally removed your mask, Father," he said, with a wry smile, as he turned to face his father. With a perverse curiosity, he gestured toward the mask where it lay at the foot of the bunk, "May I?"

"Certainly," Erik responded.

Petter lifted the mask in both hands, and peered into it. "It must be very uncomfortable," he said. "Why bother?" He had seen his father's face every day of his life, and was disturbed at the idea of his father masking himself. Somehow it seemed an unnecessary weakness in a man he had always considered so confident.

"Surely you are not naïve enough to think my deformity normal or pleasant," answered Erik.

"Well… not normal, no, but not unpleasant. It's just the way you look," Petter answered. "Appearance is not the measure of the person."

"Ah, so the saying goes. But there are some who are turned by a pretty face," Erik answered, with a glint of humor in his eyes. Petter did not understand the reason for his father's sly smile, and answered defensively. "No one cares that you lack a nose!"

Erik chuckled. "So my friends treat me. So you have only seen anyone treat me. But there was a time when I only ever ventured out in a mask."

"Why on Earth?" asked Petter, and then, as the answer occurred to him, "Were you ashamed?"

"Mm," Erik answered, and Petter sensed a looming history behind the utterance. "Your mother convinced me that it was unnecessary. Perhaps even bothersome." Erik winked at this last statement, and Petter heard the suggestiveness in his words.

Petter smiled as he recalled how often his parents embraced or kissed – when they were home of course, in private – or how often his mother touched his father's face with affection. "I imagine." His mind filled with the sensual warmth of Constance's lips against his own, and he smiled. He would not want a mask separating them. With an effort he pulled his thoughts from Constance and back to the question that had brought him to this room.

"Where is Mother – I mean, why is she in Paris? Why did she not come to London with you?" He asked the questions in quick succession, somehow apprehensive that he would not like the answers, but unable to avoid the topic any longer.

"Mm," Erik answered again, face lengthening. He moved to lean against the small desk before speaking again. "Sit down, Petter."

"Oh, Lord," said Petter, foreboding filling him, and he dropped to sit on the edge of the bunk. He had never known his parents to be separated from one another for more than an afternoon, or perhaps one of his father's short fishing trips with his sailor friend. "Please don't tell me that she is ill. Or that you… that she…"

"Your mother was well when last I saw her." After a weighty pause he continued, "And we are still very much in love."

Petter huffed in relief. "All right…" he said. A bubble of impatience rose in him as his father continued to look across the space between them, expression unreadable. He seemed reluctant to explain the situation, or to be searching for words, and this only increased Petter's apprehension. Just as Petter opened his mouth to prompt his father further, Erik spoke.

"Your mother is not in Paris," Erik said.

"But you told me…," Petter started.

"I told you I hoped we would be joining her soon. I also told you I wanted you to accompany me to Paris. Both are true." Petter pressed his lips together and waited for the explanation to the puzzle, disturbed at his father's circuitousness.

"I did not wish to worry you," Erik said after a pause.

"Father! You are worrying me. Is she ill? What is it?" Petter heard the impatience in his tone and willed himself to remain seated.

"Your mother…" Erik paused and then shook his head and sighed. "Your mother has been kidnapped."

"What?!" Petter leapt to his feet.

"It is difficult to explain…"

"Explain!" Petter interrupted, angry in his fear.

"I am attempting to!" Erik answered. A deep breath, then: "Please," he said, eyes pleading, and gestured again to the bunk, "sit down."

Petter sat, but his hands clenched and unclenched where they rested on his knees. The idea of his mother kidnapped seemed ludicrous in the extreme, but perhaps the purpose of the trip to Paris was to ransom her. Outrageous notions – kidnapping and ransom – but he would hear his father out.

"A very long time ago – long before I met your mother – I spent time in the Persian nation of Mazenderan."

"Where you met your friend, Mr. Akhtar," Petter interposed. He was confused by his father's apparently unconnected statement, but waited for the connection to his mother.

"Yes," Erik answered. "Without explaining the details, which are unimportant, I left Mazenderan a wanted man." His father paused as if expecting another interruption, but Petter held his tongue. "Mr. Akhtar was exiled for helping me… leave." Petter felt certain that his father had meant to say, "escape," but again, he waited. Intriguing as the story sounded, it was all difficult to believe, and Petter wanted nothing more at this point than for the story to reach its conclusion, so that he could attempt to digest the whole.

"Now, I have been asked to undertake a task in Mazenderan, which I am unwilling to do. A… dangerous person has taken your mother to ensure my performance, knowing that I would never return to Mazenderan of my own choice."

"Can you not ransom Mother?" Petter asked. "I assume…"

Erik shook his head as he answered, "The task is the ransom."

Petter opened his mouth to ask about the nature of the task, or why his father would refuse it when performance would secure the safety of his mother, but Erik held up a restraining hand. Petter closed his mouth again.

"As you have seen, I am injured, but even so, I intend to rescue your mother. I hoped you would assist in that endeavor," Erik said.

Petter waited to be sure his father had finished. Then he burst out, "Of course!"

"It will be dangerous," his father said. "Even after more than forty years, I may still be a wanted man."

Petter's mind twisted away from the track on which it ran to another. "Wanted for?" Petter asked. When Erik shook his head, Petter asked, his voice a whisper, "Are you wanted for murder?"

"No," Erik answered. Petter was surprised that his father's answer was not more vehement, or that it did not reflect shock and outrage at what Petter feared was an outrageous question. "I knew – know – secret information which the Shah did not want known to others."

"The Shah?" Petter asked, awed that his father would have such information, and yet relieved at the banality of the answer.

"We are going to Paris so that I can consult with the Shah's former daroga – my friend, Mr. Akhtar. He may be able to provide me with needed information."

"But, Father…" Petter stopped, unable to formulate a statement or question, his mind whirling with questions and suppositions.

"I would rather not discuss the particulars of the situation, son," Erik said. "I would not have come to you but for my injuries," he added. He ducked his head before bringing his eyes back to Petter. Petter thought he saw pleading in his father's round eyes.

Petter swallowed, and rocked his head back, eyes closed, feeling confused and pained by his father's secrecy, his mother's predicament.

"What… What if they hurt Mother? What if they kill her?" he asked.

"Then I will kill them!" Erik roared, standing from the desk upon which he leant, then turning and pounding the wooden tabletop with a fist. "I will kill as many as I can reach!" The vehemence and volume of the response startled Petter into silence. When Erik turned to face Petter, he could only stare at his father's anger-distorted visage.

"Father," Petter said, "you don't mean that. Do you?"

"With all my heart," Erik answered, although with less volume. He seemed to be panting in his anger. For a frightening moment, Petter saw a rage in his father's eyes, a savageness he never guessed could exist there. Then Erik turned away, his burning gaze directed blindly toward a wall lantern rhythmically swaying on its swing-handle.

"Father," Petter said, hoping to call to the man behind the rage. Thinking again of his mother, he asked, "Are you certain she still lives?" He was amazed that he could discuss the possibility of his mother's death with such calmness – could scarcely believe anything he had heard. At the moment, his father's rage seemed the only reality, and Petter wanted to sooth that rage, remove it from a man whom he had always known to be gentle and loving. "Father?" He rose and put a placating hand on his father's tension-bunched shoulder. He squeezed, and then left his hand resting there until the tension dissipated.

"Yes. I am," Erik answered, exhaling through pursed lips and lowering himself to lean on the desk again. Reason returned to his father's eyes. "I would have no inducement to perform the requested task if she were killed. But," he continued, raising a hand, "as I said, she is being held by a dangerous and deranged person."

Hearing the calmness returned to his father's voice, Petter released his father's shoulder. He said, "Do you think we can rescue her?" His breath quickened as he thought of the chivalrous nature of the task, but he also worried that they were embarking on a fool's mission – not that he would balk, if there was any chance whatever of helping his mother.

"Absolutely. I have certain… knowledge, certain talents."

Another peculiar gleam came into his father's eyes. Petter had a sudden unsettling notion that the floor beneath him had tilted, that his place in the world had been made unsure, that the man before him was a stranger. He thought with rising anxiety: *There is much I don't know about my father.*

Petter returned to sit on the bunk and dropped his head to his hands, as much with despair over the plight of his mother as to hide his doubt-filled face from his father.

"This is all so unbelievable." He was embarrassed to hear a quaver in his voice.

"Petter. Petter, my son." Erik limped the few steps to stand before Petter. When Petter raised his head, the stranger was his father again, compassion reflecting from eyes too moist. "I am so sorry."

Sorry for what? Petter felt lost and confused.

Petter stood, feeling like a child, and needing his father's strength and support. He sighed as Erik embraced him, and clutched at his father, holding to the solid reality of the man. He heard his father's sharp intake of breath and felt him flinch in his grasp as though in pain. Petter eased his grip and wondered again how his father came to be injured — a question Erik had declined to answer. The injury to his leg seemed not to be the only injury being borne.

When Erik released him to limp to a porthole, Petter sat again on the bunk, myriad questions rising and swirling through his mind. Erik turned away from the porthole and, obviously reading all the questions imprinted in Petter's creased brow, spoke again.

"I wish no questions. For now, son, I ask that you trust me."

"Of course, I trust you, Father," he answered. He pressed his lips together to stem the flow of questions that threatened to burst forth, and only pleaded with his eyes for explanation. When his father turned away from him, Petter spoke out of his own desperation to understand. "Can you not, then, trust me?"

"Trust you? Of course I trust you!" Erik answered, the pain of the question clear upon his face as he crossed the small room to stand again before Petter. "I trust no one else to assist me! I came to you because I honor no other man with the trust I place in you."

Petter held his father's eyes as he said, "We are going to the daroga for assistance. He must know something of the matter."

His father sighed, but did not turn away. "I am going to him for information only. Even so, I trust no one to assist me *without inducements*. Without question and without reason. I do so trust you." His father limped to the chair beside the desk and seated himself with a small groan. When Erik spoke again, his voice was low, full of sadness. "My story is not easily nor quickly told," he said. His eyes turned to a document lying on the table to his side, but he did not seem to see it. "I would not have you distracted with inconsequentialities."

Inconsequentialities? Petter wanted to yell the word, but refrained. He paced the floor thinking, *Mother kidnapped, and I am merely to trust?* But he did trust his father, with a trust that overpowered his curiosity.

"Very well, Father," he said. "I trust you to know best. And I will reward your trust in me by respecting your wishes with regard to this matter." He paused before clarifying. "Until mother is safe."

Erik understood the implication behind Petter's final statement. After a hesitation, he spoke, voice laced with sadness. "There will come a time when I will tell you all, Petter, if that is what you wish."

Petter nodded. He had another thought and said, "Does mother know what you will not now explain to me?"

"Your mother knows all," Erik answered. "She is the better half of my heart and soul – she knows all, and loves me still." Erik spoke with the quality of a man musing at a miracle, as though he spoke to himself instead of to Petter. His head rose and he looked at Petter with vehemence, rage and violence again dancing in his eyes. "And I will not lose her!" he finished.

"Of course not, Father," Petter answered, and again crossed the small room to place a placating hand on his father's shoulder. He controlled the urge to lift a hand to the pinched brow over Erik's two glazed eyes. "Of course not." He waited, hand still resting on his father's shoulder until the fire went out of his father's eyes again.

"We shall be in France soon," Erik said, as though awaking from a spell. "Be ready to disembark." He stood and moved to the mask where it lay on the end of the bunk.

"I am ready even now," Petter answered, with the same business-like tone.

"Excellent. We shall proceed with all possible haste," Erik said, lifting the mask over his head.

Petter left the cabin, intrigued by all he had learned – and failed to learn – frightened for his mother, and frightened by his father's mysterious transformation. He tried to imagine the same violent fire coming into his own eyes, but could not. Could not imagine what events in his own life would build such an internal forge. He was determined to learn. He would hold his father to his promise to tell all.

CHAPTER 15
MEETING WITH THE PERSIAN

Erik was angry. After years of sublime contentment and devotion – and yes, even inner peace – in Christine's love, he had all but forgotten the old feeling of generalized anger he now felt building in him. Since her capture, the old anger seemed to grow and expand, ready to bleed from his very pores. The need to remain civil in tone and manner to those people with whom he must interact to accomplish his goal required a talent of restraint unexercised since his days in the Opera House. Only Petter remained immune to his desire to lash out in anger, and Erik thanked the twisted fates for contriving to injure him, bringing him to seek out Petter. The boy exerted a much needed calming influence.

Erik's excitement to see Paris – the city which he had, for so long, called home – rode alongside his impatience to be finished in Paris and leaving France in search of Christine. Together, these conspired to make the carriage ride from Le Havre port to Paris seem interminable.

Erik was pleased upon their arrival in Paris to discover that, while the city had changed – as London had changed – the overall beauty of Paris was not diminished. Paris remained the rich, romantic city of his recollection. He was surprised to find himself smiling as he gazed from the carriage window at the passing sights.

As they crossed the Boulevard des Capucines – the boulevard which led to his magnificent Opera House – he wondered if Christine would find the city as beautiful as he, or whether her fright-filled escape from Paris a score and more years ago would taint her view of its wonders. At the thought of Christine, a dangerous depression threatened to settle upon him, as though not only memories but other less comfortable wraiths were descending upon him. In an effort to break away from the sudden gloom, and the anger that would soon follow, he turned to gaze at his son. Petter's likeness to Christine, and his youthful enthusiasm as he exclaimed over the passing sights washed over Erik like a cleansing light, pulling him from his lowering mood. He managed to enjoy the remainder of their ride, naming for Petter various of the sites they passed on their way.

They arrived at the daroga's flat – the selfsame flat the daroga had occupied over twenty years ago when Erik had made his home in the basement of the Opera House. Erik rang at the door, and Darius, the same devoted servant of old answered the ring, although the man was more stooped with the weight of the years. Erik removed the oversized hood he wore over his unmasked head and climbed the stairs behind the obsequious servant, remembering the last time he had climbed these stairs. Then, it had been to perform an act of deception against the mysterious man known to most Parisians simply as "the Persian." Then, he had acted from a position of strength. This time he would beg favors of the man. Erik did not like the contrast, although for many years now he had called the man friend. His desperation to save Christine and his injuries had put him in this position of weakness, and that feeling of weakness increased his anger with each step he took.

"Erik!" The once tall, but now shrunken Persian dropped his feet from a hassock and rose as Erik entered the room. Erik's anger waned in the enthusiastic glow of the greeting. "How grand to see you again! Come, come, sit." Turning to the servant, the Persian said, "Darius, refreshments for my friends."

Erik attempted a smile as he approached the open-armed man who greeted him. He moved hesitantly, due as much to the injury to his leg as to how shaken he was by the aging of the man. While Erik's hair had silvered, his body retained much of its old vigor. The dark-skinned Persian, however, seemed to have crumpled and wizened with age – he was not the strong picture of a police chief he once was.

"Faraz," he said, as they embraced and exchanged the brief kisses to each cheek as was customary between friends in Persia.

Faraz held Erik's shoulders, examining him at arm's length, still smiling. "My gracious, you've aged, Erik, but we have not aged the same number of years. You have only aged one for every two of mine!"

Erik laughed at the blunt statement of his own thoughts. He brought his hand to his own face, then ran his fingers through his silvered hair. "You are kind," he answered.

"Ah, and you must be Petter," Faraz said, turning away from Erik. "It is the greatest pleasure to meet the boy – young man! – with whom I have enjoyed correspondence all these years." Faraz extended a hand to Petter and bowed as their hands met.

"Mr. Akhtar," Petter said, bowing in turn.

Switching from the French that had been spoken thus far between the men, Faraz said, "And do you speak Persian as well as you pen it?"

Petter answered in Persian. "It would be heartbreaking indeed if one did not learn to speak such a beautiful language, given the opportunity."

"Ah, Erik. I see he has your gift with languages," Faraz said, with a pat to Petter's arm. "Your accent is flawless, young man, if I can judge such a thing after such a long time away from my countrymen." Erik was surprised to hear only good humor in the Persian's tone, without the least tinge of regret or condemnation in the reference to his exile.

"Thank you, sir," Petter answered, chest puffed with pride.

After another moment during which the smiling Persian looked between father and son, he said, "Please," and gestured to two comfortable chairs before seating himself.

"I received your letter informing me of your imminent arrival. But tell me, where is your beautiful bride?" he asked. "I had hoped perhaps to be favored with a small performance after all these years. The last I heard you sing was at your wedding, and it is too long a period to live with only the memory of heaven."

The brief comfort and good humor that had overtaken Erik at the effusive greeting of his friend evaporated on the instant, and the reason for their visit fell to rest on his shoulders as a physical weight. Erik slumped back into his chair with the sudden resumption of his burden, while Petter sat more erect on the edge of his seat. The boy seemed to be waiting with an almost greedy anticipation for Erik's answer. Irritation sparked within Erik, setting fire again to the guttering coals of anger that had momentarily cooled.

Erik sat forward and with hands braced against each knee, looked from his son to the still smiling Persian. The Persian's good humor inexplicably deepened Erik's anger.

"Daroga," he began, calling the man by his old title rather than by his given name. "Do you recall the rosy days of Mazenderan?"

The smile faded from the wrinkled face of the man before him.

"I recall those days, and many more besides," Faraz answered, puzzlement mixing with some darker emotion in his jade eyes.

"He knows nothing," Erik growled in a low voice when the Persian's eyes turned to Petter. Petter frowned, but his posture perched on the front of his seat did not change.

SKELETONS IN THE CLOSET

"Christine has been taken to Mazenderan," Erik continued. The Persian's eyes widened, and Erik noted with some detached part of his mind that the years had tinged the whites of his eyes with yellow. He wondered if his own eyes had also yellowed.

The beast that was his anger rode him and forced the next words from him. With the peremptory tone of an order given, he said, "You will help me. You owe me."

The Persian's eyes remained wide for a moment more before closing to mere slits. He rose from his chair, never taking his withering gaze from Erik. He stepped to the side of the chair and placing one hand upon its back, he turned his back to Erik.

Erik refused to allow the Persian the denial his gesture implied.

"You *will* help me," Erik repeated, frustration and anger mounting. With slow emphasis he said, "You owe me." Erik stood as he spoke. Petter looked with morbid fascination between the two men as the silence lengthened.

The Persian spoke, and his words were stilted with anger and formality.

"I cannot imagine what word or action of mine has caused me to deserve the insult you have cast upon me. I must ask you to leave my home." After another breath, he said, "Immediately."

"Daroga…" Erik growled the elongated word through clenched teeth. "I need…"

The Persian spun on him, holding a hand before his face, palm toward Erik, as if to both stop Erik's words and blot the sight of Erik from the room.

"I owe you nothing!" The angry words were no louder nor more passionate than Erik's own, but were startling nonetheless, coming from the soft-spoken man. Before Erik could respond, the Persian spoke again.

"I will admit to the services you rendered me in...," he paused as if he would choke on the words to come, "in the rosy days of Mazenderan," and again he stopped to breathe, "but those services were repaid when *I saved your life!*"

"I..." Erik began, raising one finger in retort.

"You call on me as a friend, but do not ask help of me as a friend. You demand, and suggest a burden of debt. Your insult questions our friendship and my honor, but I ask: Where is your honor in this?"

The words struck Erik as a physical blow, taking his breath from him. He dropped his raised finger, and his head with it, and all his anger flushed from him in a wash of humiliation. When he raised his head again, the Persian's palm still pressed toward him. Nothing could be seen of the man's face. Pain twisted within Erik – pain and fear at the loss of Christine, pain over the insult he had levied against his friend.

"I...," Erik began again. Erik sat rather than fall to his knees as he wished to do. "I am sorry, old friend. I have never had something to lose – someone I cared about more than life itself –

and in my pain, I forget myself." Erik stood again, but could not force himself to leave the room as demanded. He deserved no further consideration from the man, but his need – Christine's need – kept him motionless. "You have endured an undeserved insult from a thankless man. But for the sake of my wife, I beg your forgiveness and indulgence."

The Persian's hand fell to his side. The face revealed was both stern and pain-filled.

Erik forced himself to meet the Persian's sad accusatory eyes. "I am sorry, Faraz." The tall man's stiff posture eased.

"For your own sake will I forgive," answered the Persian. "For the love I hold in my heart for both you and Christine will I help."

Erik dropped his head again, feeling he could weep with shame and relief. "I can never repay you, Faraz," he said. Neither man moved from where they stood.

Petter broke the tableau when he stood and spoke. "Thank you, Mr. Akhtar."
The Persian looked startled as he turned to Petter; indeed Erik had forgotten that Petter was witness to the argument. He felt another flush of humiliation as well as pride in the son who so correctly responded to the Persian's offer of assistance.

"You are quite welcome," said the Persian. "Of course I shall help where I can." Smiling, he added, "Your father simply falls back on old habits of intercourse between us, habits long broken and best left in the past." The Persian turned to Erik, pressing his mouth into a thin line as he said, "Wouldn't you agree?" He extended a hand to Erik.

Erik took the man's hand. "Wholeheartedly," he said. The Persian nodded once, as if signaling that the matter was settled. As they embraced again, Erik said, "Again, I apologize, and I thank you."

"We shall speak no more of it," the Persian answered, and pounded Erik on the back. Erik flinched at the pain that accompanied the gesture. In response to the sudden analytical expression the Persian directed at him, Erik said, "Ribs. It is nothing."

Darius entered the room at that moment, and it occurred to Erik that the timing was more than coincidental. How long had the man waited to see the outcome of the argument? He carried a tray with three glasses of tisane and a plate of various Parisian pastries, which he deposited on a low center table before again leaving the room. The Persian seated himself and Erik and Petter followed suit.

The Persian sipped at a glass of tisane before saying with a wave of his hand, "Christine has been taken to Mazenderan." The words and the gesture seemed to erase the unpleasantness that had occurred since Erik had spoken those same words, and invited Erik to continue in his explanation.

"She is being held to insure that I complete a certain task," Erik said, and glanced at Petter. It would be far easier to explain the circumstances without Petter's presence, but Petter had already questioned whether he was trusted, and Erik would not hurt the boy by sending him away. Nor could he explain his real fear: that on learning the truth about Erik's past, Erik could well lose the affection and trust of his son.

When Erik did not explain further, the Persian asked, "She is being held by the Shah-in-Shah – the Sultan?"

"No," Erik answered. "Not by the father."

"Ah," the Persian answered, and he grimaced as he brought a hand to his chin.

"Father," Petter said, replacing his cup of tisane, and licking a remnant of pastry from his lip. Erik looked to his son, pained with the idea that to obtain any helpful information from the Persian, he would perforce need to explain more than he wished in the presence of his son.

"You have indicated that we will not be long in Paris," Petter continued.

"That is true," Erik answered, puzzled by the statement.

"I wonder if I might be allowed to excuse myself from this discussion. I would see some small part of the city if I could." Petter stood, strode to the window and looked down to the street, before he turned to face Erik again.

"Ah," Erik said, smiling at his son's understanding. "Yes, of course, son."

Faraz rang for his servant. "Darius," he said, once the servant had entered, "the young Mr. Nilsson is in want of a guide to the city." He turned to Petter and said, "Darius is a most reliable guide, and could assist you if that were your pleasure."

"Thank you, yes," Petter answered. He shook Faraz's hand, and bobbed his head toward his father, looking quite boyishly excited at the proposed excursion – which he may well have been despite the transparency of his reason for leaving.

"You must be extraordinarily proud," the Persian said, after the boy and the servant had left the room.

"Yes," answered Erik. "I am proud of my son, but not of my past. I would not burden him." It was a half-truth.

"Nor test the strength of his affection for his father," the Persian answered, speaking for the second time to Erik's thoughts.

"No, nor that," Erik answered. "I suppose the boy must learn…"

"The follies of youth are best left in the past," Faraz answered, and Erik was struck with the recollection of the same words from Mattis. "Those who love you have forgiven you," the dark man continued, "but have done so from a perch of harsh experience. Give the boy time to gain his own."

Erik glanced toward the doorway through which Petter had departed, and hoped his son had an easier road to experience than the one he had trodden. Painful memories flooded his mind.

"Christine has been taken to Mazenderan," the Persian repeated, bringing Erik back to the present. "She is in great danger if she is in the clutches of the young Sultana."

"Yes," Erik said, his tone sour.

SKELETONS IN THE CLOSET

The Persian listened through the hours as Erik explained all that had occurred, starting with the Moor seen dockside with Erik's servant, and including the Sultana's visit after Christine's kidnapping, his own capture, and his subsequent escape.

"Your injured ribs," the Persian said, nodding in sudden understanding. "Have you any other injuries?"

"My leg." Erik gestured with annoyance to his leg. "I should redress the wound if I may."

"Ah, and I had thought the cane an indication of your advanced age," the Persian said, laughing. Erik laughed with him, recognizing that the Persian's assumption was not uncalled for.

"So, now you know the situation," Erik said. His hands squeezed into fists. "I will not do as the Sultana has asked."

"I should hope not!" the Persian interrupted.

"I intend to extricate Christine from her clutches, or die trying," Erik continued. A pang of fear sliced through him that Petter would be his companion in the effort. He did not plan to place the boy into more danger than could be avoided, but with his current wounds.... "Do you have information – any information – which would be helpful to our endeavor?"

"Information?" the Persian asked. "What information would I possess that you yourself would not?"

"You were known to those highest in the Sultanate. You have a greater knowledge of the dungeons than I – if you will recall, the Sultana was not interested in… being entertained… within the confines of the dungeon proper."

"Hmm. Yes," the Persian muttered, expression darkening. He seemed lost in thought. Erik waited, hoping against hope that the Persian could provide anything that might make his task easier.

"I have maintained correspondence with several acquaintances in Mazenderan," the Persian said. "It may be possible to…" The Persian tapped at his cheek with one finger. "Hmm."

"Yes?" asked Erik, his impatience bringing him forward in his chair.

"Yes," answered the Persian. He nodded once, and rose from his chair. "I shall accompany you to Mazenderan. I feel certain I can be of service to you and, most importantly, to Christine."

"What?" asked Erik, startled at this development. "Faraz, I could not ask you to go to Mazenderan. The danger to yourself…"

"You have asked for my assistance," answered the Persian. "I believe I can be of assistance in Mazenderan. Besides," the Persian turned his head from side to side, taking in the confines of the room in which they spoke, "your visit has made me feel my age, and my complacency. I am ready for an adventure, and cannot think of a better cause." The Persian paused, and when he spoke again, there was a wistfulness in his voice. "And to see my country again. To hear the language of my people, taste again the flavors and scents of my land. I have not thought of Mazenderan for many years, but…"

SKELETONS IN THE CLOSET

Erik smiled as he listened to his friend, at the sudden enthusiasm and youthful energy generated at the contemplation of the journey. When the Persian broke from his musing and turned to Erik, Erik extended his hand. "Faraz, you are welcome." It was not said without guilt. The man was too old for this dangerous undertaking, but Erik could not insult Faraz again by refusing him. "And thank you. Thank you for everything." Despite his guilt, hope rose in his chest like a wounded bird and fluttered there.

A voice from the door startled them both. "We are returned, sir," Darius said.

"What an amazing city," Petter said from the doorway. Entering the room, he looked from Erik to the Persian, to their smiling faces, to their clasped hands. He tilted his head in question.

"Petter," Erik said, moving to stand with his son. "Faraz has agreed to accompany us in our endeavor."

"Excellent," answered Petter. "And I shall hope that two old men aided by one ignorant young man will accomplish the task!" Erik grunted as Petter nudged him in the side with an elbow, but even the pain in his ribs did not keep him from joining the other two in their laughter.

CHAPTER 16
CHRISTINE MEETS THE SULTANA

Christine awoke without the same confusion and disorientation that had accompanied her awakenings over the course of her journey. Had it been days? Weeks? The vague dreaminess and confusion that marked her memories since she had been taken made it impossible for her to judge the length of time that had passed.

She lifted her head, waiting for the expected bout of dizziness, but it did not come. She looked about, wanting to determine, first, if she was alone. For the first time since the journey began – at least to her awareness – she was indeed without visible guards. She sat up to make a more thorough investigation of her surroundings.

She was seated in a large bed, in a lavishly if somewhat garishly decorated room. She was not restrained in any way. The walls were made up of a series of tile-inlaid pointed arches, the small red and gold tiles arranged in a mosaic of geometric patterns. Most of the arches curved over recessed niches that contained statuary or potted plants. Two of the archways curved over doorways. Between each arch in the series were painted trees –

appearing to be some stylized form of palm tree – and the painted fronds met over each arch, giving an impression of being caught in the midst of an oasis. There were no windows to the outside, yet the golds in the decorations reflected with lamplight, and the golden sun centered in the dome of the ceiling, enhanced the impression of a sun-filled room. Despite the circumstances, she was awed at the splendor of the room.

Christine pulled the light sheet from atop her and pushed her legs over the edge of the bed. She was surprised to find herself dressed in a simple white shift rather than her own clothing. A brief examination of her body, using both sight and smell seemed to indicate that she had been bathed while last she slept. Her hair smelled perfumed, and felt clean and untangled in her fingers. As she pulled a lock over her shoulder, she startled at the discovery that her hair was now dark, almost black.

Why?

Her pulse quickened and she felt her face warm with blood. Somehow, this was more of a violation than the discovery that she had been bathed and dressed by… who knew?

How dare they!

She shook off her anger and uneasiness, and stood to continue her investigation while she still might. She could not know when her captors might return.

Her bare feet sank into a thick woven Persian carpet, patterned in red and black, upon which the bed was centered. The floor beyond the carpet appeared to be marble, smooth and shining in the lamp light, set forth in a checkerboard pattern of enormous square blocks in red and black. The floor was cool to her feet as she passed over it toward one arched doorway. Christine took hold of the door handle and, first pressing herself against the door to see if she could detect any sound from the other side, she tried to open the door. It was locked. She fought the impulse to pound on the door, and instead, ran to the other side of the room to try the other door. It also proved to be locked. She glanced around the room for any other door she might not have noticed, and finding none, returned to sit on her bed, again pulling her hair forward and frowning at the new color.

Guided by her nose, she saw what she had not noticed upon awakening: a silver samovar steaming with the smell of coffee, and a bowl containing chunks of meat over rice. She wondered if the food could be trusted, but a loud rumbling from her midsection decided her against concern. If they wished to poison her, they could have done so long since. She ate the meal – the lamb was tender and well-spiced – using flatbread to wipe the bowl when she reached its bottom. The coffee was strong and sweet and flavored with cinnamon. She decided that if she should be poisoned, it should be with food as savory as the meal she had just consumed.

Not that there was any reason she should be poisoned. Her captors had not taken her on such a journey, cleaned her, fed her, *colored her hair?*, and left her in such a room to kill her. She must be captive for some purpose, and that purpose related to Erik.

SKELETONS IN THE CLOSET

Erik! Had he received her message? Had he deciphered it? Did he yet live?

A panic descended upon Christine as she thought of Erik's fate. He had told her he lay under a death penalty. Had the penalty finally been exacted? Was she a widow for the second time in her life, only awaiting the terrible news?

She leapt from her bed, and again tried to open the near door – this time without any effort at silence. She pulled at the handle, rattling the door, inviting any interruption of her solitude. When this had no effect, she ran to the second door, pounded upon it, and then ran back again to the first.

Erik! I must know what has happened to Erik!

Had he escaped? Was he even now attempting to find her? As she pulled at the door, tears blurred her vision, turning the room into a garish kaleidoscope of red. *Red like blood*, Christine thought. *No. No, I mustn't think such awful thoughts. Erik is alive! He must be!* And then, with a fresh spate of tears, *Oh, Petter*, as she imagined her son all alone in the world, without either parent. She took deep calming breaths in an effort to regain control.

Having obtained no response from her captors despite her strident efforts, Christine moved around the room, examining whatever came to hand. She lifted small vases and statuary, lifted and opened decorative boxes, dropped to her knees to look under the bed and the furniture, lifted the large cushions littering the floor around a low table.

As tears came again, she thought, *What am I looking for?*

Exhausted, alone, and no further enlightened as to her circumstances, she returned to the bed and threw herself across it, weeping. She wept until she had no energy left for even that dismal occupation, and finally, she slept.

When next she awoke, the room was dark, except for the low burning of a tall lamp near the side table. Furious with herself for sleeping through an invasion into her prison cell — for that is what it was, lavish though it might be — she leapt to her feet, and ran to the near door. She tried it first quietly, hoping against hope that it had been left unlocked, and when finding it locked, she rattled the handle, and pounded on the door with her fists. She heard nothing in answer to her shouts and pounding. She might well be the only creature in an immense palace — or perhaps this room had been constructed in solitude in the center of an empty barren desert. Feeling there was nothing she could do, she returned to her bed, and this time, lay her head on the pillow and pulled the sheet over her body. Desultory tears slipped from her eyes as she stared at the dark domed ceiling — inlaid with stars around the central golden sun, as she had not noticed before — until she slept again.

When she woke again, she could tell from the red behind her closed eyelids that the room was lighted again. She covered her eyes with her hands and exhaled, in frustration, in hopelessness.

"My, you are a pretty thing," a low feminine voice said, speaking in an accented French. Christine jerked her hands from her eyes and gasped, pushing herself across the bed, away from the near voice. "But not nearly as pretty as he said."

Wide-eyed, Christine looked at her visitor. She seemed a decade or more older than Christine, with fine lines around her eyes and mouth. But she was still very attractive, with dark hair and a voluptuous body draped in colorful bejeweled veils and all manner of gold jewelry.

"Coffee?" the woman asked with a smile. Christine flinched at the smile, which seemed more akin to a cutting blade than an expression of geniality. The woman gestured with a hand, and it was not until a young girl scurried from behind the woman to place a cup under the samovar tap that Christine realized this woman was not her only visitor. She raised her eyes to find two stiffly erect male guards at the near door, and another young girl on her knees near their feet.

The near girl, apparently a servant, extended the steaming cup toward Christine. Christine blinked at the incongruity of being served with such deference while being held captive. She shook her head, more to clear it than to refuse the fragrant coffee. It was not until the cup was returned to the table that Christine recalled the words spoken to her by the opulently garbed woman: 'But not nearly as pretty as he said.'

He said! Erik!

"Where am I?" Christine asked in the same French that had been used to address to her. As her indignation rose, she pulled a lock of hair over her shoulder and thrust it toward the woman. "Who are you to dare…"

"Tsk, tsk," the woman answered, waving a finger at her as if she were a naughty child. "I dare because I may." Again the sharp smile that brought to mind the eels sold on the docks near her home in Sweden. The woman's amber eyes closed in a languid dip of lashes, then flashed open. The sinister smile was gone, her lips now pulled back over her bared teeth. Her hand flashed toward Christine, and before Christine could react, grasped a great handful of hair at the back of Christine's head.

"You will speak to me with proper respect," the woman hissed into Christine's face. "You will do so as if your life depended upon it. You will do so on penalty of instant pain."

The woman jerked Christine's head back, and something sharp touched her neck just under her jaw line. *A fingernail, a sharp edge of jewelry, a small knife?* Christine inhaled as the pressure of the sharp object against her skin increased. She froze, her only movement the rapid blinking of her eyes.

"There," the woman said in sweet tones as she released Christine's hair. "I believe we now understand each other." Again the cold smile.

"Yes," Christine answered, raising a hand to the stinging point under her jaw. She examined her fingers, caressing the small smudge of blood between them. "Yes, mistress," Christine amended.

SKELETONS IN THE CLOSET

The woman threw back her head and laughed, her eyes sparkling with good humor, the full lips of her laughing mouth looking quite natural for the first time. Christine thought the woman could be rather beautiful if not so tainted with malice.

"I approve," the woman said. "Mistress. Yes, this is how you shall address me." She gestured with one hand, and the same servant girl who had poured the coffee rose from her knees and approached.

"Coffee," the woman commanded in Persian, and with a raised eyebrow, looked back to Christine. Speaking French again, she said, "You asked where you are."

"Yes," Christine responded, then added, "Mistress."

"You are in the court of the Shah-in-Shah of Mazenderan," the woman answered. The answered chilled Christine, confirming her fears of who this woman might be. Erik had told her of the evil child Sultana of Mazenderan, and the malicious actions of the woman before her leant credence to the unbelievable stories. The woman's next words drove away any hope Christine still harbored that this woman was not who she feared.

"I am the Sultana Naheed – although you will continue to call me mistress – and you are my… special guest." The chill smile stretched into a broader smile that was all the more frightening for its childlike sweetness. Christine shuddered. Erik had also informed Christine what the Sultana did with those she referred to as "special guests."

God help me!

Christine shivered where she lay. The Sultana dipped her eyes as she sipped at her coffee. Without raising her eyes to Christine, she said, "Have you no more questions for me then?"

Christine longed to ask after Erik, wanting more than anything to know whether he lived. Terror sealed her lips.

"Come now," the Sultana purred. "I see the question in your eyes. Ask it."

"My… my husband," Christine stammered. "Is he… well?" She could not bring herself to ask the true question and allow the word 'dead' to pass her lips. She shivered and clenched her teeth in frustration as unwelcome tears once more filled her eyes.

The Sultana's eyes narrowed as she leaned toward Christine. "He is yours no longer," she said, almost spitting the words across the small space between them. "He is mine again, and will be joining me soon. We shall see if he still wants you for his own when I am through with you."

Christine flinched backward from the vehement words, and the tremors in her body nearly brought her clenched teeth to chattering.

The Sultana leaned back again, and smiled, cocking her head to one side and placing a finger on her bottom lip. Her lips closed over the tip of her finger, as though she had brought a drop of coffee to her lips. She sucked the tip of her finger once, and as she removed her finger, her smile grew. Christine imagined that this was how the Sultana would taste a drop of her victim's blood.

SKELETONS IN THE CLOSET

"Are you afraid of me?" asked the Sultana, sweetness dripping from her words like icing.

"Yes, Mistress," Christine whispered.

"How marvelous," the Sultana answered in a low voice, closing her eyes and undulating as if with sexual pleasure. Leaning toward Christine without opening her eyes, she said, "Yes, I can smell you." She sucked in a deep breath.

Christine closed her eyes. She listened as the coffee cup was deposited on the table, and waited… waited… for the blow or the stab or bite that would follow. She heard the rustle of movement, and then the opening and closing of the door. When she opened her eyes, she was again alone.

"Erik!" she cried, although her cry was little more than a whisper. "Oh, help me. I am so frightened." She lowered her head to her arms and wept until the tremors were washed from her body.

CHAPTER 17
PLANS ARE MADE

Petter returned from his walk feeling dreamy and content. Everywhere he went in the city, even just walking in the area around the Persian's flat, he imagined Constance with him, her hand clutching his arm, her parasol tilted back as she exclaimed at the sights and sounds of Paris. Although – in truth – Phoebe would more perfectly mirror his interest in the architecture. Using his Brownie, he took several photographs of the more interesting buildings – he could share these with Phoebe on his return to London.

As he entered the Persian's second floor sitting room, he found the Persian and his father bent over a large table over which a map of Persia had been spread. He drew near and listened as the men debated the rescue plans.

Rescue plans! Petter was jerked back to the reason behind his presence in Paris, despite the fact that even now he had difficulty believing the reality of the situation.

"By land or by sea is the question," Erik said, looking up at Petter. The question was not directed at Petter, but he was alert and interested in an instant.

SKELETONS IN THE CLOSET

"The farther from Constantinople," Faraz said, pointing to the map, "the less danger for you. Abdul Hamid remains Sultan, and he will not have forgotten you."

"Yes, but think of the time that could be saved taking the straits to the Black Sea… haste is of the utmost importance," Erik answered.

"And we shall be seen traversing the Bosphorus from the very windows of the Yildiz," said Faraz, with some vehemence. Quietly he murmured, "I should think your head would be of the utmost importance," but not so quietly that Petter did not hear.

"Head?" Petter asked, with some alarm.

"No one will guess 'Aqa Erik' is aboard ship," his father answered, as though he had not heard Petter's utterance.

"Head?" Petter asked again, and this time he placed a hand on his father's arm, demanding attention. Instead of meeting his eye, his father glanced sidelong at the Persian.

"Your father is rather famous across Asia," answered the Persian. "Shall we say he is highly regarded? It is much more pleasant terminology than to say he is wanted." Faraz chuckled as Erik glared at him.

Petter's frustration mounted, despite his resolution not to press his father for details or information. He squeezed his father's arm, and said, "Father?"

Erik stood. "Later, Petter, I swear to you. I will say that there are two places to which I thought – hoped – never to return. Mazenderan, and Constantinople. The first is our destination, and we must pass through the second." When Petter looked at his father with stricken eyes, Erik continued. "For your mother, we must do this. I will not be discovered in Constantinople, I assure you."

"But we need not go through Constantinople," Faraz interjected. "We could land here, near Cyprus, and travel overland from there. This area is far south of Constantinople, and you will not be recognized there."

"It is a waste of time!" Erik answered. "If we take the Black Sea to its easternmost point, we have little land to cross, and we can come to Mazenderan by the Caspian Sea. It will be much faster." Petter followed his father's finger as it roved over the map, and had to conclude that his plans seemed best. *If* speed were the only factor.

Petter bent to the map as the two men looked to each other in impasse.

"There are the mountains to consider if we go as Mr. Akhtar has suggested," Petter said into the silence.

"Yes, thank you, Petter," Erik said, and he placed an arm about Petter's shoulder, although he did not take his eyes from Faraz.

Faraz sighed and raised his hands into the air in surrender. "I only worry for you, my friend," he said.

"I must get to Mazenderan and Christine," Erik answered. "By sea then," he said, and left the room.

SKELETONS IN THE CLOSET

Alone with the Persian, Petter thought to satisfy some small part of his curiosity. After all, his father had said he would explain matters later, but had not told him he could not seek information from other quarters.

"Mr. Akhtar," he said, glancing at the door through which his father had departed. "My father's head?" he asked, not knowing how to phrase the question.

Faraz bent closer to the map, and then stood and raised his jade, wrinkle-shrouded eyes to Petter. Petter saw calculation in the man's eyes, and knew he was weighing his words.

"Your father's curse," Faraz said, "is that he is possessed of a brilliant mind."

"Secret information again, then?" Petter asked. "Father told me he was wanted in Mazenderan because he had secret information." Petter pulled at his coat, looking for a reaction from the Persian that might indicate surprise or denial. When the reaction did not come, he said, "Was he a spy?"

"Not a spy, merely a genius. A mad genius, some thought him, but he is not mad."

"But, Mr. Akhtar…" Petter started. The Persian interrupted him.

"Petter, your father is a good man, whatever questions the current circumstances may raise in your mind."

"I am not questioning that. I do not believe I could ever question that, even if he was a criminal," Petter answered, defensive on behalf of his father.

"Your father will be pleased to know that," Faraz answered. He raised a hand to ward off any further questions, and said, "Come, let us find your father. It is time for luncheon."

They lunched at a pleasant outdoor café situated on the corner of the intersection of two streets. Petter thoughts returned to Constance as fashionable young couples passed, or settled at a nearby table. His mind was fastened on thoughts of Constance's small hand on his or clutching at his arm, his arms embracing her, and the wet warmth of her mouth on his. He imagined escorting her to this café, and introducing her to French cuisine. The café was not lavish, but the newness and excitement of a Paris café would appeal to Constance.

Looking to a street vendor selling flowers, Petter thought of the flower he had painstakingly carved for Constance. He wondered where she had decided to display his gift, or if it still remained imprisoned in the gift box – perhaps resting beneath a fresh new bouquet from a fresh new suitor. His mouth turned down at the thought.

I must write to her.

Without hesitation between thought and a need to accomplish the deed, Petter stood.

"You leap as one bitten," Faraz said. Faraz looked startled and amused, and even with his the mask in place, his father's eyes glittered with humor.

SKELETONS IN THE CLOSET

"I must write a letter," he said. Glancing at their unfinished meal and flushing at his rudeness, he asked, "Do you mind if I excuse myself?"

They waved him away with good-natured laughter, and Petter rushed back to the Persian's flat, mind spinning with scraps of poetry he thought to include in his letter.

By the time Erik and Faraz had returned to the flat, more than an hour later, Petter had finished his letter. He felt certain his affections had been properly set forth (he had decided against his own poor poetry) and his promises to return to her were as fervent as he could make without feeling foolish. He had even written of the carven rose, asking her to think of him as she held it. Sadly, the writing of the letter had not eased his longing for her – nor his troubled thoughts of other suitors. In his agitation, he had written a second letter – this one to his friend, Phoebe.

He had started the letter by explaining that he would be longer on his travels than he first indicated to her father, and asking her to inform the man, with Petter's apologies. He then began to describe the city to her, including, as he could not in his letter to Constance, descriptions of the more interesting buildings, and of the differences in architecture he had noted. He was surprised to find, when Erik and Faraz entered laughing over what sounded to be a bawdy joke, that he had written six full pages to Phoebe – four more pages than he had written to his dear Constance. He rationalized that poetic protestations of love could not be too long without seeming comical, while prose regarding architecture required far more explanation. He closed the letter with a friendly valediction.

"She is a pretty girl," Faraz said, lifting a framed photograph lying near the letter to Constance.

"Yes," answered Petter, feeling a strange surge of guilt over his more lengthy letter to Phoebe. He reached for the photograph, which the Persian surrendered at once. "I took this photograph myself," he said, all thoughts of Phoebe banished as he gazed at the image of a smiling Constance.

Erik joined Faraz at the writing desk, and reaching for the photograph, asked, "May I?"

"Of course," Petter answered. Petter watched as his father examined the photograph, a quiet sadness growing in his father's eyes.

"What is it, Father?" he asked.

"Would that I had a photograph of your mother," he answered, and returned the small frame to Petter. And then with strength returning to his tone, "But I shall soon have better. I shall soon have your mother in my arms." He turned away, his dejected posture belying his optimistic statement.

"Do you have your photographic equipment with you?" asked Faraz in a bright tone. It seemed to Petter that he was trying to combat Erik's sudden darkening of mood.

"Yes, I have my camera," answered Petter.

"I would be interested to see it operate, if possible," Faraz continued.

SKELETONS IN THE CLOSET

"Certainly!" answered Petter. He pulled his Brownie and a long three-legged support from his effects. "Shall we move to the street? It is too dark in here for the exposure." When it appeared that only Faraz would follow, Petter said, "Father? Accompany us? You needn't put on your mask," – there was no reason for it – "we shan't be long and shan't go far."

Together the three moved to the street, and Petter led them toward an unpeopled yet sunny spot at the side of the building that would promise the best photograph. He began assembling the three-legged camera mount.

"That looks much like a surveyor's tripod," said Erik, showing interest in the subject for the first time.

"Yes, Father," answered Petter, "although I had to modify it. See? I've mounted a wooden platform on which to sit the Brownie. It makes for clearer pictures."

Erik examined the tripod, making small exclamations of praise, and then the camera, turning it over and over in his hands. It struck Petter that while his father looked interested, he was too old to appreciate the new invention.

"I'll take a photograph of you, Father," Petter said, taking the camera back. Erik looked self-conscious, but after a brief hesitation, struck a pose nonetheless. Faraz stood at Petter's side observing the process.

"It seems quite simple to operate," said Faraz. "May I?" Petter nodded, but not without some trepidation. He cherished his camera, and did not wish it broken. "I shall not move it," Faraz added with a smile. "You prepare everything, and stand with your father." Petter did so, smiling at his father's side.

"And now for the three musketeers," Erik said. "Can you arrange such a photograph?"

Petter's face lighted up with enthusiasm. "Actually, I can," he responded, hand darting to his pocket. He removed a delicate device he had created, which consisted of a clockwork mechanism. Dangling from it was a thin loop of horsehair twine. Erik approached to investigate. Petter spoke to his father as he attached the body of the device to the side of the platform on which the camera sat.

"This exposure lever on the side needs to be pressed slowly but steadily until the exposure is made. This, you see," and he looped the horsehair twine over the lever, "will pull downward on the lever as my clockwork mechanism winds itself."

"Ingenious," Erik said, as he first bent and then straightened in his examination of the mechanism.

Despite his pride, Petter frowned when his father cast a furtive glance about, as if trying to determine whether anyone was approaching – as if he were afraid of being seen without his mask.

"It is ready now, Father," he said. "If you will stand by Faraz, I will make certain that everything is set before I trigger the clockwork and join you." The cloud left Petter's brow as both Erik and Faraz struck jaunty poses, and he laughed as he triggered the device and ran to join them.

SKELETONS IN THE CLOSET

Later that evening, as Petter lounged with a book, he was startled to discover that his father was examining the little Brownie. Petter dropped his feet from a low stool, and prepared to join him.

"Leave him," said Faraz from the nearby chair. "He has always been fascinated by inventions, and has likely invented more ingenious devices of his own than any other one man." When Petter hesitated, the Persian raised his newspaper again, and commencing to read again, repeated, "Leave him."

"I shall buy another – two if you wish – if I harm it," Erik said from the far side of the room. When Petter looked to his father, it seemed he had not spoken, so engrossed was he in the examination of the camera.

"Let me remove the film spool," Petter said rising, "or the photographs will be ruined." Erik handed Petter the camera, and Petter rolled and removed the spool, careful to demonstrate the process to his father.

Petter sat, but could not take up his reading again. He watched dolefully as his father took the camera to pieces, thinking again that the camera was a device for the young. He retired to bed while the equipment was still in pieces, unable to cope any longer with his childish disappointment at the loss of his camera.

When he entered the sitting room the following morning, he was surprised to see the camera, assembled, looking functional as it rested on the desk where his father had worked into the night.

"I'm certain it still operates," said his father from the far end of the room. "You can test it, or, if you'd rather, I will buy you another today." Lifting the camera and turning it in his hands, Petter saw that his father had loaded a new film spool into the camera. Petter's mouth fell open in astonishment.

"Ingenious little device," said Erik, turning toward the window, "made simple for the common man."

Petter smiled as he modified his estimation of his father's inability to appreciate modern inventions, and chided himself not to underestimate his father's resourcefulness again.

CHAPTER 18
CHRISTINE TAKES CONTROL

Christine had become accustomed to the dull routine of her existence. She never left the lavish room in which she was a prisoner, she never saw true daylight. She was dressed in comfortable clothing, and she was fed thrice daily. She felt certain that if she made any reasonable request – more food, reading material, anything – her request would be granted, although thus far, she had refused to speak to anyone outside the few utterances in French the Sultana demanded on her infrequent and often painful visits. Female servants assisted her in bathing (which often included another inexplicable coloring of her hair) and dressing – the only occasions on which the male guards did not enter the room, although even then, Christine was certain that the guards would appear on the instant if the servant girls called out in alarm.

Yet despite relative comfort, Christine wallowed in despondency, or, when the Sultana visited her, in fear.

Erik. Erik was constantly on her mind. Fear for him, hopeful thoughts of being rescued by him, and then again, more fear for him. When she did not think of Erik, she worried about Petter, alone in the world, lost in the inexperience of youth. She spent much of her time lying among the bed linens that were changed and laundered almost daily, or among the cushions surrounding the low table at the far side of the room. She felt steeped in hopelessness.

Today, she sat on the edge of her bed – she now thought of it as *her* bed rather than *the* bed – eyes turned toward an indiscriminate spot on the floor. She had eaten and bathed, and felt no energy for any further movement. When the door opened, she did not look to see who had entered, assuming perhaps that more time had passed than she measured, and that her luncheon was being delivered.

She was shocked from her trance by a sharp slap to her face, delivered with enough force to knock her from her seat on the edge of the bed to the floor. She brought both hands to her stinging cheek, and did not need the sight of ring-festooned toes that swam in her vision to know it was the Sultana who confronted her now. Not taking her hands from her face, she crawled backward on her knees away from the beautiful, perfumed feet. She did not raise her eyes.

"Stand and face me, worm," came the Sultana's harsh words.

I do not wish to, Mistress Snake.

She pulled herself up to stand before the woman. Still she did not raise her eyes to the woman's face.

Another vicious slap threw Christine arching back onto the bed, feet swinging from the floor. Christine cried out, and again brought her hands to her cheek, warm tears escaping around eyelids squeezed shut. She took two deep sobbing breaths before gaining the courage to open her eyes. The Sultana stood before her at the side of the bed, glaring with an anger somehow less frightening than the wicked, sweet smile that usually adorned her face.

"Mistress?" Christine said, and drew her knees up, pulling her legs out of immediate reach of the Sultana. Even as she did so, she knew there was no escaping the woman.

The Sultana's golden eyes glared from a face distorted by rage, but the woman did not speak. She raised a hand, as though to strike again, but did so slowly. The sinuous gesture brought to Christine the vision of a cobra readying to strike.

"Damn him!" the Sultana spat. "And damn you!" She lowered her arm as she spun away from Christine toward the door. Christine watched her in confusion, until the Sultana spun to face her again. Although there was quite a distance between them now, Christine could not help but flinch farther backward on the bed.

"But, I still have you, and he will obey!" the woman screeched. The Sultana spun again and slapped at the muscular arm of a guard as she moved through the door. Christine did not move as the guards followed the Sultana through the door. She heard the inevitable sound of the lock being turned.

Erik is alive! The pain in her cheeks could not douse her joy.

But what did she mean? Did the Sultana's statements mean that he had refused to join her? Or that he had refused her conditions for Christine's release?

Erik! I need you!

How would the Sultana's anger at Erik endanger Christine? The sharp metallic fear that had come with the Sultana's slap grew into a generalized terror for her own welfare – for what the Sultana might do if Erik continued to confound her. Bruises to her face or a blackened eye could be tolerated, but Christine knew from Erik's stories that the Sultana could – and probably wished to – do far worse. She collapsed onto the bed and wept with the desolation that there was nothing she could do. What could she do? She was a helpless prisoner.

At least Erik was still alive. She consoled herself with this thought.

Some hours later, as Christine sat among the cushions at the low table, the door opened again. She clutched an unused pillow to her chest for whatever small protection it might provide, but it was not the Sultana who entered. It was a servant girl bringing her noon meal. Christine trembled in relief. As usual, two guards stood with their backs to the door as the girl set the luncheon out on the table. Christine kept her eyes on the door behind them, praying that it would not open again to let in the Sultana. Even before the girl had finished setting out the meal, Christine reached for the fragrant bowl of soup the girl had set before her. She did not take her eyes from the door, from the guards, as she took the bowl into her trembling hands. Before she could lift the bowl to her lips, it slipped from her grasp, hitting the table before tumbling to the cushions beside her. Christine shied away from the spreading liquid and the soaked cushion beside her. With small curses muttered under her breath, the servant girl wiped at the few drops of soup that had spotted Christine's shift, and then took up the soaked cushion.

"I must rinse this," the girl said, speaking over her shoulder at the guards. Turning to Christine and speaking the most simplistic Persian, she said, "Wash. I will wash." Christine turned her head away from the girl, and maintained the silence she had made her habit among the servants. When she turned back again, the girl had already disappeared through the door to the bath. One of the guards gave a short laugh, and began to speak in quiet tones to the other.

Christine reached for the warm flatbread before her, and wondered if the girl would bring more soup. She did not care. She did not focus any attention on the guards' conversation – thus far in her captivity they had not said anything of interest.

Her breath caught at the unexpected mention of the Sultana and her eyes flashed to the guards. She lowered her eyes to continue her appearance of non-interest and nibbled at the bread in her hand – but her entire attention was on the quiet words of the two men.

"It is well with me that the Sultana has left the palace – and the kingdom. She is a difficult one," said the first guard.

She's gone! Christine exulted in the information, feeling some small measure of relief suffuse her. Then: *Erik!* With the Sultana's anger of the morning, Christine felt sure that Erik was the cause of her sudden departure.

"Quiet!" cautioned the second guard, as he huffed himself into a straighter posture. "Do you want to lose your head?" He uttered the last words out of the side of his mouth.

"The girl cannot hear me," said the first guard, "and that one," – here he pointed to Christine with his chin – "cannot understand me."

Do they think me an imbecile? Christine filled with indignation until it occurred to her why the servants spoke to her in such simplistic Persian, as if they were speaking to a dim child. *They do not know I can speak their language! I have only ever spoken French – or Swedish, as when they caught me at my home!* Her pulse quickened as she realized she had a heretofore unimagined advantage. Even with so small an advantage, she felt it the hook upon which she could hang many hopes. She almost clapped her hands in her thankfulness at the silence she had maintained with the servants – a habit that she had come to imagine as childish, and had almost abandoned.

When the silent guard did not answer, the first continued speaking. "Come, you cannot tell me that you enjoy the… special demands the Sultana makes of us. I would rather go back to my detail in the Shah's guard."

The silent guard looked to the door through which sounds of splashing still came, and then looked toward Christine. Christine turned her eyes away, cursing the fact that she had not kept her eyes averted. The silent guard had not seen her attention, or did not think it mattered, for he answered, almost too quietly to hear: "I enjoy watching the Sultana's swaying rump."

The first guard guffawed and said, "And you say I should worry about losing my head!" He stiffened to attention as the servant girl came back into the room with a wet linen.

Christine slumped away from the servant girl as the girl approached and began wiping at the carpet with the linen. She turned her head away, afraid that her sudden exhilaration would be evident in her face. When the girl lifted the tray to retreat, Christine bowed her head to her chest, hoping to maintain her despondent attitude.

She waited until the lock turned before she climbed to her feet. She clapped her hands in delight as she ran and leaped upon the bed.

What have I been doing? Who have I become?

She clapped her hands over her mouth to stifle a giggle.

Shame! Shame on you, she chided herself, but with buoyant good humor. *In your youth you ran from danger and fear looking for safety and protection, and in this crisis you have reverted. But you are not the weak woman you were!*

She rolled from her stomach to her back, and brought a hand up to caress her cheek, imagining the hand to be Erik's, then imagining it to be her own, caressing Erik's cheek.

Oh, Erik. She closed her eyes and embraced herself where she lay, hands rubbing over the length of her upper arms. *After all the love and confidence you have lavished upon me, in this crisis I have failed you – failed myself.*

Christine smiled, eyes still closed. She was not smiling at her failure, but at the realization of her failure, at her knowledge that she could act, that she would act.

She sat up on the bed, and looked with fresh eyes around the room. *What do I know? What has Erik taught me?*

She stood and walked around the perimeter of the room, near to the walls, but not touching them, simply looking as she had not bothered to look before.

I know I am in Mazenderan. I know I am in the palace. I know Erik helped to build this palace.

When she had completed her circuit of the room, she walked it again, this time focusing her attention on the floor, the location of the carpets, the location of the furniture.

I shall escape this place. I do not yet know how, but I shall. I shall bide my time, I shall listen and learn, I shall be the strong woman in whom Erik has placed his faith and confidence.

Christine stumbled as the door to her room opened, and then continued her walking, slumping her shoulders forward, and adopting the attitude of the disheartened. It was the servant girl returning with another bowl of soup. Christine lowered herself to the cushions and lifted the bowl to her lips and sipped. The girl watched as Christine replaced the bowl on the table, then she nodded and said, "Good."

Yes. Good. You cannot know how good. I have not felt this good since... A little of Christine's elation bled away as she realized she could not remember when she last felt as well and alive. Not since Petter had left for London.

I have been wrong, she thought. *Not wrong to worry about or miss my son, but I am solely to blame for my feeling that my life somehow ended with his leaving.*

Erik, she thought as she took another sip of her soup. *I am coming, my beloved.*

She pictured the two of them, he pushing his way over obstacles to reach her, she climbing equally difficult ones to reach him.

We will be together again soon.

CHAPTER 19
THE OPERA HOUSE

Petter was happy to note that as concrete plans were made toward the voyage and the rescue of his mother, the rage that so often seemed to infect his father diminished. Erik still seemed filled with tension, or was struck with bouts of anger that made him snappish, but the unsettling rage did not surface to glare like an unfamiliar beast from his eyes.

Already, Erik had procured a ship that lay in wait for their use at Marseille, and the Persian had obtained the latest and most detailed maps of the Mediterranean, Aegean and Black Seas and their coasts, as well as that portion of the Russian Empire that must be crossed between the Black and Caspian Seas. From the Caspian Sea, they would proceed due south, and then both men knew Mazenderan – or at least the Mazenderan of forty years or more ago.

Despite the desperate reasons for the journey, Petter could not help but feel excitement over the adventure to come. The dangers which the Persian exaggerated (for Petter felt sure they were exaggerated) and which Erik brushed aside with brusqueness, did not seem real to Petter. He had lived his entire life in Sweden, and had enjoyed the excitement of his journey to London. He had never imagined the thrill of his current prospective travels, and had not imagined that his father – his admired and loved, but ineffably stolid father – had traveled to such an extent in his youth. The intriguing comments sometimes exchanged between Erik and the Persian, while frustrating in their incompleteness, only added to the sense of adventure.

Of course, as the more youthful and strongest member of the party, he was also suffused with the duty to act as protector of the two men he would accompany. Without doubt they had more knowledge than he, but the two were both now quite... not decrepit, but, without question, aged.

Petter was startled when, in the midst of the frantic activities toward preparation and imminent departure for Marseille, Erik suggested a tour of one of the local sites.

"The Opera House?" Petter asked, in surprise. "Why, no. I have not seen it."

"I have some reason to visit the place, and thought you may wish to accompany me." Erik said.

"Certainly," Petter answered. He became more confused when his father emptied a large traveling case and brought it along.

The hired carriage brought them to the building, and Petter gaped at the façade. "It looks like a palace," he said as they left the carriage.

"Mm," answered Erik. Petter looked to Erik, but could not decipher the strange expression his father wore. It seemed both sad and yet lustful – the expression one might wear when meeting an old lover. Petter wished for a photograph of the magnificent building, but Erik had insisted he leave his camera behind.

"Father? Shall we?" Petter asked, when his father did not advance.

"No," answered Erik. At Petter's confusion, Erik said, "You shall go. Ask for a tour, and be sure to say that you would like to go back of the stage, to see the various wardrobe and property rooms, and the dancing school." Erik removed a handsome stack of francs from his pocket and said, "Offer to pay for the tour. Do not be afraid to be generous."

"Father…," Petter began, but Erik interrupted.

"I shall meet you backstage, and complete your tour. I believe you will enjoy the beauty and… depths of the Opera House." His father smiled a knowing and secretive smile before he gestured toward the grand entrance again, and said, "Go."

Despite his confusion at Erik's incomprehensible instructions, Petter strode up the wide stairs and entered the Grand Foyer. He drew in a sharp breath at the splendor that greeted him, and stood for some minutes gaping before the sound of footsteps across the marble floor awakened him from his daze.

"It is magnificent," Petter said, not even looking at the man who faced him.

"Indeed, Monsieur," came the respectful answer. "May I be of assistance?"

SKELETONS IN THE CLOSET

Petter brought his eyes to the well-dressed man beside him. "I would like a tour, if that is possible." Petter watched the polite beginnings of a refusal disappear from the man's face as Petter removed the large stack of francs from his pocket. "I will pay any price for the inconvenience," he continued. "I am new to Paris, I am a connoisseur of the arts, and I was told this was the most magnificent of buildings."

"Indeed, Monsieur," the man repeated, this time rubbing his hands together and smiling. The hairline mustache above his lips mirrored the smile. The man smoothed his hair back unnecessarily, and checking his watch, he said, "I happen to have time at the moment, and would be pleased to assist you." The man gestured Petter forward.

Petter quite enjoyed the tour, with both the eye of a tourist, and with the eye of an architect and stonemason. The opulence was rather overdone for his tastes, but sublimely put together for all that. From the vantage of a box seat overlooking the stage, Petter indicated a desire to go backstage and his guide showed some small measure of hesitation. An additional offer of francs overcame the man's reluctance.

"There will be workers backstage," the man began, as though he thought Petter would be bothered by encountering a less genteel person than the guide.

Petter gestured to an old man sweeping the stage below them and said, "I will not be in the least discommoded. There must be many workers engaged behind this magnificent scenery." Petter reassured him with a smile. "Perhaps we may start on the stage? I have never been on a stage, despite my love of the theatre."

The solicitous guide led Petter down stairs and through side passages until they emerged on the stage.

"No, no. Please continue your work," Petter said to the man sweeping the stage when his guide would have made him leave.

The guide turned in the direction from which they had come and said, "Pierre, bring up the lights for the young master, if you would." Turning to Petter, he said, "As a patron of the arts," – Petter smiled, understanding the man's solicitousness and the impression he had given with his sheaf of francs – "you may wish to experience the stage as an actor and dancer might, with the gaslights up."

It took some minutes for the lamps to come up, and during that time, Petter wandered about the stage, curious about the grid of frail bridges overhanging him, and the assortment of ropes, pulleys, and levers which remained hidden from the audience by the hanging curtains.

When the gaslights came up, Petter was facing the old man with the push broom, while the guide stood at the far side of the stage. Petter turned toward the gaslights, smiling at the warmth of the light they emitted, and then turned back to the old man. The man stopped his sweeping, and raised his eyes to Petter's. The man's eyes widened, and the broom handle dropped from his hands. The man's mouth worked as though he wanted to say something, and he straightened spasmodically from his stooped posture. Petter was bewildered by the sudden look of fear that crossed the man's face as if a seizure had gripped him.

"The Opera Ghost," the man muttered, and when Petter took a worried step toward the old man, the man screamed, "The Opera Ghost!"

Petter froze, quite baffled at the man's behavior as he spun and ran from the stage. At the sound of a great crashing just beyond his field of vision, Petter ran to investigate. The man was unconscious, apparently having run headlong into a sturdy piece of scenery. Petter was just kneeling at the old man's side when his breathless guide ran to his side.

"My apologies, Sir," the guide huffed and motioned to two men close at hand. "I cannot imagine…"

"He said 'Opera Ghost,'" Petter said. "Or at least so I thought." The two men were now trying to revive the man, and Petter turned to the guide.

"A foolish legend, Sir," the guide said, taking Petter's arm and guiding him away from the men. "Stupid old man," the guide muttered under his breath. He seemed quite agitated, and Petter decided not to press the matter further other than to ask if the old man would recover.

"I am certain of it, Sir," the guide said. "Think no more of him." He swept Petter down a corridor, explaining the purposes of the various rooms they passed.

Petter and the guide were just passing out of a vast wardrobe room, when they were met by Erik in his now familiar mask.

Petter, shocked to see his father despite the previous promise to be met backstage, did not utter the startled "Father," that came to mind.

Erik bowed to the guide, and spoke. "Monsieur, I have been told that you are needed at the ticket office. I am to continue this portion of the tour," and here Erik bowed to Petter, "if the young master wishes to continue."

Petter stuttered his response. "I… Yes, thank you, I wish to complete this fascinating tour."

The guide looked nonplussed at the interruption by a man he seemed not to recognize, but rather than admit this, he said, "Yes, of course. Thank you." With a brief glance at his watch again, he said to Petter, "It has been a pleasure, Sir, and we hope to see more of you at our great theatre." He bowed his head, and spun to return to his duties.

Erik gave a low laugh that seemed to echo in the dark spaces around them. Petter forced a laugh in response, confused and somehow nervous, feeling as though he were engaged in a dishonesty.

"Come," Erik said. "I will show you more than that peacock would have known to show you."

Petter grew more and more mystified as Erik led at a quick pace down corridors, through a hidden doorway that opened at a touch, and through more darkened corridors lit only by the torch he carried. Petter carried the empty travel case as he followed.

"Father," Petter said as they moved down a small wooden spiral stairway. He spoke in the whisper demanded by his surroundings. "There was a man back there. He looked terrified when the stage lights came up. He cried out the words 'Opera Ghost' and ran into a wall. My guide suggested it was a foolish legend, but I must say, these cobwebbed passages bring the idea of ghosts to mind. Do you know of the legend?" Petter hoped his own discomfort at his surroundings did not sound in his voice.

Erik chuckled, and the sound echoed away from them. The skittering of small animals could be heard at its conclusion. Erik turned toward Petter, holding the torch between them raised at the level of their eyes.

"Our eyes, hmm, yes," Erik answered, and laughed again. He turned away without answering Petter.

"Where are we going?" Petter asked when they had traversed the length of a descending ramp and another stair.

"My old home," Erik answered.

"Home?" Petter asked. "Down here? How on Earth…?"

"In the Earth, I should say," Erik answered. "I built all this. I came to… escape. To build my own castle and to hide." After another several steps, he said in a lower voice, "The world is not always as kind as you expect it to be, Petter."

"You built all this?" Petter answered, looking around again, although now with some measure of awe and calculation. "How?"

"I tendered for a part of the construction of the double foundation. Once ensconced, I made free with the space. At the time I intended to hide myself forever from the eyes of men."

"Your masks," Petter murmured. He trembled at the tragic treatment to which his father must have been subjected to desire a home such as this. He followed his father without speaking, wondering – not for the first time – at the history indicated by the various bits of information he had gleaned.

"It was your mother that drove me from my home. My love for her. The dreams she set afire in my breast." And again, Petter heard the mix of longing and satisfaction.

"Does Mother know about this place?" Petter asked.

"Your mother knows everything," Erik answered. After another moment, during which Erik swept aside a curtain of cobwebs with the torch, he continued. "Your mother has been in this house." The words were tinged with bitterest melancholy. Petter had the urge to reach out and put a hand on his father's shoulder. Before he could close the distance to do so, Erik's tone lightened again.

"You must know that I met your mother in Paris," he said. Petter recalled having heard this, but had never pictured his mother and father anywhere but in Sweden. "I met her at this Opera House. She sang for me. Ah!"

With this last utterance, Erik halted, pushed open a door which appeared nothing more than a slab of rock – Petter mused that the pivot joint must be perfectly balanced – and stepped through. Petter drew alongside him. There, to one side, was what looked to be a normal wooden door, standing ajar and revealing only darkness beyond. Yet, from where they stood, Petter could also sense that in the direction opposite the door a great space – a great cavernous space – stretched before him. The air here was humid, and smelled of damp rock.

"What is it?" Petter asked, the cool and the damp bringing thoughts of ghosts unbidden to his mind again.

"The lake. I will show you. But first, to gather my tools." Erik pushed open the wooden door to his side, which opened perhaps halfway before catching against something and stopping.

Erik stepped through the doorway, and handing the torch back to Petter, began pushing at what sounded to be a large piece of heavy furniture. Quite soon, the door swung open and Erik said with a flourish and a bow, "Welcome to my home!"

Petter stepped into a room that – other than the scattered debris, the covering of dust and the smell of mold – seemed quite as commonplace as many he had seen.

"There are more torches near the door," Erik said, moving away into the darkness. Then, with an oomph of pain as though he had barked his shin, "Watch your step, son."

The torches were not far from the door – a scattering of half of dozen – and Petter lit two, leaving the torch they had used outside the door to sputter. He brought one to his father, and raised his own to look about the room.

"Your home is quite in disarray," he said, noting overturned furniture, broken lamps and dishes, and other debris too covered by dust to allow identification.

"Mm," answered Erik. Petter recognized this as his father's response when unwilling to give an explanation.

"Follow," his father said. Petter did, careful despite his curiosity over his surroundings not to trip and perhaps lose his grip on the torch. His father moved from the entry room to another, grasping at items along the floor or shelves and placing them into the carrying case he had brought. At the far end of the room, the wavering torchlight glowed on a piano and the grand candelabrum that lay toppled across its closed top.

"Did mother sing for you here?" Petter asked, as this dusty vision overlapped with his memory of their singing in their home in Sweden.

"Yes," Erik answered, "although not often." Again the answer was tinged with sadness.

"What are you gathering?" Petter asked, focusing on his father.

"My tools – some of my own invention. I will want to make modifications to our ship upon our arrival in Marseille." Erik pushed aside a large chair, and said, "Ah. Yes, this is what I've been looking for." He put the last piece – Petter could not make it out – into the bag, and said, "Come. I will show you the lake, and then we must return to Faraz. He will be wondering at the length of our absence."

SKELETONS IN THE CLOSET

"Will not the man who accommodated me for the tour wonder also?" Petter asked, as his father reached the door that led out to the lake.

Erik laughed, and this time the sound of the haunting laughter echoed throughout the large cavern, leaving Petter an impression of size far greater than his imagination had supplied. "He may indeed wonder," answered Erik, and Petter could hear the smile in his voice. "For we shall not leave the Opera House by any means of which that bag of wind is aware."

Erik led Petter to a small boat, and they pushed off onto a vast black lake. Despite the enclosing darkness, Petter relaxed as his father maneuvered the small craft, a smile playing at his father's lips as he hummed a strange but mesmerizing melody. In far less time than Petter would have thought possible after reaching the far shore, he and Erik were standing upon Rue Scribe, opposite a gated entrance which seemed unassociated with the Opera House. Petter was stunned to find himself in the afternoon sun after all the darkness of their travels, and was overwhelmed with all he had seen. They both had a layer of dust upon their clothing. They patted themselves free of the worst of it leaving a great cloud of the white-gray dust to dissipate in the breeze.

Neither spoke on their return to the Persian's flat on the Rue de Rivoli. Petter could not guess at his father's thoughts as they mounted the stairs to the Persian's sitting room, but Petter watched the older man as he moved ahead of him, caught up in the imagination of his father in his youth and the amazing underground fortress he had built. Genius, indeed!

CHAPTER 20
CHRISTINE AGAIN

Christine lay abed, restless and full of energy, desperate to be up and about the room, feeling, touching, exploring, but knowing full well that she must maintain her appearance of lethargy and despair. The servants would be in soon to bring her sparse breakfast. She had woken earlier when they came to stoke and refill the samovar with the wonderful cinnamon-scented coffee she had come to love. On every other morning, she had still been abed when the lamps were turned up and breakfast was delivered. This morning, the servants must find her there as usual.

Even knowing that she should pretend to sleep, Christine could not keep her eyes closed. Her eyes combed the dim room as she remembered the clever hidden trap doors and spy holes of their home in Sweden. While Erik was a genius at contriving new and different trap doors for each room as the architecture warranted, there was a pattern to Erik's building. Her eyes roved over the barely seen fixtures and furniture of the room hoping to discover something familiar, known.

Christine had already located three possible locations for trap doors, but she had been too afraid of interruption to investigate. Instead, she spent the day in the timeless light of the lamps trying to gauge time as it flowed from one minute to the next, one hour to the next, without any possible means of measurement. Even with the volatile Sultana gone from the palace, the only regular, predictable intervals of activity were her meals. It seemed to Christine that each meal was served at the same time each day, with the same interval between that meal and the arrival of the next. However, nothing else seemed predictable. Christine was bathed at different times of the day – sometimes before being allowed to eat breakfast, sometimes just before the lamps were turned down and she slept (although she had no way of knowing if it was "night"), and quite often, at any time between those extremes. Her bed linens were likewise changed at whatever time the servant girls must find convenient – sometimes every day, sometimes not. Then, too, servants often came into the room for no purpose related to Christine, but to clean and polish and pound cushions. Clearly, the Sultana wanted her "special guests" to feel the dissonance of luxury and terror, pamperedness and pain, mixed. Christine wondered if any "special guest" had lasted as long as she, and wondered what it was the Sultana wanted of Erik that she had refrained so long from torturing her to death. Obviously it was something only Erik could give and Christine was the lever to obtain it from him.

Lever. Knob, button, balance.

Christine's neck bent as she tilted her head back to look at the elaborate headboard rising into the semi-darkness above her.

She did not raise her hand to explore, afraid that if she found the appropriate release, a trap would open… just as breakfast was being delivered. Then another thought occurred to her: how foolish was she to assume the furniture and fixtures in the room had not been changed – perhaps several times – since the days when Erik was in the palace. Would Erik have thought of this possibility himself? He would have, and would have built accordingly. Christine's eyes moved again to the walls, to the elaborate, tiled arches, to the intervening painted oasis of palm trees. Her eyes drifted to the dark starred ceiling and she wondered if there existed peepholes among the stars. If so, she could do nothing without revealing herself. She pushed the thought away. To worry about a peephole would paralyze her. Better to be caught than to do nothing. Her eyes moved again to the walls.

The tiles. Is there a pattern, some subtle pattern that will reveal your secret to me Erik? Then, a darker thought, *What if this room has no passages? What if Erik did not build this portion of the palace?* Again, she pushed the thought away, refusing to allow doubts to dim her new optimism.

There came the sound of the lock, and the door opened to two servant girls who stopped their chatter mid-sentence. Christine fought the urge to smile at them, to speak to them, to encourage their talk. *I must maintain my advantage!* But it was strange how strong the urge to speak to the servants and guards had become when her silence was no longer a haughty refusal to speak to her captors, when she thought of all she might learn by speaking to them.

Christine harrumphed and rolled to place her back to the girls and to the ubiquitous guards at the door. She did this as much as from her own sudden frustration as because it was behavior that would not be uncharacteristic.

The servant girl cooed at her, "Coffee? I know you like the coffee…" Christine wondered if the servants – who had always treated her with kindness – were ordered to do so from some twisted cruel command of the Sultana, or whether they pitied the Sultana's "special guests" and acted from that pity. As the lamp was turned up, Christine rolled back to the girl to examine her face, to see if she could detect duty to orders or the hoped-for pity. Genuine pity might be useful.

The girl was not looking at her. Both girls now moved about the room lighting the various lamps that would bring a daylit brightness to the room.

If only I could light lamps myself when night fell. Night was the only time during which the servants did not enter her room – she knew this from the last two sleepless nights spent thinking of escape and praying that the Sultana would not return to the palace as suddenly as she had left. But the only lamp left lighted during the night was a tall and heavy one that Christine could not carry about the room, and it was turned to a dimness her eyes could not overcome. Worse, the key to the lamp could not be turned without a special tool – she had tried the previous night, and failed.

SKELETONS IN THE CLOSET

Christine coveted the long matchsticks the girls plucked from ornate boxes which they then carried from lamp to lamp, lighting and adjusting each lamp to its fullest brightness.

If only…

As the smaller and more frail of the two girls returned to Christine's bedside, Christine watched the girl from behind half-closed eyelids, trying to appear sleepy, but never losing her focus on the box of matchsticks. The girl placed the box on the side table, and again said in a singsong voice, "Coffee? Do you want coffee?" She did not look at Christine as she did this, but placed a cup under the spout of the samovar and twisted the key to begin filling the cup.

Christine feigned a great yawn and a stretch as she sat up on the edge of the bed, hoping she could reach the matchstick box, but it was too far. She allowed her feet to slip to the floor for greater leverage before she reached toward the proffered coffee cup. She sipped at the coffee and gasped, bringing her hand to her mouth and jerking the cup away from her lips. The coffee was in fact very hot, as she knew it would be – she had burned her mouth on two previous occasions when she did not let it cool in the cup before drinking. The girl before her skipped backward to avoid being spilt upon, and clucked angrily. At the same time, Christine fumbled the cup to the side table and bumped the ornate wooden box of matchsticks so that it fell to the floor. Christine hoped it looked accidental.

The hinged lid of the box bounced open as the box hit the carpet near the bed, and matchsticks burst out onto the carpet and the smooth marble floor beyond, looking like a bad throw of sticks in a game of spellicans. Christine began a patter of apologies – in French, of course – and bent to help collect the sticks. She handed all those she collected to the girl who now joined her on the floor until the girl appeared to lose her concern that Christine might being trying to secret any away. The other girl returned from the washroom with a rag with which to dry the small spill of coffee, but paid Christine no attention. Christine, with the smallest of movements, pushed several matchsticks toward her knees, and then beyond her knees toward her feet. As she stood, she used one foot to push the matchsticks farther under the bed. She remained standing in place hoping that even with the girls' vantage from where they still bent collecting the last few matchsticks or mopping at the floor, her feet would hide the view of those matchsticks now under the bed.

"Clumsy as a herd of oxen," the mopping girl murmured under her breath.

Clearly she is not motivated by pity. Or perhaps she is, making amends for her uncharitable thoughts. *Perhaps she is only human and is only unkind when I have caused her more work.*

Christine remained standing until the servants stood again, hoping that the girls would not decide that now was the time to bathe or to change the linens. Instead, the girl who had poured the coffee pointed to the remains in the cup and said, "Hot." She opened her mouth, stuck out her tongue, and fanned her tongue with her hand, before repeating, "Hot." After some small rolling of her eyes, she spun and led the others from the room.

Christine did not wait. She retrieved the matchsticks and ran to the far side of the room, poking them handle down into the dirt of a potted plant and standing back to make certain that they could not be detected in their position behind the large leaves. She returned to the fresh coffee and sipped at it, smiling, hopeful that tonight she would be able to explore the room without fear.

The rest of the day passed with a slowness that was such exquisite torture she thought she would go mad. The servants did not enter again except for delivery of her meals, so Christine could not even distract herself with watching the girls clean, or with allowing herself to be bathed. A hundred times during that day, she wondered if this day was not being purposely prolonged, or if perhaps the servants had forgotten to turn her lights down and create her artificial night, and whether she had not been waiting through two days.

Night came. Christine was escorted from her seat among the cushions to the bed. Knowing that obedience was expected, she lay down, pulled the thin linen over her body, and watched as the lamps were all but one turned down to utter darkness. She remained still for some long time afterward, hoping that it was night, and that sleep would overcome all those whose task it was to watch and guard her.

Feeling that hours had passed, she slipped from the bed, and sneaked toward the plant and the hidden matchsticks. Having retrieved one, she moved to a small lamp and lit it. She stood frozen in the sudden wash of light, hoping that no guard was so vigilant outside her door as to notice the sudden flood of light from under the door. After a full minute passed during which Christine dared not breathe, she lifted the lamp and moved to the nearest arch. She ran her fingers over the tiles that lined the interior of the arch, first at the bottom of the arch and then reaching as high as she could up its walls. Erik often chose either the bottom or the very top of a doorway to hide the trip for the door – if there was a door. She examined the patterns of the tiles to see if she could detect any variation that would give a clue to any lever or button. Then she searched all the tiles between her highest reach and the bottom, unwilling to rely on her knowledge of Erik's patterns.

Nothing.

She moved to the next arch. And the next.

After some long passage of time, she began to imagine that morning was approaching, and that she would be found, hunting the room with a forbidden lantern. Her searching became more hurried.

I can search again tomorrow night, calm yourself. But even so, she kept searching, casting occasional glances at the doorway.

She reached the archway beyond the cushions and the low table at the far side of the room. After promising herself that this would be the last of the arches she checked tonight, she passed her hands over the tiles at the extreme height of her reach, and squatted to do the same at the bottom of the arch.

There!

She felt something – some small irregularity in the smoothness of the elaborate mosaic. Her breath came fast as fear and excitement washed over her. Still squatting, she looked again to the door, needing with all her soul to explore the irregularity, and yet knowing that the sensible thing was to wait another day.

She pressed the small protuberance made by the uneven tile. There was no noise, no movement that Christine could detect. As she prepared to stand, a strange odor came to her, and she knew she had found one of Erik's passages. She inhaled. The new odor smelled of hot sand, although she felt no heat, no change of temperature. She waited, first lifting the lantern above her head, and then returning it to the floor.

Ah! At the floor, the recessed wall enclosed by the arch appeared to be lifting, showing first a centimeter of darkness, and then two.

Counterbalances! The wall is moving onto its pivot!

Christine closed her eyes, praying to God that the counterbalance or the pivoting mechanism was still functional after all these years, and hoping for the time to discover the answer before breakfast could bring her plans to an end. The minutes seemed endless, but Christine could not leave her discovery. The door first rose, then shifted to one side. She heard the smallest sound like the ratchet of stone moving on sand, and then the door was on its pivot, and it swung soundlessly away from her, revealing blackness. Christine rose and took a step into the open doorway. Holding the lantern far behind her she looked into the darkness, straining to see if there was any other light coming from any other source. She saw nothing but a blackness so deep she might have had her eyes closed. She swung the lantern into the darkness before her.

A passageway, not simply a hidden room! Christine thought her heart would burst with relief and excitement and fear. Having found what she was seeking, she backed out of the passageway and into her room. She bent to trigger the mechanism that would close the door until the following night, when she would have more time to explore.

No! I must see what I can see. I needn't venture down the passageway, but I must at least observe.

She stepped forward into the passageway again and held the lamp up. She peered as far as she could down the passageway. It ran straight and true for as far as the lamplight could penetrate. She moved around the still-open door and peered in the opposite direction down another long passage. She could not see if there were any other passages intersecting this one in either direction.

Enough! Tomorrow!

Her heart was beating with such violence in her chest that she could hear its echoes in her ears, feel the throbbing pulse at her throat.

SKELETONS IN THE CLOSET

Again, she stepped from the passage into her room. As she bent to press the button again, she saw her own distinct footprints in the dust of the floor inside the passage. She saw the distinct line of demarcation between the shining tile floor of her room and the dust of the passage.

This tunnel is never used – or has not been used in any recent time.

She pushed the button. She was pleased to see the relative speed with which the door closed, first meeting the walls of the framing arch, then lowering to the floor. Once all movement had ceased, she felt the seams between floor and door, between door and arch. She could detect no vestige of any opening.

She fought the childish urge to push the button again to assure herself that the door would work again, that she had not dreamed finding Erik's passage.

Christine backed from the door, looking for any change that might alert the servant girls – or worse, the guards – that something was amiss. In the lamplight she watched as each backward step left a dusty footprint on the shining floor. She turned and ran the few steps to the low table and surrounding cushions. She lifted several large cushions and rubbed and scuffed her feet on the carpet beneath them before she replaced them. Leaving the lamp on the table, she took a smaller cushion and wiped at the floor, doing her best to remove any trace of her footprints.

She slowed her breath even while her mind spun with what her access to this passage could mean. With a large inhale and exhale that was almost a sigh, she returned the lamp to its place and turned it out. In the lower light of the remaining lamp by her bed, she moved across the room, and with a speed spurred by the tense thought that the door would open at any moment, flung herself into the bed and covered herself.

Tomorrow, she thought, over and over, like a bell tolling within her. A warm pride mixed with the hopefulness within her, and her skin prickled with her excitement.

Tomorrow.

Knowing she would not sleep – not in her current state of agitation – she pushed her head into her pillow and pulled the linen over her, preparing her body for the impression of a sleeping woman.

Much to her surprise, she slept.

SKELETONS IN THE CLOSET

CHAPTER 21
THE SULTANA FINDS ERIK

Erik arranged the last of his masks into the case and ran his fingers and eyes over the various tinted skin creams he would use if further disguise was necessary. An assortment of costumes was already packed. The Persian and his servant were out concluding some business of their own – likely something that left the faithful Darius with the power and ability to carry on in Faraz's brief absence. Or at least Erik hoped it would be brief. But long or brief, Erik could not envision failure.

We leave today, Christine. We shall be together soon.

Erik could hear Petter in the far room, and imagined he was packing his Brownie and its various trimmings – film spools, an extra neck strap, and possibly even the modified surveyor's tripod. Erik did not see the purpose of bringing the tripod, but did not intend to tell Petter that the tripod must be left behind until such time as that became necessary. And he had faith that his son would see the necessity when it arose. Other than the boy's invariable mooning over the shallow edifice of Constance, Erik was quite proud of his son. He showed ingenuity, courage, and the ability to think on his feet – he had maneuvered his tour of the Opera House quite well, and had accepted the introduction to its dark underground spaces without fear or trepidation. He accepted the Persian's dire warnings with equanimity, and faced the coming expedition with courage. Erik could not imagine another man he would want accompanying him on this mission. Erik's recent exertions – and injuries – had highlighted his own slower reactions and his waning strength (a frustrating discovery, but one he imagined fell to many men of his age), but this was not now his only reason for wanting Petter along. The boy was a calming influence whenever Erik's anger threatened to push him to rash actions or statements – in this way he reminded Erik of Christine. The old Persian, of course, could be a liability. But perhaps he would also be of help – he could provide Erik with information, and perhaps even open useful doors.

Glancing up to assure himself that Petter was not in sight – he did not want to alarm the boy – Erik opened a cloth pouch and assured himself of its contents: several lengths of rope for use as lassos, a dagger, and a pistol, as well as a belt on which he could carry all. He was closing the pouch when a familiar scent reached his nose.

Rose oil and mint.

Without raising his head, and speaking in a low voice so as not to summon Petter, Erik said, "Naheed."

"Ah, you desert me in my time of need, and now you dote on me by calling me by name. You see, we are alike, we two. Pain and pleasure – pleasure and pain." She spoke French in quiet, intimate tones.

Erik raised his head to find her standing in the doorway, hands raised above her head and resting against the door jamb to either side of her, head tilted against one arm. She was dressed in the most provocative of the latest Parisian fashions, in a dress of low neckline more appropriate for evening wear, which tightened against her body down to a pinched waist. Her eyes remained fixed on his as the tip of her tongue emerged and licked at the center of her full top lip. She left her mouth open when her tongue returned to her mouth.

Now that she is a woman and no longer a child of ten, she has learned a woman's arts. But she is only a parody of sexuality, attempting to allure, but wanting only to cause pain. With a pang, the inevitable thought followed: *What pain has my Christine endured?*

As if reading his thoughts, the Sultana straightened and walked a sinuous path toward Erik as she spoke. "Your wife is well in my care, darling Erik," she said. "But how much longer do you intend to trust your prize to my patience? You know I am a woman of appetite, and I am becoming very, very hungry." Again she licked her lips as if to highlight her statement, but Erik did not need so obvious an indication. The unmistakable bloodlust glittered in her eyes.

She moved until she stood before Erik. She placed a hand on his chest and sliding it back and forth, said, "You are not as strong… as muscular as you once were." She smiled, and then spun away from him, as if taunting him by giving him her back. After a moment, she spoke again. "I had to come to you, if only to have your little morsel out of my reach… her screams are so delicious and satisfying that I could not trust myself to leave any of her for you."

Erik grabbed her shoulder and spun her around to face him. "If you have…"

She laughed in his face – the high, light, delighted laughter of a child. "I have said your wife is well. If you do as I ask, she will remain so. For a little while longer at the least."

"Father?" Petter emerged from the doorway at the side of the room, apparently summoned by the sound of the Sultana's laugh.

The Sultana looked at Erik with raised eyebrows. "Your son?" She purred the words. She swung her hips from side to side as she moved toward Petter. "My, you are a handsome young man." Petter flushed. An appreciative smile grew on his reddened face, and then he bowed over her offered hand.

"Madam," Petter said. He stared at the Sultana as though hypnotized, before gesturing to a chair, and saying, "Won't you please make yourself comfortable?" He moved to the chair and stood beside it, ready to assist her. Erik raised a hand and made a soft chopping motion of dismissal, but Petter's attention was focused on the Sultana and he made no indication that he saw.

The Sultana moved to the chair but did not sit. "Will you not offer me refreshment, young man? Your father has proven a want of gentility, but I see yours is not lacking." The Sultana raised a hand to Petter's cheek, and stroked it.

Petter flushed a vivid crimson before finding his voice again. "Yes, yes, of course. Do you wish refreshment?" Petter flashed a quick smile at Erik, and looked back to the Sultana as she lowered herself to the chair. She reached her hand out and stroked the front of Petter's pants as she sat. Surprised, Petter took a step back and away from her, the fatuous smile disappearing from his face. Petter looked to Erik and focused there, his uncertainty clear in his furrowed brow. Erik shrugged and rolled his eyes in disgust at the woman's behavior, and then hoped that Petter did not think the disgust directed at him. Petter's eyes remained on his.

The Sultana's scornful, piercing voice broke over the room like cold ocean spray. "You look to your father, when you should look at me!" She thrust her breasts out and opened her arms as in an embrace. Petter's mouth opened as he snapped his eyes back to the Sultana. He took another step farther from where she now sat.

"You are but a child!" she barked. "Your disgusting morality drips from you, and sours my mouth." She spat on the carpet at his feet. "You are obviously nothing like your father" – here, the Sultana looked over her shoulder at Erik, and gestured with one hand before returning her gaze to Petter – "your father, who is as cruel as he is ugly." She smiled as though she had granted Erik the ultimate in compliments, which perhaps – to her mind – she had.

Petter gasped as if he had been tapped in the stomach.

The Sultana rose from her chair and negotiated her way in languid strides back to Erik. "This is why we have loved each other, your father and I." She rolled her tongue over the word "loved," adding insinuation to implication. Still with eyes on Petter, she raised both hands and leaned toward Erik, as if to put her hands on Erik's chest before resting her head there. Erik raised a hand in a blocking motion and stepped back.

"You have never loved, Naheed," Erik growled, "and I have certainly never loved you." Anger rose in Erik at this deranged woman. She could only be adding to the questions about his own past that must be chasing through the boy's imagination. He looked to Petter to see how the boy was reacting and saw a face full of disgust – but thankfully directed toward the Sultana.

The Sultana said, with a small pout to her lips, "Oh, now Erik, how can you say such a thing to me?" She stepped toward Erik again, but this time he held his ground, raising a palm to stop her movement toward him.

Petter stepped forward, hands held in fists at his sides. "What is it you want here, Madam?" he asked. "It seems my father has little regard for you, and I assure you, I have less." Petter eyes flicked to Erik's and Erik smiled at his son's courage and sense of righteousness. Petter took another step toward the Sultana and said, "State your business, or leave, but either must be done immediately." Petter raised his chin and kept her eye.

The Sultana raised a hand to her breast in mock surprise, and then threw her head back and laughed. She bent forward from the waist and continued to laugh, seeming out of control, hands on her thighs to support her as she bent.

"Oh!" She stood and made a show of being unable to control her laughter, and again said, "Oh!" After another brief burst, she turned to Erik. "I retract what I said. I would have such an enjoyable time breaking this one." She flicked a hand toward Petter.

Whatever Petter thought – and it seemed obvious to Erik that Petter thought the comment of a lascivious nature – Erik knew to what the Sultana referred and that her reference to "breaking" was quite literal.

Petter opened his mouth to speak again, but Erik raised his palm in a halting motion. "Unlike my son, I do not have the requirement that you state your business. Leave us."

"You seem not to love your wife as much as you profess," the Sultana said, and she turned to walk among the furniture and effects of the sitting room as though looking among the wares of a shop.

"What do you mean?" asked Petter, face flushed again, but this time with anger. "What do you know of my mother?"

The Sultana turned to Petter, eyes narrowed and sparking with anger. "Do not speak to me again!" she shouted. Turning back to Erik, she said, "You must hope I do not believe you are attempting to escape my request. If I should become so convinced, your wife will begin dying upon my return and will not stop dying for as long as I can prolong her." Her face relaxed and all traces of anger cleared. She looked at her fingernails and her lips turned up in a sweet smile. "Do we understand each other?"

"Father!" said Petter, and he took a step forward, hands held out in pleading. Again, Erik raised a hand in a halting motion, but this time with greater fervency. His fear for Christine and his ability to picture any number of the Sultana's favorite torture scenarios brought bile to the back of his throat. He swallowed with some difficulty.

"Naheed, sit, and we will talk," Erik said. He raised his eyes to Petter and said, "It would be best if you retired to complete preparations." Petter's eyes and jaw hardened with determination, and Erik saw the barely perceptible shake of his head. Erik sighed and shook his own head. "Or you may stay." Erik gestured to a chair, but Petter remained where he stood, the tension in his body bringing to Erik's mind a tight spring ready either to spring forward or break.

The Sultana moved to the Persian's preferred chair, sat and raised her feet to the hassock before her. She seemed at ease as she began to speak. "I tried to bring you to my country so you could complete your task, but you fled. From all appearances, you were preparing again to flee. You must see the futility of that. I found you twice, I can find you again." She cleared her throat, and said, "And the next time I find you it will be to bring you news of your wife's untimely demise. I will even elaborate on all the beautiful details, if you wish."

SKELETONS IN THE CLOSET

"I understand," said Erik, speaking around the knot of anger in his throat. "You are correct, I was preparing to flee. I thought to sequester my son from you." Erik did not look to Petter, but knew that his son would not speak to disagree. "I see now that it was fruitless for me to attempt to escape you."

"I always knew you for an intelligent man. Now, please, I beg you, deny my request again. I am afraid our conversation has already sparked my imagination with regard to your wife." The Sultana wriggled in the chair. Again the excitement and bloodlust rose in her eyes — eyes that grew darker at such moments — and Erik knew that her statement was not a ruse or an exaggeration. He bowed his head in acquiescence.

"I will do as you ask," he whispered.

"I did not hear you," she answered. She looked to Petter and said, "Did you hear his answer?" Erik raised his head in warning to his son, but Petter apparently remembered her earlier admonition and did not speak. He remained frozen where he stood, his eyes upon Erik.

Erik looked to the Sultana, and in a pained voice said, "I said, 'I will do as you ask.'"

"Let us be clear, dear Erik. I will have no misunderstandings between us. What, precisely, will you do?"

Erik bowed his head again, loath to make explanations in the presence of his son — explanations which would require further explanations.

"Speak!" came the shrill command of the Sultana. When Erik raised his head, she was sitting forward in the chair, feet planted on the floor, clawed hand reaching to him as if to cast a spell of obedience upon him. "I am losing patience! Speak, or I shall leave you!"

"I shall travel to Mazenderan. I shall kill the Shah's newest wife. I shall kill the Shah's son." Erik waited for the sound of shocked surprise he expected from his son at this explanation. It did not come. He could not look at Petter, afraid of what he might see in his son's face.

"Aaaah." The Sultana luxuriated over the utterance, and again leaned back in the chair. "Ironic, isn't it? That every bit of pleasure involves pain? I will be pleased for you to accomplish this small task for me, but then must be disappointed in my hunger for the musical screams of your wife's dying utterances." She seemed to muse for a moment before sighing and saying, "Ah, well." She began to rise.

"What assurances do I have that Christine is, in fact, well and alive? If I have already lost my prize, I have no reason to perform." Despite his fear for Christine – the same fear that had led to his capitulation – Erik did not believe Christine was dead. Not yet. On the other hand, Erik would not allow himself to put limits on the Sultana's deviousness.

"My word of honor will not suffice?"

Erik did not respond.

SKELETONS IN THE CLOSET

"Very well, perhaps you know me too well, Erik dear," the Sultana said, flashing a simpering smile. She seemed quite at ease despite the tension flowing from both Erik and Petter like a palpable fog. "When you reach Mazenderan, my only love, send a message to the palace for one of my servant girls, Gohar. Write as her lover, Abadan. Ask her where and when you can see her next. She will respond with a meeting place and time. I will meet you there. We will finalize our plans… and…" The Sultana paused, but if she hoped for a response from Erik, he did not accommodate her. She finished, "And I will bring your Christine. You will know then that she is well and alive."

Erik stood and strode away from the Sultana. He lifted several rolled maps and began placing them in a nearby satchel. Petter still did not move from his position across the room, although Erik could see in his side vision that the boy still watched the Sultana.

Erik listened as the footsteps of the Sultana crossed the room toward him. From behind him, her hand reached to close gently on his neck. He refused to flinch or otherwise acknowledge her touch, but continued placing map rolls into the satchel. Her fingers curved so that her nails bit into the side of his throat, then began to move toward the back of his neck, undoubtedly leaving marks. Erik reached up and gripped her hand, jerking it away from his neck. He did not turn to look at her.

"I am not your play thing," he growled. He released her hand.

"Do not bring your dismal friend, the Old Daroga. I have never liked him." She spoke to his back. "You can bring your son of course. Perhaps he will be my play thing."

Erik listened to her laughter, listened as it accompanied her down the stairs behind him. He heard it through the open windows as she left the flat. The sound reminded him of the needles she used for the purposes of torture, with much the same effect on him.

Erik was startled from his thoughts by a hand closing over his arm.

"Father, is this what she asks of you? You do not mean to kill those people?" Petter asked.

"Of course not," Erik answered, tone sharp. "I intend to rescue your mother, as I have always intended. But the Sultana is a dangerous woman to deny – as you may have gathered. I assured her to prolong your mother's life until we can achieve her escape." Erik mused for a moment and said, "I hope to accomplish the escape immediately upon our arrival in Mazenderan, and before having to meet with the Sultana."

"Hideous woman," Petter muttered under his breath.

Erik turned to his son with a bitter smile. "You thought her quite beautiful when first you saw her."

"Looks are not everything, Father. I assure you, I was cured of my initial impression very quickly, and now cannot even recall that first vision." Petter shuddered as he spoke.

SKELETONS IN THE CLOSET

Erik chuckled but it was a bitter sound. "I last saw Naheed as a child of ten. I promise you that she was no more attractive a person then. She laughed more freely, I suppose, but even then, for the wrong reasons." Erik lifted the satchel of maps and the travel case containing his masks from the table and deposited them at the side of the door. "Be certain everything is ready for when the Persian returns. We leave for Marseille at first light."

CHAPTER 22
THE VOYAGE

Petter was surprised that his father did not mention the Sultana's visit to the Persian. He almost mentioned it to the Persian himself, feeling it the only fair thing – to divulge to a man who was accompanying them what had transpired. However, Petter also respected and admired his father more each day and as he gained more information about his father's past – fragmented as that information was. His curiosity had heightened, of course, but the frustration that first accompanied his curiosity had lessened to the point of nonexistence. He trusted that his father would tell him the story of his past, and now trusted that he would not be disappointed with the knowledge – and would not be disillusioned, as seemed to be his father's fear. He had questions, to be sure – for example, why the Sultana would seek out Erik for such a task – but no real doubts. The Persian and Christine knew of Erik's past, and they still loved and admired the man.

Thus, rather than tell the Persian about the Sultana, Petter kept his silence. If his father chose not to tell, there must be a reason.

SKELETONS IN THE CLOSET

The reason, when Petter discovered it, was rather mundane. They were not long into their carriage ride to Marseille when Erik told the Persian of the encounter.

"Yesterday, Faraz, while you were out, Naheed came to your flat," Erik said.

The Persian looked to Petter. Erik said, "Yes, she is now acquainted with the fact that I have a son – not something I would have wished, but alas – and he is acquainted with her. She made no attempt to disguise her nature."

"Ah," answered the Persian, and the glance he gave Petter was filled with pity. Directing his words to Petter, he said, "I pray you never have reason to renew or... expand your acquaintance." The Persian's eyes dropped to his hands, and a grimace of pain passed over his face as if in recollection of an unbearable loss.

"I have promised to commit the murders she has requested," Erik said. Petter looked to the Persian, wondering at his reaction to this shocking statement, and was pleased to find no disapproval there. The Persian nodded as if Erik's answer to the Sultana were the only one reasonable. "She warned you away from accompanying me," Erik continued, but the Persian snorted and waved a dismissing hand.

"There is no reason to modify our plans, I presume?" the Persian asked.

"None. This is why I did not tell you of her visit before we departed. I knew we would have time to discuss this en route, if you thought it necessary, and did not wish for delay. Also, I did not perceive of any immediate danger to you, friend. I hope you agree."

The Persian contemplated and said, "I may wish to change residences upon our return, which is unfortunate after my years of comfort, but is no matter of importance."

"I am sorry, Faraz," Erik answered.

"You did not purposely draw the little Sultana to my home," the Persian answered. He pulled the satchel of maps from the floor beside his feet, withdrew a roll from within, and spread it upon his lap. "I do not suppose you have changed your decision to go through the Bosphorus Strait and Constantinople?" he asked. He did not seem to wait for Erik's answer, but began looking to the map of the Russian Empire beyond the Black Sea.

Erik and the Persian reviewed their travel plans in detail on the journey to Marseille. Having met the Sultana and now more fully understanding the danger to his mother from such an evil woman, Petter listened all the more intently to the plans. Even the cities they passed en route to Marseille – Dijon, Lyon, Avignon – cities which, with his earlier sense of adventure, he had longed to see – no longer intrigued him. For the first time, he appreciated his father's need to get to Mazenderan with all possible haste. His father's earlier statements of the dangerous nature of the person holding his mother did far less to persuade Petter – who could not comprehend such things – than mere minutes in the presence of the Sultana had done.

SKELETONS IN THE CLOSET

Once in Marseille, they proceeded to the docks, and received a comprehensive tour of the ship Erik had purchased. Erik praised the crew for their thorough preparations, and granted them all leave to go about town for the next several days. He even declined the offer – a wise offer to Petter's thinking – to have several of the men remain to guard the ship and its inventory.

"We shall stay on the ship ourselves," Erik answered, quite to Petter's dismay, for he had thought they would either embark immediately, or, should delay be necessary, to take a room in town with all the pleasant amenities it might offer.

"We have work to do," Erik said as the last of the crew departed, apparently reading Petter's disappointment on his face. "Gather my tools, if you would."

That night and the following day were filled with strenuous labor. Petter was glad of the strength and stamina he had earned through his work as a stonemason, although in the instant case, they worked only with wood. He assisted his father in creating invisible trap doors from one cabin to another, from the floor of a cabin to the hold below, and in two cases, crafting storage boxes so that they appeared full of linens and other sundries but contained a space under the linens in which a person might hide.

"Why…?" Petter began as they started work on another trap door.

"Give me no whys or wherefores, Petter. Time is short, and we must away," his father answered, huffing as he drew a short saw through a plank.

Petter broached the subject again with the Persian when he paused for a meal. "Mr. Akhtar, why is Father…?"

"Constantinople," the Persian answered. "He tells me I worry for no reason, and yet takes these precautions." The Persian barked a short laugh.

"Perhaps he takes precautions so that there will be no reason to worry," Petter answered, partially in defense of his father, and partially because this was very likely his father's reasoning. He asked no more questions.

They were soon underway, the crew unaware of the various modifications Erik had made to the ship.

Once at sea, Erik began what looked to be a rough architectural rendition of a large and complex building. Petter thought it to be a distraction, an activity in which his father engaged to pass the time. Several of the dimensions were intriguing, and Petter bent over the sheet.

"What are you drawing?" Petter asked, thinking to engage his father into a further distracting conversation.

"The palace in which I believe your mother is being held," Erik answered. Petter's eyebrows raised, but he said nothing. Erik lifted the top plan to show a different floor. "This is the dungeon level," Erik flipped the page on which he had been working back to its place, and said, "but I am attempting a re-creation of the entire palace plans, as I may have need…" His voice trailed off as he tilted his head and examined what he had drawn, then erased several lines and redrew them.

SKELETONS IN THE CLOSET

"You designed this?" Petter said. "You built this?"

"Yes," Erik answered.

"A palace," Petter murmured in awe. He examined the plans he had thought a creative fantasy, and tried to imagine creating something of similar scope – and even more, of re-creating such plans from memory after an absence of decades. He examined the placement and proportions of the rooms and of the great halls and hallways, and then too, of what were obviously secret passages interspersed so as to give no indication from within the various rooms or hallways that such passages existed. After long minutes, Petter sighed and moved to sit on a bench at some small distance from where his father worked.

Petter had been trained in his craft by his father, and had come to believe that he knew enough of the craft to be both artist and technician, that he would someday create amazing structures. He was a novice, despite all the praise of Mr. Evans and even Lord Pendleton, and would never achieve his father's talent. He said as much to his father, although he was not sure, with Erik's concentration, that he was heard.

Erik pulled the straightedge further along the line he had been drawing, and continued the line. He dropped his pencil to the table, and placing his hands at the small of his back, stretched backward.

"Nonsense," Erik said, straightening again, a frown furrowing his brow. "Come, you will spot certain mistakes I made." Disconsolate, Petter roused himself, and moved toward his father.

"Here," Erik said, pointing. "What would you have done here?" Petter examined the plans and, to his amazement, did see the error his father indicated. He explained the simple correction that would economize the lines and spaces.

"Yes, and tell me what else you see."

Petter bent to scrutinize the plans, and saw again to his amazement – now that he was critically examining the grandiose plans – that there were several other areas in which he could suggest improvements.

"But, Father," he said, ashamed to find that he did feel somewhat bolstered by the discovery of small errors to the plans, "I could never have designed all this to begin with, so it is of no consequence…"

"Again, nonsense!" Erik answered. "It is simply that the English do not have this level of imagination, not that you couldn't exercise your own should the situation require. The Persian Shahs and Sultans think on a grander scale. Honestly, what could you do with unlimited funds in unlimited space, under a demand that you build to the fullest extent that your talent and poetic sense could create?" Erik looked back to the plans and said, "You would not have made the mistakes I made when I was your age."

Petter stood, wanting nothing more than to embrace his father for the praise, but hesitating to interrupt the man who again was leaning over the unfinished plans. He was not at all convinced that his father's praise was deserved, but he cherished it, nonetheless. He spent the rest of the evening memorizing all he could of the plans his father painstaking reconstructed, knowing he may well need the information for his mother's rescue. He slept that night, dreaming of fantastic palaces that included all manner of spaces and opulence and frivolity.

***

It was not until the ship had traversed the Dardanelles and entered the small sea of Marmara and they were surrounded by the Ottoman Empire that anything occurred of more import than eating, sleeping and studying the plans. Erik and the Persian argued over whether the Persian should take to hiding once they began entry of the Bosphorus Strait. (Petter thought it ironic that the argument was over whether the Persian should hide after all the dire warnings that it was Erik himself who would be in danger traveling through Constantinople.) The Persian conceded once Erik recalled Naheed's admonishment. There was no knowing what obstacles the Sultana might have placed in the way of the Persian's passage through the Empire. The crew would state without hesitation that the ship contained an all-French crew and three French nationals as traders, and while this was true, the Persian would be too readily recognized from any description the Sultana might have provided.

"And if we are searched?" Faraz asked. "How is it that you and Petter will divide yourselves to become three? Or have you a crewman ready to pose with you?"

Erik laughed, and said, "You must trust me, Faraz. I tell you, there will be no danger."

"You and your need for mischief," Faraz answered.

Thereafter, Faraz sequestered himself in his cabin, prepared – although not without some complaining – to lock himself into the bottom of the disguised box of linens.

Petter's curiosity and worry brought the inevitable question. "What shall we do if we are searched?" he asked Erik.

"We have all the necessary paperwork describing you as Pierre Nouveau, myself as your father, Erik Nouveau, and our companion as Jacques Martin."

"And who shall play the part of Jacques Martin?" Petter asked.

"Do not worry yourself. You will recognize Monsieur Martin, should the need arise."

Petter grimaced at his father's amused look and knew he would obtain no further information. He decided to put the puzzle out of his mind. He was convinced, given the quiet nature of their voyage thus far, that there would be no trouble in passing by Constantinople. For this reason, he was quite alarmed when the cry went out that a ship was approaching from Constantinople, and even more alarmed when it became obvious they were to be boarded.

"Father, what shall we do?" Petter asked, when Erik returned from assisting the Persian into his box.

"Everything will be fine. Do not become alarmed when I become ill and retire to my cabin," Erik answered.

SKELETONS IN THE CLOSET

"Are you ill?" Petter asked, but his father winked, and seated his mask at the neck where it entered his shirt.

"Come with me to greet our boarders," Erik said, and led the way to the deck.

Several Persian soldiers stood on the deck, armed, but not yet wielding their arms. One soldier stood speaking to the Captain, but with little effect, as the Persian did not speak French, and the Captain did not speak Persian. Petter was not surprised when Erik feigned ignorance of the language. There was some delay as a young soldier who spoke French was brought from the Persian ship. The translator explained that they were searching for rebels – members of the "Young Turks" threatening to overthrow the Sultanate – and that all ships passing through Constantinople were being thus searched.

Erik stepped forward weakly and announced himself the lead merchant of the expedition. he wiped his brow several times and brought his hand to his mouth to deliver a wet belch – a sound Petter had never heard from his father in all their years together. Erik apologized to the translator, saying that he was feeling quite ill. He bowed to the leader of the soldiers, and presented their papers. When this did not calm the air of suspicion that enfolded the Persian leader, he bowed again and invited the men to search the ship. Erik and Petter both led the way to the lower level, which contained the sleeping quarters, accompanied by several soldiers and the translator. All the while, Erik pressed at his stomach, and wiped at his brow, and again, bringing his hand to his mouth, apologized for his illness.

Petter's knees became weak in their sockets when Erik led them to the Persian's cabin. Erik entered, saying, "This is my cabin." He went to a small wardrobe and flung the doors open and opened the box in which the Persian lay buried. He rushed for the water bowl, and gave such a convincing demonstration of vomiting that Petter wondered if his father had somehow poisoned himself to achieve the result. The soldiers and the translator gave only the most cursory look about the cabin before excusing themselves.

"Go with them Pierre," Erik said, standing and wiping at his mouth. "See that they have everything they need."

"Yes, Father," Petter answered. As he closed the door, he heard again the sound of his father's quite convincing sickness. He led the men to his own cabin, that being the next in line. He stood aside as it, too, was searched. When they left his cabin, the sounds of illness could still be heard from the first.

Not knowing what to expect, and finding his own brow covered with perspiration, Petter went to the door of Erik's cabin and knocked.

"Come in!" came a deep timbered voice from within. After a brief hesitation during which Petter's mouth opened and closed again, he opened the door.

There, in a mask Petter recognized from his father's packing case, sat Erik. Petter was too stunned to say anything, but stepped into the room to permit the entry of the Persians.

SKELETONS IN THE CLOSET

"What is meaning of this?" Erik asked.

Petter hesitated before answering. "These men are searching for Turkish rebels," Petter answered, adding belatedly, "Monsieur Martin."

"Rebels?" Erik answered. "Good gracious." Standing and puffing his chest out, he said, "We are hiding no rebels here. We are a trading vessel. Surely this was explained to you."

The translator stepped forward, and looking at the papers he still held in his hand, he said, "You are… Jacques Martin?" He pronounced the sibilant at the end of the first name.

"Indeed," answered Erik, puffing himself up to even greater proportions.

"We will be just a moment more, Monsieur," the translator added, clearly intimidated by the loud man he faced. "We have no wish to disturb you in your mission, Sir."

Erik maintained his ground, looking irritated as his room was searched.

The translator turned to Petter and said, "We need only search the men's berth and your hold."

"I will lead you," Petter answered.

"Be certain nothing is taken, Pierre!" Erik bellowed to his retreating back.

In the cramped hallway, Petter again heard the sound of vomiting from the Persian's room.

"Your father is quite ill," the translator said, as his eyes darted toward the far cabin. He looked green with sympathy.

"Yes, apparently so," Petter answered. He stifled the nervous laugh that threatened to escape as the sound of another bout of illness came from behind the small door. Petter smelled a faint odor of illness in the hall and wondered if his father's mystifying illusion extended to scent, or if it was just his imagination. Petter did not envy the guard stationed to maintain watch in the hallway, for between the sound and the odor – imagined or not – Petter's stomach churned in discomfort.

The men completed their quick but thorough search. Erik, in the person of a pale and still weak Erik Nouveau emerged from his cabin, and stood with Petter to oversee the disembarkation of the soldiers. Petter supported his father as they went below deck. He fought the irrational concern that his father was truly ill, so convincing was the act, and only overcame his concern by reminding himself that in the disguise of Jacques Martin, he had been quite well.

Once below deck, Erik said, voice still weak with illness, "We must see to Faraz." Petter led the way to the Persian's room, as his father followed, supporting himself against one wall of the corridor. Once inside the room, Petter locked the door, and turned to watch his father lower himself into a chair.

"Father?" Petter asked, approaching with a rising level of alarm.

"A moment, son," Erik answered, and then shook himself as a dog might shake water from his pelt. Inhaling, he stood, smiled, and said, "I believe I was rather convincing." In two strong strides he was at the linen locker, lifting out linens and pulling at the latch that would reveal the hidden Faraz. Petter watched without helping, amazed at the illusion of the two very different men presented by his father in the space of two moments.

Faraz emerged, bending his neck to and fro as if to relieve a crick and brushing with some irritation at his suit pants.

"The boarding party is gone, I presume?" he asked. He moved his hand to his head as if to adjust a cap that was not there, and then smoothed at his sparse hair.

Erik smiled his triumph.

"Mr. Akhtar, you would not believe what father did," Petter started. He heard his own amazement and admiration in his voice.

"I would believe anything of this incorrigible man," the Persian answered, his irritation at his confinement still coloring his tone. "I can see from his self-satisfaction that he enjoyed another of his mischievous pranks."

Erik laughed, and patted the Persian on the shoulder before seating himself on the bunk. "Yes, yes. I was quite the genius," Erik said, eyes twinkling with merriment. Sitting forward and regaining a level of seriousness, he continued. "Faraz, my friend, we shall soon conclude our travels and arrive in Mazenderan. There the true danger arises. I do not believe Naheed will have alerted the Shah to my imminent arrival – it would spoil her plans – but may have alerted him to yours. Are you certain you do not wish to give me what information you can, perhaps the names of people you can trust to be of some assistance, and then abandon this journey?"

The Persian maintained his sour grimace, and then his face softened. "No, Erik. I will not abandon you – nor Christine. I have come this far. My country beckons in my memory, and," the Persian brushed at his coat front and straightened to stand as tall as he might, "my honor demands I assist the plight of even the most frivolous of my friends."

Erik laughed again, and this time the Persian joined in the laughter. The laughter was reprised that evening at dinner when Petter was permitted the opportunity to tell of Erik's diversion of the soldiers.

CHAPTER 23
CHRISTINE AND THE SULTANA

It had been some time since Christine had discovered Erik's trap door, but even so, she had only made two exploratory midnight trips into the tunnel. This was not for fear of discovery – although that fear sometimes paralyzed her – but because she must conserve her matchsticks. The servant girls, simple as they were, would not likely provide Christine with another opportunity to gather more, nor believe that such an attempt was again accidental.

The first night she entered the tunnel, Christine had proceeded slowly, terrified that her lamp light might be seen glimmering through a peephole or behind a mirror. She was therefore relieved to discover that each peephole was covered, and each mirror draped. She did not lift the coverings for fear of having her lamp observed, and she was in no way prepared to traverse the tunnel in darkness.

That night she traveled the tunnel toward the right, noting the number and placement of the various peepholes, mirrors and trapdoors, and traversing some small way down several adjoining tunnels doing the same. When she felt in danger of expanding the mental map she was building beyond her ability to remember, she retraced her steps, testing her memory against the reality of the return trip. Once at her room again, she walked the same tunnel to the right, noting the number of steps needed to reach each memorized peephole, mirror, trapdoor, or cross tunnel. She used a memory trick Erik had taught her – changing each number of steps into a musical note, and assigning a whole-, half-, quarter-, or eighth-note to the four different types of landmarks. As she explored, she strung the notes together to form a crude melody she could remember. She dared not hum it aloud, but a third repetition of the right-hand tunnel secured it in mind. She repeated the task in an exploration of the tunnel to the left, and added to her initial melody. Hours later, in bed, she sang to herself, adding words to the melody. She was pleased with herself.

On her second night of exploration – some several nights later – she tested her memory, and finding it adequate, expanded her exploration, and added to the melody. At no time and in neither direction of travel did she come to the end of the tunnel, despite the fact that she had traversed more meters of tunnel than existed in their entire home in Sweden. And at no time did she come to what appeared to be a trapdoor leading to the outside. She began to despair. The tunnel maze seemed endless.

Without discovering a door to the outside, Christine could only let herself into another room of the vast palace, and thus far, she still had no idea which rooms were behind each peephole or trapdoor. In fact, if the rooms were particularly large, several of the trapdoors could lead into the same room. She lay abed that night

SKELETONS IN THE CLOSET

singing her melody and wondering whether she should prepare to travel the tunnels in darkness and use the peepholes to explore the rooms beyond hers, or whether she should stop trying to build her mental map and attempt to find an exit to the outside.

But what would she do once outside? No doubt she would remain on the palace grounds, and no doubt those grounds were guarded. She needed more information.

This night she determined to travel the tunnels without light. She would look into each room as she came to it, and hope to discover something useful. She opened the hidden door to the tunnel, still unable to help peering toward the locked door of her room as she waited for the hidden door to open. Her heart pounded as she stepped into the dark space beyond. She closed her eyes – there was no difference to the blackness – but then opened them again, feeling more at ease with the thought of facing the darkness. Perhaps she would see some scrap of light where none had been visible to her in the lamplight. She reached her hand to the near wall, and began counting the steps of her melody. She thrilled when the correct number of steps brought her to the first peephole. She held her breath as she slid aside the cover.

Her excitement was dashed as she discovered that the room beyond was dark. She could see nothing. Or perhaps the peephole had been covered over? She moved on to the next, and the next, and the next. Her bright hopes for the evening crumbled to ashes as she discovered that most of the peepholes revealed nothing but more darkness. Only in the occasional room did a lamp remain lit, and often it was dimmed to the point of providing Christine little clue as to the size or purpose of the room, and no indication of whether the room was occupied. She continued with her task even through her growing despondency.

She wondered as she counted her steps toward the next landmark if she could dare to enter the tunnel during the day when the rooms would be lighted – either by lamp or by daylight. She could conceive of no way to do this without being discovered.

Christine reached the end of her melody, the end of her explored section of the tunnel maze. She began to turn to complete her return trip and then stopped and blinked into the darkness. Was the unbroken darkness of the tunnel causing an illusion of some small brightening ahead of her? Did her eyes in craving vision create a ghost of one ahead of her? She blinked again, but vision did not fade. She turned and gazed into the blackness from which she had come, and then turned again to the path ahead. There was a definite brightening before her.

She moved forward, counting her steps from the end of her melody. The brightness increased as she walked, and came from a long way from where she had previously stopped. After some seventy-eight steps, she reached her goal. It was a huge drapery that must shroud the back of the greatest mirror Christine had ever seen, and from the edge of the drapery, light. Christine held up the skirt of her nightclothes to prevent it from settling in the dust and squatted. She lifted the bottom corner of the drape to peer into the brightly lit room.

SKELETONS IN THE CLOSET

It was a fantastic bedchamber, far more lavish in its appointments than her own, reducing her room to a mere cell in comparison of size and luxury. The mirror itself seemed two stories high and was wider than the large bed at the far end of the chamber. Christine's eyes darted about from colorful mosaics to gleaming silver, from crystal to gold, until they fixed on something that brought her pounding heart into her throat. It was an immense painting, larger by far than Christine, and depicting in larger-than-life size the one person who could bring instant dread to her – the Sultana. Christine dropped the edge of the drape and brought fluttering fingers to her chest before remembering that her hands must be covered in dust. She remained squatting, reminding herself that she was hidden from view and forcing her breathing to return to a more normal pace. She had no doubts as to whose bedchamber lie on the other side of the mirror. She could imagine no one – not even the Shah himself – being so fond of his daughter as to face that portrait in their bedchamber. No one, that is, except the Sultana. Christine shuddered as she lifted the drape again.

She looked from side to side to the extreme limits of her vision, trying to determine, where – if at all – a trapdoor might have been installed which could grant her entry to this room. She could not imagine ever wanting to enter the room, but this was the first room into which she had been able to see, and she must know if there was a secret entry. She dropped the drape again and began walking through the darkness back in the direction from which she had come. Her hands combed the wall beside her searching for anything that might indicate a trap door.

There! Only ten steps. She ran back to the mirror and tried to peer in that direction. She could see the corner of an oversized, ornately decorated wardrobe that appeared to be the correct distance from the mirror. The trapdoor must open into the back of the wardrobe.

Satisfaction and dread warred within her as Christine started her slow journey back toward her room. Her pulse pounded twice for every step she took, keeping a syncopated rhythm to her memory melody. She did not know how this information could help her – she wanted to get as far from the Sultana as possible, not to enter her bedchamber – but still she clung to the information with a brightness that matched the red spots before her light-blinded eyes.

***

Days passed, nights passed, and even with explorations through the darkness, Christine did not expand her information much. The internal map she tried to build in her mind of the configuration of the palace beyond the dim rooms she could see solidified in her mind. She began making plans for expanding her exploration of the tunnels, and for the building of a longer melody. It would be easiest to expand down the left tunnel, in the direction of the Sultana's bedchamber, for this melody could be added to the end of her existing melody, while an expansion down the right tunnel would need to be added to the middle. She was far more interested, however, in expanding away from the Sultana's chambers. She lay abed, musing with the task of breaking the melody into two separate songs – one for the right tunnel and one for the left – this would allow her to build on the end of each – when the door to her room opened. Christine looked toward the figures entering expecting the delivery of breakfast. Her eyes widened and her fists clenched in the bed linens.

The Sultana stood in the open door. Her stance and her cold, cruel smile brought to mind the portrait Christine had seen hanging in the far bedchamber.

"You do not look happy to see me," the Sultana purred. "Your husband was pleased to see me again. Very pleased, I should say." The Sultana swayed her hips forward and raised one hand to brush against her own breast.

Christine said nothing. The unexpected appearance of the Sultana had brought such a level of fear to her rattling insides that she could not even muster anger at the woman's ridiculous insinuation. Instead, her mind flew to her last meeting with the Sultana, and she edged further from the door, and closer to the far side of the bed.

"He sends you his love… through me, of course." The Sultana undulated toward the bed and, without taking her eyes from Christine, walked to the foot of the bed. She paused, then smiled again, this time with apparent warmth. Her eyes closed, and she inhaled as if lost in a sweet memory. She opened her eyes again and rounded the foot of the bed toward the side on which Christine now sat. Christine did not dare move away.

"Do you not want the love he sent?" She moved closer to Christine. Christine could not think what to expect. She could only imagine that she would be struck again and for one brief second entertained the fantasy that Erik had struck the Sultana – that this was the "love" the Sultana would deliver in return.

The Sultana's hand rose, and Christine flinched away from what she thought would be a blow, but the hand, instead of striking, closed on the back of Christine's neck. For a moment neither moved, and Christine's eyes clouded with the welling of tears and the searing attention of the Sultana's eyes. The Sultana lunged toward her, and Christine felt the woman's lips on her own, and a warm questing tongue forcing its way into her mouth. Christine gagged and tried to pull away, but the Sultana clamped her hand all the tighter, and with the other arm now locked around Christine's shoulder and back, pulled her closer to continue the kiss. Christine's arms flailed against the other's shoulders, trying to push her away, but slipping against the smooth fabric she wore. Christine thought to bite down on the Sultana's tongue, but fear of the consequences kept her from acting. The Sultana pulled her closer still, until their breasts were pressing against each other, and pushed her mouth even more savagely against Christine's until Christine's teeth were cutting into her own lips. Christine cried out, but the sound, muffled as it was by the Sultana's mouth, sounded distressingly like a moan of pleasure. Tears surged from her eyes like a fountain.

In a sudden movement, the Sultana released her and threw her back on the bed. Christine, weeping, brought her hand to her lips, and with her tongue licked at the bruises and cuts her teeth had made on the inside of her lips. Her fingers smelled of roses.

"Does Erik not kiss you with such passion?" The Sultana raised an eyebrow and raised one side of her mouth in a smirk.

Christine shook her head and tried to quell her tears.

"No? Ah, well perhaps Erik's kiss was meant for me after all." The Sultana mused and said, "Would you care to give it back to me?"

Again Christine shook her head. Her hand remained over her bruised lips.

The Sultana gazed at her, and with a pouted pucker to her lips and a shrug of one shoulder, began moving around the bed, and back toward the door.

"Erik never would have kissed you, unless you took it from him as you did me," Christine said, without removing her hand from her lips. She realized her mistake as soon as the words were out, and prayed that she had not been heard. She prayed in vain. The Sultana whirled on her.

"What. Did. You. Say?" She spoke with deliberation, somehow punctuating the words through clenched teeth.

Christine shook her head again, hoping somehow to deny her words.

The Sultana now walked toward the bed again, for the first time not swaying her hips in the over-dramatization of a woman's walk, but moving forward with the stealth and control of a hunting cat.

"You have no idea what has and still does exist between Erik and me," the Sultana said. Gone was the characteristic purr, the false smile. Her mouth was stretched taut, her lips barely parted for her words, her teeth showing in a snarl.

Christine shook her head, and still her hand remained on her swollen lips. She said, "No. No, you are right. I do not know." Her mind whirled with thoughts but one stood out like a scream.

Oh, but I do know. I do. I know all about you. How could I have been so foolish as to say what I did?

The Sultana seemed to tower over her where she crouched on the bed. Christine's tears were flowing again. The Sultana turned away from her, and took several steps toward the door. Christine gasped with relief before she heard the Sultana's next words.

"Guards," she said. "Hold her."

The four guards rushed toward Christine, two coming over the bed toward her, and two racing around it to the other side. "No!" Christine screamed and tried to leap from the bed, although where she might escape to she had no idea. She was overtaken and brought back to the bed. Once on the bed, one guard gripped each of her limbs, and held her spread like a starfish across the loose linens. Christine struggled, then subsided as she realized the uselessness of her fight. The only sound she could hear was the panting of her own breath.

It was then that the Sultana turned to face her again. She smiled at Christine as she advanced. When she reached the edge of the bed, she turned and sat. She put her hand out to stroke Christine's forehead as though Christine were a sick child and she, the tender mother.

"I have given you what Erik directed I give you," she said, and this time Christine nodded in agreement.

"Yes. Yes, thank you," she said. She tried to smile, but could tell from the contortion of her mouth that she had failed. Her tears rolled down the side of her face into her ear.

"And, now, I shall give you something I have been longing to give you." She looked away, hand reaching for something out of Christine's sight. She lifted her hand to show a short dagger she must have had hidden in her clothes. Holding the dagger handle between thumb and forefinger, she twirled the jeweled handle so that each gem glittered in the light.

"No, no, please," Christine whispered. "I was wrong in what I said. I was wrong." As one, the guards turned their heads away from Christine, as if they did not wish to see what the Sultana would do next. Or perhaps she forbade them to watch?

"You were wrong," answered the Sultana. "But I have wanted to do this for so long… so long." She seemed almost to swoon. Her eyes closed, then opened again. She looked at Christine with a face that spoke of love, but Christine saw the madness behind the amber eyes.

What did Erik tell me about her? What does she need? Want? Other than the pleasure that comes with mutilating people?

The dagger approached her cheek. She wanted to shake her head in denial of what was to come, but was afraid that the movement might lead to greater injury.

The Sultana pressed the dagger point to Christine's cheek, just under her cheekbone. Christine gasped as it pricked there. The gasp turned into a scream – a scream so powerful and loud that Christine did not believe it came from her own body – as the knife sliced down her cheek toward her chin. Her head jerked away from the Sultana even while her eyes tried to keep sight of the evil woman. No amount of pulling and jerking at her limbs seemed to loosen the guards' grip. She felt locked in stone as she screamed again, the pain of her face seeming to radiate with a burning heat as she opened her mouth to let the sound escape. She smelled and tasted her own blood, and wondered if the knife had cut all the way through her cheek.

The Sultana stood and turned Christine's face toward her again. The muscles in Christine's neck strained as she tried to oppose the action, but then gave way, and her wounded cheek pressed to the pillow. Christine whimpered and relaxed, pressing her cheek harder to the pillow.

Yes, yes. I must stanch the blood flow.

SKELETONS IN THE CLOSET

The Sultana leaned all her weight on Christine's head, trapping her injured cheek to the pillow, and brought the knife to Christine's other cheek. Christine thrashed as she realized what was to come next, but with a futility equal to that of her other struggles. She could see the glassy look of near ecstasy in the mad woman's eyes.

Think! What did Erik tell me? Outside of pain, she loves power over the powerless, she loves control, she loves witnessing fear and despair. She does not merely kill.

"Mistress!" she cried. The last syllable elongated into another scream as the knife bit her other cheek and sliced again. She was still screaming when the Sultana released her head. Her pain and fear-widened eyes flicked to the Sultana and terror welled in her like a living beast. The Sultana's eyes begin to move over her body as if she was contemplating where next to place her dagger. The terror clamped her throat and cut off the scream, and with barely time to gasp for breath she was speaking again.

"Mistress," she said, her voice quivering so the word was unintelligible, even to herself. She swallowed and tried again. "Mistress?" This time her voice was quiet, almost calm. "I was wrong to doubt someone as powerful as yourself," she said, feeling at once that her words were foolish, but willing to say any foolishness to stop further pain. "I have known from the start that you are powerful – far more powerful than I have ever been."

The Sultana's eyes stopped their roving examination of her body and rose to meet Christine's.

"Yes, of course," she said matter-of-factly.

"And now you have won," Christine continued. She had the Sultana's attention, and intended to keep it. "You have won in every way against me. You have taken my husband from me, and now you have taken my beauty as well." She inhaled and continued, imagining that she saw some semblance of sanity returning to the eyes, even if only in the form of self-satisfaction. "Even if you had not already taken my husband from me, which I cannot doubt as you are a much more powerful and beautiful person than I, he could not continue to love me as I am." She hiccoughed, and finished, "As ugly as I am." She dropped her eyes as they welled with fresh tears. The warmth of their flow from her eyes to her hair joined the warmth of the blood on her cheeks. She toyed with a final phrase, first deciding to say it, then deciding against it, fearful of the response it might illicit, hopeful that she understood the Sultana well enough to accomplish an end to the torture. She thrust the sentence forth, not certain that at the moment she did not mean it.

"You have won so completely over me – perhaps it would be better if I were to die, here, now." She held her breath and pressed her lips together, then released both as the pain in her cheeks flared again.

The final sentence worked even better than Christine hoped. It seemed to descend upon the Sultana like a slap waking her from a trance. A frown creased her forehead as she stood. Without looking at Christine again, she said, "Release her."

Looking to the nearest guard, she said, "Fetch the surgeon. Tell him to do his best work." She beckoned to the other three guards and said, "Come." Christine heard her final words as the wicked woman and the guards strode out of the room. "I will not ruin my bargain for a bit of fun."

Alone again, Christine pressed both sides of the pillow up and against her cheeks, pressing as hard as she dared against her bleeding wounds. And again she wept, but this time out of profound relief as well as pain.

I must find a way to escape soon. I may not be able to stop her next time.

CHAPTER 24
IN MAZENDERAN

By the time they reached Baku on the western edge of the Caspian Sea, Erik and Petter had donned disguises and looked as Moorish as the Persian himself. Faraz wore no disguise at all other than a change of costume. Petter had darkened his skin using one of Erik's tints, and Erik, of course had donned yet another mask – this one complete with false beard.

Erik laughed as Petter wriggled his nose and contorted his mouth in his effort to manipulate the skin of his face.

"Why do you laugh?" Petter asked pettishly. "This tint itches unbearably, and you've told me not to scratch."

"I told you not to scratch while it was wet. It is dry now. Feel free." He chuckled again.

"It did not itch this much when it was wet!" Petter lifted his darkened forefinger and rubbed it back and forth over his upper lip. "You only need wear it around your eyes, while I am covered in this abysmal concoction. What is it made from, anyway?"

"Don't ask," Erik answered, and this time both he and the Persian laughed. Petter scowled as he continued to rub at his cheeks and at the tips of his ears. It was the first time Erik had seen his son seeming less than enthusiastic since London, but he could not blame him. The unguent did make the skin itch.

"Petter, if you cannot bear it, remove it," Erik said.

Petter sobered, and after one final rub at his chin, lowered his hands. "I can bear it," he answered. He reached up and adjusted his turban. "At least, other than this turban, the clothing is comfortable. Far less constraining than suit coats and shirt collars."

They obtained passage south on a boat going to Mazenderan. It had two planned stops along the coast, but seemed the fastest way to reach Mazenderan without drawing undue attention.

Once in Mazenderan and having secured several adjoining rooms near the palace, the Persian donned what little disguise he intended – a beard, like Erik's, although far fuller and covering more of his face.

"Having been gone so long, and with this beard, I do not believe I will be recognized," the Persian said after examining the effect in a small mirror.

"I do not recognize you as the same man I traveled with yesterday," Erik answered. In fact, the addition of the beard highlighted the man's cheekbones and filled in the gauntness of his cheeks. Even Faraz's eyes seemed to deepen in his face. "However, I worry that your plan is too rash, given the Sultana's warning against your coming to Mazenderan."

"Someone must conduct reconnaissance, and I am best suited for the task. I feel I can trust the several people with whom I have maintained a correspondence," the Persian answered. "I will succeed where you would not."

"It is easy to maintain a friendship when the correspondent is in France. That trust may not withstand the strain when your friend discovers you here and endangers his own life by assisting you," Erik said.

The Persian did not answer. He turned for another look at his beard, used a small amount of tint to further darken his eyes, and strode to the door. "I shall return… soon. In truth, the longer I am away the better indication of my success." He paused and fondled his beard as though it was a normal addition to his face. "Unless of course, I lose my head in the palace courtyard," he continued, and then flashed a smile.

Erik scowled. He did not think the jest at all humorous.

"I will not be longer than two days," Faraz finished.

"Be careful, honored friend," Erik murmured as Faraz stepped through the door.

Faraz did not return that night, nor did he return the following morning. In that endless time of waiting, Erik fretted and paced, and castigated himself for not coming to Mazenderan alone. He would likely have succeeded without the Persian's information. He would likely succeed – despite his injuries – without his son. His injures were no longer crippling and with his current level of tension, he regretted having brought either man. He thought the Persian dead, and could not shake the waking nightmares that his son, too, would perish here. He spent hours watching Petter as the boy studied the palace diagrams. He looked away whenever Petter raised his eyes, afraid the boy would too easily read the haunted look he knew must scream from his eyes. He would wait the two days Faraz had indicated – until the following morning – and then he must find a way to send the boy home.

Faraz returned that evening, just as Erik and Petter prepared to step out for a hasty supper. Erik's tension broke not with relief, but with anger.

"Faraz! Damn you, man. Where have you been!"

Faraz backed a step, surprise evident on his face, but did not answer. Erik looked from the tall man to Petter. His son was smiling.

"It is good to see you well, Mr. Akhtar," Petter said, and gestured that he should come further into the room. The calm statement brought Erik to his senses. He exhaled, allowing his relief to gain the upper hand.

"Yes, Faraz, yes. Come in. You had me worried, my friend, so I bark when I should leap with joy." He stepped forward and embraced Faraz and pressed his masked cheeks to each of Faraz's bearded ones. When he backed again, Faraz was smiling, although weary. His eyes seemed even darker than when he stepped from the room a day and a half ago, and Erik guessed the man had not slept since that time.

"Success?" Erik asked, the doubt plain in his tone.

Faraz lowered himself into a chair with a groan before answering. "Success of a kind, I suppose," he answered. "I stand before you with my head."

Erik forced himself to sit rather than to pace, or worse, to shake the information from the Persian. He did not speak.

"But," Faraz said, sighing and bending to remove his boots, "nothing more."

"Nothing? You could not reach your friends?" Erik asked.

"I spoke with several, to include a friend still employed in the palace," Faraz answered. "I have discovered that the Shah-in-Shah does have a son, and found where the mother and child are sequestered in the palace – she has her own quarters with the boy, because the Shah does fear for the boy's life." Faraz looked about as though searching for something and said, "I will show you on your diagram later, if you wish."

"Christine?" Erik asked.

"Nothing," Faraz answered. "She is unknown to any with whom I spoke. There are not even rumors of a golden haired woman visiting the palace. It seems certain that she is not being kept in the dungeons – this, third hand of course, from a guard who would know. She may not be in Mazenderan at all, for all I learned of her."

"She is," Erik said, no longer looking at the Persian, but gazing at his own entwined hands. He pounded a fist into his open palm, and said, "She must be here." Lifting his head, he said, "She is here. I am to meet with Naheed to gain the details I will need for the murders, and Naheed assured me she would bring Christine to the meeting as proof of a bargain kept. She is here!" Erik slumped as he sat. "I had hoped to free Christine without need of seeing the Sultana, but that is not to be." Erik remained lost in his thoughts until Faraz spoke again.

"I must sleep," he said, rising to return to his room.

"Yes, of course," Erik said. "Thank you for your efforts, Faraz. You learned much, although not all."

Before the evening was over, Erik had written the coded letter to "Gohar," and signed with the name Abadan, as directed, and had the letter messengered to the palace. There was nothing more left to do except wait. Erik expected the wait to be overlong, knowing the Sultana's propensity for torture – even such indirect torture as making Erik wait. In this, at least, he was wrong. The return letter arrived the following day, indicating a meeting time that same evening. He refused to consider allowing either Petter or the Persian to accompany him.

Erik waited at the appointed time in the exclusive restaurant the Sultana had indicated. He had been shown to a private room with a large low table and sufficient space and cushions to seat more than a dozen. He ignored the tea he had been served, and instead fingered the Punjab lasso and dagger where they lay hidden beneath his tunic. The time for the meeting came and went, and Erik's impatience mounted to rage. Knowing the need for calmness and rationality in the upcoming meeting, he closed his eyes and began a meditative sequence timed to follow the tick-tick-tick of his fingernail against the point of his knife. Each slow intake of breath and each slow exhale contained an inaudible two-syllable word: "Chris-tine." He would see her soon. Soon.

He opened his eyes at the sound of a faint rustle. There, before him stood Naheed, veiled this time, but recognizable to Erik, nonetheless. He looked past her before saying, "Where is my wife?"

The Sultana did not move or respond.

"Naheed, where is my wife?" This time the words were an impatient growl.

"Ah, darling Erik," she answered, lifting the veil and moving toward him. "I was not sure it was you, but I could never mistake your voice burred with anger." She smiled and moved around the table as if she intended to seat herself on the cushions beside him, but paused. She bent to peer into his eyes, and – apparently not trusting what she saw there – she turned and lowered herself to the cushions at the opposite side of the table. She wriggled as she pulled several cushions into better positions and settled herself. "That is a mask, is it not? Quite ingenious."

Christine cannot be dead! A flush of fear thrilled through him, and purged whatever calmness he had managed to achieve. His rage reawakened, and his own breath came in pants as he envisioned leaping the table and snuffing the life out of the monster before him. Incongruously, he also envisioned Petter – Petter who had tried on so many occasions thus far on their journey to sooth Erik's explosive rage – and felt an immediate return of his composure. Taking a deep breath, he said, "My wife."

"Ah, yes, your wife," she answered. She twirled a bit of her long black hair around one finger watching the motion as though fascinated. "It occurred to me that you intended a rescue. And further, that I might not live through the rescue attempt... and I intend to live a long, long life." She smiled as she spoke as if she were discussing some inconsequentiality, rather than accusing Erik of contemplating her murder.

Erik's face flushed at her words – he was thankful for the covering of his mask – for that had been his plan. Not the murder of the Sultana, unless it became necessary, but certainly the rescue of Christine.

When he made no answer, the Sultana laughed and said, "You see, my love, we know each other so... intimately." She shrugged one shoulder and licked her lips in a long, slow motion.

"We had a bargain," Erik said.

"Yes, her life for your deed," she answered, still smiling, smiling.

"And that you would bring her to this meeting," he said.

"No. You," and here she jabbed a finger in his direction, "added that condition, and it is a condition of which I do not approve." Her eyes flashed at him, and her smile turned cold but remained.

"I will not do the deed," he said.

"You condemn your wife to slow death," she answered. Their words lashed at each other like the blades of two duelers. But Erik knew he had lost. He lowered his head.

"If I do as you ask, what assurances do I have that you will return Christine to me. Alive. And unharmed." He added the last two phrases in full knowledge that the Sultana would find a sick humor in returning Christine's corpse.

"I will do as I say," she answered, and running a fingertip along the tabletop toward him, she asked, "Do you not trust me, my love?"

Erik huffed a small derisive laugh, lowered his head, and raised it again to meet her fluttering eyes. "If you do not, I swear to you now, I will kill you myself. Look into my eyes and understand that I make this oath with the greatest of solemnity."

A spark of fear crossed the usually impregnable face, and Erik hoped the fear did not arise from her own certain knowledge that Christine was already dead. But then, her smile returned, and with it, the confidence she always carried.

"Why speak to me thus, Erik? We have loved each other too long to quarrel in this manner." She affected a pout, and walked two fingers toward him on the tabletop. "I have already told you I intend to live a very long life. I tell you again, you silly man. Christine is my special guest" – Erik shuddered at the words, remembering well how she treated her "special guests" – "and will remain so. If you do as I ask, I will do as I say."

Erik nodded once. "Do you have a plan?"

SKELETONS IN THE CLOSET

"Of course," she answered. Smiling and raising herself she said, "Shall we dine, or…"

"Speak, Naheed. I will break no bread with you."

Again, the pout, but she lowered herself to the cushions again. In a languorous manner and sugared with many endearments, the Sultana explained. She named the night for the deed – only three days hence, which seemed to Erik both impossibly far away and surprisingly soon. She explained in excellent detail where he would find the mother and child, and how to move past the guards of those quarters. She did not refer to the hidden tunnels, and neither did he. If she remained unaware of their existence after all these years – her father, the Shah, not having trusted her with the information – so much the better. She told of her own alibi: a reception for a visiting ambassador where she was sure to be seen. Through all this, Erik listened, having no intention whatever of committing the deed, but waiting to learn the conditions of Christine's return. When the Sultana finished her account without that explanation, Erik's patience ended.

"And my wife is returned when? How?" He barked the words.

"I wish to see proof of the deed," she said, "naturally." She explained her desires to Erik's growing horror. "Then, my love, I will take you to your wife." She paused, and with an arch of her back and the lifting of one knee, she said, "Unless you wish to claim another prize?"

Again Erik fought the recurrent urge to leap across the table, to strangle the creature before him. He felt confident that the Sultana had left orders for Christine's immediate death if she failed to return from this meeting. Erik conjured the earlier calming vision of Petter – Petter's concerned eyes, his placating hand to a shoulder. With a shuddering exhale, he said, "I have never wanted you, Naheed." He stood and walked around the table, feeling ill. He needed fresh air. He needed to be quit of her presence and her scent.

"Oh, Erik, you lie," he heard her soft words behind him, uttered with sadness. "You lie. We have always been lovers in our hearts." He closed the door behind him and heard no more of her mad utterances.

CHAPTER 25
CHRISTINE PLANS FOR ESCAPE

Christine had dared much since the Sultana had cut her face. Tonight she must dare more – for now she had a plan.

She brought her hands to her cheeks and shuddered as she recalled those horrible woundings.

The Sultana had only come to her room once since that morning, and had stayed only a moment. Christine melted into violent shivers as the Sultana approached her, unable to speak even to plead, her mind tearing and twisting in an incoherent tangle of terror. But the Sultana just ordered the bandages to her face removed so that she could inspect the stitches. Then she demanded the bandages replaced with new ones, and without meeting Christine's stricken gaze, had spun and left the room. As the lock turned in the door, Christine had shaken in one great final spasm and vomited up her lunch, spattering her clothing and the bed linens. She had crawled away from the mess to the cushions at the far side of the room and had wept, careful to lean forward to keep her tears from soaking the bandages. That night she had slept, too exhausted to enter the tunnels.

By the following evening, the pain in her face had dulled, her resolve to escape had redoubled, and she had entered the tunnels after her lights were turned down. She no longer feared discovery so much as the return of the Sultana and her sharp little dagger.

That night, Christine took her lantern and one of her three remaining matchsticks into the tunnels. She traveled the tunnel in the blackness until she reached a peephole that looked into a room that had always been darkened, had never revealed the low lamp light she had seen in other rooms. She reasoned that the rooms that remained lit – even with low light – were rooms in use, and she dared not enter those.

Her heart pounded in her ears as she felt her way to the near trapdoor. She tripped the catch and held her breath as the door slid aside. Its mechanism was as noiseless as she could have hoped, and she again blessed Erik's genius. She slipped into the dark room, and stood, straining to hear any small sound, perhaps the sound of a sleeper who preferred darkness to the low lamp light. She heard nothing. She reentered the tunnel, and closing her eyes to preserve her night vision, she struck a matchstick and lit the lantern, turning the flame to low. With the lantern held before her, she again ducked through the open doorway and surveyed the room.

It was another bedchamber, similar in its appointments to her own. No figure lay across the bed. With the skin-prickling feeling that someone stood at her back ready to touch her or speak to her, she swung the lantern about, searching for the room's occupant. In the low lamplight, too many shadows remained. She turned up the flame, and again turned about.

Nothing. No one.

She tried to calm her breathing, tried to assure herself that the doors would not open, that she was as safe from being discovered as she would be in her own room. She went to each of the two doors and pressing her ear to each, tried to hear anything from beyond. She heard nothing. Heart still pounding as if she had been running, she searched the room – cupboards, armoire, shelves – hoping to find something she could use to facilitate her escape. Perhaps a weapon, or matchsticks, or… or… She was unsure of what she hoped, but she searched nonetheless. She found nothing of use. The room was as bare of such useful items as her own room.

Cursing with the frustration of having risked so much for no gain, she hurried back to the trapdoor and the tunnel. She closed the trapdoor and stood, panting, but filled with relief at having again reached the safety of the tunnel. She again imagined the interior of the room she had just left, confirming in her mind before she moved on that she had searched all she could. She wanted any second thoughts to occur to her now, when she could reenter without much risk, rather than later, as she lay in her bed. She could think of nothing.

That had been all she had dared that first night.

Beginning at breakfast the following morning, she started putting aside bits of flat bread from each meal. When she could, she stuffed the bread with rice. She did not bother with trying to put aside meat or vegetables, both because the meals were so fragrant with spices that she thought their scent would lead to their discovery, but also because she thought they might spoil faster than the bread or rice. At first, she kept the flatbread under her mattress, but the regular changing of her linens made her fear its discovery. Thereafter, she tucked the bread into the dirt at the back of the potted plants in her room. What would she care of a small bit of dirt, if she managed to escape and needed food?

As the days passed, she also began using the voice control tricks Erik had taught her to practice mimicking the voices of those around her – that of one of the youngest of the guards whose voice was still high-pitched, those of the two servant girls who most often attended her, and, with an inward shudder at each attempt, that of the Sultana. The guard and the girls gave her ample opportunity to listen to inflection and habits of speech. She did not wish the same opportunity of the Sultana – in fact, she hoped never to be in the presence of the Sultana again, as unrealistic as that hope might be.

If only I could observe the Sultana without being in her presence. With a flash of sudden insight, *Perhaps I can!*

That night, Christine made her way through darkness to the large mirror that looked into the Sultana's bedchamber. She waited as several servant girls tidied and readied the room, working without the chatter Christine might have expected. As she waited, Christine's eyes kept returning to the oversized portrait of the Sultana, vision drawn there against her will. No matter how many times she pulled her eyes away from the towering vision, they always seemed to return.

She was looking at the portrait again, at the amber eyes so faithfully preserved even to the glint of haughty superiority, when she heard the voice of the Sultana. Christine gasped and released her hold on the drape, returning her to a world of near blackness. Her face flushed, heating her cheeks, and she placed her cool hands upon the now unbandaged flesh, feeling the line of the healing scar tissue under her fingers.

I don't need to look at her. I only need to listen.

The Sultana spoke as peremptorily to the girls as she spoke to the guards, and the girls answered in quiet and respectful tones, saying as little as necessary. Despite Christine's fear, she was drawn to watch the Sultana as she spoke, not through any voyeuristic desire, but through the desire to observe her movements and mannerisms. Ducking her head, Christine raised a corner of the drape. She almost dropped the drape again, but fear made her freeze. The Sultana stood before the mirror, turning, and plucking at her clothing as if to watch the fabric rise and fall against her skin. Christine only began to breathe again as she realized that the Sultana was not looking down in her direction, but was examining her own reflection.

Christine relaxed as the Sultana moved about the room. She studied the Sultana's walk, listened to her tones and words, noted the small flick of her shoulder that preceded an order to one of the girls. She watched her hands, which seemed restless and ever moving, even when one of the girls assisted in removing her rings. Christine watched as various jewels were removed from the woman's hands, arms, neck, hair and feet, and thought that with only a part of that wealth, she might be able to bribe a guard or a girl to help her. But perhaps not. What was wealth compared to a life – a life that would be forfeit – to assist a woman they did not know, or like, or trust? Besides, the jewels might be missed.

Christine's attention became focused as the Sultana removed first one dagger and then another from her clothing – one from her waist at the small of her back and one from the area of her thigh. Christine could not see how the daggers were secured or hidden, but she noticed that they were placed in a case containing several such daggers. Would the Sultana miss one of those?

What am I thinking? I cannot and will not enter this room of all rooms!

Christine lowered the drape when the Sultana moved to her own washroom. She had observed enough for one night.

She returned down the tunnel to her own room, but thrilled with excitement and too wakeful to sleep. She practiced walking and talking as she had watched the Sultana do, careful to keep her voice quiet, but determined to improve her imitation. After only a few minutes of this, her bristling, fear-tipped energy drove her to the tunnel again. She would enter and search another darkened room.

Thus did Christine's days and nights proceed. She spent her nights watching the Sultana, and twice more entered and searched darkened rooms. This latter she gave up after discovering that the darkened rooms were rooms like her own, empty and without any useful items. Her days she spent stealing and storing food. And always with a mounting fear that this day would bring the Sultana back to her room with her small, sharp, jeweled dagger and the crazed bloodlust shining from her wicked eyes.

She now had a plan. She needed one small bit of information to put that plan to action – and, of course, no way to extract it. She could only listen to the servants and guards, and wait, and pray through the unbearable tension of her days that she would not die before her chance came.

Then, quite suddenly, her prayers were answered.

Christine sat at the low table, eating the luncheon that had just been delivered. She watched as the servant girls changed her bed linens, waiting for the moment when she might hide her bread. The girls chattered in low voices as they always did. Christine listened without watching them, afraid of alerting them to the fact that she understood them. The guards stood at the door, the eyes of one on the nearer servant girl, the other bowing his head and picking at a back tooth, as though he had just eaten and was attempting to dislodge some tenacious particle of food.

"I don't understand why you see him. He is boorish in his manners," the shorter, slimmer girl said.

"He may seem boorish to you, but I appreciate his directness," the rounder girl answered. "And his hands." She giggled as she pulled and straightened the bottom linen.

"Ugh," answered the other. "You only ever think of the one thing."

"And why shouldn't I?" the round girl answered. She wriggled her bottom, and even without looking directly at the guards, Christine could see that the one appreciated the movement. "I am seeing him again tonight," she continued.

"What? With the Sultana gone for the entire evening, we girls were planning a small party – relaxation, food…"

"You relax in your way, and I'll relax in mine," came the response, with a wink and another wriggle of her bottom. Christine hardly heard the words, but saw the wink and the wriggle because her eyes had snapped up to look at the girls.

With the Sultana gone for the entire evening.

Christine's eyes lowered again to focus on her stew, although the bit in her mouth now seemed too large to swallow. She forced it down as she might a stone, feeling the pain of its progress down the passages of her throat and neck.

Tonight. Tonight. Will I be ready?

Christine inhaled through her nose, and then exhaled through pursed lips, trying to relax the tension that had leapt into her shoulders. She sat with her eyes closed, running over the plan again in her mind.

I am ready.

For the first time, her mind tried to move beyond the walls of the palace, to think through what she would do if she did manage to escape the palace grounds. For all that they were hopeful thoughts, she could not bring herself to focus on them, realizing that she could not plan so far ahead, could not know what she might do once quit of her prison, could not know what opportunities or obstacles would present themselves.

Erik...

Without even having escaped, without even knowing that she would be successful, she felt closer to him.

She finished her meal with some speed, feeling somehow that the hours and minutes before she could act were speeding as well.

Once alone again, she stood and began walking the room. She swayed her hips as she walked in the Sultana's exaggerated manner, and flicked her fingers up to look at her imaginary rings. She placed a hand on her opposite shoulder and pulled it toward her breast. She flicked her shoulder and whispered an order – "Turn down the bed." Using the voice of the lascivious girl who had just left the room, she answered herself: "Yes, Sultana."

Over and over, refusing to allow herself to fall out of the character of the Sultana, Christine walked, spoke, wiggled, touched various items around the room. She flashed her eyes at an imagined affront, some failure of comportment on the part of one of the servants.

"I shall not *accept* such behavior. Either you will *do* as I have instructed, or I..."

Christine broke off as she heard the lock turning in her door. She clapped her hands to her mouth, realizing – too late, too late! – that she had been speaking at a normal speaking volume.

The door burst open and a guard rushed into the room. His eyes swept the room, not even pausing over the figure of Christine standing near the foot of the bed. Christine lowered her hands from her mouth to stand with fists clenched at her sides. A second guard entered the room behind the other, although without the same hurried manner. He too looked about the room, then raised an amused eyebrow and cocked his head unseen at the back of the guard that stood several paces into the room. The first guard turned to the guard behind him.

"I thought..." He paused and glancing around the room a last time, shrugged his shoulders and said, "I really thought I heard her."

"Perhaps you should smoke a little less hashish at lunch," the second guard answered, with a small laugh.

Together, and without another glance at Christine, they turned away.

"Foolish, foolish woman!" Christine whispered as the lock turned once more. She smiled as she realized that her impersonation must have been convincing – at least through a closed door. Excitement rising – *tonight!* – she walked around the bed, body undulating, arms swinging, fingers twiddling in the Sultana's affected fashion. With a small laugh, she threw herself onto the bed. Her stomach fluttered in denial of her forced confidence, and she thought she would be ill.

No! She pushed her unease away. *Tonight I escape. I will not entertain fear!*

CHAPTER 26
ERIK ENTERS THE PALACE

"But Father, it makes no sense!" Petter slapped a hand on the table, and turned away from Erik. Before Erik could respond, his son spun back and said, "You are injured – and don't think I haven't seen you favoring your leg and ribs. You asked me to assist in rescuing Mother, and after all this travel and preparation, now you say I will not enter the palace with you!"

Erik wanted to explain his true reasons for the current plan, wanted to say that he could not bear the possibility of losing both his wife and his son on this night. But Petter would not accept this – would not consider his own mortality for many reasons, his youthful inability to believe in his mortality not being the least of them.

He also could not explain the new plan he had developed since meeting with Naheed three days ago – the plan outside of rescuing Christine – for then both Petter and the Persian would think him mad and either forbid him to go at all, or insist on coming into the palace with him. However, mad or not, he intended with this new plan to secure his future safety, and that of his wife and son, once and for always. He intended to insure the Sultana could never endanger his family again.

"Petter, son, I have explained this to you," Erik answered.

"You have told me you need an 'outside man.' I understand that, but Faraz can be that man, can he not? Why the both of us?"

Erik sighed, bent over the table, and pulled the rough palace plans toward him. He gritted his teeth in the effort to hide how his ribs pained him with the motion. "There are two possible ways for me to get your mother out of the palace. If she is in the dungeons…"

"I have told you she is not," Faraz interrupted with no special vehemence.

"I know what you have told me, but I must plan for all eventualities, must I not? What if your source was incorrect? What if Naheed moves her there? What if the other passages have been blocked or changed?"

"Go on," said Petter, somewhat subdued from his earlier heated manner.

"I need one of you here," he pointed, indicating the spot. "However, if Christine is in Naheed's wing – where she traditionally kept her 'special guests' – then this passage would be the best, and I need someone here." Again he pointed. He raised his eyes first to Petter, who was examining the plans, and then to Faraz. The Persian returned his look with an analytical tilt of his head – clearly suspecting that Erik was not divulging everything – but uncertain enough to hold his peace. Erik looked away.

"Why not one set of horses – perhaps here," Petter pointed to a spot between the two Erik had indicated, "so that regardless of the exit you use…"

"No," Erik interrupted. Petter was too intelligent to accept Erik's simplistic explanation, and was nettling at the ruse Erik had adopted to keep Petter from going into the palace.

"I am not a child, Father. Explain it to me."

Again, Erik sighed. He would need to tell part of the truth. "I will explain my reasoning, but it will not make you happy." He straightened his back and turned to his son, placing his hands on the younger man's shoulders. "I know you are not a child, my son, so you must listen to what I tell you, and you must accept it as a man. I will have no further argument as to the plans after my explanation."

Petter, with a stubborn set of his chin which reminded Erik of Christine, said, "If your reasoning is sound, I will argue no more."

"You know I love your mother more than life itself. You know I love you as much," Erik said. He blinked as his eyes clouded with unwanted moisture.

"Of course," Petter answered.

"I do not intend to leave the palace without your mother. I will… die before I will leave the palace without your mother." Erik paused to let the words sink in. "I will give your mother directions for how to find her way to you, and I will protect her exit with my life, if need be." Petter's lips twitched in protest. Erik continued, "I have no intention of sacrificing my life unnecessarily, but you must understand that your mother may be the only one of us to return to you. And if she is injured, if she is ill, if I cannot…" He stopped, words failing him. "I want you here," he stabbed the two points he had indicated earlier, "to help her."

Petter said nothing for a long moment. In a low voice, he said, "Father, I understand all you have said. Will you listen to what I have to say?" When Erik could not bring himself to answer past the lump that had risen to his throat, Petter said, "Father?"

Erik swallowed and said, "I will listen."

"If I entered the palace with you…" Erik raised his hand and shook his head in negation, but Petter said, "You said you would listen!"

With a sigh, Erik nodded.

"If I entered the palace with you, we could both help Mother if she needs help. We could also protect each other, giving us a greater chance of escape."

Erik nodded again, and hesitated as though he were considering his son's words. "And a greater chance that tonight will see the end of us all. I have not lied to you. I have not told you that this rescue would be without risk and danger. I do not wish to die. I do not wish your mother to die, although we may both perish without achieving her freedom. If this is the case, I would not have you dead as well." He squeezed Petter's shoulders and said, "Your mother would agree."

"But why did I come if not to help?" Petter's frustration brought the words out with a squeak.

"I was injured. I am better now. And you *shall* help. You will get your mother safely away and out of Mazenderan if I do not return. I am counting on you."

"You talk as if you *know* you will meet your death," Petter said. His eyes were questioning pools of sadness and anguish.

"I intend to escape death or injury. But I want the assurance that if I do not, you will be there for your mother."

Petter closed his eyes and tucked his chin to his chest. He raised his head and without opening his eyes nodded.

Erik exhaled a long slow breath. He had accomplished what he had set out to do. Petter would not enter the palace. The new plan was far too dangerous to allow Petter to accompany him.

He stepped away and began wrapping a length of rope about his waist for possible use as a lasso. He tucked a small knife into his boot. Into a pocket he placed two small candles and a box of matchsticks. When he felt that neither man was watching he tucked several small vials into his sleeve. "I will leave now," he said. "You will go to get the horses and proceed to the rendezvous points. If all goes well, tomorrow we shall leave Mazenderan forever." He smiled in an attempt to show lighthearted confidence.

"I will wait at my assigned post until you emerge," Petter said.

"Until your mother emerges. I intend to be with her, but you must not wait beyond that." Erik waited until Petter nodded. He stepped forward and embraced the boy – the man.

Turning to the silent Persian, Erik said, "Thank you, Faraz, my honorable friend." He was thanking the man for his silence, for his lack of addition to Petter's arguments. Then, "Take care of my son." He had already given the man instructions.

Faraz nodded and walked with him toward the door. Speaking quietly in a clear attempt to keep Petter from hearing, Faraz said, "You have not told all, friend." He reached for Erik's sleeve, and clutched through the cloth at the vials hidden there.

"You are a good man, Faraz," Erik said. "I will see you again, if Allah wills it."

"If Allah wills it," responded the tall man. He stepped back with resignation, understanding that Erik would not explain further. "May Allah go with you and watch over you."

***

Erik's entry into the palace was not without its difficulties. He did not see or alert any guards, knowing entries that were still secret and therefore unguarded, but he did injure himself twice – once flipping over a low wall and further bruising his injured ribs as he slid over, and once stumbling over a raised flagstone and bumping his leg in his effort to keep from falling. For the hundredth time since leaving Sweden he damned old age and injuries. Maybe Petter was right. Maybe without Petter's strong arm he would fail in his mission.

Christine's face floated in his mind's eye.

No. I will not fail.

Despite the Persian's information that Christine was not in the dungeons, Erik determined to make certain. He had not lied when he explained that he thought it possible the Sultana had moved Christine there in the hopes of securing her while Erik committed the hoped-for murders. Once in the tunnel warren and with the assistance of a small candle, Erik found a barrel holding several dry torches, and near that, a smaller bucket of oil which still contained a small amount of the combustible substance with which he could revive the torches. Thus equipped, he moved through the tunnels toward the dungeons. Twice he made wrong turnings and had to backtrack. Again he damned the vagaries of age, although not with as much vehemence – after all, he had been many years away from the palace of Mazenderan and had made no effort until now to recall the many convolutions of the place.

For what seemed an endless time, Erik traveled the dark tunnels. His thoughts of Christine hastened his footsteps, and increased his limp. The bobbing of the torchlight on the walls of the dusty tunnels gave the impression that the tunnels themselves were rocking and pitching, as if he were aboard a ship destined for hell.

When Erik reached the dungeons, he stomped out his torch, and moving from peephole to peephole, looked into each cell. There were few prisoners. Erik scrutinized each one in the low light, each of dark skin, each of dark hair... and none with the golden hair of his Christine – of that he was certain.

Now he must proceed to Naheed's wing – if he could remember the path through the twisting maze. His passage to the dungeons had wounded his confidence in his memory, but he determined – even if he must walk these tunnels for days – he would make his way. With a new torch lit and a spare tucked into his belt, he moved out of the area of the dungeon. As he walked, he noticed that several parts of the passages were regularly traversed – by the Shah, he presumed. This came to him not in evidence of footprints or similar signs, but in the lessening of the sandy dust beneath his feet and the utter lack of spider webbing. He moved through these areas with as much speed as possible, not wanting to meet the Shah.

He came finally to what he recalled to be Naheed's wing. He had not walked far when he noticed, for the first time, distinct footprints in the otherwise heavy dust. Small footprints, a woman's footprints.

Naheed!

When Erik had built the palace, the Shah had forbidden Erik to tell a soul of the tunnels and passages and trapdoors, and Erik had sworn never to do so – an oath he had kept. The Shah's young daughter had not been aware of the tunnels when Erik had escaped Mazenderan. Clearly, the Shah had had a change of heart and informed Naheed, or the devious woman had discovered the tunnels on her own. The small footprints were evidence of as much.

Erik's heart skipped and sped as he realized he must be close to his goal. Moving forward, he followed the path of the footprints as they stretched before him. Several times they moved some small distance down a side tunnel, but the bulk of the prints concentrated in the main passage. After determining this, he stopped straying from that corridor. He approached a trapdoor that showed evidence of numerous entrances and exits. Naheed's bedchamber? He thought not. The prints looked recent, and Naheed had no need to use the tunnels to enter or leave her bedchamber.

Christine! This must be Christine's room! Naheed has come upon her in secret!

Throwing the torch some distance down the tunnel, Erik peered into the room. It was a dim bedchamber, small and simply furnished. Not Naheed's room – even as a child of ten she had occupied far more lavish quarters. After watching for some minutes and seeing no movement, Erik triggered the mechanism that would open the trapdoor. He stepped into the room. It was unoccupied. He strode toward the unmade bed. As he bent to look beneath it (at no small cost to both leg and ribs), he noticed a small cloth enfolding molded bread and grains of strewn rice – the whole crawling with insects.

No one has been in this room for quite some time.

SKELETONS IN THE CLOSET

He moved to the armoire. He expected to find the armoire stocked with clothing, but instead it was empty. He stopped in the act of closing the doors again when something at the bottom of the armoire caught his attention. Shoes. A pair of shoes. *Christine's* shoes.

Erik bent and gathered the shoes to his chest. He threw his head back unsure whether to laugh or howl her name. He did neither, but instead, turned and looked about the room again.

Where is she?

He replaced the shoes and closed the armoire. He went to the near door and tried the handle. Unlocked. He opened the door. A washroom. Also empty. He moved to the far door, and again tried the handle. This door was locked.

"Naheed!" he whispered through gritted teeth. "What have you done with her?"

Frustration welled in Erik like a balloon of acid rising in his throat. To have come so far, to have found Christine's room – Christine's shoes! – and to have failed to find Christine in the flesh.

In the flesh. The thought, twisted as it was with memories of Naheed and the games she played with human flesh, took on a gruesome meaning. In that instant, like the crashing certainty of his own pulse in his ears, Erik knew. Knew.

My Christine is dead.

His rage at the thought blossomed behind his eyes all but blinding him to the room in which he stood. He knew what to do.

He would leave this room. He would find Naheed's chambers. He would lie in wait for her. And he would kill her.

No calming vision of Petter will save you this time!

He moved to the open trapdoor and into the tunnel. The thrown torch was still guttering and he used it to light the fresh one he held, and then closed the trapdoor. Examining the patterns in the dust at his feet, he began moving away from the direction in which he had come, moving into an area that had been even more heavily traveled.

This will lead me to Naheed's bedchambers.

He stopped each time the footprints evidenced entry through some trapdoor, and peered through the peephole. In his fury and frenzy, he was careless of the light of the torch, and did not extinguish it. He was peering into the third such room when the shock of near voices caused him again to throw the torch away from himself. He could see no one from his vantage point, but he could hear their words.

"I wish nothing from you. Be gone!" It was Naheed speaking, he was sure of it! Why had she returned to the palace? Why endanger the careful plans she had arranged to be away from the palace and surrounded with indisputable alibis?

Well, whatever the reason, Erik thought this development all the better. His face stretched in a feral smile. With a limping run toward the torch, he kicked it farther down the tunnel. He returned and triggered the trapdoor, and stepped into the darkened room. He walked toward the open doorway, listening again for the voice of the woman he sought. Just as Erik brought his head around the edge of the doorway, a young girl moved past the door, then entered the next room. She did not see him. Erik eased his head around and looked in the direction from which the girl had come.

There! Just turning into another corridor. *Naheed.*

He slipped from the darkened room into the wide, bright corridor and followed, heedless of who might try to intercept him. His fingers moved of their own accord upon the rope, twisting it with practice into a lasso.

CHAPTER 27
CHRISTINE ESCAPES

Christine could not eat her dinner when it came. Her giddy confidence of earlier in the day had abandoned her and her stomach had turned molten. It churned and rumbled.

I cannot be ill. I cannot be so weak!

She clutched at her stomach as the servant girl approached the low table. Christine's stomach chose that moment to rumble again, and the girl looked at her with pity as she gathered up the untouched meal. She leaned toward the water pitcher with its upturned glass over the top, and said, "Drink." She left the pitcher when she took the rest.

Christine did drink, hoping the water would steady her stomach. She moved to her bed and waited with a shivering impatience for the final visit of the evening, when the lights would be turned down. The girl returned sooner than Christine expected, apparently thinking that with Christine ill, an early night was in order. Or perhaps it was just a desire to be finished with her duties for the evening so that the planned "party" among the servant girls could begin.

That must mean that the Sultana is gone from the palace by now.

SKELETONS IN THE CLOSET

With the lights all turned down save the one by her bed, the servant left her in near darkness. As the lock turned, Christine leapt from the bed. She stood panting, and tried to assess her illness. Better – the water had helped.

She ran to the washroom and took a small wash linen from the shelf. Back in her room, she reached behind a large plant to recover her food. She shook each piece of bread as she removed it and brushed at the dirt before placing it in the center of the cloth. The topmost pieces were hard and crusty, but the more buried pieces felt damp and not at all palatable. She moved back to the lamp near her bed and inspected them, and then dashed the cloth to the floor. The dampness from the servant girls' watering of the plant had caused the deeper pieces to mold, and small white worms moved over them all.

Useless!

She did not pause, but ran to another plant – the one that hid her last remaining matchstick. She triggered the trapdoor, and while she waited for the counterbalances to do their work, she lit her lantern. Traveling the tunnel in darkness would grant her greater safety, but the lantern would allow her greater speed. At this moment, as she prepared to gamble her safety on a mad plan for escape, speed was of greater importance.

Once in the tunnel, she paused long enough to close the trapdoor behind her before running in the direction of the Sultana's bedchamber.

Please! Let no one be there!

She extinguished the lantern as she approached the massive drape of the Sultana's mirror. She bent and lifted the drape, and then cursed under her breath. A lone servant girl was tidying the bed linens and arranging the numerous pillows at the head of the bed.

"Farida, let's go!" The voice came from the direction of the Sultana's washroom. A servant girl emerged from the washroom, and approached the girl at the bed. "It is perfect. Now, come!" She tugged at the girl's clothing. After a final pat to a pillow, the two girls left the room, both giggling and whispering as they went. Christine exhaled and counted seconds until a full minute had passed.

Now, I must go now. But still she hesitated, fear filling her at the thought of the daring acts she contemplated, causing her to pant several times through pursed lips.

Now!

Without allowing herself further thought, she moved to the trapdoor that opened into the back of the wardrobe. Again, she listened, but hearing nothing, she triggered the door. She reached forward into the dark. Her fingers brushed against fine fabrics, and she ran her hand from side to side across the width of the full wardrobe. She bent to feel whether there were any objects on the floor of the wardrobe. There were not – she would not trip as she stepped in. She pushed the clothing aside and stepped into the wardrobe, wishing that she could chance dressing before emerging, but without light, she did not believe she could accomplish the task. Again she stopped and listened for voices. Silence. She pushed the wardrobe door open and stepped into the lighted room.

Her first sight was that of the oversized portrait, the eyes glaring into Christine's own, shining with victory. Christine had to force herself not to reenter the wardrobe to escape their evil gaze. She looked into the wardrobe, and with a final resolute puff of breath and a nod, she reached for the various articles in which she would drape herself – the ballooning pants, the small top which would not fit her as well as it fit the more voluptuous Sultana, and the various veils and wraps. She knew what to choose and how to dress from her nights watching the Sultana and did so, hands shaking. Then the jewelry. Then the daggers. She could not determine how the Sultana carried the daggers and just slipped the blades into the waistband at her back and adjusted the shoulder veil to be certain it covered the weapons. She hoped she would not need them.

Adjacent to the washroom, Christine seated herself at a large vanity table and painted her eyes in the manner of the Sultana. Her hands were shaking and the effect was not as precise as she wanted, but she hoped no one would look closely enough to notice – and if they thought her the Sultana, no one would be bold enough to comment on her eye paint.

She pulled a veil over her hair and pinned one side over her face, leaving only her eyes visible – the red scars on her cheeks would destroy the disguise in an instant. She had not seen the Sultana veiled, but she assumed that the woman must sometimes dress so. She topped the ensemble with a jeweled chain that fitted well enough to center the jewel on her forehead. She turned to the enormous mirror and stood motionless looking over the details of her costume, pulling at this, adjusting that. Her darkened hair still held her natural curls – unlike the Sultana's straight hair – but the veil covered enough to keep the difference from being noticeable… she hoped. Whatever the Sultana's motive in coloring her hair to the same brown-black, the decision served Christine's current needs. Christine flipped the loose strands of hair over her shoulder and with a slow sinuous stride, moved toward her image.

"Why Sultana, you look mystifyingly beautiful," she purred. And then again. She had never heard the Sultana say those words, but she mimicked tone and sultry insinuation.

"Yesss…" She drew the word out. She flashed her eyes at her reflection, and she flicked one shoulder as she turned. Without hesitation – after all, she was the Sultana, and the Sultana never hesitated – she moved toward the large double doors from which she had seen the Sultana enter.

Christine faced a wide corridor that led away from her endlessly. The corridor was lined with doors at well-spaced intervals, some open, some closed. A servant girl was moving away from where she stood, and after a few moments, the girl knocked upon a door and entered it. The girl had not seen her. She lifted her hand preparing to check the security of the veil covering her face, but lowered it without touching the veil. The Sultana would not check the veil.

SKELETONS IN THE CLOSET

I am *the Sultana*.

She began walking. Not quickly, despite the fact that she wanted to run, but not too slowly. She was not walking for effect; she was on business and, as the Sultana, did not want to be disturbed.

Christine was abreast of one closed door when it opened and a girl emerged. It was the round servant girl who brought her meals. As startled as Christine was, she was less so than the girl, who shut the door behind her, and backed, bowing.

"Sultana," she said, breathless.

Christine glared to cover her startled reaction and snapped, "What is it girl?"

"We were told…" the girl stammered, unable to finish. "We were told…"

"Yes, well, what were you told, you fool? Speak!" She took a threatening step toward the girl. Only her iron control kept her voice from shaking.

"We were told you were out for the evening," the girl squeaked. Her eyes moved to the door from which she had just entered the hall, and Christine guessed that the room contained a certain "boorish" male occupant.

"My plans changed," Christine said with a flip of her hand, and she turned to continue down the corridor. The girl followed for several steps.

"Is there anything…," the girl started.

"I wish nothing from you. Be gone!" Christine flipped her hand at the girl and turned away again. The skin of her scalp bristled as she waited for what the girl would do – Shout out? Hold her? – but instead she heard the soft patter of retreating footsteps and the opening and closing of a door. She did not look back as she so wished to do, but continued, although at a faster pace. She turned down the next corridor for no reason other than to put a wall between herself and the servant girl.

Her thoughts veered away from questions of whether she had done something wrong or behaved in a suspicious manner – the incident was behind her – and instead directed her thoughts forward.

Where am I going? How do I escape this place? What will I say if I am questioned by guards or if they insist on escorting me?

She was thus lost in her thoughts when her worst fear was realized. Just as she was passing an open door to a lighted room, she was snatched from behind in strong arms and thrust through the doorway. Before she could scream or even decide whether she should scream, a hand clapped over her mouth, and something – not a hand, a rope perhaps – wrapped about her throat. She was held until she heard the door close behind her, and then she was thrust face down into a gathering of cushions arranged in the near corner of the room. A hand pushed her face into the cushions, silencing whatever sound she might have made.

"Make a sound, and it will be the last sound you make. Understand me?" the voice growled.

SKELETONS IN THE CLOSET

She recognized the voice and shuddered in a paroxysm of joy.

Erik!

Tears sprang to her eyes as her worst terrors evaporated on the instant.

"Understand me?" he growled again. She nodded.

"My wife. I want her. Dead or alive, I must be with her."

Christine tried to roll over, tried to lift her face from the pillows, but the rope around her neck tightened.

"Do not move. Do not make a sound. Listen, for once," he said.

Christine again nodded and the rope about her throat loosened again.

"I love Christine more than you will ever be able to comprehend, you mad murderess. If she is dead, you die. No one will hear you. No one will come to your rescue. If she lives, you will tell me where to find her. Now. If you do not, I will assume she is dead, and – again – you will die."

Erik patted at Christine's veiled hair and down her back until he discovered the two daggers. He pulled them both from her waistband and threw them across the room. Her body thrilled at his ungentle touch as he patted her thighs. "Do you have any others?"

Christine shook her head, swallowing painfully around the rope at her throat. If she could have, she would have laughed through her tears at the thought of being killed by her beloved rather than rescued by him – and, ironically, on the night of her own attempted escape.

"Roll over. You will answer my questions. For your sake, I hope you have not deceived me, and that my Christine is well."

The rope did not loosen as she moved, but did not tighten either. She rolled, both afraid to provoke Erik and in painful breath-stealing anticipation of seeing his face.

His face! He wore no mask. There was no impediment to seeing – until her eyes filled again, and he blurred from her sight. She inhaled in a silent sob of joy and blinked, unwilling to lose a moment of the vision floating above her.

Such anger in his eyes. The hand that did not hold the lasso came up to pull her veil from her face and paused hovering. Christine blinked away fresh tears, and sobbed again as the anger faded from his eyes, and his brow furrowed in confusion.

"Your eyes," he said. "She doesn't have your beautiful blue eyes." Then: "Oh my God, Christine!" as his hands both worked at the lasso. As soon as it was loose, he lifted her into an embrace, one hand clutching at the back of her head, their faces cupped in each other's neck. He rocked her there, saying her name over and over, as she repeated his through quiet laughing sobs. He released her and with hands to her shoulders eased her away from him. His hand came up to the veil, which, although still clasped, was askew. He released the catch, and pulled the veil from her head.

Erik's warm, love-filled eyes fixed on the still healing scars on her face – first one and then the other – and hardened to stones. She raised one hand to her cheek – in embarrassment, in apology. He raised his own to her other cheek, but did not touch her.

"Do they pain you?" he asked. His voice was as hard as his eyes.

She shook her head and seeing his disbelief, said, "Honestly, there is very little pain now. A little tenderness."

With hands to her shoulders again, he drew her closer. His eyes widened and warmed and were filled with love and pain as he spoke to her. "You are beautiful, my wife." He pulled her closer still until their lips met.

"I love you, Erik," she breathed against his lips as they parted. His answer came in another kiss, this one as tender but containing more hunger, and lasting – it seemed to Christine – for an eternity of sweetness. When they broke from the kiss they were both breathing heavily.

After another long look, Erik stood and reached a hand out to help Christine to her feet. Catching at a loose curl of her dark hair, his forehead furrowed.

"Why…?" His face cleared as he continued. "Ah, yes. I know why. Clever she-devil. No wonder there was no report of a golden haired…" He smoothed her hair over her shoulder and continued, "… goddess… in the palace."

Tears threatened again as Erik pulled Christine towards him, kissed her forehead and embraced her. Trembling from his touch, she gratefully returned his embrace.

Without another word, he gathered up the Sultana's two abandoned daggers and first handing the smaller to Christine, secured the other in his own belt. Christine watched his every move as she replaced her veils, filling her eyes with his presence. He moved away from the door to the opposite wall, and within moments had located the lever to trigger another door into the tunnel. Hand clasped in Erik's strong, warm grip, she stepped with him into blackness.

CHAPTER 28
ERIK AND CHRISTINE

Erik pushed the trapdoor until it latched and they were engulfed in blackness. He was paralyzed by the touch of Christine's hand in his own, by the lingering taste of her mouth on his lips. He pulled her toward him and again, they were in each other's arms. He spoke into her hair as his eyes burned with tears of relief. His voice quivered as he spoke.

"You're alive, oh my heart, you're alive."

She spoke through his words, "You came for me."

Again their mouths met, and for long moments the only sound in the tunnel was their breathing and the sweet wet sound of their mouths tasting each other.

"Let's move away from here," Erik whispered. "Wait just a moment." Erik sought out the candle in his pocket, and before long it flared to life. He looked along the tunnel and fixing in his mind the path he had taken since leaving the tunnel in search of Naheed, he whispered, "This way." He took Christine's hand and kissed her palm before leading her to the place where he had dropped the torches. The newer of the two still burned where he had left it.

Lifting the torch and raising a finger to his lips to enforce a continued silence, he led Christine back the way he had come, past her room, past the footprinted dust to an area that looked long unused. After checking the nearest peepholes to see if the adjacent rooms contained occupants, he said, "Now, we can talk." He leaned toward Christine for another kiss, and then said, "How is it you come to be walking the palace halls in the guise of a mad woman?" He frowned as he remembered how he had treated Christine when he thought her Naheed, and said, "Did I hurt you?"

Christine smiled and shook her head.

"I was escaping," Christine said and giggled. "It sounds so ridiculous, but the Sultana was gone, and I thought… I thought… I don't know what I thought. I had to get away." The last was said with a painful vehemence, and Erik winced as Christine's hand stole to her cheek.

"Yes, she is away tonight. She is away so that she will not be held responsible when the Shah's newest wife and only son are killed tonight."

"Killed?" Christine asked.

"Yes. It is the ransom I must pay for your release."

Christine lunged into his arms, and said, "Oh Erik. I am so sorry." After a moment, she pulled away, and said, "What will she do when she finds me escaped and the deed undone. Is there anywhere we can hide? Anywhere we can be safe?"

"No," he answered. Seeing her stricken look, he continued in more tender tones: "Yes, of course, temporarily." He brushed a hand along the line of her chin, on the soft skin of her neck, bewildered to have her so near. "But we shall forever be looking over our shoulders. I will not live that way."

"And Petter?" Christine asked, clutching at Erik's shirt.

"He is safe." Erik saw the doubt and worry in her eyes, and continued, "He is here. He is waiting outside the palace walls to aid in your rescue."

Christine's brow furrowed and then cleared. "Yes, I suppose he is safer, here, with you, even on this mad venture, than he would be alone in London." If Erik had not been so relieved and happy to have Christine alive and before him, he might have been disappointed to hear the familiar lament over Petter.

"Come, I'll take you to him," Erik said. "He will take you back to our rooms, and we can leave Mazenderan at first light."

"Take me?" she asked. "Are you not coming?" The confusion was plain on her face.

Erik was loath to explain, but knew he must. "I have unfinished business in the palace. I do not intend to live our lives under the shadow of Naheed's mad demands."

"What?!" Her confusion melted into shock and anger. "What do you intend?" – and here Christine clutched at him again and did her best to shake him – "Erik, I refuse to allow you to endanger yourself. We are free. Let us go!" She did not seem to notice the wince elicited when her clutching hands contacted his ribs.

"We are not free, my love. We shall never be free," he answered. He made no attempt to free her hands from his shirt, happy to be held by her in any way at all.

"And what? Do you intend to kill her?" she asked.

"I do not," Erik answered.

"You threatened as much when you thought I was she," Christine answered, apparently unbelieving of his calm denial. Her eyes were bright and brittle in the light of the torch, and Erik pondered whether she approved or condemned the act.

"Yes, when I thought you dead at her hands. Her disgusting life for yours. I thought it a fair trade at the time." He brought his hands up to enfold her own, and pressed them to his chest. "With you before me, alive and well, I am myself again."

"Then *what?*" Christine asked, her voice rising several levels above a whisper. Erik brought a hand to her mouth in caution. "Then what?" she repeated in a harsh whisper. "I will not leave you!"

"Shh, love," he whispered, and pulled her to him.

"I will not be placated with your kisses!" she whispered, but she did not push him away. She clutched at him with desperation and again their lips were pressed together. He tasted the salt of fresh tears. After a heated time in which she pressed her body against his and her mouth devoured his, her hands released his shirt and began to move in near frenzy through his hair, over his back, down his buttocks to his thighs, up the front of his thighs. Somehow her hand missed moving over the wound on his thigh, but he would not have stopped her if it had. Her hands seemed to leave burning tracks where they touched him.

He explored her body – at once so familiar to him and yet so longed for, so new under hands that had not touched her in so long. He was not surprised that his body reacted to her touches, to her kisses, but was startled when her hands moved at his belt, at his pants. He thought to put a stop to their recklessness, but again her mouth was on his, and her hands moved over his now bared groin. He moaned through their kisses under her urgent ministrations.

"Yes, Erik, yes," she whispered. She turned in his arms, and his hands – guided by hers – cupped her breasts from his position behind her. He buried his face in her hair and panted, matching her wild breathing with gasps of his own. Without realizing that (or how) she had removed so much of her clothing, he felt his own exposed body pressing against the soft, warm skin of her bare bottom. Her hand guided him into her depths. She undulated against him, ready for him, welcoming him, and his eyes fell to her hips, to their bodies, moving together in the glow of the flickering torchlight. He knew the erotic vision of this frenzied moment of hunger and need would stay with him for the rest of his days.

After some time, they held each other panting in the silence of their satisfaction. In the intoxication of the moment Erik did not wish to release her – indeed ever again – and thought to abandon his plans, to leave the palace with Christine in his arms.

"Thank you, my love" she whispered, and he tightened his arms about her.

She pulled from him, and began the rearrangement of her clothing. "What is your plan, Erik? What is this unfinished business?"

Her words struck him like a sluice of cold water to his chest, constricting his heart and spasming through his limbs.

He pulled at his own clothing as he spoke. "Will you allow me to lead to you safety? Will you allow me to do as I must?" he asked.

She smiled sweetly and raised herself to her toes to kiss him, and he thought she had capitulated. Then she spoke.

"I would sooner scream – and die with you where we stand – than leave you again. We are a pair, we two. I would not have these past moments – as sweet as they were," she brought her hand to his cheek, "be the last time we make love, or if so, only because we have perished together." She bent for her abandoned veils and taking several steps away from Erik, shook the dust from them. "Now, what is your – *our* – plan?"

Erik sighed, closed his eyes and shook his head. His son, and now his wife, and their damnable stubbornness. But, it was the fire within Christine's soul that had first made him love her. He could not wish it away.

He opened his eyes to see the iron in her own. He sighed again, and defeated by his love for her and her demand, explained his plan. When he finished, he said, "And now, I ask you again. Will you let me first lead you to safety?" He held little hope for agreement.

SKELETONS IN THE CLOSET

"It is a good plan," she answered. "I can help you." She turned and took two sinuous steps away from him, then turned again to face him. With the lower pitched voice of the Sultana and the lift of one brow, said, "After all, I am the Sultana."

Erik shuddered at the perfection of the illusion. "Please. Do not."

When she spoke again, it was with her own voice. "I can lead you through the palace. No one will question me. You need not try to find your goal through this impossible maze of tunnels."

Erik did not answer – could not answer against the force of her argument.

"You have said you must hurry. You have said that you have little time." She smiled and licked her lips. "I have stolen a good part of that time for my own selfish purposes…"

"Hardly selfish," Erik interposed, another rising tingle in his groin.

"… and now I can help return that time to you," she finished. "Please, let me help you."

Erik raised his arms and Christine stepped into his embrace. "I love you, wife," he said. He kissed her and taking up the torch again, began leading her down the passage. "I will bring us out in Naheed's wing. We can go from there."

CHAPTER 29
MOTHER AND CHILD

Christine squeezed Erik's hand as he led her through the dark tunnels back the way they had come. The exhilaration that filled her – brought about both by the joy of Erik's hand in her own, and the excitement and tension of what they prepared to do – threatened to bring tears to her eyes again. Tears! The realization brought her to a halt against Erik's insistent pull.

"What is it?" he asked.

"My face," she said. When he looked his lack of comprehension at her, she said, "I am sure my face is quite disordered. Can you see the eye paint in this light? Is anything amiss?"

Erik leaned toward her without bringing the torch any closer. His hand moved up to brush at the skin under one eye.

"I am afraid so," he said. "Just as well. I will proceed as I originally planned." He turned away from her.

"No. Can you take me back to my room?" she asked.

"Your room?"

SKELETONS IN THE CLOSET

"I can lead us to the Sultana's room from there. I can fix the eye paint." When Erik hesitated, she said, "It will take little time, I assure you."

Erik nodded and turned to continue on his way. Christine's heart filled with love and admiration for the speed with which Erik arrived at his decisions, and then acted upon them. She remembered the many fears and hesitations of her imprisonment.

Thank goodness Petter is more like his father in that respect.

With the unexpected moment of insightful comparison, she remembered the reasoning Petter had presented upon making what seemed a sudden decision to go to London. She sighed.

I have been wrong and unfair. Unfair to myself, but even more unfair to Petter and to Erik. I belong with Erik. But Petter belongs to the world.

Christine recognized the approach to her room before reaching it. "Keep going," she said in the barest of whispers. Erik did not look back at her, but squeezed her hand in acknowledgement.

"Here," she said as they reached the Sultana's room. She bent to peer into the room at the corner of the mirror and said, "I will return immediately."

"I'm coming with you," he said.

"Don't be silly. I can explain my presence in 'my' bedchamber, but not yours." When Erik raised a hand and opened his mouth to protest she kissed his chin and triggered the trapdoor. She was being unfair, insisting that she would accompany him in his plan and then denying his ability to accompany her, but she ducked into the wardrobe without hesitation, and crossed the room, not stopping to see if he followed. At the vanity table, she worked to fix the paint around her eyes, and only once dared a glance toward the open wardrobe and the mirror. She imagined Erik on the other side of the mirror, watching her as she worked, and her imagination moved to thoughts of undressing before that mirror, knowing he watched, but unable to see him – and of what would follow.

The excitement of freedom from my imprisonment and his proximity have combined to make me hungry! She smiled as she completed her task. Her hands were not shaking as they had the first time she applied the eye paint. The result was far more precise.

Within minutes she was with Erik again in the tunnels. She left the trapdoor open. "We could proceed from this room, if you wish," she said, gesturing through the wardrobe.

"No, it would be safer to start from farther along Naheed's wing," he answered. He pulled the wardrobe door closed and reset the trapdoor.

"You shall have to lead me while making it appear that I lead you," she said. "I am unfamiliar with the palace."

Erik grunted his understanding as he pulled her back toward and then past her own room. He stopped at a room that appeared unlit through the peephole.

"Are you ready?" he asked. Christine exhaled once and nodded. She reached for her head veil to secure it over her face,

SKELETONS IN THE CLOSET

but Erik stopped her hand and kissed her once more before helping her with the veil.

In moments they were into the darkened room, and then to its door. Christine took a deep breath and wriggled relaxation into her tense muscles before opening the door. When she looked back to Erik, she was in control of her persona as the Sultana. She gestured to him imperiously, and turned away from him, but not before the darkness returned to his eyes with another small shudder.

They walked the corridors of the palace without speaking, except for Erik's occasional directions. "Left, and then up the stairs." Then later, "Right, down this hallway." Christine did not nod or make any other acknowledgement as he spoke. She did not look behind to be sure he followed, and did not turn to see if he walked with head high or bowed low. The Sultana would expect to be followed without question. Only twice did they pass servants in the halls. The servants bowed as she passed. She did not respond or react in any way.

"There. The door with the guards," Erik whispered.

Christine strode toward the guards. They granted her the barest of salutes. Their loyalty was not to the Sultana, although they recognized her position as the daughter of the Shah.

"I wish to enter," she said, lifting one shoulder in a flicker of a shrug and raising her chin, the picture of haughtiness.

After the smallest hesitation, one guard opened the door to the room, entered, and closed the door again. The remaining guard kept his eyes forward, looking neither at Christine nor at her mysterious companion, but Christine felt his careful watchfulness just the same. After another moment during which Christine examined her fingernails and made small impatient clicking sounds by running her thumbnail against a ring, the door opened again.

"You may enter," the reappearing guard said, and stepped aside to let Christine and Erik pass.

Before them a young, plump woman was rising from her position amongst the cushions. To Christine's eyes she seemed very young, but very pretty in her more modest and sedate attire. Her eyes, which Christine thought might often contain laughter, were narrowed with confusion and suspicion at the obvious unexpectedness of this visit.

"You wished to speak to me?" the young woman asked. Her voice was tight with strain. Her long-lashed eyes flickered to Erik and back to Christine.

"Yes," Christine answered. She turned and looked to the two guards who stood at their backs. "I wish to speak to you alone," she said, and flicked a hand at the guards in a gesture of dismissal. Neither guard moved or even looked at her.

Again, the woman's eyes moved to Erik, and this time lingered there. Christine could not blame her – Erik's unmasked face often drew attention – but she was surprised to find curiosity rather than revulsion in the woman's eyes. The woman raised her rounded chin and bringing her eyes back to Christine, said, in a warm contralto, "Guards, please step outside. I will call if I need you."

The guards saluted, and left the room. The door closed on their retreating backs. Christine allowed herself a brief exhale of relief although she did not change her posture. She had done it. She had gotten Erik into the presence of this favored wife of the Shah.

Erik stepped forward and bowed. "Honored wife of the Shah-in-Shah," he said, and the young woman nodded. "I beg your indulgence, and ask that you listen to what I have to say, and do not raise a cry of alarm." The woman brought her hand to her bosom, and Erik continued, "Your life is in danger. Yours, and the life of your young son."

Her lips moved as though she whispered a name or a prayer, and her head turned toward a curtained alcove to her side. Christine knew the fear that must be thrilling through this young woman and she felt an immediate camaraderie. She wanted to embrace her, and comfort her, but forced herself to maintain her stance.

"I come to warn you, and to save your lives if I can," Erik said, and as the woman looked ready to cry out, "I beg you, do not cry out – not if you value your son's life."

Her lip trembled and her eyes again scoured Erik's face. She raised her chin, and turning her attention to Christine, she said, "What know you of this, Naheed, daughter of my husband?" Her voice again was sharp with suspicion. Knowing the Sultana as she did, Christine could not fault the woman's suspicions.

Christine unhitched the veil covering her face, and speaking this time in her own voice, she said, "I am not the Sultana." She took two diminutive steps toward the young woman – walking without the Sultana's customary swagger – and curtsied. "I apologize for the need to deceive you and your guards, but the deception was necessary. This man speaks the truth. Your lives are in danger."

Christine kept her head bowed and waited for the response. Would the woman shout out, or would she listen?

The silence stretched as none of the three moved to break the tableau. Finally, Erik said, "Will you allow me to explain? I speak as the father of a beloved son, and come to be the savior of yours."

After another hesitation, the woman's warm voice said, "I will listen. I should not, perhaps, but Naheed is no friend to me or to my son, and that fact that you are not she," and here she nodded to Christine as her hand came up to touch her own unmarked cheek, "relaxes my suspicion."

"Thank you," whispered Christine. She took another step forward, and the young woman said, "Do not approach. You will remain where you are, and you will speak quickly and convincingly, or I shall raise the alarm." Her hand disappeared under her veils and emerged with a dagger. "And know that you will die before you harm my son." Her eyes blazed as she spoke the last sentence, and again Christine felt a kinship with the woman, knowing the fierceness with which she would fight to protect Petter.

SKELETONS IN THE CLOSET

Christine backed the step she had taken, and Erik backed two steps to stand beside her.

"Honored wife of the Shah-in-Shah," Erik began. "You are not wrong to mistrust Naheed." He told of the Sultana's plans for their deaths this night. She listened without speaking until Erik finished, never relaxing her defensive posture, nor lowering the dagger still gripped in one fist. Only when Erik explained the reason for his own apparent complicity – including the explanation of Christine's capture and the ransom Naheed required of him – did she soften. She raised her free hand toward Christine's face and gestured across the small distance, and while her eyes remained on Christine, she spoke to Erik.

"Your wife has suffered at the hands of the Sultana." She touched her own cheek, dropped her hand to her side, and turned to Erik. "How much easier for you to have done as Naheed required, rather than to warn me. Why have you warned me? What am I to you?"

"Please do not take offense when I say that you are nothing to me. But I have a wife whom I love deeply, and it is well known that you are the favorite of your husband. I have a son for whom I would die, and you are a mother. Apart from that, I do not share Naheed's black heart, and have no taste for killing."

For the first time, the young woman relaxed her stance, and after a glance again toward the curtained alcove, said, "I have listened. What now do you intend?"

"I would have your husband, the Shah, learn of this plot," Erik answered. "Both for your safety, and for ours."

"You have risked much," the woman said, and sighed. "But favorite though I am, I do not think my husband will believe this of his daughter. He is blind with his love for the wretched woman, and I do not think he will accept your word over hers."

"Naheed herself told me that your husband begins to suspect her nature. He will believe," Erik said, but the woman shrugged her shoulders and lowered her head.

Christine, seeing the pain and resignation in the woman's eyes, could no longer contain herself. She took a step toward the woman, hands raised before her. "My husband has a plan," she said. "Will you listen for a small time longer?"

The woman did not raise the dagger again at Christine's forward movement – as Christine thought she might. She looked to Erik and nodded her willingness.

"Honored wife of the Shah-in-Shah," he began again.

"Delara," she interrupted. "You may call me Delara. It means…"

"Beloved," finished Erik.

A tiny smile bent one corner of Delara's mouth as if she found her name ironic or as if Erik had amused her, and then she nodded.

"Delara," Erik began again. "My plan is to show your husband the true nature of his daughter. Surely he would believe her nature if he were given the proof of it?"

"How do you intend to do this?" she asked.

Erik paused before speaking, and Christine could see how he struggled with what he must say, with how he might gain her trust enough to complete his plan.

"You have no reason to trust me, outside of the fact that I have put my life, and the life of my wife, in your hands. I know you need only call the guards and our lives would be forfeit."

"I know it," she answered matter-of-factly.

"I ask you then to trust me," he said. His voice was low, but full of fervent pleading.

"In what should I trust you?" she asked. The suspicion was returning to Delara's voice.

Erik cleared his throat and said, "I ask you to allow me to administer the Mazenderan scent to you. And to your son," he said.

"Absolutely not!" she answered, her voice rising above the calm quiet volume in which all three had been speaking. Her dagger was again extended between them. Heart pounding, Christine turned to look toward the doors, expecting the guards to enter, but the doors remained closed.

"I will explain," Erik continued, but Delara shook her head.

Again, Christine could not restrain herself, although she was interrupting Erik's careful explanation. "Delara, please," she said. "I too am a mother – the mother of a son I have had the pleasure of raising to manhood. He is my pride and delight, and although I have had trouble releasing him into the world…" Christine turned to Erik, and taking his hand, said, "Yes, I see now that I must." Erik squeezed her fingers, but Christine could not take time to bask in the warm approval of his gaze. She turned back to the young mother before her. "I cannot imagine losing him. I cannot imagine not having had all these years with him – and all the years that are to come, seeing what he will make of himself. I cannot imagine losing him through murder. And not if I could do anything to prevent that murder."

Delara again shook her head, but not as vigorously as before, and Christine thought the gesture now represented a denial of the thought of her son's death.

Erik spoke into the pause. "Come, you must know that if your deaths are not achieved this night, the Sultana will attempt to procure your deaths at some other time through some other agent. Can you hope for another warning?"

Delara closed her eyes in painful acknowledgement of Erik's statement and shook her head.

"I am offering you a chance to live," he added.

Christine again took up her impassioned plea. "Again I beg you, as one mother to another, as one beloved wife to another, take the chance my husband is presenting you to save your life and the life of your son – not merely tonight, but forever."

After a moment, Delara spoke. "And of course, to save your lives as well."

"Yes," answered Erik, and again he squeezed Christine's hand, although he did not look toward her. He seemed to hold his breath as he waited for the young woman's answer.

SKELETONS IN THE CLOSET

With a slump to her shoulders, Delara said, "What is your plan?"

Erik explained. Delara's face twisted with anger and outrage when Erik got to the point in the explanation where the Sultana wished to gloat over their dead bodies, and his plan for evading that wish. As he finished, he removed a vial from his sleeve, and said, "So will you?"

Defeat was plain on Delara's face – defeat and fear and sadness. She said, "I will."

Erik stepped toward the young woman, hand outstretched, the vials resting in his open palm. Delara reached toward the offered vials, and then dropped her hand. Her eyes narrowed as another look of suspicion tightened her face.

"Give a vial to your wife. Prove it does not kill," she said, lifting her chin.

"No, I…" Erik began, but Christine interrupted him. She knew what she must do for Delara to overcome her suspicions. It was important to the success of Erik's plans.

"I will take it," Christine said, and rushing forward, she snatched a vial from his hand.

"Christine, I must get you out of the palace," Erik said, and his frustration was evident in the low burr that entered his voice.

"Come back for me then," she said. She put a hand to his face and mouthed three words: I love you. Turning to Delara she said, "Now I must trust you as we are asking you to trust us." Without waiting for any response, she pulled the stopper from the vial. As Erik moved toward her, she bent over the small bottle and inhaled deeply of the rose scented fluid. The room swam in her vision. She reached toward Erik, felt his arms go around her, and then felt nothing at all.

Her last vision before blackness claimed her was of Naheed looming over her, twisting a jeweled dagger. She reached for Erik through the darkness, but he was gone.

CHAPTER 30
ERIK FINDS THE SHAH

Erik caught Christine in his arms even as the open vial fell from her fingers to the floor. He lifted her and pressed her limp body to his, holding her against him to counter his impulse to shake her in his frustration. He raised his head to look at the woman who had forced this upon them, but upon seeing the now complete acceptance in her eyes, he realized that Christine had done well to do as she had. Lifting Christine's head, he brought his forehead to hers, and with eyes closed, whispered, "I will return for you, my wife."

"You love her very much," Delara said. "And she trusts you with her life."

He raised his head to see warm tears in Delara's eyes. He said, "May I lay her down?"

"Of course," Delara answered, and as he moved toward the cushions in the near corner of the room, she said, "No, please, bring her into my bedchamber."

Delara pulled down the bed linens and threw several pillows to the floor. "No one will enter here this night," she said. Erik lowered Christine to the bed and arranged her head and limbs into an attitude of peaceful sleep. As he straightened, eyes still looking down at Christine, he felt a tentative hand on his arm. "I would promise you her safety, but at the moment, I am not assured of my own. If this night goes as you say, if I and my son live to see the sun rising over this palace…" She did not finish, but shrugged and turned away, returning to the room in which they had first spoken. Erik knew why she did not finish her sentence. Even as a favorite wife, she had little power and little protection she could promise. When Erik joined her in the outer room, she was just closing the doors outside which the guards waited.

"I have told my guards that my guests have left through the other guarded entrance to this suite. They believe I am retiring for the night."

Erik nodded, but did not speak or move. It was Delara who must make the next move.

Delara stood rigid, hands behind her and back pressed against the doors as if summoning her courage for what was to come. She walked toward the curtained alcove. She drew aside the curtain and motioned to Erik. When he approached, she said, "My son." She smiled as she gazed into the alcove.

Erik looked into a bassinet at a young boy of no more than two years – probably less. "He is a handsome boy," he said.

Delara dropped the curtain and turned toward Erik with a jerk. She raised her clenched fists and bringing the knuckles of her fists together before him hissed, "*Swear*, on the life of your wife and son, that no harm will come to my son. *Swear it!*"

SKELETONS IN THE CLOSET

Erik backed a step. "I give you my oath that I intend no harm to you or your son. I give you my oath that all I have told you about Naheed and about my plans is true. Beyond that, we are all in the hands of Allah."

Delara murmured a brief prayer under her breath, eyes closed. She pushed the curtain to the side and lifted the small boy into her arms. She moved to the cushions on which she had been seated when they first entered the room, and lowered herself to them. The child stirred in her arms as she settled, and she made small quieting noises as she placed him onto her lap. There were tears in her eyes as she raised her hand to Erik. He unstoppered the small vial and gave it to her. She lowered her head again to her sleeping son, and bending close to him whispered several long phrases. Tears now coursed down her round cheeks and fell on the face of the boy. Drawing the vial toward her own face, but not too near, she inhaled lightly, and said, "Ah, yes," as though confirming the scent as one she knew. She held the vial close to the boy as he breathed several times in the long, deep breaths of sleep. The child's breathing lengthened and became quieter – almost silent. Delara leaned close to the boy's face to confirm that he still breathed. Without raising her eyes from her son's face, she brought the vial to her own nose and sucked in a breath. The hand holding the vial fell to the cushions beside where she reclined, and her body crumpled forward over that of her son.

Erik retrieved the vial, and then pulled Delara's upper body up and laid her back on the cushions.

Now to arrange the bodies where they must be found.

Erik sighed as he lifted the boy from the arms of his mother. He weighed almost nothing. He dreaded moving Delara, for her weight, slight as it would be, could not be carried without paining his leg. He gritted his teeth, determined to complete his task.

***

With Delara and the boy arranged, Erik moved now through tunnels that were clean and obviously frequented. He was near his goal, and he stopped several times to peer into the rooms beyond the tunnel through peepholes and mirrors. Finally, he found what he had been seeking. The Shah – looking older than Erik remembered, for all that he had a very young wife – sat at a desk, reading what appeared to be correspondence. He was turned sideways to the desk, and one bare foot lay propped on a low stool. His mustache, which Erik remembered well, was gray, although it retained its fullness, and still extended in an almost straight line from under his hooked nose to several centimeters beyond his gaunt cheeks. His chin was bare, and his substantial and now gray eyebrows limned deep-set eyes that still seemed bright with intelligence.

This man had placed Erik under a death sentence for knowing the maze of tunnels within the palace in which he lived, and now Erik planned to step from those tunnels and into the Shah's personal presence. Erik drew a long breath and pulled the

SKELETONS IN THE CLOSET

Sultana's jeweled dagger from his belt. All would depend on the next few moments.

He thought of Christine sleeping in Delara's bed – still within the palace, damn it! – and reminded himself of all that would come of his failure here. He had given the Persian strict orders to get Petter out of Mazenderan if neither he nor Christine emerged from the palace by morning, but he worried what Petter might do.

Enough! He steeled himself and pressed the lever that would open the trapdoor into the Shah's chamber. He stepped through into the light.

The Shah raised his head to look at Erik and brought his foot down from the stool, but did not otherwise move, and did not show alarm or surprise.

"I thought you dead," said the old man. He still spoke with a deep and almost musical inflection, although his voice had grown huskier with age. His face remained expressionless. Erik noted the surreptitious movement of the Shah's hand behind the desk and guessed that the man was reaching for a knife or a pistol as he spoke. Erik did not think the man would attack blindly, but his body sprouted perspiration nonetheless. The Shah continued: "I would think you a ghost but for the fact that ghosts do not age, and you have done that."

"Most honored Shah-in-Shah, I have not come to haunt you, but to help you," Erik answered.

"Yet you carry a weapon," the Shah answered, with the lift of one thick eyebrow.

"I carry the dagger that Naheed would plunge into your heart, Sire," Erik answered. For the first time, a fleeting expression of anger or concern entered the man's dark eyes. Erik took a step toward the seated man, but before he could speak again, the Shah's hand lifted from behind the desk. Erik froze as the barrel of an ornately decorated pistol pointed at his face.

"Sire," Erik said, turning the dagger so that the jeweled haft extended toward the older man. "You would not kill the man who would offer your daughter's traitorous knife to you, and in so doing, would save the life of your son."

"My son!" the Shah exclaimed, and jumped to his feet. He still held the pistol pointed at Erik's heart, but now the barrel trembled in the outstretched hand. "What do you know of my son? Speak now or… or…"

"Your son is safe, although your daughter would not have it so," Erik answered. Holding the blade, he extended the dagger toward the Shah, and took another step toward the desk. The Shah backed one step from the desk and kept the pistol raised. When Erik could, he reached forward and placed the dagger on the desk, and then backed with his hands raised.

"I have no other weapons," Erik said, and with arms still raised, turned a slow circle. "I appeal to your honor, Sire. I have made you a gift of my only weapon, and ask that you accept that gift in the spirit of friendship in which I make it."

"Friendship, bah!" bellowed the Shah. "I ask you again, what of my son? Why do you speak so of Naheed?"

SKELETONS IN THE CLOSET

"I do not wish to die, Sire," Erik said. He had not yet received the response from the Shah for which he hoped. He nodded at the pistol, and kept his arms raised.

"Sit down!" bellowed the Shah. Then in quieter tones, "I will not kill a man who is unarmed after presenting me with his weapon. As you know, I am an honorable man – even to a man whom I have already ordered beheaded." Erik lowered his arms, although the Shah had not yet lowered his pistol. He did not sit despite the order, and would not until the Shah himself sat or unless he was ordered yet again. He had dealt often with the Shah during his time in Mazenderan and knew the protocols. The Shah said, "You speak of my son. If my son has been… harmed," – clearly the man could not speak of his son's death – "you will hope for a death as swift as a beheading."

"I will explain, Sire. I am at your service in this, as in all things." Erik bowed as he spoke.

The Shah lowered himself into his chair but still did not lower his pistol. The anger faded from the Shah's face, and again he faced Erik with complete lack of expression. Erik could not help but admire the man's self control. "Speak," he said.

Erik sat. "You have sired other sons. Only this one has survived." Erik watched for a reaction but saw none. "Naheed," Erik said. He let the one word hang in the silence before speaking again. "Naheed was responsible for the deaths of your other sons, and would not have your newest son survive either," Erik continued, and finally the stoic expressionlessness crumbled.

"This cannot be so," said the Shah, but the pain that creased his face belied his belief in his statement.

"It is so, and I can provide you the proof of her current intentions," Erik said.

"This cannot be so!" shouted the Shah, and again he stood, with such force that his chair nearly overturned.

Erik stood. "I can explain."

The Shah crumpled to his seat again, and placing the gun on the table, rubbed his fingers along his forehead above his eyes. "Damn you to your infidel's hell," he said. Then: "Explain, and quickly."

Erik explained.

When he finished, the Shah asked, "What do you suggest? What you tell me sounds far-fetched, even if I were to admit that I have come to suspect Naheed of certain… intrigues within these walls." The Shah's voice was weary.

"I suggest you summon guards and come to a place where you can see the truth of the treachery."

The Shah rose, lifted the pistol and the dagger from the desk, then turned away from Erik. When he returned, he was flanked by four palace guards, and no longer carried the pistol. His daughter's dagger was tucked into the front of his belt.

"We wait," said the Shah. He seated himself, and again raised a foot to the small stool. The minutes passed in silence, with the Shah at ease and the guards stiff in their positions behind their seated ruler, eyes fixed on Erik. At last a fifth guard entered the room and saluted.

"Speak," said the Shah.

"They are not in their rooms, Sire. There is a strange woman in your wife's bed, whom the guards say entered earlier this evening in the guise of the Sultana. She entered with your wife's permission."

"What is this?" said the Shah, snapping his head to glare at Erik.

"My wife," answered Erik, and wiping his perspiring palms on his pants legs, he turned to the guard. "What have you done with her?"

The guard addressed the Shah. "She could not be roused, Sire. We left a guard but did not disturb her. What are your wishes?"

"Leave her under guard," the Shah said. Turning to Erik he said, "My wife. My son. Do you know where they are?" His narrowed eyes were a mixture of knife blades and concern.

"They are well. I will take you to them," Erik answered.

"Lead," the Shah said. He rose as he spoke.

Erik moved around the other side of the desk from the Shah and his guards, unwilling to give the guards cause to fear for their Shah. "We will need to go to Naheed's wing," he said.

As they approached the proper wing, two guards came into view, both of whom rose from the squatting positions they maintained with their backs pressed against the walls. Both saluted the Shah. The group had almost passed the guards when the Shah turned to one of the now erect guards. "Has the Sultana Naheed returned?" he asked.

"No, Sire," the guard answered. His eyes were directed at the wall ahead of him, and not toward the Shah. The Shah grunted in response, and Erik again began walking. He wondered if the guards would report this strange late night entourage to the Sultana when she did return.

Erik led the Shah to Naheed's bedchamber. "With your permission, Sire," Erik said. The Shah stepped past him, and threw open the doors. Erik led the man to the washroom. The guards followed.

Erik crossed the lavish washroom, around and past the enormous sunken tub. The Shah, losing what small patience he had retained thus far, roared, "Where do you lead me? What is the meaning of this? This is a wash room!"

"With your permission, Sire, may I request that your guards stay in this room, while we enter the next?"

"Sire!" The largest of the guards stepped forward, interposing himself between Erik and the Shah. "This cannot be permitted!"

"Cannot?" asked the Shah. "Do you doubt your king's ability to protect himself against this…," his eyes raked Erik and his hand raised and lowered as he gestured with disdain to Erik's thin frame, "one man?" In truth, even in the slight stoop of the Shah's age, he stood taller and stouter than Erik.

SKELETONS IN THE CLOSET

"N-no," stuttered the guard. Then with a backward thrust of his shoulders and a forward thrust of his bearded chin, he said, "May we be permitted to search your most honored guest?"

"He is not my honored guest. He is a fly in a festering wound," the Shah grumbled. Then with a gesture to the guard, "Search him."

Erik allowed himself to be searched, pleased with his own foresight in leaving his boot knife in the tunnel.

"Proceed," growled the Shah. "But I warn you, if nothing comes of this charade, not even my well-earned reputation for justice and mercy will save you." Erik heard the harsh words, but knew that they masked a grave uncertainty on the part of the Shah toward his daughter, and a growing fear for his son. Without that uncertainty and fear, Erik could not have led the Shah this far. Erik smiled as he opened another door at the far side of the washroom and gestured the Shah to enter. For the first time the Shah hesitated.

"It is a room for linens and such. And it is dark," he said.

"This room is more than it seems," Erik answered. "And there is a light, although dim. Your eyes will adjust."

"This is ridiculous," said the Shah.

"This is necessary," Erik answered. "I have promised you information and the safety of…" Erik paused to choose his words. It would not do to refer to the safety of the Shah's son, or the possibility of the son's murder. The already anxious guards may not then allow themselves to be restrained. "…certain personages of importance to you." Erik pointed into the room toward what appeared to be a small window from which a dim light emerged.

The Shah grunted and stepped into the room. When a guard tried to stop Erik from closing the door, Erik said, "Sire, no light must enter this room." The Shah nodded with a jerk of his head and gestured toward the guard. The guard stepped back and Erik pulled the door to.

Erik did not yet move toward the lighted window. Instead he said, "You must believe me when I tell you that your wife and son are well, although they will not appear so. It is a deception to which your wife agreed. With the deception, you will learn much of your daughter's intentions."

"Enough of your circuitous babble!" the Shah said.

"Step to the window, Sire," Erik said. He stood back, already knowing what the Shah would see, and unwilling to stand too close to the man in the moment of shock he knew was coming.

The old man ambled through the darkness to the window, and after peering through it, gasped and turned his back to it, head bowed, cupped hands raised to his face. Erik heard several murmured prayers. When the Shah raised his head, Erik could see nothing of his expression, only the outline of his head against the window. The old man took a stumbling step toward Erik, and Erik reached out arms to support him. The Shah righted himself and lunged at Erik, one hand closing on Erik's throat. The coolness of a knife blade kissed his neck above the Shah's constricting hand.

SKELETONS IN THE CLOSET

"They are dead, and now you will die," the Shah hissed between clenched teeth. "Tell me, traitor, before I open your throat. What was the purpose of your treachery?"

Body lifted onto his toes, chin raised in an effort to escape the blade at his throat, Erik spoke. "They are not dead, Sire, I swear it. They merely appear so. Your daughter demanded to see the bodies. If you will but have patience…"

"I will not. I am tired of your lies!" The knife bit into Erik's neck.

"Sire!" The word burst from Erik. "Time will prove me correct and you will have killed an innocent man who has saved the life of your son. If I am lying, your wife and son will be no less dead for the passage of time. I will not be able to escape this room without your knife avenging you, and even if I could, your guards would not leave me alive." The pressure of the knife eased. Erik panted once and said, "Sire, my life is in your hands. I beg you to patience."

The knife fell away from Erik's throat. The Shah moved to the window again, and when he spoke, his voice was rough with emotion. "There is much blood," he said.

"A ruse, Sire, nothing more," Erik said. He touched his throat where the knife had bitten him, then rubbed his thumb against the viscous liquid coating his fingers.

The Shah was silent as he continued to peer through the window. After several minutes, a light knock sounded at the door. The Shah went to it, and after cracking it to peer at the uneasy guard, said, "Do not disturb me. I will emerge in my own time, whether or not this mongrel dog emerges with me." He closed the door again and returned to the window.

"What is that room?" he asked after another long silence. "I was to have the complete plans of the palace, but I know nothing of this room."

"You have the complete plans of the palace, Sire. Your daughter refers to this room as the 'chamber,' and it was constructed for the… special entertainment of the young Sultana. This room is labeled as one of the Sultana's rooms on the plans."

"I have not explored my daughter's rooms," the Shah answered. Then, as though speaking to himself, "Perhaps I should have done." After several more minutes, the Shah said, "How long am I to wait? How long am I to look upon this terrible scene?"

"I do not know when the Sultana will return, Sire. Only that she will."

"I cannot stand this sight." The Shah grunted and moved away from the window. Erik moved to the window and took up the watch. The interior of the chamber below had changed much since he last had seen it. Only a few of the large mirrors remained, and much evil equipment had been added. And there, on the floor, the bodies of Delara and the Shah's son, appearing quite dead.

The only sound while they waited was that of the impatient pacing of the Shah behind him.

CHAPTER 31
THE SULTANA

An interminable hour passed, with the Shah pacing and Erik standing at the window, looking down at the gruesome scene below.

Would the Sultana come this night as she said she would? Would she stop and look in on Christine first? How would she react, finding Christine gone?

The darkness and the quiet and the length of the wait left Erik ample opportunity to plague himself with second thoughts. How long would Petter and Faraz wait? Would Petter leave his post at the Persian's urging if a new day should dawn without the emergence of either Erik or Christine? Would Petter attempt to enter the palace?

Just as Erik began his own pacing in the small room, the unmistakable voice of the Sultana sounded from the room below.

Speaking? To whom would she be speaking?

Erik turned to the window, only to be pushed aside by the Shah. Erik eased back for a view of the torture chamber. Shoulder to shoulder, the men stood looking down on the scene unfolding below them.

The Sultana – dressed in the splendor appropriate to her evening engagement – slid into view. She slapped her palms together like a delighted child as her eyes fixed on the bodies. Speaking over her shoulder to a person not yet visible, she said, "Wonderful!" and clapped her hands together several times. "Do you not agree?"

Erik gasped as a second figure came into view. It was Faraz, looking somewhat green despite his dark complexion, and turning his eyes from the scene before him.

"Oh, come, Faraz. Can you not share my pleasure?" she purred, and then she threw back her head and laughed.

"Who is this man – this Faraz?" asked the Shah, too loudly. Eschewing protocol, Erik hushed the man with a hand to his mouth, hoping the Sultana's laugh had covered the Shah's question. The Sultana did not appear to have heard. Erik breathed his relief in one long, low breath.

"Who is this man?" asked the Shah again, whispering this time.

"A friend," Erik answered. His mind whirled as he tried to fathom the reason behind Faraz's presence in this room with the Sultana. Did Naheed discover him and threaten him into accompanying her? Or perhaps this was the Persian's way of gaining entrance to the palace to look after Erik's own safety? His mind returned to the Sultana as she slithered toward the prostrate wife.

SKELETONS IN THE CLOSET

Naheed stood above Delara turning her head this way and that, as though appreciating the beauty of the apparent corpse that lay at her feet. With a feral snarl, she pulled back one leg and kicked at the woman's ribs, and then hips. The Shah jerked against him, and Erik heard a small gasp.

"How dare she?" The Shah whispered, and Erik could tell from the hiss of the words that he whispered through clenched teeth. Erik did not respond.

Erik's eyes moved to Faraz, who had not advanced any further into the room. Faraz's head swiveled as he glanced toward the ceiling and along each of the walls. The man's knowing eyes paused when they reached the small window at which Erik and the Shah stood watching. To any person within the torture chamber, this window would appear to be another small mirror, but Faraz was familiar enough with the chamber to recognize the window for what it was. Erik wished he could give Faraz some sign that the bodies were not corpses, that these proceedings were being watched, but he could not do so without also alerting the Sultana.

The Sultana walked a slow circle around her father's wife and crouched to poke the woman in the cheek. "Still warm," she said. "Oh how I wish I could have done the deed myself!"

"She is mad," whispered the Shah.

"Yes," whispered Erik in return. For his own part, he hoped Naheed would not bend and lick at the blood that lay pooled under Delara's head – as she might. She would know then that she had been deceived.

Erik almost sighed aloud when the Sultana stood, and then he flinched as she again kicked at the unmoving body of the woman.

"I will send my guards," said the Shah.

"That may be best, Sire."

Clearly the Shah had seen enough of Naheed's performance to be convinced of the truth of Erik's accusations, and leaving Naheed any more time with the bodies may indeed be fatal.

The Shah turned away from the window just as Faraz spoke his first words. He spoke loudly and clearly, and Erik knew from the man's second quick glance toward the window that Faraz hoped to elicit more information. "Now that you have accomplished these deaths, what do you plan for the future, Naheed?"

Erik clutched at the arm of the retreating Shah, and drew him back to the window. "Wait, Sire," he said. "You may yet learn more."

The Sultana glanced over at the body of the little boy, and then turned back to Faraz. She leapt over the body of the prone woman and walked toward Faraz. The movement of her hips from side to side was heightened even over her normally exaggerated sway. She lifted and lowered one shoulder and arm and then the other, as if she swam in the air. "I have won," she said. "I have won again. I will soon marry some ambitious idiot and rule when my father dies."

SKELETONS IN THE CLOSET

She reached the Persian and running a finger from his cheek down the front of his shirt in a wavy downward movement, she asked, "Would you like to be that man?"

Faraz stiffened and stepped back from the woman as her finger reached the front of his pants. "Certainly not," he said.

She laughed. "I would not allow it," she answered as she walked around Faraz, one arm extended toward him, the hand running around his shoulders and back as she walked. "I told you I need an idiot, and you are far too intelligent to qualify. Besides, I don't like you." She turned away from him and back to the sight of the woman and boy lying in what appeared to be their own blood. "My brother," she crooned, and began to walk toward the boy.

"The Shah is still hale," the Persian said. "Or do you have plans for his demise as well?"

The Sultana turned to face the Persian, but continued her sinuous progress toward the boy by stepping backwards.

"No," she said. "He allows me all the time and leisure to do as I like – and you *know* what I like." She raised both arms into the air and twirled like a ballerina as she passed the body of the woman. "Of course," she went on, "I may have to poison him if he takes too long to die, or is rude enough to bear another son," she said. She giggled, and continued her slow approach toward the boy.

The Shah stiffened and a low growl sounded in the small room.

"The guards, Sire," said Erik, turning from the window and walking toward the door. He felt certain that the Shah had heard enough, and he did not want Naheed harming the boy with the same vicious kicks she had delivered to the mother.

Erik did not need to press the Shah. He preceded Erik, who paused only long enough to close the door to the viewing room they had just vacated.

"This way, Sire," Erik said, as the Shah gestured to the guards. They ran, although Erik had to clutch at his ribs as he ran, and his limp became so exaggerated that he stumbled twice.

"There," said Erik, pointing to a door. He was panting, and stood bent from the waist, both arms now clutched about his middle.

"Quickly!" said the Shah. The four guards burst through the door, with the Shah close behind them. "Arrest them!" the Shah bellowed.

Two guards rushed to the unmoving Persian, who stood his ground and allowed them to bind his hands. The two others ran to the Sultana. The Shah loped with powerful strides to his son.

"Father," the Sultana cried. "Thank Allah you have come. I have found the man who has killed your son," she yanked an arm free from one guard and pointed to Faraz, "although I did not arrive in time to stop the murders." She sobbed once as if heartbroken, bringing her wrist melodramatically to her forehead. When the guard again gripped her wrist, she progressed from sobbing to anger.

"Release me!" she shrieked. "Father!"

SKELETONS IN THE CLOSET

The Shah did not give any indication he could hear his daughter's protests. The old man bent and lifted the limp body of his son, bringing his ear first to his son's mouth, and then to his chest. When he raised his head again, his eyes moved to the struggling Sultana.

"Father, don't you hear me?" She struggled against the grip of the guards as she spoke. "That is the man who killed your son! We must question him. He may have compatriots." She ceased her struggles, and tilting her head to one side in the attitude of a very young girl, said, "Father, tell these men to release me."

"No, Naheed," he answered.

"I don't understand…" she began, a look of innocence widening her eyes.

Erik limped another two steps into the room, gaining Naheed's attention. Her eyes narrowed to mere slits as her innocent face melted into a look of malevolent hatred. "Noooo!" she howled. The howl continued as her struggles resumed.

"Take her away," the Shah said. "Put her under lock and key in the dungeon – do not return her to her quarters." Naheed continued to struggle and shriek, and the guards were forced to carry her as she kicked at them. Her head veil fluttered to the ground and her hair flipped and twisted about her face as though caught in a great storm.

Erik, limping toward the Shah, turned to Faraz where he stood, still flanked by two guards. He smiled grimly at the tall man, but Faraz did not return the smile.

"My son lives," said the Shah. He pulled the small body tighter to his chest.

Erik bent and rolled Delara onto her back, cradling her head in one hand as he did so. He bent to listen for her breath, and felt at her neck for a pulse. "As does your wife, Sire, as promised."

The Shah bowed his head, eyes closed, and then raised his head to Erik again. He straightened his posture to his full height, and said, "You are free to go. They say, 'The wise enemy lifts you up, the ignorant friend casts you down.' It seems I have many ignorant friends, and I thank Allah you are a wise enemy." Again he bowed his head to Erik.

Erik said, "Why enemy, Sire? I have never broken faith with you. I have tonight accepted your friendship with the gift of my knife and been witness to your heroism. Is there no Persian saying about the wise friend?"

"No," the Shah answered as he turned away.

Erik's attention was drawn toward several additional guards entering the room at a half trot.

"Remove my wife to her quarters," the Shah said. "See to it that she is cleaned and cared for." Turning to Erik he said, "She will awaken soon?"

Erik nodded.

"You are free to go," the Shah repeated. "You have won your reprieve." Erik opened his mouth to speak but the Shah spoke over him. "This reprieve will last for the one day necessary to leave Mazenderan forever. If you speak of what you know," and the

Shah rolled his eyes about the room, which Erik understood to indicate the palace and its numerous tunnels, "your reprieve will be revoked. If you ever return to Mazenderan, your reprieve will be revoked."

The Shah hefted the boy in his arms to more securely carry him, and turned toward the door.

"Sire," Erik said, stepping forward to intercept him. "May I retrieve my wife? I will go under guard, of course."

The Shah considered, then nodded and said, "A wife for a wife." The Shah attempted to step around Erik, and again Erik blocked his way.

"I beg your indulgence for a moment more. Will you also release my friend?" He nodded toward Faraz.

"I will not," the Shah answered, and turned to peer at Faraz. He took two steps in the direction of the motionless man and said, "I know this man. He is Akhtar, my old daroga. He was exiled for bungling my orders to put you to death, and now I see that he did not merely bungle. He failed utterly. He will be put to death as a failure to his Shah." Faraz's dour face folded into greater grimness, and he bowed his head.

"Sire," Erik persisted. "This man was instrumental in causing the Sultana to reveal herself to you. In so doing, he has shown nothing but the utmost loyalty to his Shah." When the Shah did not answer, Erik said, "I ask this of you. I, the man who, this night, saved the lives of your family."

The Shah shook his head and said, "No." He strode toward the door.

Stricken, Erik looked to Faraz. His mind whirled with how he might extricate the Persian from this terrible fate. He barely noticed when the Shah stopped at the door and turned toward him again.

"If the man, Faraz," the Shah said, his voice resounding through the room, "ever returns to Mazenderan, he will face immediate death." The Shah jerked his head in the direction of the Persian. It took several seconds for his words to register upon Erik's tumultuous thoughts.

Erik bowed, and said, "Thank you, Sire. You are indeed as merciful as you are just."

"In this case, I am neither merciful nor just. I refuse to acknowledge having seen this man here tonight. The man whom I have exiled has never returned to Mazenderan. He would not be foolish enough to do so." Turning to the guards, he said, "Release this man and escort him from the palace." Motioning toward Erik with his head, he said, "Lead this man to his wife, and then escort him from the palace as well. See that this is done immediately."

"Thank you, Sire," Erik said to the Shah's retreating back.

Faraz approached Erik and held out his hand. "It is good to see you again, old friend."

"Yes," answered Erik. "There were several times this night when I thought we might never meet again."

SKELETONS IN THE CLOSET

"It is as Allah wills it," Faraz answered. He threw an arm about Erik's back, and helped Erik limp from the room.

CHAPTER 32
PETTER RETURNS TO LONDON

It was not until the ship passed from the Aegean to the Mediterranean Sea, and Crete could be seen off the bow that anyone would agree to salve Petter's burning curiosity. The journey from Mazenderan to this point was thus disappointing to Petter for two reasons: He was locked in the doldrums which come at the end of any adventure, and even worse, those doldrums were not alleviated by any fanciful tale telling.

"Your mother needs to rest," was the first excuse Petter heard for not being told what had occurred within the palace. This excuse held a great deal of weight for Petter. He had been horrified when first he saw his mother, dirty, tired, and with those awful scars on her face. He was not horrified with the disfigurement so much as he was horrified in his contemplation of the pain she had endured receiving the scars. He wondered more than once if her body bore other scars that were not visible, but he could not bring himself to ask. He was not certain he wanted to know.

Christine had slept almost the entire first three days of their journey, waking only to eat between sleep periods. Petter fussed over her as much as his father would allow, which was not much.

But after those three days of sleep, Christine had seemed her old self – energetic and cheerful.

"Your father needs to heal, dear," had been the second excuse. Petter did not accept this excuse for more than a day, as his father had been injured before even coming to London to gather Petter into the adventure, and had not allowed those injuries to slow him much. In truth, it seemed those injuries had been exacerbated during Erik's hours in the palace, but not so much that Erik couldn't sit and talk.

"Wait until we've passed Constantinople, and left danger behind," had been the final excuse. "Until then, we are all too tense and too ready for catastrophe to wish to discuss much at all." Though unhappy, Petter had accepted this final excuse because it seemed to him that this one included a finite deadline that would soon be reached.

Petter forced himself to stand at the rail until the Aegean Sea and more than half of the Island of Crete was behind them. With a firmness of jaw and a resolute stride, he went below decks to make his demand for information.

He knocked at the door to the largest cabin – that shared by his father and mother – and entered when answered. He faced his mother, his father and the Persian, all sitting about a small dining table spread with a veritable feast.

"Now see here," he said, closing the door behind him. He was greeted with good-natured laughter by all.

"We've been waiting for you, dear," Christine said, motioning to the bench on which the Persian sat. "We made bets as to how long after we left Constantinople you would wait." She smiled as Erik chuckled again.

Petter moved toward the offered seat, "Who won?" Again this was answered with laughter by all.

"I certainly lost," answered Erik. "I didn't think you would wait until we reached Crete."

"If it makes you feel any better, Petter," Christine continued, after pouring him a cup of wine and passing it to him, "Not one of us has heard the story of the other. We were not so rude as to salve our own curiosity whilst rebuffing yours."

"Do you wish to start by telling your tale?" Erik asked him.

"My tale?" Petter asked. "I stood around with horses, counting the hours and getting sore feet!"

Again, gentle laughter. Erik sobered and said, "And staying safe."

"Yes, and staying safe," echoed Christine. She put a hand over his and patted it. She reached for a bit of dark bread as Erik reached for cheese. The Persian occupied himself with flatbread and a chickpea spread.

"So?" Petter asked. "You've made me wait this long and now we're going to eat in silence?"

"I think your mother should start," Erik said. "I have only heard the barest of details myself."

SKELETONS IN THE CLOSET

"Which is more than I've heard," Petter muttered to himself, but he could not maintain his pique. He gathered a bunch of grapes into his palm and prepared to listen.

Christine told her tale as a storyteller might, creating sumptuous images in Petter's mind – of her lavish prison room, of the fear she felt in the presence of the mad Sultana, of her discovery of Erik's tunnels and her explorations thereof.

"You must never speak of these to anyone," Erik admonished the others, but he was waved to silence by all.

Thankfully, Christine did not spend much time or description over the Sultana's maiming of her face, for Petter had already used his own imagination to great effectiveness in that regard. Finally, she told of her bold plan to impersonate the Sultana and achieve her escape. It was not quite coincidence that this happened to be the night on which Erik infiltrated the palace, for – as Erik explained – this was the night on which the Sultana absented herself, making certain that all in the palace knew she would be away.

Erik and Christine laughed as they recounted their nearly disastrous meeting in the halls of the palace.

"But how did you come to be searching the halls for the Sultana, Father?" Petter asked. "You thought her out for the evening. I didn't think wandering the palace halls was part of the plan."

"It was not," Erik said. "Perhaps I should back up and explain my doings before finding your mother."

He explained.

"But Father, if you found Mother so soon after entering the palace, why the hours before you emerged?"

Erik looked to Christine, but she said, "You had better continue the narrative from here."

"Yes, do," said the Persian, "for I, like Petter, was not aware of any additional plans outside of Christine's rescue." He cocked his head at Erik as if annoyed, and then allowed his pursed mouth to melt into a knowing smile.

With an embarrassed sigh, Erik explained his plan to keep the Sultana from ever disrupting their lives again.

Even though all had ended well, Petter was aghast to learn of Erik's secondary plan – the plan to entrap the Sultana into revealing herself to the Shah – and even more horrified to hear of his mother's involvement. And, again, even though all had ended well, Petter could not control his outraged response: "Father, you might have been killed!"

"There was no great danger to me," Erik said. Faraz snorted.

"To mother then," Petter said.

Christine spoke, "I involved myself. Your father tried to dissuade me."

When Petter cast a look of doubt toward his mother, Erik said, "She threatened to scream and bring the palace security down on us if I did not let her accompany me. Impetuous woman!" He brought her fingers to his mouth to take the sting from the exclamation, and said, "And you, son, are much like her. With my wounds near healed…" – Petter guffawed – "it is why I did not want you in the palace with me. Much as I trust and cherish you, I thought you might do something rash!"

"We have both learned from a master," Petter shot back, and then laughed at his father's wounded expression.

"Now, you, Faraz. How is it you came to be with the Sultana in the torture chamber?" Erik asked.

"With the Sultana?" came the response from both Christine and Petter at once. Petter muttered, "Everyone in it but me."

"I am ashamed to say that the Sultana surprised me," Faraz began. "It seems my instincts as a police officer are waning." He coughed into his hand and continued. "After she playfully admonished me for entering Mazenderan against her wishes – you know how the woman operates – she asked the purpose of my sentry duty. I explained that I was waiting for you and Christine to emerge, so that we might be away. She laughed again and told me that neither of you would leave the palace with your lives, and told me I should go. When I refused, she insisted I accompany her – not doubt to dispatch me as well – and the speed with which she produced a dagger was compelling. Of course, I believe I could have overtaken her. Instead, I allowed her to believe her threat convincing, and accompanied her. I hoped once inside the palace that I could prove of some service to you."

"And so you were," answered Erik. "The Shah was distraught over Naheed's apparent desire to destroy his wife and son, but her confession of an intention to commit fratricide was a worse crime in his eyes."

"What will he do with Naheed, do you think?" Christine asked.

"Do you worry for her, wife, even after her treatment of you?" Erik asked.

"I do not like the idea of anyone being executed – murdered," Christine answered.

"Yes," Erik answered. "Your son has inherited your forgiving heart. He brought me back to rationality several times during our journey when my worry for you and my rage threatened to overtake me." He mused and said, "Thank goodness for you both." He leaned across the table to grip Petter's hand then raised a hand to Christine's face, ran a thumb under the scar there.

Christine brought her hand up to meet his. "These are nothing," she said. Petter could not agree with that assessment, but did not respond to her statement.

"It is true she has not marred your beauty one whit," Erik answered and leaned toward Christine to kiss her on the cheek. "Your beauty has always been within you."

"As yours is in you," she answered. They gazed into each other's eyes. Petter could not help rolling his eyes to the ceiling, feeling the air in the room thicken with their sentimentality. The Persian, apparently agreeing, coughed into his hand.

Christine giggled and blushed as she looked away from her husband. "So," she said. "The adventure is concluded and life goes on. What are your plans, you two?" She looked from Petter to the Persian and back.

"With Naheed restrained, I shall return to my flat on the Rue de Rivoli and take up my rather placid existence," Faraz answered. "Despite my insistence on helping my friends, this adventure was more than I thought it might be, and I will return to my quiet comfort."

"And you, son? Will you return to London?" Christine asked.

His mother would not be pleased with his answer – she seemed to worry over him to excess. He braced himself for tears and pleading, and ducked his head as he spoke. "Yes, London. As you know, I have hopes of establishing a career."

"Wonderful! I know you shall, for you are as brilliant as your father, and had better training than he," she answered. Petter raised his head in astonishment. "And," she continued, after giving him a tiny wink, "I understand you have a young girl there, a love interest."

"Y-yes," Petter stammered, looking between the two smiling faces of his parents. "Constance. She is quite..." He could not finish his thought. He realized with a jarring sense of loss how long it had been since he had thought of Constance. The smile that had started at his mother's new acceptance of his decision to go to London faltered and fell from his face.

"Quite...?" prompted his mother.

"Quite… beautiful," he answered. His mood spiraled down as he realized he did not feel uplifted at the thought of seeing Constance again, but instead was worried at her displeasure over his long absence, and over what new suitors he may have to fend off.

"I should like to meet her before we leave London," Christine said, but all her brightness could not lift Petter from the worries that now had him chewing at the inside of his lip.

CHAPTER 33
PETTER AND HIS LOVE

After the conversation aboard ship near Crete, Petter's impatience to be back in London became acute. He fussed and fretted over a letter to Constance, and then wrote a more comfortably composed letter to Phoebe, telling both of his imminent return. He posted the letters upon their arrival in Marseille. For all his excitement over the idea of returning to work with Mr. Evans and to his friendship with Phoebe, he was sick with worry over Constance. What gift could he bring her from Paris that would be sufficient? What excuse could he give for not having written more often? He could not tell her the details of his daring adventure, for it would require explaining too much about his father's past, and what little Petter had learned had aimed him toward caution. The need for caution was emphasized when upon reaching Paris, Christine declined Erik's invitation to visit the Opera House where they had met.

At Erik's suggestion, her eyes had first brightened, but then she had smiled sadly, and said, "I think not, my love. I do not wish to be recognized."

The Persian had agreed. "You are thought to be deceased, my friend," he said. "It might be best not to raise questions."

"Yours is all the music I need," Christine had said, rising on her toes to kiss her husband's disappointed face. Petter's curiosity over these enigmatic statements was blunted by his hope that his mother's refusal would hasten their departure for London. His hopes were quickly realized, for the next day – after a brief shopping excursion during which Petter bought Constance a magnificent Parisian scarf – they began the last leg of their journey.

"I must first see Constance alone," Petter told his parents when, upon arriving at his London flat, he found her invitation to call upon her.

"Of course," answered his mother with a knowing smile. "We can meet her after you have been reunited." Petter could not understand the scowl that crept over his father's features, but he did not puzzle long over it. He set about writing a note announcing his return to the city and asking for an immediate appointment. Her response was prompt, and it was only then, in the effusiveness of the moment, that Petter could say, "And you must meet my employer. He is a most generous man, and seems to appreciate my work. You will like him. Father did."

"Indeed, I did," answered Erik. "And his lovely daughter."

"Yes, Phoebe. She's a darling friend," Petter said as he tightened his tie over a fresh shirt. With a peck at his mother's jaw – he was too afraid of hurting her to kiss her cheek although he had seen his father do so – he said, "I must be off. I mustn't be late."

He was still bursting with energy when he arrived at Constance's residence. He tucked the elaborate gift box under one arm and pulled his jacket into proper submission. He nearly ran past the sedate butler in his haste to see, once again, his beautiful Constance.

"Petter, how nice!" she said upon his entrance into the sitting room. On the entire ride to her residence, he had imagined the two of them rushing into each other's arms, and while he was prepared for such a heartfelt reunion, he faltered as he approached her. Instead of rising to enter his arms (he had imagined the crush of her against him), she remained sitting, one hand stretched out toward him. Her smile was so fetching, so blinding, that he could not speak through his own stretched lips. He adopted a more respectful approach as he raised his hand to take hers.

"Constance," he said as he bent over her hand. He allowed his lips to just brush the smooth skin of her knuckles. In his mind, he called her "my love," but he could not bring himself to say the words. He felt a renewing of her affection was necessary before turning to such endearments.

"Sit, Petter," she said, and gestured to a facing chair. He stopped himself in the act of turning to join her on the couch, and moved to the indicated chair. The worry that had overwhelmed him since just before reaching France seized him again, and his eyes fluttered to the side table and the fresh new bouquet of roses that sat there. He turned back to Constance's smiling face.

"Did you get my letters?" he asked, not knowing what else to say. She dropped her eyes and a slight blush crept up her cheeks.

"Yes, Petter. You flatter so prettily," she answered. When she said nothing more, Petter once again could think of nothing to say. He glanced down, and only then remembered the gift box he carried.

"I brought you a gift. I got it in Paris." He stood to present her with the box, fluffing the ribbon as he held it out to her.

"Oh, Petter, how nice," she said, with another fetching flutter of her lashes, but she did not reach for it. "Of course, I cannot accept it."

"What?" Petter said.

"Why, it would be improper," she said, and again she dropped her eyes, "now that I am engaged to be married."

Petter backed the few steps to the chair he had vacated, and then fell into the chair as his knees gave way. "Engaged?" he asked. "I've only been gone a short time."

"He is the loveliest young man," she said, brightening. "You would like him. He already has money of his own, and he is due to inherit five thousand pounds a year on his father's death." Nodding in open-faced sincerity, she said, "He's just the loveliest young man."

"I see," said Petter. He could barely utter the words through the bitterness that filled his mouth. He lifted one hand to scratch at his forehead and lowered his gaze to the floor. For a wild irrational moment, he thought to drop to his knees and plead with her, but his mind took him back to the first time he had called on her. He recalled the disdain on her face as she spoke to a disappointed suitor. *Don't be such a bore.* He could not remember the man's name, but then, perhaps neither could she.

With pain and something akin to disgust making his limbs heavy, he raised his gaze from the floor to Constance. There she sat, still smiling, still beautiful after a fashion, but now utterly unattractive to him.

He stood, and holding himself erect with his gift box again tucked under his arm, he said, "I congratulate you, Constance. I wish you the best." He bowed his head to her, and said, "Thank you for agreeing to see me. I will take up no more of your time." He pushed his words through the dull pain blossoming in his chest.

"Must you go?" she asked, and she tilted her head and puckered her perfect lips into a pout. Petter was incredulous.

I have been a fool, he though. *But no longer!*

"I must," he answered. He bowed more deeply this time, turned, and walked from the room with all the dignity he could muster.

She called from behind him as he crossed the threshold. "I hope you will call on me another time, Petter. I always find your visits so pleasant."

Petter shuddered as the butler closed the door behind him. What had he ever seen in the greedy, manipulative girl? She was not *that* beautiful.

He brooded on the return trip to his flat. What would he tell his parents? After all the ruckus he had raised over the girl, what would he say? He glanced at his watch and decided that he would take them to meet Mr. Evans. This would allow him to say little and distract them all, giving him time to think. He was nearly to his flat when he stopped, and with a bow, handed the gift box to a passing elderly woman. She was poorly dressed, and had he been of a lighter mood, her surprised expression would have made him laugh.

His demeanor on reaching his flat must have told more than he meant his parents to know, for as soon as he entered, his mother said, with an uncertain quiver to her voice, "How did your meeting go?"

"Not well, but do not be concerned." Forcing a humor he did not feel, he said, "Would you care to meet Mr. Evans, my employer?"

"Indeed!" his father responded. He donned his mask, and with nothing more said about Constance, they were on their way.

***

"Petter!" Petter heard Phoebe's animated greeting before he saw her. She rushed to him from her drafting table, her dark eyes radiating the pleasure evident in her smile. She paused before him, eyes glittering as they met his. She turned to Erik, and with a small curtsey, said, "It is a pleasure to see you again, Mr. Nilsson."

"And you, my dear," Erik said. He smiled as he took her hand and bowed over it.

"This is my mother, Christine," Petter said, and again Phoebe curtseyed.

Phoebe's eyes returned to Petter. "I am so happy to see you, Petter."

Her eyes – beautiful eyes, Petter thought – kept unabashed contact with his.

"How was your voyage? Did much good come of it?"

"I am reunited with my mother," Petter said. "She needed a bit of rescuing." He chuckled as he said this, knowing that Phoebe would not imagine how literally he meant what he said.

Phoebe turned to Christine and said, "Trapped by clingy friends or family I suppose. How nice that your husband and gallant son came to your rescue."

"Indeed," answered Christine. Christine smiled warmly at Phoebe.

"I am afraid my father is not in the shop," Phoebe said. "I do not expect him to return this afternoon. He will be sorry he missed you. I hope your stay in London will allow you another visit." Phoebe walked as she spoke, leading the group toward Petter's drafting table. "He kept your table open, Petter, saying – as you can imagine he would – that no one could replace you."

"Have you done something different to your hair?" Petter asked. The words were out before he knew he intended to say them, and he flushed as Phoebe turned to him.

"Yes," she said. There was no Constance-like coy downturning of her eyes, no flutter to her lashes. She looked at him squarely as she said, "Do you like it?"

"Yes, it's lovely," Petter answered, a smile growing over his face as his own cheeks warmed further. Looking into her steady eyes, he thought, *Why did I ever think Phoebe plain?*

The silence between Petter and Phoebe was interrupted by Erik's small noise as he cleared his throat.

Phoebe flushed as she turned away, and placed a hand on Petter's drawing table. She turned back, a shy smile competing with the sudden crease in her brow.

"Petter," she said. "I am afraid I took a liberty with your plans while you were absent. It seemed to go well, so I hope you will forgive me." Her brows remained drawn as she took her bottom lip into her teeth.

Despite a small thrill of annoyance, Petter kept his voice calm as he said, "What liberty?"

"Well… Several gentlemen came to see Father about developing certain plans. They were from New York, in America. I could not help overhearing their requests, and I thought, 'My goodness, they sound like they would be interested in one of Petter's plans.' I asked Father, and he agreed wholeheartedly."

SKELETONS IN THE CLOSET

"Yes...?" prompted Petter. His annoyance was blossoming into excited hope.

"They did like your plans, one especially, and they left a request to meet with you to discuss your overseeing the project. Of course, they mean to build it in New York."

Petter could only gasp in happy bewilderment. He stepped forward and wrapped an astonished Phoebe in his arms. He released her, and said, "My word, Phoebe, but you're wonderful!" Turning to his father, he said, "Isn't she?"

"Indeed." Erik was smiling at Petter with evident pride, and the warmth in his eyes as he turned to Phoebe was unmistakable.

Petter returned his gaze to Phoebe – a Phoebe made beautiful by the flush on her cheeks and her smiling eyes. He felt as dazzled by her as he ever had by Constance's façade.

"Which plan did they like?" he asked.

"This one. I'll show you!" Phoebe half ran to her drafting table, from under which she drew his portfolio. "I kept it under lock and key," she said. Opening the portfolio, she pointed to the top plan. "This one," she said. She seemed even more excited than Petter was himself. Petter could not look away from her, and gripped his hands at his side to keep from taking her hand in his. He dropped his eyes to the indicated plan.

"This is the plan you helped me modify," Petter said.

"Well, I..."

"I shall correct the legend to reflect your name as well as mine," Petter continued.

"Petter! I only…" Phoebe's eyes were wide with her surprise.

"I plan to go to New York," Petter continued.

"Yes, of course…" Phoebe began, and her eyes dropped.

"I would like you to come with me," he finished.

Phoebe opened her mouth, and closed it again. When she spoke, it was a whisper. "What did you say?"

Petter reached forward and took her hand in his. Her fingers closed over his. His mind took him to all the times on his journey he had thought of her, of the photographs he had taken for her, of the warmth and companionship he felt when she was in his thoughts. The warmth that suffused him now was far deeper, far more overwhelming than the shallow flashes of excitement or desire Constance had inspired. Meeting Phoebe's beautiful eyes with all the sincerity and force he could muster, he said, "Phoebe, I want you to come to New York with me." He took a breath, and said, "Will you?"

Her eyes grew moist, and then a smile warmed her face like a sunrise. "Yes, Petter, I will," she said.

Paying no heed to the fact that his parents stood at his back and that any number of journeymen worked at their stations across the large room, Petter took Phoebe into his arms, and kissed her. After they bumped noses and separated long enough to laugh, he kissed her again, and this time, allowed himself to be swept away.

CHAPTER 34
CHRISTINE AND ERIK

Christine held Erik's warm body close against hers. It was late at night and the hotel room was dark, but the sound of the still-active London streets beat its way through the pane of the closed glass.

In the aftermath of their lovemaking – a lovemaking far more passionate than the pleasant but despondent unions of months past – they had both lain so still that she thought Erik asleep. She was startled when he spoke into the silence.

"I would rather it was the sound of the ocean," he said.

"Yes," she answered. She moved herself into a more comfortable position against him as she had not dared to do when she thought him sleeping.

"So what shall we do now, my wife?" he asked. "I have conquered the dragon and saved the fair maiden. Shall I now take her back to my castle?"

"Sweden?" she asked. She shifted her head onto his chest and pulled closer still.

He gave a deep-throated answer. "Yes, Sweden."

"I love hearing your voice in your chest, hemmed in by your heartbeat." She tightened her arms around him and said, surprising even herself, "No. We had a long and wonderful time in Sweden, but I am ready for something new."

"Ah, some new place. Let's see…" Christine lay against him, waiting for him to voice his thoughts. "Do you speak Spanish?" he asked after some while.

"You know I do not," she said. She laughed and lifted her head to look at him in the low light. "Can you not think of any place in the world where they speak a language I have already learned? I have had enough adventuring in the last months to want at least the comfort of a known language."

He was silent for another long moment, and Christine drifted toward sleep. When he spoke again, she could hear the hesitation, the searching nature of the question. "Would you like to go to New York? We could be close to Petter."

She sighed in self-reproach for the depressed attitude she had forced Erik to live with after Petter left for London. "No, not to New York either." She squeezed her husband again and said, "Thank you for asking, Erik. I know you did so only out of regard for me. But I have come to realize – to accept – that we have had all of Petter we can claim. He must walk his own path. I love him, I will always miss him and be happy to see him when the opportunity arises, but he has a life to live. I only hope that it is as exciting, as fulfilled, as successful as mine has been." She sighed again, this time with release. She had been meaning to explain her changed feelings to Erik for some time now, but had not had the opportunity. "And with Phoebe… I think he has found a wonderful woman with whom to walk that path."

Erik chuckled, the laugh bouncing her head as it lay against his chest. "I thought so from the moment I met her. I hoped Petter would come to realize it."

Erik stretched and then rolled to cup his body around hers. "You have not told me where it is you would like to go," he said into her ear.

"I do like the idea of going to America," she answered after some thought. "But perhaps to the frontier, rather than to a city." When Erik did not answer, she said, "Although, you might miss the ocean."

Erik tightened his arms about her. "I will miss nothing so long as I am with you," he said.

She yawned and snuggled into his arms. "At least they speak English there," she said sleepily.

Erik spoke through his own answering yawn. "If you can call what they speak 'English,'" he answered.

She smiled as she fell asleep, wondering what new adventures tomorrow would bring.

***

Less than two weeks later, Petter and Phoebe met Erik and Christine at the docks. Christine was pleased to see how happy the young couple looked – gleaming even in the somber London weather. Phoebe smiled as she held Petter's arm and leaned close to him.

"Are you certain you don't want your father and me to stay for the wedding?" she asked. It was the one aspect of their quick departure that troubled her. She and Erik needed to return to Sweden to wrap up their affairs there and the sooner the better. Then they would take the promised world tour and – assuming they did not find another place to settle – America.

It was Phoebe who answered. "Mrs. Nilsson, Petter and I are already married in our hearts, and you see us as happy today as we will be that day." Christine thought this was probably so, and embraced the young woman.

"We're having a very small wedding, in any case," Petter answered with a smile. He turned to gaze at Phoebe with glowing eyes. Christine's eyes clouded as she reached to embrace Petter as well.

"When do you go to New York?" Erik asked.

"We nearly have the contract finalized, Father," Petter answered. "I'll let you know where we've settled when you write with your own whereabouts."

"I am very proud of you, son," Erik said. His voice sounded suspiciously choked with emotion as he clasped Petter's hand and then embraced him.

Petter waited as Erik also embraced Phoebe, then said, "I have a gift for you, Father." He reached into his jacket pocket and took out a square of stiff paper.

SKELETONS IN THE CLOSET

Erik took it and Christine leaned close to examine the gift. It was a photograph of Erik and Petter, standing at the corner of a brick building.

"How lovely," Christine said, and lifted her gaze to Erik.

Erik held the photograph a bit longer, swallowed heavily, blinked back tears and smiled before placing the gift in his breast pocket. "Thank you, son, most sincerely." His smile broadened. "And I'll have you know that I have already procured a Brownie of my own." Erik embraced Petter again and then took Christine's hand to lead her away.

"Father," Petter said, stopping him. "You still owe me the story of your youth."

"Yes, I suppose I do," he said. "One of these days, perhaps we can find a quiet time for the long and unhappy tale."

"I will hold you to that," Petter said.

"I am certain you will," Erik answered with a smile. "I am certain you will."

- END -

Davyne DeSye

Thank you for taking the time to read
Skeletons in the Closet!

If you enjoyed it, please leave a review on Amazon!

Made in the USA
Middletown, DE
21 July 2017